Praise for *R*

"*Rules for Ghosting* is the kind of book you want to live in. This gorgeous debut marvels at new life and does not shy away from life lost. It cracks open the meaning of the word 'haunting'—whether that be of discarded identity, hidden yearning, or literal ghosts. Best of all, Shelly Jay Shore has written the soft-Jewish-trans-boy-who-sees-dead-people of our literary dreams. If I read a million pages about Ezra Friedman, I'd still be left wanting more."

—Haley Jakobson, author of *Old Enough*

"Fully immersive from the first page, Shore's writing grabbed me by the throat and never let go. Part ghost story, part Jewish family epic, part romance, *Rules for Ghosting* is a meditation on life, death, and healing, told through a queer and trans lens that is at turns bitingly funny and deeply moving. Shore is an immense talent. Ezra's world will live in my heart for a long time."

—Anita Kelly, author of *Love & Other Disasters*

"*Rules for Ghosting* is fun as hell. It's giving TJ Klune, but instead of supernatural children, we've got dead people. Same sexy queer longing, though (and honestly, also some supernatural children). I'm sure you can even read it if you aren't trans, but I don't even care to think of the cis people right now. Because this is fun and it's *for* me."

—A. E. Osworth, author of *We Are Watching Eliza Bright*

"A tender, heart-filled novel, *Rules for Ghosting* is a beautiful story about identity, family, faith, community, and first love.... A breathtaking debut."

—Ashley Herring Blake, author of *Delilah Green Doesn't Care*

"As unabashedly queer as it is loudly and beautifully Jewish, *Rules for Ghosting* is one of the most unique, poignant novels I've read in a long, long time. Ezra's journey through self, complicated family dynamics, and opening up to new love was one I'll never forget. Throw in a looming ghost or two and this book truly has it all."

—Carlyn Greenwald, author of *Sizzle Reel*

"*Rules for Ghosting* has everything: a family funeral home and a main character who can see ghosts, an adorable pit bull named Sappho, a mother coming out at seder dinner, a trans love story, a fiery climax that brings everything to a head, humor, heart, and so much more. It's about finding your place in the world, in your family, in partnership and, finally, within yourself. It was a joy to read, and I can't wait to see what's next from Shelly Jay Shore."

—Celia Laskey, author of *So Happy for You*

"A movingly wrought story about the ways queerness, Jewishness, grief, and joy intersect in messy, painful, and beautiful ways."

—Lev AC Rosen, author of *Lavender House*

RULES *for* GHOSTING

A Novel

SHELLY JAY SHORE

Dell
New York

A Dell Trade Paperback Original

Copyright © 2024 by Shelly Jay Shore
Book club guide copyright © 2024 by Penguin Random House LLC

Published in the United States by Dell, an imprint of Random House, a division of Penguin Random House LLC, New York.

DELL and the D colophon are registered trademarks of Penguin Random House LLC.
RANDOM HOUSE BOOK CLUB and colophon are trademarks of Penguin Random House LLC.

ISBN 978-0-593-72394-4
Ebook ISBN 978-0-593-72395-1

Printed in the United States of America on acid-free paper

randomhousebooks.com
randomhousebookclub.com

2 4 6 8 9 7 5 3 1

For the eldest daughters, current and former—
this is your reminder to exhale.

RULES *for* GHOSTING

twenty years ago

In the showroom, the caskets are arranged with care, from the gleaming mahogany to the sturdy pale poplar with the embellished lid.

Ezra has touched them all, ranking them by comfort and scent, how the fabric feels against his skin, whether he can see through the tiny holes bored through the bases to allow the dirt of the burial plot to seep inside.

Clients linger in that room, debating this engraving or that one, crepe lining over velvet. They murmur over the prices, typed neatly on stationery and tucked into plastic frames, each containing a handwritten legend: EACH CASKET HAS BEEN BUILT TO THE HIGHEST STANDARD OF KASHRUT, IN ACCORDANCE WITH JEWISH LAW. The script is his grandmother's, graceful and sloping, every card carefully prepared at the kitchen table while Ezra watches with his head on his hands, lulled into meditation by the smooth flow of her fountain pen filled from the indigo inkwells his zayde buys her each birthday.

"It adds a human touch," Bubbe tells him, the cards spread out across the kitchen table as the ink dries. When Ezra looks closely, he can see the tiny imperfections where the ink has blotted, smudged. "That's what people need when they're grieving. They don't want a factory funeral—they want to know that a real person, with a face and a name, came and took care of the person they lost. That they weren't just thrown away."

Ezra nods and lets her run her fingers through his hair, the curls his mother won't let him cut thick and loose and falling to his shoulders.

Zayde props the lids open and encourages the clients to take their time, to think, to touch, to choose what feels right.

"The body *must* touch the earth," Zayde says in his accented English, Polish still clinging to the edge of each word, as he leads Ezra and Aaron through the room. They trail after him like ducklings in his tall, thin shadow. Years later, Ezra will have a philosophy professor who lectures the same way and will imagine the life Zayde might have had, if the world had been kinder.

By the time he's six, Ezra can recognize the names of his siblings and parents and grandparents and cousins when they're written out in front of him. He has memorized seven books, he can count to fifty-six, and he can recite the rules of Jewish burial customs like a poem, learning them at his grandfather's knees the same way he learns the aleph-bet and the colors of the rainbow. *For a casket to be kosher it cannot be constructed on the Sabbath and it must be made of wood: no metals in the hinges or fastenings or handles; the linings must degrade over time.*

Because the body must touch the earth.

When Zayde leads clients on his tours of the room, they drift without fail toward the shinier models, the ones with their bright finishes and soft velvet. But Ezra's favorite is the flat pine box that sits away from the others. He likes the way it smells, lingering juniper and sandpaper instead of wood polish and wax. When he climbs inside and turns to lie on his belly, the pinpricks of light shining through the holes sting his eyes, just enough hurt to make them water and blur.

Aaron kicks him in the ankle when Ezra climbs out again, rubbing his eyes and complaining about the light. "The people in there wouldn't be looking," he says, rolling his eyes.

Zayde swats the back of his head. "Don't kick your sister." His voice has a gravelly rasp, and he rarely raises it. But his stern whisper is more commanding than their father's shout.

"Yeah," Ezra says, sticking out his tongue. "Don't kick your sister."

Aaron makes a face. Ezra makes one back. Zayde sighs, long-suffering, and turns up the sound on the ancient radio.

"Don't tell your brother," Zayde will tell him, with a conspiratorial wink and a second toaster waffle, "but if you were a boy, I'd hand this place over to you."

Every morning, from the time he's old enough to walk until the spring he turns seven, Ezra follows Zayde across the yard that connects their family house to the funeral home. Holding Ezra's hand, Zayde unlocks the staff entrance, and Ezra trails after him as he walks from room to room, turning on lamps and adjusting thermostats, fluffing the drapes, checking on the eternal light in the chapel, making sure the little signs on the display room caskets are arranged *just so*. Once everything is arranged to his satisfaction, he leads Ezra down into the basement, where Ezra sits at the rickety staff table in the kitchen and eats a toaster waffle and watches his grandfather start the first pot of coffee, then sit down to read the obituaries.

"I *could* be a boy," Ezra says, every time, and Zayde pats his head and tells him to eat, nudging the bottle of maple syrup across the table toward him with a conspiratorial wink. Extra syrup is a sacred secret they share.

Ezra tells himself that it's silly to feel hurt over these dismissals. He doesn't know how to explain how much he hates the long hair his parents refuse to let him cut, the skirts Mom insists he wear on Shabbat. Aaron gets to wear pants.

"I swear, sweetheart," Mom tells him. There is an exasperation in her voice. She has sent him up to his room, the third Saturday in a row, with firm instructions: Change your clothes. "I am ready for you to be *done* with this phase."

When he looks back, years later, Ezra's never sure why he always turned to his grandfather—what support he was hoping he'd get, what he was hoping Zayde would say. Whatever it was, he never said it, and Ezra, reluctant and pouting, would give in.

The morning before Zayde dies, Ezra resists. He sits on the stairs and refuses to go to shul if he has to wear a dress. He wraps himself around the banister, arms and legs both, and ignores his mother's attempts to cajole, guilt, and coerce him. Becca, just a year old, is squirming and fussy in her arms. It's not until Dad threatens to change him himself that Zayde steps in.

"I'll stay home today," he says, stopping any argument in its tracks. "You go on."

They go, Aaron the only one who waves at Ezra on his way out the door, and that's what makes Ezra cry. He unwraps himself from around the banister and puts his arms around his knees, burying his face in them, crying like Becca does, loud and without rules. He is frustrated and confused and hurt, and not sure why.

Zayde sits down next to him, his bones creaking audibly. He pats Ezra's shoulder. "Your mother isn't angry at you," he says. "But you should listen to her."

Ezra wipes his nose. "It's a stupid rule," he mutters.

"Maybe," Zayde allows. "But you still need to listen."

Any other morning, it wouldn't be a betrayal. But on this one, with his skin already prickling and his heart already sore, it was.

"You don't understand," Ezra says.

"Well," Zayde says. "Why don't you tell me?"

Ezra shakes his head. "No." He pushes his arm off. "I don't want to. I'm going upstairs."

Zayde says his name, but Ezra ignores him. He stomps up the steps and slams his door behind him. Sitting down with his back against it, he listens for the sound of footsteps on the stairs and hears them, the heavy, weighted tread of Zayde's gait. After a moment, there's a knock at the door.

Ezra pushes more firmly against it, just in case, and doesn't answer.

Zayde sighs. "I know that sometimes we ask you to do things you don't like," he says, the words chosen slowly, carefully, as they almost always were. "But it's part of being in a family. Even when it's hard."

"Then maybe I don't *want* to be part of the family," Ezra retorts. "Maybe I'll just stay here. By myself. Then I don't have to do *anything*."

There's a smile in Zayde's voice when he says, "That sounds lonely."

"I don't care," Ezra says. "I just want to do what *I* want. And I want *you* to go *away*."

On the other side of the door, Zayde takes in a breath—and then sighs. Ezra holds his own breath, waiting, because he knows, *knows,* that he's said something cruel.

A few seconds later, Zayde's footsteps fade down the hallway.

The sound of him walking away hurts, and the hurt twists itself into knots of anger again. Ezra climbs to his feet to open the door and slam it again, just because he can, before pulling the quilt off his bed, crawling under it, and refusing to emerge for the rest of the day, not when everyone returns, nor when his mom calls him for dinner. He waits, sure that if he waits long enough, someone will come and tell him that they were wrong, and he was right. But nobody does, and Ezra falls asleep, his stomach growling, his skin too tight for his body.

Zayde doesn't come to get him for their morning rounds. Ezra stares at his closed door, chewing his bottom lip and watching the sky outside his window get lighter, until his aching stomach and the promise of waffles lure him out of bed. He dresses carefully, putting on a shirt he knows Mom will like. It doesn't mean he's sorry.

The hall outside his room is quiet when he pokes his head out, but no one comes to scold him, so he tiptoes down the stairs and out the back door. His shoes are damp from the dewy, fresh-cut grass by the time he gets across the yard and climbs up the steps to the STAFF ONLY door of the funeral home, and he wipes them carefully on the mat before reaching up to try the handle.

Usually, Zayde has to unlock it, but the knob turns easily under his hand. Inside, the corridor is dim and still, painted gray by the pale sunlight filtering through the windows.

He finds Zayde there, just where he starts every morning, standing tall and straight to check the Ner Tamid, to ensure it hasn't gone out overnight.

"Zayde," he says. He doesn't really mean to whine. "You didn't come get me."

Zayde turns toward him, and stills. He stares at Ezra across the pews, deep lines furrowing in his brow. He opens his mouth, but he doesn't speak. He frowns.

"I'm sorry I told you to go away," Ezra says. "I was just—I was mad."

Zayde looks at Ezra as if he's seeing him for the very first time.

"Zayde?"

Nothing. Ezra steps forward. His hand comes up without him realizing it. Reaching.

"Sweetheart, *there* you are."

The voice behind him comes out of nowhere, and Ezra shrieks. Mom drops to her knees and sweeps him into her arms before he can register why he's crying. He feels strange. *Wrong.* Mom strokes his hair, rocking him gently. When he squirms away from her, she lets him go.

"Where have you been? We've been looking everywhere for you."

"With Zayde," Ezra says through his tears, bewildered as much by the redness of her eyes as his own overwhelming confusion. "Like always."

Mom's face goes a shade paler; her eyes, behind her thick-rimmed glasses, are shiny with unshed tears. She isn't wearing makeup, and the skin under her eyes is thin and dark.

"Honey," she says, and stops. She shifts, still crouched in front of him, and uses her thumbs to wipe away his tears. "I need to tell you something about Zayde, okay?"

She says the words, but Ezra doesn't hear them. He doesn't see her face when she says them, either. He's looking past her shoulder, at the doorway to the Chapel, where Zayde is standing, solemn and thin in his black suit.

Silently, Zayde touches a finger to his lips.

Then, like a candle going out, he's gone.

now

I

Being psychic is more trouble than it's worth.

Ezra sees the world in double vision: air that's empty one instant, and thick with the dead the next. Sometimes, they look like everyone else, indistinguishable from the living—until he tries to touch them and his hand phases through them. They look solid and alive but feel *off*, the air around them colder. Other times, they are hurt or sick or broken, their gaits the hypnic jerks of sleeping limbs.

There are a thousand moments when he almost tells someone: Aaron, in the early weeks after Zayde dies; when Aaron asks why Ezra never wants to play in the showroom anymore; Becca, when she's six and asks why he keeps staring at nothing; why sometimes he looks suddenly, randomly ready to cry. When his college roommate finds him hyperventilating in the bathroom after a pale-eyed shade no older than eighteen appeared in his shower stall.

He never says a word to his parents. He thinks that some part of him knew, even as a child, that this would be one confession too many. He was queer when he was fourteen, a boy when he was twenty—adding *Oh, and I see dead people, and did you know there are ghosts everywhere?* would just be too much.

Instead, he learns to keep his feelings off his face. To keep his breathing even and suppress his startle reflex and keep himself from shivering when the air goes cold. He swallows the impulse to flinch from the hovering dead, and tries to keep his eyes on the living.

It's not all bad. Sometimes they're peaceful. Calm. Sometimes he can read them and try to . . . not *fix* things, but maybe *help*. Once, he'd caught a typo in a funeral program and corrected it, reprinting the cards twenty minutes before a service, and got a beaming smile from a dead English professor before she vanished in the space between blinks.

He's not sure *he'd* haunt his funeral over a typo, but maybe the dead have different priorities.

It makes apartment hunting harder. He can manage the casual ghost sighting, but he refuses to have a repeat of his first rental out of college, with its disappearing-reappearing old woman who stood by his bed and *cried,* night after night after night.

The relative lack of ghosts was what drew him to the tiny studio he's lived in for the past three years, despite the rattling pipes and the light fixture in the bathroom that never stopped flickering no matter how many times he changed the bulb. There was only one spirit haunting the place, a young blond woman, who seemed content to occasionally appear long enough to watch episodes of *The Great British Bake Off* on the lumpy futon.

And it had been a good home, while it lasted. The first night he'd brought Sappho home, fifty pounds of adopted pit mix so anxious she might as well have been a puppy, they'd slept together on the futon because she was too scared to get up on the bed. He'd done his first T shot in the tiny bathroom. He and Ollie had their last first time on his lumpy mattress, and afterward, Ollie hadn't even laughed at Ezra when he cried.

He and Ollie had their last breakup here, too, sitting miserably together as they decided once and for all that they'd be better off as friends.

Unfortunately, his affection for the place hadn't been enough of a reason for his landlord to resist selling the building to a condo development group. So here he is, wedging the last of his packed boxes into the trunk of his car to drive across town to yet another new home, while Nina leans against the passenger side door, Sappho's leash looped idly around her wrist.

But he feels good about this new apartment. Ollie's lived in the house for years, including the last year of their on-again, off-again relationship. If there were anything spectral lurking, he'd have felt it by now.

He doesn't realize that he's been muttering a mantra of *Stop freaking out, it's going to be fine* under his breath until Nina interrupts it, cutting right to the core of his simmering anxiety in the way only she ever has, brutal as the surgeon her mother's still annoyed she decided not to be. "You know," she says, "I still think it's weird that you guys are moving in together. You two only broke up for good, like, what, two months ago?"

"Three," Ezra says. Not that he's been counting.

Her skeptical look makes his cheeks go hot, but for once, she doesn't comment. "Still sucks," she says. "Especially since you're going to have to get used to roommates again." She shudders. "I love you, but if I had to do that after living alone for three years, I'd just buy a tent and set up under the nearest overpass."

"You once told me that you need five bubble baths a week to live," he says dryly.

Nina sniffs. "I'm very adaptable." She eyes his trunk skeptically as he picks up the last box. "Is that going to fit?"

"Maybe. Probably. You could help, you know."

Nina, all five feet eleven of her looking more like she's ready to walk onto the nearest runway than help him move, reaches down to give Sappho a pointed pat on the head. "I'm holding the dog." Sappho gives an entirely unhelpful huff, tongue lolling happily as she leans against Nina's leg. Ezra makes a face at both of them and starts wedging the box into the improbable remaining space in the trunk.

Technically, he and Ollie aren't *really* moving in together. There are three apartments in the building, and Ezra's taking over the abruptly vacated room in the unit below Ollie's. According to both Ollie and Lily, one of Ezra's new roommates, the doors of the two apartments are so consistently open to each other that they might as well be a single unit, but Ezra's clinging to the justification of not-actually-roommates like a lifeline. It had been sheer luck that Ollie's downstairs neighbor had moved out two weeks ago, and her roommates wanted to fill the spot with someone who wasn't a complete stranger.

It's fine. They'll be fine. This is going to be fine.

With a last shove, he fits the box into the car, then slams the trunk shut. "That's as good as it's going to get," he says, wiping his face. "Let's go."

Sappho hops obediently into the back seat when Ezra opens the door for her, and settles her head on the armrest between the two front seats as he and Nina climb in. "So," Nina says, twisting to scratch Sappho's ears while Ezra pulls out of the driveway, resisting the urge to take a last backward glance at his former home. "Are you freaking out about the Ollie thing, the living-with-roommates thing, or some other problem you've made up to stress about?"

"Wow." Ezra takes his eyes off the road just long enough to shoot her a sour look. "Rude."

She shrugs, flipping her hair over her shoulder. "Don't shoot the messenger."

"Who says I'm freaking out about anything?"

"Well, I've met you," she drawls. "So."

"Uh-huh." Ezra turns on the radio. "It's a seven-minute drive. Think you can handle not trying to make me talk about my feelings for that long?"

"I'll endeavor to suffer through it."

Someday he'll have a best friend who doesn't make fun of him constantly. That day, apparently, is not today.

Despite a few threatening clouds, the weather's still holding dry ten minutes later when they pull up in front of the old renovated Victorian that houses Ezra's new apartment. Ezra manages—with some wrangling—to get Sappho to sit still long enough to get her leash clipped on before she bolts from the car. He has her leash around one wrist and a box in his hands when his phone starts buzzing. He props the box against the side of the car with his hip and digs his phone out of his pocket, then groans.

If it were anyone else, he'd send them right to voicemail. Unfortunately, he doesn't want to be murdered. He shifts the box to get a better grip, mouths *sorry* to Nina, and picks up the call.

The first words Mom says are "Did you see my email?"

"Hi, Ezra," Ezra says, leaning against the car and trying not to let Sappho yank his shoulder out of its socket. "How are you, Ezra? Oh, I'm good, Mom, thanks for asking! How are you? Oh, I'm great, Ezra! I just wanted to call my favorite child and—"

"That's not nearly as cute as you think it is," Mom says, like he can't hear her exasperated smile over the line. "But yes, okay, hi. How's the move going?"

"It would be better if I could use both my hands." He meets Nina's eyes and gives her his most pleading look, and she heaves a long-suffering sigh, taking the box and setting it on the hood of the car. He tries to convey an enthusiastic thank-you via eyebrows alone, rolling out his shoulder. "What's up?"

"I was asking if you saw my email."

"That's like asking if I noticed the sun was out." His inbox is forty percent Mom emails. They have their own filter. "Can you be a little more specific?"

Something clatters on Mom's end of the line, followed by a muffled "Fuck!" Ezra winces. "How's Becca?"

"Stressed," Mom says, packing an impressive amount of dry irritation into the single word. "The email was about your bubbe's Pesach recipe binder—Becca thinks you have it."

Sappho, having realized that Ezra isn't going to let her go to the house without him, hops up on her back legs to brace all her weight on his chest and begins to lick the side of his face. He gets her into a delicate headlock to remove her tongue from his neck, and she starts slobbering on his shirt instead. "I have it somewhere," he says. "But it's probably buried in boxes, Mom. I don't really have time to go digging for it if you still want me there by four today."

Mom sighs. "I still can't believe you planned a move for today."

"Yeah, well, take it up with my ex-landlord." Ezra tries, and mostly fails, to get Sappho's tongue out from under the collar of his shirt. "Didn't you two plan this menu, like, weeks ago?"

"You know your sister," Mom says, which, yes, fine, but so not helpful. "Is there any chance you can take a look before you head over here? You're so organized, I'm sure you know where your books are packed."

Ezra turns his face skyward. No divine intervention appears. "I will do my absolute best," he says. "Mom, I really need to go. Sappho's going to eat my face."

He can practically hear her wrinkling her nose. "Right," she says. "And you're . . . sure your new roommates can't watch her for you when you come stay with us?"

"Am I sure that I'm not going to ask the people I've met literally twice if they want to babysit my dog for three days? Yeah, I'm sure." Another lick to his face. "I'm hanging up now. I'll see you in a few hours."

"I'll try to dog-proof the house before you get here."

"I love you, too," Ezra says dryly, and hangs up.

"That sounded fun," Nina says. She's lounging against the car, scrolling through her phone and deliberately not helping him with the dog.

"You know my mom," Ezra says. "There's always something." He picks the box up again, gives Sappho a firm look he hopes conveys *Don't you dare yank my arm out of its socket,* and heads around the corner of the long driveway toward the front door.

Nina scoops up another box from the back seat and follows him. "And yet, somehow your response is never to tell her to . . . not do that."

"You want to tell her that?" Ezra says. "Be my guest."

Nina shudders. "Hard pass. That woman scares the hell out of me." She abruptly stops, and Ezra nearly crashes into her. "Um—I don't want to alarm you, but I think someone's trying to break into your house."

Ezra gets Sappho's leash under control, fixes her with a stern look that she returns with wide-eyed innocence, and follows Nina's pointing finger.

The house is a gorgeous three-story Victorian, built— according to his new roommate Lily, who's apparently obsessed with old architecture and spent most of Ezra's just-checking-that-you're-not-a-serial-killer tour rattling off trivia—in 1900 and converted into apartments back in the seventies. The exterior is painted a flaking, faded yellow and ornamented with random balconies and decorative railings. There's an octagonal tower on one side and a narrow turret on the other, tacked on as if an afterthought. A questionably stable porch wraps around the entire first floor.

And there is, indeed, a man on said porch, attempting to pick the lock.

It's broad daylight on a Sunday afternoon. Ezra's a little impressed by the nerve.

"Uh," he says loud enough to be heard over the slightly pathetic scraping of whatever metal tool this guy is using—is that a paper clip? *Jesus*—to get the lock open. "Can I help you?"

The guy's head snaps up so fast Ezra honestly thinks he might get whiplash. *Does,* actually, if the face he makes is any indication. "Oh, hi," he says, and then takes in the box in Ezra's hands, the keys dangling from Ezra's forefinger, and his own position crouched in front of the door. To Ezra's surprise, his face lights up, as if in recognition. "Oh, hi!" he says again, much more brightly. "You must be the new guy on the second floor?"

It's alarming, Ezra thinks, how much a smile can transform someone's face. Even crouched under the door like an amateur burglar, this guy is handsome. Objectively. But it's his smile that changes everything, the crinkles at the corners of his eyes, set behind a pair of thick-framed glasses, softening his dark brows and turning the strong line of his jaw into an easy warmth.

Ezra's messy hair and the blooming sweat stains at his neck and armpits suddenly feel very obvious. Just his luck.

He's also probably been quiet too long. Ezra clears his

throat. "Yeah," he says, and shifts the box onto his hip to hold out a hand, Sappho's leash still looped around his other wrist. "Ezra. This is my friend Nina."

"Jonathan." He climbs to his feet and shakes Ezra's hand, firm and warm, and smiles at Nina. "I'm on the first floor."

Ezra eyes the paper clip in Jonathan's hand. "You sure about that?"

"I locked my wallet and keys inside," Jonathan says, smile turning crooked and a little self-deprecating. It's a good look on him. "I'd offer to show you my ID to prove it, but . . ."

He looks like a kicked puppy. Ezra could never resist a stray. "Hold on," he says, and pulls out his phone.

Ollie answers on the first ring. "Hey," he says, cheerful, and Ezra tells the part of his chest that leaps in gleeful optimism at the sound of Ollie's voice to simmer the fuck down. "Are you back?"

"I'm on the porch with someone who says he lives on the first floor but doesn't have a key. And was trying to break in with a paper clip," Ezra says, biting back a grin when Jonathan shoots him an offended look. "Ring any bells?"

"Tall guy, dark hair, major Nice Jewish Boy vibes?"

Ezra looks Jonathan over again. He doesn't *not* give off NJB vibes, breaking-and-entering attempts aside. "Pretty much, yeah."

"That's Jonathan, you can let him in. Oh, hey, let me put my shoes on. I'll help you with the rest of the stuff in your car."

"About time you did some heavy lifting," Ezra teases, and hangs up on Ollie's indignant squawk. "He says you check out," he tells Jonathan, who grins.

"Nice Jewish Boy vibes, huh?"

Ezra's cheeks heat. Beside him, Nina looks like she's ready to burst with delight. She's barely restraining it. "You heard that?"

"You have your volume up, like, *really* high." Jonathan nods at the box in Ezra's hands. "Carry that up for you? Least I can do."

"Oh, that's okay—"

"He'd *love* that," Nina interrupts. Ezra shoots her a dirty look, but she grins breezily. "Dog wrangling, you know? The extra hands would be *great*."

"Sure," Jonathan says.

There's a tiny glint in his eye. He's completely aware that Nina isn't even bothering to be subtle. Ezra can absolutely carry this box himself, but screw it, he's not going to turn down a good-looking guy offering to carry it for him. His legs are tired. "Sure." He passes it over, then unlocks the front door and lets Jonathan go in ahead of him. "Stop that," he hisses to Nina when she starts to follow.

She widens her eyes at him. "I don't know what you're talking about."

"I'm firing you as my best friend."

"Please," she says. "You'd be screwed without me." She steps inside and raises her voice to shout up the stairs. "Oliver! You'd better be ready to help move some boxes!"

Ezra rolls his eyes and follows her inside, past a door on the first-floor landing that must lead to Jonathan's apartment. The stairwell is narrow enough that they can't walk side by side, so Ezra falls back a step behind Jonathan and Nina, reining in Sappho's leash to keep her from pushing past Nina to sniff at the new guy's feet.

"So, Ezra," Jonathan says, looking over his shoulder. "This is maybe a weird question, but have we met before? You look really familiar."

Is that a pickup line? Ezra genuinely can't tell. "I don't think so." Jonathan has one of those faces where it's hard to tell his age. He looks like every grad student Ezra saw on campus at Brown, cute and a little tired. Ezra knows the first-floor apartment is another three-bedroom, which means Jonathan's either got roommates or a decent income. "We could play Jewish geography, if you want."

Jonathan lets out a startled laugh. "Unfortunately, I think we'd be here all day, and I have plans tonight."

Not flirting, then. Probably for the best. Ezra already has one ex under this roof; he doesn't need to start something that'll end up giving him another one.

The door to Ezra's new apartment is propped open with a novelty garden gnome wearing leather pants and proudly waving a rainbow flag. Ezra has no idea who owns it, but he's in love. Jonathan holds out the box, and when Ezra takes it from him, he catches a flash of metal—a plain band on his left ring finger.

Definitely not flirting. It was a nice moment of fantasy. "Thanks for the help."

"Right back at you." Jonathan grins, nodding back toward the front door. "See you around, Ezra. Nice to meet you, Nina."

"You too," Nina calls after him.

She watches him go down the stairs and then waggles her eyebrows pointedly at Ezra. He rolls his eyes at her and nudges the door the rest of the way open to find Ollie, Lily, and Ollie's roommate Max all leaning toward the door, clearly eaves-dropping.

"Wow," he says, carefully moving the gnome with a foot and letting the door close behind him. "Hi. This isn't creepy at all."

"In our defense, none of us have seen him talk to anyone in weeks," Max says. She's dyed her hair since the last time Ezra saw her, her tight curls now a deep turquoise that pops against her brown skin. "He's been kind of a hermit lately."

Ezra puts the box down and rolls his shoulders, then his neck. "He seems like a good guy."

"He is," Lily says, getting to her feet with a grin as Sappho starts pulling toward her, leash taut in Ezra's hand. Lily's the kind of gorgeous that Ezra used to think only showed up on Instagram, all airbrushed and stunning long legs and cascading dark hair. She's a paralegal who stepped out of a Bollywood movie poster. "But more importantly, *hello*, my *real* new roommate. Come here, precious baby, I'm gonna be your new mom."

Ezra takes the hint and drops Sappho's leash. She leaps across the floorboards to Lily, nearly knocking her back through the door, all muscle and enthusiastic slobber. Lily either has experience with dogs or possesses the strongest thighs of anyone Ezra's ever met, because she braces herself and scoops Sappho's face into her hands, nuzzling their noses together. "You are going to get *so spoiled*," she says. "Did you know that? Did you know that you are going to be the most popular good girl in the whole apartment? *Yes*, you are."

"She comes with a very nice walk schedule, too," Ezra says. "If you want to hang out with her at six in the morning."

"Ew, no," Lily says, straightening up with a last kiss to Sappho's nose. "I'm strictly an afternoon dog aunt, thanks. Noah might take her, though, if you ask him very nicely. He's basically nocturnal."

Ezra hasn't met Noah yet, other than a quick *Yo* in the group chat Lily added him to when he signed the lease. He knows three things about Noah so far: He's a graphic designer who works mostly with overseas clients, the kombucha in the fridge is his, and he communicates primarily through memes.

"Wait, let's go back to Jonathan," Max says. "Because I was getting a flirty vibe from that."

"*See?*" Nina says, dropping onto the arm of the couch next to her and reminding Ezra abruptly why he hates letting her and Max be in the same room. "It's not just me."

Ezra keeps an eye on Sappho out of habit to make sure she doesn't get too out of hand, but he can't help the quick skeptical look he shoots Max. "You got a flirty vibe from fifteen seconds of overheard conversation?"

She shrugs. "I have a sense for this sort of thing," she says. "I matchmake for a living."

He blinks. He thought she worked in an art gallery. "Since when?"

"Since never," Ollie says, eyeing her with a mix of exasperation and affection. Ezra has been on the receiving end of that look more times than he likes to admit. "It is her side hustle, though."

"I'm very good at it!"

Ezra's reference points for matchmakers are *Fiddler on the Roof* and *Mulan*. Neither of those will serve him well here. "I don't think you're on track with this one," he says. "I'm pretty sure he's married."

Lily wrangles a lolling Sappho down onto the rug for tummy rubs. "He's not," she says. Ezra raises his eyebrows, then holds up his left hand and wiggles his ring finger pointedly. Lily shakes her head. "He *was*," she clarifies. "His husband died, though. Like—what, a year ago?"

"Something like that," Max says. "It was really sad. Totally out of nowhere."

Oh, okay, *hard* nope. "So then he's *definitely* off-limits," Ezra says. "I don't want to be someone's grief rebound, that's the worst."

"But he's totally your type," Ollie protests.

Ezra gapes at him. "Et tu, Brute?"

"How is he Ezra's type when *you're* Ezra's type?" Max says, clearly skeptical, looking back and forth between them.

"I was a fluke," Ollie says cheerfully. Nina audibly snorts. "Right?"

"You were kind of a fluke," Ezra says. Ollie's dark-haired and dark-eyed, too, but he's fine-featured and slim, more *Let's go tour a museum* than *Shoulders for days*. Ollie used to joke that Ezra was using him for his mom's Korean cooking, and Ezra usually just shot back that Ollie was in it for Ezra's mom's brisket. That was easier than either of them admitting that at a certain point, they were both just in it for the familiarity. "I can't be held responsible for sporadic lapses in my taste."

Lily gives Sappho a last pat and moves back to the couch, slinging her legs over Max's lap. "Wait, are we going to talk about this? I thought we were all going to just act like you guys never slept together and that this wasn't super weird."

"Nosy," Ollie tells her. "Very nosy. Ezra, back me up."

Ezra shrugs. "They're your friends, I just live here."

"Oh, no, no, no," Max says, grinning at him with just a hint of dangerous glee. "You're part of the madhouse now, cutie-pie. Welcome to the mortifying ordeal of being known."

The urge to ask for his security deposit back and bail is overwhelming, but his alternative—moving back in with his parents—is worse, and at least this apartment is a three-minute walk from a good coffee shop.

"Yikes," he says. In his head, he says a prayer: that his thought process is not visible on his face, that it's written in invisible ink. "Okay. Can I at least start the ordeal with someone other than just me carrying the rest of the stuff up from my car?"

"I already helped," Nina says, settling on the floor. Sappho, the traitor, flops immediately into her lap.

"You carried *one box*."

"Yeah, but I also helped you get all your stuff out of your studio."

He gives up. "Ollie?"

"I already said I'd help you, drama queen," Ollie says, climbing to his feet. "Come on."

He's grinning, but when they round the corner on the stairwell, out of immediate earshot of the conversation in the living room, he nudges Ezra's shoulder with his. "Hey. You okay?"

Ezra's skin tingles where their arms touched. "What? Of course. Why?"

Ollie shoots him a familiar look, the one that says *Come on*. That says *We've done this too many times for you to lie to me*. That says *I know you*.

Their breakup was months ago, but that look still makes Ezra want to drop his head onto Ollie's shoulder. It was easier back when he knew he wouldn't have to wake up the next morning alone.

Past the timeworn but classic exterior of the house, the apartment itself is full of what Ezra's sister would call *character* and his mom would call *an absolute hell to dust*. It's all nooks and crannies and built-in shelves and cabinets and original hardwood floors and crown molding that someone, for a blessing, decided not to paint over or rip out during renovations. None of the rooms fall at right angles and there are windows *everywhere*. Compared to his studio, with its lack of sunlight and terrible eighties carpet, it's like a breath of fresh air.

"You're lucky, you know," Ollie says idly, helping Ezra carry another box into his room. "I almost stole this room when Cait U-Hauled out with her girlfriend. The light's incredible."

He nods at the large, east-facing windows, his fingers fidgeting around the edges of the box like he's itching for a camera, and Ezra can't help but grin. Ollie's a photographer; he's always been picky about natural light. "Why didn't you?"

He sets his box down on the bed that Cait had left behind. Gorgeous lighting aside, it's a small room, most of its space taken up by the bed and the dresser he's inherited from Cait. He thinks there will be room for the desk and chair from his studio, and even for them to be usable if he's clever about re-arranging things, with enough room left over to spread out a yoga mat to practice in the mornings.

"Max threatened to disown me," Ollie says, a little glumly. "How long do you have before you need to head out?"

Ezra checks his watch and bites back a swear. "If you ask my mom? Negative ten minutes," he says, rubbing a hand over his face. "So much for having enough time to shower."

Anything sympathetic Ollie might have been about to say is abruptly interrupted by Nina bursting into the room like a hurricane, slamming the box she's carrying onto the dresser. "Did you see Ivy's email?"

What is it with the emails today? "What?"

Ivy is the director of the Providence Queer Community Center, where Ezra teaches yoga four days a week and Nina manages the youth outreach programming. He's technically only a part-time employee—the pay's not great, but it gives him health insurance and a reliable paycheck. Nina keeps try-ing to nudge him to ask about a full-time gig, maybe joining the constantly hiring program or education teams, but Ezra's true love is still his birth doula work, and he doesn't want to lose the flexibility he has to take on new clients. He's only been doing it for two years, but working in birth has been such a refreshing departure from the world of death and dying he grew up in that he can't imagine doing anything else long-term, even if the income isn't as predictable. "No, my phone's . . . somewhere. I haven't been checking it." He turns his work notifications off on the weekends—if someone needs him badly enough, they'll text.

Nina pulls out her own, taps at the screen a few times, and shoves it at him. "We have a problem."

Ezra takes it, frowning when he recognizes their boss's email address at the top of the screen, right next to a subject line marked URGENT. He feels around for the edge of the bed and sits down without looking, scrolling through the email as nausea starts to curl in his stomach.

FROM: ivy@provqcc.org
TO: team@provqcc.org
SUBJECT: [URGENT] RENOVATION UPDATE & EMPLOYEE SAFETY

Dear Team,

As you all know, we've been excited for our building renovation since the success of our capital campaign, made possible by our incredible Development team.

This evening, we took our first step in that direction by meeting with a state building inspector in order to acquire our permits and permissions. During this inspection, we discovered significant instabilities in our building's foundation, as well as additional flaws in some of the key support structures and electrical wiring. The inspector's conclusion, which I have reviewed and agree with, is that our building is not safe for occupation at this time, and will not be until some critical infrastructure has been repaired.

Effective immediately, we will be closing the Center's physical operations in order to ensure the safety of our employees and participants. Because this represents a significant loss for us in anticipated program revenue and

funding eligibility, <u>all nonessential employees will be
furloughed until the building is safe to reopen.</u> We will
continue to provide employee health, disability, and paid
leave benefits. At this time, we estimate that this will be a
furlough period of approximately eight to ten weeks.

Payroll will be processed at your standard salary or wage
through the end of this pay period, at which time we will be
reducing all nonessential staff payroll to 25% of your usual
rate. In the interest of continuing our policy of transparency
and organizational commitment to equity, I will also be
reducing my own salary to this 25% rate, and the rest of the
executive team has committed to a salary reduction of 50%
during this period in order to ensure we are able to continue
to provide some support as we—

He stops reading. Nothing good is coming after that.
"Fuck," he says.

Nina sits next to him with a huff. "Yeah."

Ollie nudges Ezra over to peer at the screen. "What's going
on?"

Ezra passes the phone over, putting his head in his hands.
He wishes he'd unpacked his pillows, to have something to
scream into.

"Are you panicking?" Nina asks. "I'm panicking."

She doesn't sound like she's panicking, but when he picks
his head up to look at her, he can see the ticking tension in her
jaw and the too-wild look in her dark eyes. For Nina, that's
practically an anxiety attack. "Are you okay?"

"Oh, sure," she drawls, sarcasm dripping. Ezra winces. Unlike him, Nina works full-time at the Center, running education programs and support groups in addition to teaching
dance classes. "This is great for me. I love finding myself spon-

taneously unemployed because nonprofits can't handle running regular building inspections."

Ollie hands Nina her phone back. "I don't even know what to say," he says. "I mean . . . Is there anything I can do to help?"

Nina scoffs, swiping over the screen. "Find me a rich husband so that I can live the trans girl trophy wife life I clearly deserve?"

"I'll see what I can do," he says, and then looks at Ezra. "Hey. Breathe."

"I'm breathing," Ezra says automatically.

Nina freezes, her head snapping up. "Ezra, oh my God," she says. "You're literally about to go to your parents' house. Your mom's gonna *freak*."

Yes. Yes, she is. Ezra rubs his eyes. "Maybe she'll be too stressed about the seder tonight to pick up on anything."

"Has that ever worked for you?"

"Never." His mom has a sixth sense for anything that might potentially get him back under her roof.

A new thought occurs to him, and he snaps out a hand to grab Ollie's arm, hard enough that Ollie almost falls off the bed. "You can't say anything about this."

"*Ow*," Ollie protests. "Say anything to who?"

Ezra gestures to the door with the fingers he's not digging into Ollie's wrist. "Them! I *just* moved in, it's not like I can tell them I just lost almost all my income—"

"Hey, no," Ollie says. He pries Ezra's death grip off his arm, but doesn't let go of his hand, squeezing his fingers firmly. It's not an unfamiliar touch, but it doesn't reassure him like it used to. "They're not going to evict you. We'd figure something out."

Ezra shakes his head. "I just met them," he says. The words come out more desperately than he means them to, his voice cracking. He swallows hard. "I can't."

"Okay, okay." Ollie huffs out a sigh. "Fine. Be a secretive little gremlin. I just think—"

There's a knock at the door, and Ezra almost jumps out of his skin. It's just Lily, poking her head in. "Hey," she says brightly, and then falters at whatever she sees on their faces. "Am I interrupting?"

"Not even a little," Nina lies, her face perfectly straight. "What's up?"

"Noah's home, and we were going to order dinner," she says, waving her phone. "Ezra, I was thinking we should do some kind of welcome-to-the-apartment thing. Can we treat you?"

Ezra musters a smile. "Rain check," he says. "I actually have to run—I'm having dinner at my parents' place tonight."

He braces himself—he really doesn't want to be the weird antisocial roommate who moves in and then immediately vanishes—but Lily just shrugs. "Next time," she says. "Ollie? Nina?"

"Sure," Ollie says, before Nina can open her mouth. He gets up, pulling Nina with him. "We'll come look at a menu."

Nina purses her lips at him. They've all known one another since college, but Nina was Ezra's friend first, and has always reserved the right to go hot and cold with Ollie based on whether he and Ezra are currently on or off. So far, she's been unmoved by Ezra's insistence that this *off* is permanent but that they're staying friends. "You're buying," she says finally, then turns back to Ezra. "Are you sure you're going to be okay?"

"I'm fine," he says, going for smooth and easy and probably landing in the vicinity of wobbly. "If you see Sappho, can you leash her? I'm just going to make sure I've got everything for tonight."

"Your funeral," Nina says, but she leans down and presses a smacking kiss to his cheek before she lets Ollie nudge her out the door.

Ezra watches them go, then huffs a sigh and drops onto the bed. He rubs a hand over his face, trying to gather himself back into something like a normal state so that he can get Sappho and get out the door without looking like a breakdown waiting to happen. To buy himself a minute or two of productivity, he reaches for the backpack he'd tossed onto the end of the bed earlier, dragging it over and unzipping the largest pocket, as if inventorying his toiletries will settle his nerves.

The air shifts. Ezra pauses, hand halfway into his bag.

He knows what's coming before he looks up.

It's been long enough since that first sighting, so many years ago, that he's rarely surprised to see the ghosts anymore, and he doesn't fall over himself at the sight of a strange man standing in his doorway. That sixth-sense tingle is whirring to life, cataloging the cooler air, the too-bright glow of otherworldly eyes.

All the same, Ezra stares.

The ghost stares back.

He's tall, broad in the shoulders, dressed in a cable-knit sweater and dark pants. For one heartbeat, Ezra sees him in kaleidoscopic vision: He is a man in his early thirties, dark-haired and light-eyed, pale and calm as he meets Ezra's gaze—and then bleeding and bloodstained, his face twisted in the agony of dying.

Ezra blinks. When he opens his eyes, the ghost is whole again, and the broken afterimage has vanished, leaving only a man, tired and just off the edge of normal. He blinks again, and the hallway is empty. The tingling in the back of his head subsides, and his fingers begin to warm again.

If it were any other day, he'd at least try to figure out who that ghost was. If they're haunting something, there's a reason, and when that something is a some*where* and that somewhere is Ezra's apartment, it's pretty motivating.

But honestly?

Ezra narrows his eyes, looking at the spot where the ghost had stood, in case it reappears.

It doesn't.

"Okay," Ezra says out loud. "Not today, Satan."

He zips his backpack, shoulders it, and leaves the room, hitting the light switch on his way out.

2

Technically, the Friedman family seder isn't due to start for another two hours, but a full day of scrambling is as much a part of Passover as the meal itself. When Ezra was a kid, he'd spend the day darting back and forth between helping his mother and both grandmothers in the kitchen and keeping Becca out of trouble. As Becca got older and started getting interested in what was happening in the kitchen rather than undoing all the cleaning Ezra was trying to do, it had been his job to keep her from cutting off any fingertips, supervising her grip on the kosher-for-Passover knives that spent most of their lives in carefully wrapped boxes in the basement for fifty-one weeks of the year.

It's still weird to think that the kid he once had to lecture about keeping her fingers out of the food processor can now French cut an onion in twenty seconds. And that she knows what French cutting even is.

The front door is rarely locked. Ezra lets himself in, unclipping Sappho's leash and letting her set off into the living room at an eager trot while he shrugs out of his jacket. The house smells like roasting vegetables and frying oil, and he gives himself a moment to breathe in the scents of old family recipes and listen to the duet of Mom and Becca's shouting match, competing with—and, somehow, winning over—the blender.

The reverie lasts only a few seconds. "Ezra!" The shout comes from the kitchen, taking him out of the brief foray into pleasant calm. "Your dog is trying to get into the oven!"

Ezra tucks his overnight bag into the nook by the coatrack and jogs into the fray to find Sappho's nose wedged under Becca's arm, Becca holding her face out of the oven with one hand and attempting to stick a meat thermometer into the roast beef with the other.

He whistles. Predictably, Sappho ignores him—she's decently trained, but it's not like she lives a life filled with quality kosher meat—and Ezra tugs her firmly back by the collar, ignoring her whining.

"Sorry," he says. "Sappho, sit. *Sit.*"

Sappho gives him a canine pout and slinks away, curling up under the kitchen table with a huff. Ezra sticks his tongue out at her and then turns to his sister. "Hi."

"Hi!" She yanks him into a hug hard enough to eject the air from his lungs. Becca has always been deceptively wiry. "Finally decided to show up once all the work was basically done?"

Ezra eyes the state of the kitchen over her shoulder. Becca tends to move through the world with the oblivious power of a natural disaster, and the kitchen looks like every other room his little sister has spent more than half an hour in, which is to say it resembles the aftermath of a tornado. Every surface is covered, cutting boards and rolls of Saran Wrap and mixing bowls and vegetable scraps and three empty tins of Manischewitz Matzo Meal. There are pots and frying pans on the stove, three out of four burners going strong, the Passover crockpot is stewing along in the corner, and—Ezra squints—there are at least two roasting pans in the oven.

"Yeah," he says, reaching around her to make sure the wiggly stove knob is set all the way off, before the open gas line sends them all up in smoke. Dad's been trying to convince Mom to replace the stove for years, but she insists it's perfectly safe, as long as no one accidentally knocks it. He's pretty sure that, sentimental attachment to the house aside, half the reason his parents refuse to sell the house and move is that they'd have to repair the ancient gas lines running through the place. Sometimes, Ezra's genuinely amazed they're all alive. "It really looks done. Definitely everything is chill here and you absolutely don't need more help."

"I want it on record that your sass is unappreciated," she says tartly.

Ezra grins and boops her nose, looking her over the way he always does when it's been a few days since he's seen her. There is something protective and feral knocking beneath his breastbone, making sure she's still in one piece. At twenty-one, she has yet to outgrow her baby face, and with her oversize glasses and tendency to use pens to hold her hair up, she looks like Ms. Frizzle. But the deep circles under her big brown eyes are new. "You feeling okay, monkey?"

Becca wrinkles her nose at the nickname but shrugs. "School," she says. Becca's living at home while she finishes her culinary arts degree at Johnson & Wales, and what little Ezra knows about her schedule makes him want to run for the hills. "It's okay. This is the last semester, and then it's just"— she wiggles her fingers—"the real world! So fun."

"So fun," Ezra says, proud of how straight he keeps his face, because now is not the time to tell her that sometimes the real world yanks your income out from under you and leaves you sprawled out on your ass in an apartment full of your ex-boyfriend's friends.

"Okay, okay, enough sibling time," Mom says, shooing Becca back with an exaggerated wave of her hands. "Mom hugs."

Ezra lets her fold him into her arms. He rests his chin on her head the way he always does, the way that makes his mother lament the fact that she never quite topped five feet. She smells like she always does in the kitchen: roasted chicken and sautéed onions and the floral, stinging scent of sweat and perfume. She has a pair of swimming goggles propped on her head, holding back her nest of gray-streaked curls. "Horseradish?" he asks as he pulls back.

She returns his grin, her eyes bright and cheerful. Working in the funeral home, her fashion has always trended toward conservative and modest, catering to the lowest common denominator of the clients they serve, but the one exception has always been her glasses: She favors large, thick, colorful rims in teal or yellow or pink or purple. As a teenager, he'd been embarrassed by them, had even accused her of spending half the family's budget on frames she might have found sold with a Barbie. But her bright frames serve to distract—or at least attempt to distract—from her thick lenses, which magnify her hazel eyes and refract even the subtlest emotions into the obvious.

It's the first thing he looks for when he comes home—any tiny microexpressions of unhappiness.

She seems calm enough today—or at least, he amends, as calm as she can ever be in the hours before the first night's seder, when there's always a certain amount of chaos in the air. Ezra kisses her cheek. "Sorry I wasn't able to get here for biur chametz," he says, and means it. The ritual burning of the symbolic pieces of dry pasta or Cheerios before leavened foods are banned from the house for the week of Passover— and the candlelight search that precedes it—is one of the few Jewish rituals where all his childhood memories are fond.

Mom shakes her head. "Dad was a bit put out, but I think he's over it. You know how he is; as long as he gets to set something on fire, he doesn't really mind who's around for it."

Ezra bites back a grin. "Sounds like him," he says. "How can I be helpful?"

Mom cranes her neck to look at the clock on the microwave. "We're actually heading to the point where I need Dad and Aaron to start moving things around in the dining room," she says. "Can you run across to the office and grab them?"

The office is how Mom refers to the funeral home. As a kid, it seemed strange—Dad called it the Chapel and most of the people Ezra talked to in the community called it Friedman's, but to Mom it was always *the office*. She never said why, but Ezra assumed it was because Mom had married into the business, and while she was good at it, she would never have picked it for herself. By making it just another office, just another place where she ran logistics, she didn't have to think about the fridge of bodies, lying stiff and silent across her tulip-lined yard.

Abner Joseph Friedman founded the Friedman Memorial Chapel in 1969. He had arrived in Providence twenty years earlier—thirteen years old, orphaned, and with a genocide's worth of trauma neatly packaged in the back of his mind, never to be touched except in the most strategic of moments to apply the weight of all his murdered family members' hopes and dreams and legacies onto his children and then, later, his grandchildren.

To the Jewish community that adopted him—and that he adopted in kind—he was Mr. Friedman, the kind but imperious funeral director. To Ezra, he was just Zayde.

In the photos scattered around Ezra's parents' house, Zayde Abner is a solemn, world-weary man, with deep circles beneath his eyes even in black and white. Ezra's brother, Aaron, four years Ezra's senior and—as far as their Zayde knew, since it would take Ezra another decade to come out—the only boy, was the heir apparent. Even when they were children, the assumption was that Aaron would join Dad as a funeral director, and so Aaron was the only grandchild to give a eulogy at Zayde's funeral.

Ezra was still refusing to believe that Zayde was dead at all by the time of the service. How could he be, when Ezra kept seeing him, tall and stern and solemn and sad, everywhere he looked?

Becca, barely a toddler at the time, only knows him through photos and their parents' stories. But Ezra remembers him by his woundedness and warmth, as someone who always made time for an Ezra he knew by a different name.

Ezra had been ten when he finally learned why.

"Your Zayde was the middle child, too," Mom told him, very quietly, holding Ezra's hand as they left services on Yom Kippur. "He had a brother and a sister, just like you. Now it's just him. I think that's part of why he does the work he does. To remember. And help other people remember."

Even then, Ezra knew a little bit about being haunted. Nothing like what Zayde knew, but a bit.

It made him understand Zayde a little more.

Which was why it hurt so badly, as the years passed and Ezra became less and less the little girl Zayde loved so much—if he'd ever been that little girl at all—that his grandfather looked more and more disappointed. Every time Ezra turned a corner in the Chapel and ran directly into his ghost, Zayde was there to greet him, brow furrowed and eyes unreadable. It's one thing to suspect your deceased family might not have approved of the person you grew up to be. It's another to see it. Zayde's spectral silence makes it impossible to know: Is it Ezra's abandonment of who he once was or his abandonment of the place where he was raised that Zayde finds so terrible?

Is it better or worse that he'll never know?

Ezra lets himself in through the employee entrance, sending up a prayer that he'll get through this visit without a glimpse of the dead. On the surface, the Chapel hasn't changed much since Zayde was in charge. The exterior of the building is still neatly kept and landscaped, the entryway rug well cared for but worn by decades of grieving footsteps, the furniture in the waiting room identical to the pieces that were there when the doors first opened. It's curated to be both welcoming and impersonal—not devoid of identity, but adaptable to anyone who might want to find a place for themselves inside it.

It's intentional, Ezra knows now, and probably one of the most genius things Zayde ever did—creating a blueprint for incremental changes, one year to another, a Theseus's ship of tiny shifts in color and décor to give a sense that the place never looked different, even as the pieces within it changed.

It's a sharp contrast to his family's home, just across the yard. If the Chapel is timelessness and calm and careful neutrality, the house exudes more personality per square foot than it has any right to. Nothing ever quite matches, the styling changing eclectically from room to room, something always mid-project, mid-renovation. When Ezra got permission to redecorate his room before he started high school, he jumped at the opportunity to turn it into a zen garden. It immediately became—even more than it had been before—Aaron and Becca's refuge, the three of them retreating to the cool, mossy oasis of Ezra's bedroom when everything else got too loud.

Metaphorically and not.

The employee entrance takes him in through the walk-in basement. There's a young woman sitting shmira by the cold room, a candle burning on the small table beside her. For half a heartbeat, he catches the shape of another woman, sitting cross-legged on the floor beside the first, with a sweep of dark hair and a soft, calm look on her face. He blinks, and the shade is gone.

He shakes his head to clear his vision and continues through the hallway, past the two preparation rooms and the display room, and up the stairs to the public space of the Chapel. Dad's office door is closed, but Aaron's is open. Ezra raps his knuckles against the doorframe but finds the room empty when he pokes his head in.

The door to Dad's office opens, sound rushing out into the hallway. "Like we said," Aaron is saying, clearly mid-conversation, his voice tight and tense. "We appreciate the offer, but we're not interested in— Oh, fuck." He breaks off at the sight of Ezra, clearly taken aback, one hand still on the doorknob, a leather folio and his laptop tucked under his other arm. "What are you doing here?"

"Hi to you, too," Ezra says dryly.

Aaron holds up a finger, sticking his head back into the office. "Ezra's here, Dad," he says.

"Ezra?" Dad comes out, followed closely by a tall woman with sleek blond hair and a suit so sharply tailored, Ezra's willing to bet it cost more than his car, adjusting the strap of her handbag over her shoulder. She's too well put together to be a client, Ezra thinks, and the irritated look on Dad's face that his professional façade hasn't quite covered confirms it.

"Hi, Dad."

"Chag sameach, kiddo." Dad presses a kiss to the top of Ezra's head, on the opposite side of Mom's. "How was your move?"

"It was fine." Ezra eyes the woman in the suit. "Sorry if I'm interrupting."

"You aren't," Aaron says flatly. "Ms. Lawrence was just leaving."

She gives him a customer service smile, all teeth and too high in the eyebrows. "Of course," she says. "You have my card, Mr. Friedman."

"I'll show you out," Dad says. "Ezra, I'll see you at home."

"Uh," he says. "Sure?"

The woman's mouth twitches. "Enjoy your holiday," she says.

Ezra watches warily as Dad directs her firmly away in the direction of the main exit, then turns to Aaron.

Aaron holds up a hand. "Please don't ask."

Ezra narrows his eyes at him. Aaron looks exhausted, his dark hair mussed, his usually impeccable suit a little rumpled around the edges. "Should I be worried?"

"No," Aaron says, too quickly.

"Wow." Ezra was already planning to be worried, joking questions or not, but now he frowns, looking more closely at his brother's face as if he can catch some clue he might have missed earlier. "So definitely yes, then."

"I will give you my second helping of kneidlach at dinner if you don't ask me any more questions," Aaron says.

He *really* doesn't want to tell. "Fine," Ezra says, but he nudges his shoulder against Aaron's. "You *can* tell me, though. I can keep a secret, if I need to."

Aaron smiles, but it doesn't reach his eyes. "Yeah," he says. "I know you can." He sighs, pulling Ezra into a one-armed hug. Ezra can still feel the tension humming through him, but his grip is firm and affectionate, and he ruffles Ezra's hair when he pulls away. "Wasn't expecting to see you over here. I know you avoid the whole building like the plague."

"I don't *avoid* it," Ezra protests, which is at least ten percent true.

"Sure you don't." Aaron gestures to his laptop. "I have to put this away. Did you come over because Mom needs us?"

Ezra lets him change the subject. "Furniture."

"My favorite. Let me drop this stuff upstairs and I'll be right there." He starts to turn, then pauses, giving Ezra the same once-over that Ezra had just given him. "What about you? You're looking tired. Everything okay?"

Ezra can't do everything, but he can do this. He pastes on a smile and lies through his teeth.

"Everything's great," he says. "Just glad to be home."

3

"So you noticed, it too?"

Ezra finishes the buttons on his shirt, glancing at Becca in the mirror. With fifteen minutes before they're supposed to be groomed, company-ready, and in the living room, Becca's somehow miles ahead of him, showered and changed and sprawled across his bed, Sappho half in her lap, scratching her ears with one hand. It soothes him to know that she's just as comfortable barging into his room as she ever was, as heedless of his state of undress as she was when she saw him as a sister, instead of a brother.

"Aaron being really shady? Kind of hard not to, after what I walked in on." He turns to her. "Does this look all right or am I going to Mom jail?"

Becca sits up on her elbows, studying his clothing and then giving an approving nod. They've always walked a fine line dressing for major holiday meals, finding the sweet spot between Nice Enough for Family Photos and Comfortable Enough to Eat Way Too Much. Becca's trended toward dresses and jumpsuits the last few years, and tonight is no exception, an orange one-piece that brings out all the subtle notes of gold in her brown eyes. Ezra tried on about six different outfits before he finally settled on a white button-down and a pair of khaki joggers—he can wrangle a French tuck and a half-open collar and get away with it, as long as neither of his parents looks too closely and realizes he's wearing the same pants he'd throw on to teach a yoga class.

"You look good," Becca says. She studies him for a moment more. "Can you really breathe in that thing?"

"You can say the word *binder*, it won't bite," Ezra says dryly. "And yes. They're literally designed for me to be able to breathe in them." They're *not* designed to be worn as many hours a day as Ezra wears his, and he's been on the receiving end of more of Nina's lectures about it than he cares to count—not that Becca needs to know that. Top surgery is expensive, even with his mostly decent insurance, and it's not like he has the time to take off for the recuperation period. He'll be stuffing his tits into nylon and spandex for the foreseeable future. "How long's it been going on? Aaron and Dad?"

She hums, pulling Sappho a little closer and resuming her ear scratches. Sappho whacks her tail against the wall. "At least a few weeks," she says. "Let me do your hair. Are you still putting that cheap stuff in it? I thought you were going to get better products."

"Not all of us can put curl cream on Mom's credit card, Rebecca," he drawls, but caves and pulls the—expensive, for his budget (he'd caved after her last rant about sulfates)—styling cream he uses out of his bag and tosses it to her. He sits in front of her so she can thread it through the longer curls at the top of his head, scrunching it through and twisting the individual curls around her fingers until they sit how she likes them. Ezra loosens them a bit when she's done anyway, because it's always funny to make her object and because he doesn't like how stiff it looks.

"Seriously? Weeks?"

Becca nods. "I think that woman's from the bank or something. It's gotta be a money thing. Remember how Dad used to get?"

There had been a few months of financial precarity during his junior year of high school, and Dad had been sharp with all of them, his temper on a hair trigger. They'd all walked on eggshells until things evened out. No surprise that it would fall on Aaron now. Uncle Joe, whose easy manner balanced Dad's short fuse, had resigned and moved out to the Cape two years after his wife died, and Dad would never let any of the regular employees know if they were in trouble.

"Not great," he says. Becca gives him a look, as if to say, *Understatement, bitch,* and he drops a hand down to Sappho's rump, scratching absently. She thumps her tail harder. "Have they said anything?"

"Have you met them?"

Yeah, he should have expected that. "Great. Excellent. Very helpful."

"In their defense," Becca says, "we come from a glorious tradition of absolutely not dealing with our shit."

"You don't do such a bad job," he says, reaching over to tap her nose with one finger.

"You used to give me Disappointed Mom Eyes until I talked to you about my feelings," she says, but she's grinning when she bats his hand away.

"Ezra!" Mom's yell comes from downstairs. "Rebecca! People are going to be here in five minutes. Will you come be social, please?"

Becca sighs. "Duty calls," she says, climbing to her feet. She leans down and cups Sappho's face in her hands. "Will you be the best girl and sit near me so I can use you as an excuse to not talk to people?"

"Hey," Ezra says. "Get your own dog." Sappho enthusiastically licks at Becca's hands. "Traitor."

"Ha," Becca says.

"Now, please!" Mom's second shout makes them both jump and head for the stairs.

Despite Mom's panic, the dining room is already set, Aaron and Dad sitting in the living room, glasses in hand and a bottle of plum brandy on the coffee table. "Pregaming already?" Becca teases, plopping down on the couch next to Aaron and peering at his glass. "Bold move, lightweight. Are we forgetting the great fourth glass of wine incident of 2017?"

"Don't tease your brother," Dad says. He looks a little more relaxed than he had when Ezra saw him earlier, though he's still wearing everything but his tie. Ezra briefly considers going back upstairs for shoes, a little worried about being sent up if he doesn't, but Becca seems perfectly at ease in bare feet.

Then again, Becca's the baby, and could probably murder a man in the living room and get away with it. She mischievously attempts to wrestle a sip of Aaron's drink while Dad looks on and does absolutely nothing about it.

"Are you two really drinking already?" Mom asks, drying her hands on a towel as she comes in from the kitchen, frowning at them. "We're about to spend the night going through about six bottles of wine."

"Aiming low tonight, I see," Becca deadpans. Mom gives her a pointed look, and she abandons her efforts to steal Aaron's glass. "Just saying! There are what, four glasses to a bottle, and if there are going to be eight of us—"

Ezra blinks. "Eight?" He'd known one of the local rabbis was planning to come, along with his wife—which is confusing, because Ezra thought clergy always worked on Passover, but hell if he's going *anywhere* near Providence congregational drama by asking—but the last he'd heard, that was it. "Who else is coming?"

"Their son-in-law," Dad says. "His plans with his family fell through at the last minute, apparently."

The doorbell rings and Mom goes directly into hostess mode, her face doing a strange transformation as she turns *Mom* off and slips into *Mrs. Friedman,* the funeral director's wife, pillar of the community. It's never failed to freak Ezra out, and he manages to successfully pluck the drink out of a momentarily distracted Aaron's hand—"Hey!" Aaron protests, too late—and drains it in one go.

It turns out that Ezra *has* met Rabbi Isaac Resnick and his wife, Judy, several times—almost always at family gatherings like this, where they blend into the sea of other Upstanding Jewish Community Members in Their Sixties that he files away in the back of his head in a little mental box labeled OPEN WHEN NECESSARY FOR SOCIALIZING. Fortunately, they seem to know both his name and his pronouns, so he gets through a few minutes of small talk without too much difficulty, and much *less* difficulty when Becca casually slips a glass of wine into his hand as they schmooze with Rabbi Resnick—"Call me Isaac, please," he says, shaking Ezra's hand, laugh lines deep around his eyes. "I'm off the clock."—while Mom and Judy retreat into the kitchen.

"You," Ezra tells Becca under his breath, as she knocks her shoulder against his, settling in with her own glass, "are my favorite sibling."

"Duh," she retorts. "Mom and Judy are talking shit in the kitchen, it's hilarious."

"Surprised you didn't stay."

"I got the sense that their desired topic was about to be talking shit about their kids," Becca says dryly. "I'm only so much of a masochist."

Ezra hides his laugh with a sip of wine—and then nearly chokes on it.

There's a ghost by the front door.

A familiar one.

He looks different in the golden light of late afternoon. More solid, less like a shadow. But Ezra recognizes him all the same as the ghost he'd seen barely a few hours ago, standing in the doorway of his bedroom. And that's . . .

That's not how it works. He may not understand why the ghosts he sees are there or what they want, but after twenty years, he's managed to scrape together a handful of rules he's pretty sure they have to follow. One of them—one he's always been grateful for—is that the ghosts don't *wander*, at least not any of the ones he's ever seen; they haunt the space around their bodies or they haunt the place where they died. They don't amble from place to place.

This isn't just a ghost drifting from one room to another. The Chapel is halfway across town from Ezra's new apartment.

"Ezra?"

He shakes himself back to reality, and the ghost disappears between one blink and the next. "Sorry—what?"

Becca frowns at him. "Are you okay? You went all spacey."

Ezra shakes his head. "I'm fine." The doorbell rings again, and he jumps at the distraction. "I'll get it—keep an eye on Sappho?"

Becca looks at the dog, currently parked by the coffee table and staring mournfully at the cheese board. "I think I can handle it."

Ezra hands her his wine and goes to the door, then nearly does his second spit take—this time without the benefit of actually having a mouthful of wine, which is just embarrassing—at the sight of Jonathan standing on the front porch.

He's dressed up since Ezra saw him at the house, and he looks as startled to see Ezra as Ezra is to see him.

"Um," Ezra says. Either the alcohol's already going to his head or this guy just makes him feel tongue-tied, and neither of those options can mean anything good. "What are you doing here?"

Jonathan blinks right back at him. "I was invited?" he says. "And . . . hi, again, I guess?"

Ezra isn't sure whether to relax or not. "Hi," he says. "Are you—" His brain, belatedly, catches up with his two sips of Aaron's brandy and half glass of wine, and he mentally smacks himself. "You're the son-in-law."

Something Ezra can't quite place flashes across Jonathan's face, but then he's all smiles again. "Yeah," he says. "Got a last-minute invitation—are you a stray, too?"

"I live here," Ezra says. *Jesus, Friedman, pull it together.* "I mean—my parents live here."

Jonathan's face lights up. "Oh my God, that's how I recognized you earlier." Ezra bites back the urge to cringe—*Please don't be a horrible this-one-time-my-kids story,* he thinks—but Jonathan's face softens as quickly as it brightened, turning kind, and a little sad. "Your dad handled my husband's funeral. I saw your picture in his office."

Oh. That's so much worse. "I'm sorry for your loss," Ezra offers, because *God, I hope it wasn't one of the ones where I still look like a girl* just seems like way too insensitive a thing to say.

Jonathan inclines his head in the graceful way Ezra has seen from widowed spouses before, that universal *There's really no good response to that, and I'm not sure why you're apologizing in the first place* half nod. "He made it as easy as he could," he says. "He's great at his job."

"Yeah," Ezra says, and then, way too belatedly realizing he's still standing in the doorway, shakes his head and steps back.

"Sorry, come on in, we'll get you a drink. Your— Everyone else is already here."

Aaron, thank every God that's ever been deified, recognizes Jonathan and greets him with an easy handshake, guiding him over to the makeshift bar. Ezra takes the reprieve and makes a dash to the bathroom, pulling out his phone as soon as the door locks behind him.

Rainbow Gnome Fan Club

> well, i figured out why Jonathan-from-downstairs thought I looked familiar 😵

Noah

> 👀 👀 👀

> YUP

> apparently my dad did his husband's funeral and there's a picture of me in his office

> SO THIS IS ALL VERY COOL AND NORMAL

Noah

> YIKES DOT GIF

Lily

> Did you actually just type that out instead of putting in an image

Sometimes I like to let y'all choose your own adventures

Also my wifi is garbage right now

Max

Ollie just spat his water all over the floor FYI

Ollie

I AM. WHEEZING.

OH MY GOD.

EZRA. ONLY YOU.

Noah

fwiw I was really banking on it being a summer camp hookup kinda thing

????? he's like?? five years older than me???

Noah

. . . did people not hook up with their counselors at your camp

Lily

Therapy. All of you.

Ezra shakes his head, slipping his phone back into his pocket. He flushes the toilet and—for appearances—washes his hands, and then makes his way back toward the living room.

He detours past the kitchen to double-check that Mom doesn't need any last-minute help—she wouldn't ask for it if she did, but she'll absolutely guilt him for not asking—and stops in the doorway at the sight of Mom and Judy sitting at the kitchen table, heads pressed together. Mom has her back to the door but he can see Judy's face, set in a tight, uncertain almost frown. She's younger than Rabbi Isaac, all glossy auburn hair and surprisingly youthful skin. She looks like someone who's usually smiling, and there's a wrongness to the tension of her face that radiates off her, even though he does not know her at all.

"Bobs," she's saying, barely audible from where Ezra's standing, caught between interrupting and running for the hills. He can only catch every few words, but the line of Mom's shoulders tells him they're not going over well. "I know you're frustrated, I get it, but this is already such a hard time of the year—with everything, you know what we're dealing with. This just isn't—*right*."

No one calls Mom *Bobs*. Dad calls her Bubbe; everyone else calls her Bobbi. Ezra has heard her introduce herself as *Barbara* exactly once, and that was to an overfamiliar telemarketer. Ezra hovers, caught between the temptation to eavesdrop and the urge to bolt.

Mom heaves a sigh and pushes her chair back, wood scraping linoleum. "We should get into the living room," she says, voice weary in the way Ezra recognizes from a hundred overheard almost arguments between her and Dad. It means *I'm not happy, but there's nothing to be done about it*. He's been on the receiving end of it a thousand times. "It'll be candlelighting in a few minutes."

"Bobbi," Judy says, something pleading in her voice. "I don't want us fighting."

Oh, no thank you. Ezra has enough to deal with keeping Mom and Dad's drama straight. He's not getting involved in Mom's friend fights, too. He makes a strategic retreat to the living room, pointedly ignoring Becca's curious look as he re-unites with his beloved wineglass and drains it just in time for Dad to check his watch, climb to his feet, and call everyone in to light the candles.

4

The thing about hosting a Passover seder year after year is that it becomes predictable. A few thousand years of doing the same thing the same way the same night of the year will do that.

At this point, Ezra and his siblings have found enough similarities from year to year to make bingo cards.

Those were great, while they lasted. For a fantastic four years, they pooled thirty bucks and bought a cake for whoever won once the holiday was over and they could all eat leavened desserts again. The cake was always too big for one person anyway, so it was a win-win—until Mom caught Becca surreptitiously filling her card out under the table. After a lecture that lasted well past dessert, they'd agreed that Friedman Family Seder Bingo would be retired.

Thus, the Friedman Family Seder Drinking Game was born. The rules range from ritual (Someone picks an inappropriate sing-along tune for listing the parts of the seder? *Drink*) to scholarly (Debate about why the Haggadah contradicts itself and can't decide if matzah is the bread of affliction or the bread of freedom? *Drink*) to conversational (Any of the three of them are asked when they're getting married? *Double drink*). Rules have been removed due to lack of use ("Any cis man outside the immediate Friedman family helps with dishes in any way, shape, or form") or way too much use despite alarming specificity ("Ezra is misgendered by a well-meaning but clueless relative over the age of seventy").

It's probably not any subtler than the bingo cards, but at least the lack of props makes it harder for Mom, over her own glass of wine, to do much more than give them the Disappointed Eyebrows.

Having an actual rabbi at the table means they blow through some of the more obscure rules earlier in the evening, and Ezra is pleasantly tipsy by the time they're halfway through maggid. Becca has had to kick him twice under the table for tilting into Jonathan's side when something makes him laugh too hard, muttering, "Oh my God, you *lightweight*" under her breath. Jonathan clearly picked up on what was going on the second time Aaron knocked back a glass of wine when Dad and Rabbi Isaac got caught in a frenzy of vigorous "debate," which was more like an enthusiastic series of agreements at an escalating volume. After that, he starts subtly playing along.

Which is, Ezra thinks, just unfair, because off-limits men should not be attractive, funny, *and* willing to casually join informal drinking games.

He mentions this to Becca when they go into the kitchen to "choose another white wine" and also subtly chug down a glass of water each.

"Please," she says. "Like that's ever stopped you."

Ezra finishes his water, considers the glass, and then refills it at the sink. "I'm making better life choices."

"Maybe stop looking like you're trying to play footsie with him, then," Becca says. She plucks his glass from his hand, pours half of it into hers, and downs it in one gulp. "Also, can we talk about how cranky Aaron looks about being across from Dad? Line of fire."

"Better him than me," Ezra says, though he'd found it a

little weird that Aaron ended up there instead of Rabbi Isaac, ostensibly the guest of honor. But Judy had taken the seat next to Mom, and Rabbi Isaac the seat next to Judy, and Aaron and Jonathan had exchanged five seconds of *not-it* eye contact before Aaron caved and took the seat at the head of the table, opposite Dad. Ezra refills his glass again. "It's his lot in life as the firstborn."

Becca nods, solemn. "We'll send him a fruit basket," she says, and pulls a bottle of moscato out of the fridge. "All right, let's go before someone restarts the Great Matzah Debate."

They slip back into the dining room, Becca depositing the bottle in the center of the table and Ezra meeting Aaron's *How dare you abandon me* glare with an apologetic widening of his eyes as he takes his seat again. Aaron rolls his in response.

"Now that everyone's back," Dad says, leveling a look at Ezra and Becca that has *You're not nearly as cute as you think you are* written all over it before opening his Haggadah again. "Ezra, why don't you pick up for us with Arami Oved Avi on page—"

"Actually," Mom says. "There's something I'd like to say before we go any further."

Something in her voice—a steady steel—slices through the room. Out of the corner of his eye, Ezra catches Becca's eyebrows shoot up, and the immediate, apprehensive look Aaron darts across the table toward Dad. For all they joke that Mom runs the family, major meals are usually Dad's domain. He has systems; he likes to play stage director, to make sure all the good beats of the story get their due time without anyone ending up hangry.

Dad tucks a napkin into his Haggadah to mark his page and sets it down on his plate with a gentle tap of paper on porcelain. "Of course," he says, like it's perfectly normal for them to go off script mid-seder.

Mom opens her mouth, and then pauses. She glances at Judy, who glances back, and they exchange a long, searching sort of look, the kind of look that speaks volumes of intimacy, untranslatable to everyone.

Everyone but Ezra.

After a moment that lasts an eternity, Mom extends a hand.

Not to Dad.

After a heartbeat of hesitation, Judy puts her hand into Mom's. They lace their fingers together.

Oh, Ezra thinks. *Oh*. Fuck.

"Um," Becca says. "Hi. What the fuck?"

"Language," their parents say together. Becca's mouth drops open. Ezra reaches over and puts a hand on her leg under the table, digging his fingers into the meat of her thigh.

Out of the corner of his eye, Ezra catches Jonathan using everyone's preoccupation with Mom and Judy to subtly pick up the bottle of moscato and refill his wineglass to the top.

"Bobbi," Dad says, voice carefully calm. "What's going on?"

Mom and Judy exchange another look. By some silent agreement, Judy speaks first. "Leo," she says, and then breaks off, looking across the table. "Isaac," she adds. "I—we—love you both very much. And we know this is going to be hard for you to hear."

Becca's hand clamps down on Ezra's. Across the table, Aaron looks like he's rapidly putting puzzle pieces together and getting increasingly alarmed as the picture starts to match the box.

"And—it's been so hard to find the right time to tell you this," Mom says. She looks at Judy, and if she were anyone else, Ezra would take out his phone to snap a picture of the literal stars in her eyes, shining with open affection. "But this whole seder is about freedom, and redemption, so we thought—*I* thought—"

"We've been in love for two years," Judy interrupts. Rabbi Isaac, who had just picked up his glass of water, drops it with a clatter. "We want to get married."

No one ends up eating dinner.

Ezra attempts—valiantly, in his opinion, though there's enough alcohol in his system that he can admit it's probably not nearly as smooth as he'd like to think—to cut the yelling off at the outset. There was probably never a chance of that working, especially when Judy's announcement is greeted by not one but two yelps of "What the *fuck*?" from opposite sides of the table, Becca and Aaron chorusing with the kind of synchronicity Ezra historically sees from them only when they're ganging up on *him*.

To absolutely no one's surprise, that doesn't set a precedent for a calm, rational discussion, and everything goes to shit from there. Dad and Rabbi Isaac start talking over each other immediately, each attempting to take control of the conversation, attempting to talk to his own wife, attempting to talk to the *other's* wife. Mom keeps looking around the room with wide eyes, as though she can't imagine why everyone's reacting the way they are and yammering about *living her truth* and *the importance our family puts on openness and respect*. Ezra catches and pointedly ignores the *back me up* looks she repeatedly sends his way; the fourth time, he gives up and snaps "Do *not* drag my queer ass into this" so dryly that Jonathan, next to him, chokes on his water and has to be thumped on the back by Aaron.

Judy puts the final nail in the coffin of any chance at a calm discussion by bursting into tears. After that, Dad kicks everyone whose marriage isn't actively going to hell out of the dining room without ceremony, and Ezra leaps on the opportunity to take Sappho on a loop around the block, leaving Aaron, Becca, and Jonathan standing in an awkward semicircle in the living room.

At least the night air is crisp enough to sober him slightly. Ezra's phone is going wild, but it's all in the group chat with his siblings, so he silences it and shoves it back into his pocket. He briefly considers texting Nina, or maybe his new roommates—if they thought his small-world Jonathan message was fun, he thinks, this'll *delight them*—and decides against it.

Mostly because he is absolutely not sober enough to walk the dog and text at the same time.

No one is left in the living room when he gets back. Ezra pauses by the dining room long enough to hear Judy shout, "Do *not* bring your *mother* into this, Isaac!" then hastily retreats to his bedroom, clicking his tongue at Sappho to follow him.

To his surprise, Aaron is on the floor of his room, a bottle of slivovitz in one hand and his phone in the other. He's abandoned his tie and his shoes. "Yo," he says, when Ezra slips in and closes the door behind him.

"Hi," Ezra says. "Don't you have your own room?"

"Your rug's comfier, I always floor-drink here." He lets out an *oof* as Sappho flops down against his stomach. "Jesus. She weighs a ton."

"Shush, you'll give her a complex." Ezra makes kissy noises at her until she rolls back up to her feet and trots across the room to him as he takes a seat against the side of the bed. "Where's Becca?"

Aaron takes a drink straight from the bottle, coughs, and gestures toward the door. "She said something about screaming into the void."

"Great. Don't suppose you stuck around the dining room to hear how things were going?"

"I bailed when I heard Judy bring up her and the rabbi's dead kid. The phrase 'emotional competency' was used."

"Hard *yikes,*" Ezra says, just as Becca slips into the room.

"Please tell me you have alcohol," she says by way of greeting, shutting the door behind her. Aaron holds up the bottle of plum brandy, and Becca groans, slumping back against the carpet. "Fucking *gross,* I hate this holiday so much. Why couldn't Mom make her marriage-ruining announcements on Purim?"

Aaron rolls his eyes and passes the bottle over, leaning up against the side of Ezra's bed. Becca unscrews the cap and takes a straight swig, then chokes. "Oh my God," she croaks. "That's a hate crime."

"No kidding," Ezra says. "Give it here."

Becca hands it over. The yelling from the dining room is audible through the closed door. "Where did Jonathan go? Are we terrible people for not inviting him to come be weird and drunk with us? I kind of feel like we're terrible people."

"We're good, he bailed *right* out of this madhouse," Aaron says. Ezra takes a sip of the slivovitz and promptly coughs as it burns its way down into his chest. "I saw him calling an Uber when I went to steal this."

"Oh, well," Ezra wheezes, trying to clear brandy out of his lungs. Aaron plucks the bottle out of his hand and takes another, much smoother sip. "At least we're not bad hosts."

"This is ridiculous," Becca says. "Like—this is ridiculous, right? Do you think it's a prank? Maybe the four of them are in some kind of weird open-relationship wife-swap kind of thing, and this is their way of easing us into it."

Aaron squints at her. "By having Mom say she had an affair? And then descending into a screaming hellscape?"

"Ew," Ezra says, taking the bottle back from Aaron. If they're going to sit here and have this conversation during the one week a year when they can't escape to IHOP to drown their feelings in pancakes and chemical syrup, he's not going to be any more sober than is absolutely necessary. Unfortunately, the slivovitz doesn't get any better with repeat exposure. "You're the one who's with them the most," he says to Aaron. "You really didn't have any idea this was going on?"

"Obviously not," Aaron says, with remarkable disdain for a guy who probably hasn't spent more than an hour out of earshot of one or both of their parents for five years. "First of all, I'd tell Dad. Second of all, I'd tell *you*."

"Please," Becca snorts. "You'd tell Ezra before you'd tell Dad, and then make Ezra tell Dad *for* you."

Aaron sticks his tongue out at her but doesn't argue. For a funeral director, Aaron avoids conversations that require any kind of emotional intimacy with an impressive level of skill. He often seems to forget that emotions exist.

Somewhere in the house, a door slams hard enough to rattle the walls, and they flinch in unison. Ezra passes the bottle back to Aaron as they fall quiet, reluctantly listening. The yelling seems to have stopped, but that doesn't necessarily mean anything. There's a thick expectation to the quiet that feels more like it's the eye of a hurricane than the passing of a storm.

Becca breaks the silence, her voice, uncharacteristically, very small. "What do we *do*?"

Ezra looks over at her. She's drawn her knees up to her chest, her arms looped around them as she worries at the skin between her thumb and forefinger, a nervous tic that Ezra and Aaron share. He reaches over and takes her hand before she can start digging her nails in, lacing their fingers together. The sugar in the alcohol is settling unpleasantly, but he can't tell if the stirrings in his gut are coming from his liver or his psyche.

"Probably nothing tonight." Approximately nothing good will come of them trying to wrangle any order out of this kind of chaos. Ezra's spent enough of his life trying to wrestle his parents and siblings into a baseline of *Can't we all just get along?*, at least for major family events—he knows when not to bother.

He wonders if it's worth seeing if there's any dinner left to salvage, but decides he's not actually sure his stomach can take it. Instead, he stretches a toe across the rug and nudges Aaron's leg, because Aaron's gone from looking like he's hoping to find the presence of God somewhere in the slivovitz bottle to mindlessly scrolling through his phone. "Hey. What about you? You okay?"

Aaron looks up. "What? Yes. I mean." He scrubs a hand over his beard. "I'm—well—"

"Oh my God," Becca says. "Spit it out."

Aaron shoots her a sour look but puts his phone down. "Not to make this shit about work, but Mom does, like, half the shit that keeps Friedman's running on the back end, and I can't imagine her showing up after chag ready to dive back into the office, and now I'm realizing how fucked me and Dad are going to be."

Ezra blinks. "Oh," he says. "Fuck."

"Yeah," Aaron agrees. "Which, you know, sure, but am I supposed to take all this as a resignation letter?" He winces. "Which I wouldn't even know what to *do* with, because Mom handles half the paperwork for personnel."

"Yikes," Becca says. Aaron shoots her a hopeful look, and she flings her hands up. "Absolutely not," she says. "I have my practicum, and even if I didn't, I am *not* cut out for the funeral business. Hire a temp."

"Right, because we're just *brimming* with people who want to hop into a family funeral home with a fresh round of HBO-level drama. Yeah, I'll type that 'help wanted' ad job listing *right* up."

A horrible thought starts percolating in the back of Ezra's head.

He doesn't like it. He *really* doesn't like it.

"If I happened to have some time opening up in my schedule," he says, hating every word as it comes out of his mouth, "what kind of work are we talking about?"

5

Ezra wakes up with a pounding headache, a nose full of dog fur, and his phone trilling in his ear. He groans and smashes his face into his pillow, which turns out to be less his pillow and more Sappho's neck, and gropes around for his phone to try to turn it off before the shrillness of it makes him throw up. It stays infuriatingly out of reach, and he forces his head up, squinting against the too-bright sunlight streaking through the curtains Cait had left on the window.

SUNRISE YOGA CLASS IN 1 HOUR!!! the notification tells him helpfully, and Ezra groans, jabbing his thumb against the screen to cancel it. He thought he'd deleted all his recurring class alarms in a fit of petty stress last night, but apparently he managed to miss the one set for *six in the morning*.

His reflection stares back at him from the blank screen, bleary-eyed and pale. He looks like roadkill—light brown curls smushed up to one side, clinging to the remnants of the product Becca had scrunched through them last night, the hazel eyes he normally actually likes shadowed with dark purple circles.

At least his skin is still clear—a hard-won victory over the second puberty his testosterone prescription had slammed into his pores.

Sappho snuffs at the side of his face. "Yeah," he sighs. "All right. Okay."

He starts a pot of coffee in the kitchen as a favor to his post-dog-walk self while Sappho noisily inhales her breakfast, and then forces himself to slog through two laps around the block in the early morning damp. Sappho gives him a resentful look when they turn toward the house, and he scratches her ears apologetically. "I'll take you for a better one in the afternoon," he promises. "Since apparently I don't have anywhere to be."

Steve the Pride Gnome is propping open the apartment door again, and the murmur of voices reaches Ezra well before he hits the landing. Sappho's entire body goes rigid with excitement at the sound of potential people to pet her, tail wagging so hard he genuinely worries she might sprain it, and he barely manages to wipe her paws off on a towel and unclip her leash before she goes racing inside, all skittering claws and delighted panting.

Ezra shakes his head after her, then startles at the unexpected eruption of greetings from the living room. Rounding the corner, he finds Noah and Max at the kitchen table and Lily passing a mug of coffee to Ollie where he's sprawled across the couch. They're in various states of readiness for the outside world considering it's barely six-thirty on a Monday, Max's paint-splattered, oversize RISD T-shirt and apparent lack of pants looking far more appropriate for the time than Lily's neat dress and an intricate fishtail braid.

"Look what the dog dragged in," Lily says, as Ezra gives them a bemused wave, shuffling over to pour himself a cup of coffee. He's suddenly glad he thought to make a full pot. "I thought you were going to be gone for a few more days."

"Change of plans," Ezra says. He joins them in the living room, lifting a socked foot to prod pointedly at Ollie's hip until he moves over on the couch to make room for him. Getting a rideshare after midnight on a weeknight in Providence, especially one that was willing to take a dog, had been a pain, and he'd spent half an hour sitting on the porch of his parents' house waiting for the car to show up. It was worth it to not have to wait for Aaron to sober up enough to drive him home—he hadn't wanted to spend any more time in the cloud of tension and fury that hung over the house than he had to. "Family drama happened. I staged a strategic retreat. Got home at, like, one."

Ollie, who has never in all the time Ezra has known him been a morning person, snaps his head up from where he'd been listing into his steaming mug. "Friedman family drama? And you didn't text me?"

"I will reiterate," Ezra says dryly, "that it was one in the morning."

"Time is fake," Ollie says. "Spill."

"You might as well," Max adds, reaching over to pluck a slice of avocado off Noah's plate. He wrinkles his nose at her but doesn't try to take it back. "You know he won't stop nosing until you do."

Ezra does, unfortunately, know that.

He gives them the highlight reel of last night's seder from hell. Ollie does an actual spit take when Ezra tells them about Mom and Judy's mid-seder bombshell, the story briefly derailing while Ollie chokes and sputters and Lily has to go get him a towel.

"Jesus," Noah says when Ezra stops talking. It's only the second time Ezra's met him in person, and Ezra can't help but think that no person should look that good this early in the morning. Like Lily, he's dressed for work, though more casually in jeans and a button-down with sleeves rolled up to expose the tattoos that run from his wrists to his elbows. His tight, dark curls are swept up into a loose messy bun, drawn back from his face with a yellow headband that makes his deep brown skin and eyes pop. The black polish on his nails is enviably un-chipped. He looks like he rolled out of a magazine shoot, not a bed he probably crawled into at two in the morning. "I want to start coming to your family dinners. Mine are boring as hell." Lily, coming back from the kitchen with her own coffee, smacks Noah's arm. "Ouch! What? What did I say?"

"He's having a *crisis*," Lily says, taking her seat and reaching down to pat Sappho's head. "Don't be insensitive."

"No, he's right," Max says idly. "I'd go to Ezra's family dinners. You need a date for your next one?"

Ezra cocks an eyebrow. "Are you willing to put up with a lot of invasive questions about your willingness to convert?"

"I could be!"

Noah holds out a hand. Max slaps it.

"Okay, but wait," Ollie says. "Can you go back to the part where you're going to be doing your mom's job?"

"That's a good point, actually." Lily props her chin in her hand. "What about your actual job?"

"I'm a doula," Ezra says. "It's not exactly a nine-to-five any-way."

Max leans forward, interest sparking on her face. "Wait, that's so cool."

He never knows how to respond when people say that. He loves it, but it's just his job—it's not any cooler than anything else. "Thanks." He clears his throat, carefully avoiding Ollie's eyes. It feels wrong to lie to them, not when they've only been good to him in the tiny amount of time he's known them, but the idea of telling them everything makes his stomach flip in a way he knows has nothing to do with his lingering hangover. He goes with a half-truth instead. "I teach yoga on the side, but I've been wanting to scale that back and do something a little more stable anyway, and someone has to do her job while she's—doing whatever she's doing. So it's a win-win."

"Right. Except that you'll be spending all your time there," Ollie says. "Which you hate."

"Ooh, insider info." Max tries to take another piece of Noah's avocado. This time, he pulls it out of her reach. She sticks out her tongue at him, then turns hopefully back to Ollie. "Say more!"

"Do *not* say more," Ezra says before Ollie can open his mouth. "And I don't *hate* it. It's just complicated."

He does hate it, and Ollie *knows* he hates it, because he's been on the receiving end of Ezra's rants about it for years. Ezra meets his eyes over the edge of his mug and tries to pour every iota of *Please don't make this a thing* he can muster into his face.

Ollie frowns at him, but he doesn't push.

That was the thing with Ollie, though. He never did.

Ezra spends most of the day on Nina's couch, texting his siblings and pretending he's not avoiding his own apartment.

Becca had managed to talk a friend into picking her up shortly after Ezra left last night and hasn't been home since, and has been alternating choppy single text messages with paragraph-length dictations. That's baseline for her in the initial aftermath of a crisis. Her crash always comes a week or so later, when she's run out of steam and inevitably breaks down.

Aaron confirms that Dad is functioning, albeit in something of a daze—at least enough to handle the immediate calls that are coming in, since even though funerals don't take place on chag, death doesn't stop just because it's a holiday. They've been staying in their respective offices for the most part, and Dad has been communicating only through their work email server.

Mom, evidently, left with Judy last night, and no one seems to know where either of them went.

if it turns out they have a secret love nest somewhere, Becca texts at one point, i will riot. shit 😳 will 😳 burn 😳

Ezra can't say he blames her. He texts back another reminder that he loves her, that she should remember to drink some water and not just stress-chug energy drinks all day, and tries to remember that she's old enough to not need him hovering over her to make sure she's okay. In his head, she's the kid who called him every single night his first month of college to ask when he was coming home, even though he'd gone to school only fifteen minutes away.

He starts and deletes about fifteen messages to his mom, chewing the inside of his cheek until he starts to taste copper and Nina takes his phone away. "Unless you're going to go track down your mom or haul your dad out of his office, you're just stressing yourself out," she tells him.

"But—"

"No buts. You can have this back when I think you'll be responsible with it. Now, come snuggle and let's watch some terrible reality television."

They spend a few lazy hours watching old episodes of *The Bachelorette,* Sappho snoring contentedly on the floor beside them. Ezra inches his way closer on the couch until Nina finally rolls her eyes and slings an arm around him to pull him against her side, and something animal and unsettled inside him quivers and then goes limp and loose at the touch.

He puts his head on her shoulder, feeling suddenly exhausted. "Thanks," he mumbles.

It's quiet enough that it's almost swallowed by the sound of the television, but Nina shifts to look at him, one brow cocked. "For what?"

He shakes his head, not knowing how to put it into words. Normally his family would be having their second seder tonight, just the five of them. It doesn't feel right to be somewhere they're not, somewhere he can't make sure they're okay, especially when he knows they're not. The rational knowledge that there's nothing he can do to fix any of this doesn't make the clawed scratchings of *useless, useless, useless* at the back of his head any easier to bear.

None of that is her problem. "I don't know."

Nina gives a little sigh, tinged with fond exasperation, and slides a hand into his hair, stroking through the longer, messier curls at the top of his head. She'd been the one to finally haul him out of his dorm room freshman year, insisting he do something other than talk to his baby sister. She knows all his bad habits by now, and has her own opinions about how often she's willing to let him get away with them. Tonight, she seems willing enough to give him a pass. "You're staying over?"

"Can I?"

It comes out more hopefully than he intended, but she smiles. "Not like it's the first time. Besides, you're the only guy in my life who doesn't steal the covers."

Her smile softens the words. Ezra gives a noncommittal hum and drops his head back onto her shoulder. There's still a jittery, anxious energy under his skin. Maybe Nina wants her bookshelves dusted? Everyone's bookshelves can use dusting.

"I know that look," she says, and nudges him off her. "The last time you looked like that you got rid of half my closet. It did *not* spark joy."

"You said you wanted a capsule wardrobe."

"In *theory,* not in practice. You know I'm a maximalist at heart." She gets to her feet and pulls him with her. "You need to relax. Go take a bath."

He grimaces. "You know that's not really my thing."

"You can turn the lights off." She gives him a pointed shove down the hallway. "Go. Put some music on, drop in a bath bomb, try not to give in to the temptation to drown yourself. It'll be good for you."

Ezra gives up. It's not like he's ever won an argument against her anyway. "Can I at least have my phone back?"

She purses her lips but hands it over. "For ambience *only*," she says. "I'll send you a playlist."

He salutes her, then heads off down the hall.

Ezra doesn't take baths often. It's a long time to spend naked and alone with his body, and while there are plenty of things he doesn't mind doing with his body—even plenty of things he doesn't mind doing with his naked body—there's something about the length of a bath and the heat and stillness of the water that reminds him of being suspended in time. But sometimes, when his brain is fussing and fidgeting and too much, and he doesn't have it in him to quiet everything down enough for a yoga session, heat and stillness are the best he can do.

Turning the bathwater to somewhere between Fires of Mount Doom and Fire Cannot Kill a Dragon, he crouches down to poke through Nina's box of spa supplies where it's tucked under the sink next to the sharps container for her estrogen injections. He chooses a candle that claims to smell like grapefruit, peach, and hydrangea, a stick of jasmine incense, and a bath bomb labeled Deep Sleep. The clear water fizzes into a milky foam of violet blue when he drops it into the tub, swirling like a galaxy. Ezra tests the temperature and sighs softly in relief when his fingers all but vanish beneath the surface, the water satisfyingly opaque. When he turns off the light, leaving only the soft glow of the candle he places on the rim of the tub, he can see the level of the water and the outline of his body but not much more than that, and he's glad for it.

It's easier when he doesn't have to *see*.

He undresses, piling his clothes on the closed toilet seat. He's careful to fold his packer securely into his underwear—the last thing he needs is a repeat of the time it fell out on the way from the bathroom to Nina's room, and he still has nightmares about her throwing it none too gently at his head with a yell of "Stop leaving your dick in public places, Ezra!," which would have been mortifying even under the best of circumstances. Laying his binder on top of the pile, he runs absently through a few stretches, rolling his shoulders and neck as he turns the water off and climbs in.

It's . . . nice. Between the dark room and the violet water, his only awareness of his body comes from what he can feel, not anything he can see. The tub isn't that big—one of Nina's biggest complaints about her apartment is never being able to submerge her nipples and her knees at the same time, but then again, she's a lot taller than he is—but he doesn't mind exposing his knees to the cooler air if it means his chest is fully under the water.

His phone vibrates on the edge of the tub, nearly falling in before he catches it with his elbow. He gropes for a hand towel, dries his fingers, and picks it up, then nearly drops it again at the sight of Dad's name. It's a new group chat, Ezra realizes, just his dad and siblings, Mom's number conspicuously absent.

Dad

> Omer starts tonight. Don't forget to count.

Well. It's proof of life, at least. Ezra looks at the message, thumbs hovering over his keyboard, suddenly sweaty in a way that has nothing to do with the bathwater.

He's never done the nightly counting that tracks the seven weeks from Passover through Shavuot, despite his dad's repeated attempts. He'd tried, once, after he first came out, to prove that he wasn't abandoning their customs just because he'd rejected the name they chose for him for the one *he* chose. He had taken away their oldest daughter, sure, but he wasn't erasing the rituals they'd raised him with, the practices they'd worked so hard to teach him to love.

He'd given up somewhere in the third week. It had felt hollow, more recitation than ritual. Now he wishes he'd tried a little harder.

He's waited too long to reply. Ezra sighs and unlocks his phone again, the screen gone dark while he drifted, lulled into memory by the water and the subtle scent of jasmine in the air.

Thanks:)

It doesn't feel good to make it seem like he'll be practicing this year, but at least it lets Dad know he's there on the other end of the line. Ezra waits until Dad texts back a thumbs-up, then a few more seconds to see if he'll send anything else. When he doesn't, Ezra chews his bottom lip, tapping a finger against the side of his phone, then gives up and calls Aaron.

Aaron picks up on the first ring, sounding simultaneously wired and exhausted. "Hey."

"Hey," Ezra says. "How's Dad?"

"Avoiding me. I was about to go lurk outside his office to make sure he was still breathing."

"He's not talking?"

"You know how he is. Earlier I asked him if he wanted to have dinner together since obviously we're not doing a seder, and he told me he was going to catch up on paperwork. That was"—there's a pause—"five hours ago."

"Oh."

"Yep." Another pause. Ezra knows the next question before it comes. "Have you talked to Mom at all?"

"No." He knows that if any of them are going to, it'll be
him, but he just . . . doesn't have it in him yet. Out of pure
blind hope, he tries, "You?"

Aaron lets out a humorless laugh. "You don't want me
talking to Mom right now."

That's . . . true, probably. Aaron's far better at managing his
temper than Dad, but he's still twice as quick to snap or yell as
Ezra. "I'll call her tomorrow."

"You don't have to."

Of course he does. "I want to." The lie rolls off his tongue,
practiced and smooth. "It'll be fine."

"If you say so." He can hear rustling, the quiet clatter of
dishes.

Good, Ezra thinks. *At least he's eating.*

Aaron clears his throat, too loud over the line. "So—hey.
About Mom's work, at the Chapel—I know we didn't really
talk logistics—"

Ezra sighs, tilting his head back against the tub. In truth,
he's been regretting his promise to help ever since he'd impul-
sively offered it last night, but the hope in Aaron's voice kills
any chance of him backing out now. "I'll come in early tomorrow."

Aaron's sigh rushes through the line, thick with a desperate sort of relief. "Thank you."

Ezra tucks the naked gratitude in his brother's voice away,
so he can find it again the next time he's aching under the
weight of memory that clings to the Chapel's haunted halls,
ghosts both literal and emotional lingering in every room.
They had all grown up there, surrounded by death and ritual
and strangers, but only Ezra could see the faces of the dead.

The Chapel was Aaron's birthright. It had been Ezra's playground, until it became his haunted house. He'd left as soon as he was old enough to run. He'd hoped it would feel better, to be going back by choice, but there's only that old anxiety, tight and hot and prickling across his skin.

"I'm happy to help," he says.

He expects the acoustics of the room to amplify the words, make them flow and echo off the walls. Instead, they slip out, too quiet, too heavy. They leave him in a murmur and sink beneath the water like a stone.

6

The walls of the building haven't crumbled under the weight of familial drama by the time Ezra walks into the funeral home the next morning.

It's more of a relief than he expected.

He follows Aaron through the staff entrance, shivering slightly in the cold morning air and then in the chill of the air-conditioning. It's still chag, so there won't be much happening until the holiday ends after sundown and ritual work is permitted again. The building is quiet without the constant hum of voices and shuffling feet that usually fill the halls, mourners gathering and staff moving quietly and efficiently around them, readily available yet invisible until they're needed.

Despite the early hour, there are voices coming from the open door to the main staff office as they make their way down the hallway. "Melissa," Aaron says by way of explanation when Ezra shoots him a questioning look. "She said she wanted to come in to get some paperwork done, and I wasn't going to tell her no."

"Is that you, Aaron?" Melissa, one of the other funeral directors, pokes her head into the hall. Her reading glasses are tucked on top of her head, her regular pair perched on her nose and magnifying the laugh lines around her eyes. She's worked for the Chapel since Ezra was eight, and he's never met anyone else with her ability to go in less than a minute from pastoral compassion to putting the fear of God into a doctor who forgot to sign a death certificate. "Oh! And Ezra!"

"Hi, Melissa." Ezra accepts her hug, remembering to turn his head to avoid being poked in the eye by one of the pens stuck haphazardly through her hair to hold her bun in place. "How were your seders?"

"Calmer than yours, from what I hear. I can't believe your mother would just quit on the spot like that after all these years."

"Tell me about it," Aaron says, remarkably smooth, before Ezra has a chance to look at him. "Fortunately, Ezra's volunteered to step in and cover us while we figure things out."

"Mensch that he is," Melissa agrees, squeezing Ezra's arm. "It'll be good to have you back around, honey. We've missed you haunting the halls!"

"Ha," Ezra manages. "Yup. Looking forward to it."

Aaron clears his throat. "Is Jonah in?"

"Not yet," Melissa says. "I think he was on daycare drop-off today." Jonah, a tall, wiry man around Aaron's age, took over the vacant funeral director position when Uncle Joe retired. He has three kids under the age of six and Ezra has never seen him looking anything other than absolutely exhausted or without a travel mug of coffee the size of his head. "Bless him," she adds.

"Or something," Aaron says with an exaggerated shudder. "You know he and Lori are thinking about a fourth?"

"More power to them, I suppose," Melissa says. "I was happy to be one and done." The phone rings behind her. "I'd better get that. Ezra, we'll catch up later, okay? I want to hear all about everything you're up to."

Ezra has enough time to wave before she's ducking back into the office. He catches the way her voice shifts into smooth professionalism as she picks up the call.

"'Can't believe she quit on the spot'?" Ezra murmurs as they head down the hall, not sure if they're quite out of earshot.

Aaron has the grace to grimace. "I had to tell her something," he says. "But I wasn't going to spill all the gritty details. Not without Dad saying it was okay."

"It's Melissa," Ezra points out. "She can sense gossip six miles away."

"I'm counting on the post-Passover rush to distract her," Aaron says. There's always an influx after a major Jewish holiday, the elderly and sick who were holding out for one last gathering or ritual finally willing to let go.

"Good luck with that."

The door to Dad's office is shut when they pass, the soft murmur of Dad's voice just audible through the heavy wood, surprisingly calm. Aaron pauses by it, his fingers fidgeting at his side as if preparing to knock. Then he seems to think better of it, shaking his head and moving on down the hall.

Unlike Dad's office, all dark wood furniture and unremarkable art prints and severe lines, Aaron's feels organic. The soft gray walls make the green of the plants scattered across the windowsill and coffee table and shelves seem brighter, proof of life. There's texture to the chairs and the area rug around the little coffee table in the other corner of the room, a few extra tchotchkes and photos on the desk and bookshelves.

"You've redecorated," Ezra remarks, dropping onto the sofa.

"*Becca* redecorated," Aaron corrects, sitting down in one of the chairs across from him. "Three months ago, maybe?

She said it was enough for me to be taking over Dad's old job, I didn't need to keep his office the same."

Ezra spares him a smile. This room had been Dad's before Zayde died, the big office next door remaining empty for almost two years after his death until his father was convinced to take it over. Ezra might be the only one who can see ghosts here, but Zayde's presence lingers, and Dad is haunted, too. "The plants are a nice touch."

"Also Becca," Aaron says. "Though she keeps telling me she's going to switch me to fake ones if I don't stop killing them."

Ezra raises his eyebrows at the little cluster of pots in the center of the table. "They're succulents," he says. "You have to, like, *work* to kill these things. I had one that I didn't water for like six months because I thought it was fake, and it *still* didn't die."

"I don't have Mom's green thumb," Aaron says glumly, eyeing the plants.

The mention of Mom thickens the air, summoning a weary tension that hangs between them like a fog. Aaron's eyes dart toward the wall that adjoins Dad's office, just briefly, and then he slumps back in his chair, pushing his glasses up so he can rub a hand over his face. It's a gesture they share, picked up from Dad and Zayde when they were still too young to notice where it came from. Becca does it, too, though more delicately, mindful of her makeup.

"Has he said anything?" Ezra finally asks.

Aaron scoffs, shaking his head. "Come on."

Did you *ask,* Ezra wants to press, but he knows the answer. Aaron and Dad get along as well as they do because they never rock the boat. Maybe it was wishful thinking to hope that this might be enough to make Aaron push against the boundaries of Dad's well-established comfort zone, but apparently not. He lets it go. "I'm still trying to figure out what to say to Mom."

"You could wing it."

"Not really my style." He can't really remember the last time he said something important that he hadn't run through at least twice in his head. "I'm going to try to text her tomorrow, maybe tonight if I can get my head around it, I'm just . . ."

"Hey, it's not like I blame you." Aaron gives him a crooked half smile. "She wasn't exactly subtle about trying to get you on her side the other night."

Ezra huffs. "Noticed that, did you?"

"I'm not *that* oblivious." Aaron grimaces. "I mean, she'd already dug a pretty deep hole for herself, but trying to drag you in with her with the whole *Well, we're all gay here so clearly you should be on my side* bit was shady."

"Thanks for the solidarity." He toys with a loose thread on the hem of his shirt. "I'm not used to not knowing what to say to her. Even when she's driving me halfway out of my mind, I still usually know how to talk to her like she'll eventually listen to what I'm saying. But this is . . ."

He trails off, not really sure what he can say. Aaron gives a quiet hum in response but doesn't offer any advice. Aaron has always been happy to play the protector and the spokesperson, but whatever gene that was supposed to bestow sage wisdom upon eldest siblings seems to have skipped over him. "What's Becca say?" Ezra grimaces, and apprehension dawns over Aaron's face. "You haven't talked to her about it?"

Ezra rubs at the web between his forefinger and thumb, pinching the skin absently. "She's taking this so hard already," he says. "I don't want to make things worse for her."

"She'll have to talk to Mom eventually," Aaron points out.

Ezra shakes his head. "Let me mellow them out a little," he says. Trying to get Mom and Becca to come together smoothly is like trying to force two magnets to join at the same pole. "Then they can talk."

Aaron looks at him, thoughtful and quiet.

"Okay," he says. "You know best."

Ezra takes over Mom's office out of practicality, since everything he'll need to do her job is already there.

But it's strange to be here without her. Mostly because it doesn't . . . *feel* like her anymore. When she wasn't playing the dutiful Funeral Director's Wife, Mom's energy—large and loud and sweeping—filled any room she entered. Now it seems dull and blank and almost devoid of character. It's as tasteful as almost every other room, done in cool greens with undertones of gray, with framed abstract black-and-white art prints on the walls and a few succulents scattered across the room. When Ezra snoops through her shelves, he finds mostly books on workplace culture and employee development, as well as a smaller section that seems to focus mostly on Jewish rituals and the funeral industry as a whole.

The only things that still make the room feel at all familiar are the family photos lining the desk—snapshots from Aaron's bar mitzvah, Ezra's college graduation, the trip they took up to Vermont the summer after Becca finished high school. He spends a good five minutes studying them, looking from one to the next in chronological order, as if he can place the exact moment Mom checked out of her marriage by staring at her body language, before giving up and flopping into the desk chair with a sigh.

Cool air prickles against the back of his neck. He doesn't bother turning his head. "Don't start," he says, hoping no one walks by the open door and catches him talking to an ostensibly empty room. "I'm not here because I want to be."

He can picture Zayde's frown without having to look. When the unpleasant chill doesn't go away, he glances over anyway, just to be sure.

Zayde *is* frowning, but it looks more concerned than disapproving. Ezra frowns back. "What?"

Zayde purses his lips and then disappears.

Ezra stares at the empty space where he'd been standing, then drags himself to his feet to go find a cup of coffee.

Halfway through his second day, Aaron pokes his head in and asks if he has a suit. Ezra's blank expression must be answer enough because Aaron shoves a credit card at him with instructions to go get one tailored by the end of the day. "I forgot how often Mom came to the services to help with logistics," he says, ushering Ezra toward the exit and out into the parking lot. "We've got two lined up tomorrow, and not enough ushers, and you know the basics."

"Okay, but I don't know where—" Aaron's already jogging back inside, phone in hand, and Ezra slumps against the side of his car. "Cool," he says, and sends a mass text to everyone he thinks might know where to find a trans-friendly tailor on extremely short notice.

The amount he ends up charging to Aaron's card makes him wince, but it's worth it when he looks at himself in the mirror at the tiny tailor's shop in Cambridge, his shoulders broader and the lines of his torso straighter than he's ever seen them.

It's worth it all over again when he shows up at work the next morning and catches Jonathan in the smaller of the chapels setting out discreet boxes of tissues with a VOLUNTEER USHER badge pinned to his lapel. In response to Ezra's hopefully subtle question, Melissa tells him that Jonathan has been doing more volunteer hours with the Chapel for the past few months—mostly chevra work, but generally making himself available for whatever is needed. Including, apparently, weekday funerals.

"I don't think he's working full-time yet, poor thing," Melissa had said, sympathy in her voice. "Not that I can blame him."

With the amount of time Jonathan spends there, maybe Ezra should be more surprised that they haven't crossed paths sooner. But then again, he'd spent the last several years avoiding the place like the plague.

When he sees the way Jonathan's eyebrows fly up at the sight of him, recognition and amusement sparking in his face, Ezra suddenly regrets not visiting more often. "Don't you clean up well."

The way he says it is light, teasing, but there's a touch of heat to the words. Ezra feels an answering warmth creep up his neck. "Don't tell my roommates," he says. "They think I only own yoga pants and joggers, and I want to keep it that way. It keeps expectations low."

Jonathan laughs. "My lips are sealed."

Ezra's saved from having to watch the way his dark eyes crinkle at the corners when Jonah calls him over to put out the cones in the parking lot.

If his cheeks are still flaming by the time he gets there, Jonah is polite enough to pretend not to notice.

He spends the better part of a week learning the systems that keep the Chapel running: software, filing systems, decoding the complicated way Mom organizes to-do lists. There are things that he already knows from growing up here—how to answer the phone, how to fill out the first call sheets, how much information he's allowed to take before passing an intake off to one of the licensed funeral directors. His office is tucked out of the way of most of the foot traffic, and he goes back and forth between enjoying the quiet and desperately missing the buzz and barely organized chaos of the QCC.

Ezra never finds out the specifics of what Aaron tells everyone about what happened at their seder from hell. Dad makes himself scarce, as much a ghost as the occasional spirits Ezra catches out of the corner of his eye, appearing to talk with clients but otherwise barring himself behind a closed door, leaving Aaron in charge by default. Melissa and Jonah take Ezra's presence in stride, and other than getting a little tired of introducing himself to the newer volunteers and burial society members, the transition goes smoothly. Whatever Aaron said, it got the point across.

But maybe he should give Aaron a little more credit. For all the contrasting ways Ezra's used to thinking of him—the golden child groomed for the responsibility of the family business, the human disaster Ezra's been emotionally managing since he was about four—he's also a professional. More important, he's a professional in a horrendously close-knit community with generations of gossip and baggage. Rumors are already spreading, given that Rabbi Isaac heads up one of the most well-known synagogues in the area, and Aaron's smart enough not to hand out any information that might throw fuel on the fire, no matter how much he trusts the people who work at the Chapel to be discreet.

Whatever Aaron said, or didn't say, no one asks any questions.

The walk through the Chapel at the end of each day feels miles longer than it should, like the very floor of the building is trying to keep him from leaving. He finds himself staring down at his feet so he doesn't make eye contact with any wandering ghosts that appear almost purposefully in his path the moment he tries to leave.

It's harder than he expects, guilt prickling over his skin with every step, and he can never manage to resist one last look back over his shoulder before he walks out the door.

But then Zayde will be there, his lined, somber face determined, standing between Ezra and the corridor. He shakes his head and nods at the exit. Pointed. Firm.

Is he protecting the ghosts from Ezra, or Ezra from the ghosts?

Ezra takes the hint, and goes.

7

It's strange, being back here.

Growing up, he'd been constantly in his parents' way, possibly a subconscious attempt to punish them for making him spend so much time surrounded by the cold, tingly feelings that came along with everything he couldn't talk about. He might have been the only one aware of the ghosts, but everyone seems conscious of the other specters in the air—the decisions made based on what Zayde would have wanted, the looming pressure of being his legacy, the weight of thirty-six murdered family members none of them had ever met lingering like smoke from an ill-kept fireplace.

By the end of the first week of fitting himself uncomfortably into his mother's shoes, Ezra's bracing for a crash. It's not just about the cold spots and crawling chills that let him know something is there that shouldn't be, the effort of remembering to keep an impassive face when he sees something no one else will notice—it's knowing that he'll have to provide constant, unending availability to Dad and Aaron. When he was younger, Ezra was the go-to for complaints and venting and airing of grievances, about working with each other and working with clients and the emotional weight of the world. He can't imagine it'll take long before he's back there again.

Nina tells him he has a miserable case of chronic Eldest Daughter Syndrome, and that's why he can't tell them to manage their shit themselves like grown men should. "It transcends gender," she'd said dryly when he narrowed his eyes at her the first time she threw out the term. "If you were raised the eldest daughter, you're stuck with it for life."

In the end, he's half right to expect it. The barrage of texts he's used to getting daily from Aaron turn into near-hourly visits to Mom's office, Aaron dropping into one of the chairs across from Ezra's desk that are meant for clients and promptly launching into a tirade about whatever's driving him up a wall, regardless of whatever Ezra's working on at the time.

He's working through Mom's giant inbox and trying not to spend too much time glancing up at the clock as it ticks closer, closer, closer to five, flying high on feeling halfway competent and the absence of a single ghost sighting all day, and is thinking about the possibility of another cup of coffee when someone raps at the doorframe of the office.

"Ezra?"

A zing of recognition flashes through him before he looks up. That's . . . more than a little embarrassing.

I've met this guy three times, and I already like how he says my name. Ezra clears his throat. "Hey."

"Hi," Jonathan says, leaning against the doorframe, all long limbs and broad shoulders and warm eyes. "Do you have a minute?"

The to-do list Ezra started this morning has doubled since he got to his desk, with only about a third of the tasks crossed out. "Yes?" he offers.

"You sound very confident about that," Jonathan says, mouth quirking slightly at the corners.

His hair is doing something different today, more of a

sweep of dark curls over his forehead rather than the combed-back style that Ezra assumed was his usual. It makes him look a little younger, a little softer. Ezra slams the door to that thought shut and swallows the key.

"I've got a minute," he says. "What's up?"

Jonathan's easy smile falters into something almost cha-grined. "Is there any chance you have time to help with a taharah?"

Ezra blinks. "What?"

"I hate to ask," Jonathan says, and sounds like he means it. "But I can't get a fourth member of the chevra out here for another hour, and we're supposed to be starting in"—he checks his watch and makes a face—"twenty minutes. We can manage with three, but I really prefer a full four. Normally Aaron or your dad would fill in when we need an extra set of hands, but they're both running ragged. Which you probably knew." He gives Ezra a small, hopeful smile. "Aaron said you'd done it before and I could ask you, but he mentioned you weren't super into it. I won't be offended if you say no."

"Oh," Ezra says. He and his siblings had been taught the traditional pre-burial practices when they were in high school. The sex-segregated nature of the rituals meant that Ezra had learned from his mother, caught between discomfort and wonder, watching her maneuver rigid limbs with the same tenderness she used to brush the hair from his forehead.

It wasn't until he put two and two together in college, fi-nally having the space for his gender identity to puzzle into place the way he'd never been able to put into words, that he realized it wasn't the ritual that had made him uncomfortable. It had been doing it for women, who were only supposed to be seen *by* other women. Some secret, hidden part of him had known he didn't belong.

"I might need a quick refresher," he says. "But I can do it."

Jonathan's face is like the sun breaking through a fog. "*Thank you,*" he says, so emphatic that red starts to creep up Ezra's cheeks again.

"No problem," he says quickly. "I mean, I'll have to finish, like, two quick things here, but—" A thought occurs to him, an *obvious* thought. "Oh—hey. Um, there's one thing."

This never gets easier.

"I'm trans," he says. Jonathan's face doesn't change, so Ezra pushes on before he can lose momentum. "Which you probably picked up on, but if it's going to be an issue, like, on the religious side—"

"*Oh.*" Jonathan looks alarmed. "Oh my God. No. Of course not. Sorry, I should have— Sorry. Let me back up." To Ezra's surprised amusement, he literally takes a step back out into the hall, gives himself a little shake, clears his throat, and steps into the room again.

"Thank you for telling me," he says, looking Ezra in the eyes with a kind of steady sincerity that Ezra doesn't know what to do with. "I'm sorry you felt like you had to— That's fine. We wouldn't— It's gender identity that matters. I wouldn't have pressed you."

". . . Oh." That damned earnest look. Ezra wants to wave off the whole conversation and hide under his desk to avoid it. He takes the easy route. "I'm happy to help, then."

"Thank you," Jonathan says, his warm, open face flooding with relief—and is *he* flushing a little? *What the fuck,* Ezra thinks. Jonathan's hands twitch slightly at his sides, and Ezra catches the motion as he turns his wedding ring around his finger, a nervous little fidget Ezra recognizes from all his partnered friends.

"You'll probably want to change, too," Jonathan adds. Ezra raises an eyebrow, and Jonathan motions to his own casual clothing. "We'll be dealing with a lot of water."

"I remember," Ezra says, wincing. "I keep some stuff across the yard at my parents' house, I'll grab something. I'll meet you downstairs in twenty?"

"Fifteen, if you can swing it," Jonathan says, and gives him a quick, grateful wave.

By the time Ezra makes it down to the preparation rooms, his dress pants swapped out for a pair of threadbare jeans he'd found in the back of his closet, Jonathan has been joined by two men Ezra doesn't recognize. One looks to be in his late forties, the other older, closer to Dad's age. They both shoot him slightly curious looks, but Jonathan does a smooth round of introductions, presenting Ezra as "Leo's younger son" as if it's obvious who he is, and the other two men seem to take it in stride, shaking his hand and giving their names, which Ezra does his best to commit to memory.

Jonathan passes him the taharah handbook outside the door, a slim booklet stapled with the chevra kadisha's logo stamped on the cover. "That refresher you wanted," Jonathan says, giving him a wink. "The text is still taped to the walls inside if you need a quick reference. I'm going to go check supplies, and we'll get started when you're ready, okay?"

Ezra spends the next several minutes frantically attempting to re-memorize liturgy while the other two men talk a few feet away and Jonathan rummages around on the other side of the door, silent except for the occasional sounds of a wheeling cart and rustling fabric. There's a girl sitting shmira in the nook at the end of the hall, reading quietly aloud from a battered copy of *The Many Adventures of Winnie-the-Pooh,* her voice a gentle murmur. As if sensing Ezra's presence, she gives him a small smile.

A daughter or granddaughter of the deceased, probably, going by her age. Ezra wonders if she volunteered for this, or if, like him, it never occurred to her to say no. He looks away.

When Jonathan pokes his head out again and cocks an eyebrow at him, Ezra musters a thumbs-up, handing the booklet back and rolling up his sleeves.

Like nearly every other Jewish practice, taharah starts with a handwashing, a ritual pouring of water without any soaping or scrubbing. Jonathan slips his wedding ring off and tucks it into his pocket before he puts his hands under the water, and Ezra catches the flash of sorrow that crosses his face before he smooths his expression back to something carefully neutral and calm. He glances around a moment later, as if to make sure no one noticed, and Ezra quickly looks away.

Hands washed and aired dry, they enter the room in traditional silence.

It's cool inside, the only sound the soft hum of the cold storage unit across the hall. The telltale shape of a body lies flat on the table, covered by a plain white sheet. Moving with practiced ease, Jonathan picks up a box of matches and lights the candle waiting for them. He blows out the match and gestures for them to put on their surgical gowns and gloves, and then begins laying out the burial garments in their careful order. Ezra helps the other men prepare the casket, surprised to find that his hands remember the order of the work, laying out the lining cloth and the simple tallit. He runs his fingers over the tzitzit, arranging them carefully, and uses a pair of scissors to cut one down, rendering it unusable for prayer.

The movements come back to him with an ease he doesn't expect, the liturgy even more so. He recites the words like it's been days and not years since he'd last done this, the familiar phrases of blessings and psalms—prayers for the burial society, for the dead man's forgiveness, for the blessing of the dead.

Jonathan uncovers the body with steady hands, and they begin.

Taharah is at once an intricate and simple process, somewhat modernized but relatively unchanged over centuries of practice. One area at a time, the body is uncovered and gently cleaned using lukewarm water and soft cloths. Then the ritual washing begins, the pouring of water over the body, carefully placed and timed to ensure an unbroken flow, simulating immersion in a ritual bath for purification.

The pouring is repeated three times, and then the body is dried and dressed before being placed with care in the coffin, wrapped in the tallit and then the sovev, the lining cloths. Pottery shards are laid over the eyes.

Ezra finds himself moving through each step as if he's underwater, the light and sound of the world falling away into muted silence. The usual urges to look constantly over his shoulder disappear, leaving him almost buoyant.

The room is quiet, the murmur of voices blending into the rippling flow of the water. Ezra lets his hands move the way they will, at once disconnected and more present than he's felt in months. He follows the cues of the other men, goes where he's directed, lifts limbs and pours when his turn comes around again.

He can't quite stop his eyes from drifting, time and again, to Jonathan.

If Ezra is moving mostly on muscle memory—not without care, but not with deep spiritual investment, either—then Jonathan moves with absolute intention. His eyes are simultaneously focused and soft above his mask, an absence of the subtle lines of tension at their corners that Ezra realizes he's grown used to seeing. His gloved hands are tender as he touches the met, an elderly white man with hair gone pale with age and a face etched with deep lines, and Jonathan handles him the same way Ezra might handle a newborn baby, with reverence and care.

The man is a still, linen-wrapped form when they finish, anonymous and silent, but to the young woman reading as she sits shmira in the hallway, to the people who will come to his funeral early tomorrow morning—he was known, loved.

More than a body.

More than a ghost.

Afterward, Ezra finds himself unable to shake off the silence, even after they take off their gloves and complete the final rounds of handwashing, one just outside the taharah room for sanitation, the other at the sink outside the funeral home itself, accompanied by a quiet series of verses. The last washing is done with cold water, and Ezra shivers slightly in the cool late afternoon air, sitting on the steps outside the back door.

He's alone. The sun has crept lower in the sky, and Ezra lets the wind ruffle his hair. Something in him needs this quiet calm, to sit in silence as the last remaining water droplets shrink and vanish from his skin. Normally he'd have his phone in his hands, scrolling for the sake of scrolling, but it's as if all the parts of his psyche that bang against the cage of his ribs have washed away, out to sea, with the tepid water.

The door behind him creaks open and then closes with a soft *click*. "Hey," Jonathan says quietly. "Mind if I join you?" Ezra shakes his head, and Jonathan sits on the step beside him, drawing his long legs up to rest his elbows on his knees. The posture makes him look younger. "You did a good job in there."

"Thanks."

"Sorry." Jonathan laces his fingers together loosely. "I know it wasn't your first time, or anything, but—"

"It's okay, I know what you meant." He does. There are people who hold it together during taharah and then break down afterward, people who can't handle performing it at all.

Ezra never had the option to fall apart.

"You're still quiet," Jonathan observes. "I know we don't know each other that well, but I don't get a sense that *quiet* is your baseline."

Ezra will give him that one.

"Want to talk about it?" Ezra raises his eyebrows, and Jonathan shrugs. "It can be a lot. The first one. Or the first one back, after—after a break."

Something flickers across his face, soft and wistful, and Ezra thinks, without meaning to, *Oh, there it is, there's your trauma. I was almost worried that you were too good, that you didn't have any, that I was going to ruin you.*

It's a shitty thing to think, and he shoves the thought away before it can slip any closer to the front of his mouth. *Jonathan's a sweet guy who's had a horrible loss, and he doesn't need you taking advantage of him for trying to be nice*, he tells himself, channeling his mother's stern tone. Then, before he can stop himself, he lets out a half-hysterical bark of laughter, because *wow* does that tone lose its moral weight when she's just flounced off with another married woman.

Jonathan says, a little nervously, "You okay?"

"I'm going to hell," Ezra says automatically, and then, when Jonathan looks alarmed, adds, "Oh, fuck, no, not for anything in there, just with—" He gestures vaguely at himself in a way he hopes conveys *all of this;* from the immediate bloom of understanding and the wry, generous smile that curves Jonathan's mouth, the message gets across. "No. Sorry. Do you ever have an internal monologue that just gets away from you and you kind of want to just, like, take yourself directly to church?"

"We're Jewish," Jonathan says.

Ezra waves a dismissive hand. "And yet."

Jonathan laughs. It's not a sound Ezra's heard from him before—it's a full-throated, open sort of laugh, warm and genuine and slightly too loud, that lights up his whole face, and Ezra pushes his hair off his forehead, wrapping his arms around his knees and pillowing his cheek on his arms to watch him. The soft gold of the sunlight shines on the lighter strands in his dark hair, and Ezra says, the words slipping out in the unfiltered rush he thought he had figured out how to dam up, "You have a good laugh."

"Oh, God, I *really* don't." Embarrassment flushes across Jonathan's cheeks. "I used to get picked on as a kid for being so loud." Ezra gives him an incredulous look. "Seriously! Well—okay." He ducks his head, still grinning. "I used to snort a lot more. I grew out of that. Mostly."

Ezra tries to picture him as a little kid, chubby-cheeked and chortling, snorting with every giggle. His own mouth turns up at the corners. "Still sounds cute."

"I'll let the kids at my high school know," Jonathan says, dry but still smiling.

They spend a few minutes in an oddly comfortable silence. Ezra feels acutely aware of the distance between their shoulders, close enough that he can just feel the warmth of another body next to his. Jonathan has put his wedding ring back on and is toying with it again, twisting it around his finger, and Ezra is glad to see it—it's a reminder that Jonathan's a safe guy to look at, to flirt with a little, but that he still deserves better than Ezra's haunted baggage.

Finally, Jonathan sighs, glancing at his watch. "I'd better get back inside. There's another taharah scheduled in half an hour and I need to get the room reset and update the supply lists."

Ezra shoves down a small flare of disappointment. "Need any help?"

"No, I'll be okay. Besides, if I keep you too much longer, your brother will never let me hear the end of it." Jonathan gets to his feet, brushing himself down, and then pauses. He looks down at Ezra like he wants to say something and isn't sure how, that faint flush back on his cheeks, and Ezra feels, suddenly, pinned down.

There's uncertainty to it, but a little bit of heat, too, and Ezra thinks, *Oh, fuck,* because he knows what's coming, and that sucks, because now he's going to look like an *asshole*.

"Listen," Jonathan says. "I'm sure you're busy, with everything going on, but I really appreciate the help today. Could I take you out to coffee or something? As a thank-you?"

And there it was. "I . . . don't think that's a good idea," Ezra says, praying the reluctance he feels doesn't show up in his voice. "Like you said, there's just— There's a lot going on right now."

Jonathan's glasses aren't as thick as Mom's, amplifying every trace of expression by ten, but he doesn't seem to have much of a poker face, either. Ezra can see every emotion as it flickers rapid-fire over his features, disappointment-embarrassment-calm, before settling into a grin that's so obviously a mask it almost hurts to look at it.

"Fair enough," he says, easy, like it's nothing. "But really. Thanks for your help."

Nothing like a weird rejection to ruin a good vibe. Ezra plasters on a smile. "You got it," he says. "See you around."

Jonathan's smile turns a little more genuine. "We do live in the same building," he says, dry but good-humored. "It seems pretty likely."

Ezra waits another five minutes before he follows Jonathan inside, just long enough to hopefully make sure they won't run into each other in the hallway. The main floors of the Chapel are kept at a comfortable seventy degrees year-round, but the basement level is cooler for obvious reasons, and Ezra shivers slightly as he lets the door close behind him.

It's only a few degrees of difference from the air outside, but it's enough that Ezra doesn't notice the tickling sensation at the back of his neck until he nearly walks past the ghosts.

There are two of them, standing by the girl sitting shmira outside the cold storage room, so still and half shadowed that Ezra almost doesn't see them.

One is the man whose taharah Ezra just finished. He looks different in movement—they always do—and Ezra sees that his eyes are a lively blue, cloudy with age, and the lines around his face are from smiling, creasing as he watches the young woman read. A grandfather, Ezra thinks, or a well-loved uncle. He wonders what's making him stay.

Maybe he just wants to hear the end of the book. Sometimes it really is that simple.

Ezra looks at the second ghost—and freezes.

He recognizes this one, too. He's seen him twice. In two different places, which has never happened, not in all the years that Ezra has been seeing the dead. With everything that happened the night of the seder, the unexpected sighting had nearly slipped from his mind.

This makes three. Three buildings. One ghost. Tall and handsome and with eyes so sad that it cracks something in Ezra's chest, for he seems so whole and solid he might still be breathing.

The ghost glances up and acknowledges him with the barest tilt of his head.

Ezra stares, unmoving, rooted to the floor.

"'And how are you?' said Winnie-the-Pooh. Eeyore shook his head from side to side. 'Not very how,' he said. 'I don't seem to have felt at all how for a long—' Oh!" As if sensing Ezra's presence, the girl breaks off her reading, looking up at him with wide eyes. "I'm sorry—am I in the way or something?"

Ezra shakes himself back into reality. "No," he says quickly. "No, sorry, you're fine, I—"

Just thought I saw something, he almost says, but then remembers that that's the worst possible thing to say to someone in a funeral home. "Just zoned out a bit," he finishes instead. "Sorry, it's been one of those days." He tries to muster a smile. "Are you okay here? Can I get you anything?"

She returns the smile, small and a little sad. "I'm okay, but thank you."

He leaves her with an awkward little wave and carefully doesn't react as the two ghosts turn, as one, to watch him go.

Pages rustle behind him as she opens her book again, the sound of her voice following him down the hallway.

"'Not very how,' Eeyore said," she reads, a murmur that echoes on the tiled floor. "'I don't seem to have felt at all how for a long time.'"

8

After that, Ezra stops trying to ignore the ghosts.

It's not hard to find them. He may have left, but they were always here.

Most of them are fleeting. Their bodies are here, waiting for burial, so they hover—in the little family rooms, in the preparation rooms, drifting, listless, uncertain. Many are peaceful, old men and women who died of failed hearts or lungs or a stroke or any of the other tiny events that add up to *natural causes* on the death certificates it's Ezra's job to hunt down. Others are too young, and furious about it, whatever futures they had planned forever out of reach.

Once they're buried, most fade. Some attend their own funerals, where Ezra lingers in the wings, bottled water and extra tissues at the ready, a ghost himself.

Worse are the ghosts that stay. Shades he remembers from childhood, most of their names long forgotten, some of them—maybe most of them—dead before he was even born. Others are family, like Uncle Joe's first wife, Maddie, who worked in reception until Ezra was ten, when her second breast cancer diagnosis came too late, and still lingers around the offices, her brow furrowed when the phone rings too long without an answer.

Then there's Zayde, who's everywhere.

In the days and weeks after his grandfather's death, Ezra avoided the Chapel with a desperate stubbornness. When he reluctantly went back, Dad all but ushering him across the yard to help with gathering up discarded programs and emptying trash bags between one service and the next, Zayde was there, too, with his dark suit and mournful eyes, watching with that familiar critical frown as the chairs were reset and tissue boxes arranged.

Except for the silence, it was almost as if he hadn't died at all.

Ezra couldn't understand it. At first, he thought that maybe Zayde was angry with him, and that explained his refusal to respond when Ezra tried day after day to talk to him. He would reach out to try to touch his grandfather's hand, to hold it the way he used to on their morning walks, but it always felt like plunging his fingers into icy water, a feeling so cold it burned.

After a month, his parents sat him down and told him, gently but firmly, that he was too old for imaginary friends. That talking to the empty air was confusing Becca, and his insistence that the empty air was their grandfather was making it worse. That they understood he missed Zayde very much, they all did, but there were better ways to grieve than pretending he was still there.

"It's time to be a big kid," his mother said, not unkindly, as Ezra chewed the inside of his cheek until his mouth tasted salty and sharp. "No more imaginary Zayde. Okay?"

"But—" Ezra started to protest, and then, catching the brimming ferocity around his mother's eyes, thought better of it. It was fine, he thought, even though his chest felt hot and tight. He could pretend. "Okay."

*   *   *

Zayde is in the chapel and in the offices, in the taharah room and the supply closets. He hovers on the fringes while Ezra cleans the caskets in the showroom, running spectral fingers over the pine and flicking the lingering specks of sawdust. He's at the edges of services and on the periphery of intake calls, and follows every processional to the very edge of the door, watches as every hearse drives away.

This morning, he's standing over Ezra's desk like a shadow. Ezra tries to ignore him, still sorting through the mess of Mom's inbox, but then Zayde's leaning turns into lurking.

"Can I actually *help* you with something?"

Zayde straightens up. In Ezra's memory, he's large and imposing, but seeing him now, he's slender, the gaunt memory of starvation permanently etched into the shadows of his face. He tilts his head toward the open door, and Ezra frowns.

"What?"

Another significant look. Bemused, Ezra gets to his feet and follows his grandfather down the hall and down the staff stairwell into the basement where the prep and taharah rooms are, shivering at the familiar drop in temperature from one floor to another. Trailing in the wake of Zayde's steps, it's hard not to feel like Ezra's doing the haunting. He touches his fingers to the wall to feel something solid beneath them, reassurance that he's there, that he's real, that he's breathing.

Zayde stops outside the closed door of the taharah room. Crossing his arms, he looks at Ezra again, then at the door.

Then he's gone.

Ezra stares at the empty spot of floor. As though if he stares long enough, he can see the echo of footprints there, proof of presence.

The hallway is quiet, empty of murmuring voices—the funeral directors coordinating their schedules, members of chevrei kadisha beginning or concluding a taharah. A quick check of the sign-in sheet on the wall shows no rituals until the afternoon, the most recent one scheduled to have ended an hour earlier. There's no sign of disarray, nothing he can think of that would warrant his grandfather's summoning.

On the other side of the taharah room door, someone hitches in a breath, then goes quiet. The universal sound of bitten-back tears, of not wanting to be heard crying, even alone, even in an empty room. It's not an uncommon sound in these halls, and for a moment, Ezra hesitates, reluctant to intrude on someone's grief.

He also knows, with an exhausted surety, that if he goes back upstairs, it'll be less than a minute before Zayde is glaring at him again.

Ezra taps his fingers on the door. There's a startled gasp on the other side. "Sorry," he says. "I'm just— Is everything okay?"

There's a beat of silence, the familiar quiet of a person collecting themselves. He's not expecting to recognize the hesitant voice that says "Ezra?"

Ezra opens the door.

Jonathan looks young and small, sitting on the floor with his knees drawn up to his chest. He's pushed his glasses up on top of his head, holding his hair back from his brow, and he blinks up at Ezra with damp, red-rimmed eyes. "Hi," he says, his voice cracking on the word. "Sorry. I was trying to be quiet."

"You were," Ezra says. He steps into the room and closes the door, careful not to let it slam. "I just happened to be down here. Are you okay?"

Jonathan gives him a watery smile. "Fine," he says, and if it's a false answer to a foolish question, Ezra can't object. "Just." He nods his head toward the table. "It was a hard one."

Ezra follows his gaze to the closed casket, still and silent with a candle flickering at its head.

It's a very, very small box.

"Oh," he says.

Jonathan lets out a trembling breath. "Yeah."

It's not the first Ezra's seen, or even the smallest. But it cracks something in him all the same. It's a too-sharp reminder that he's miles away from his doula work, from spending his time in breath and life.

So far, he's been lucky. He's terrified of the day he won't be.

He sits beside Jonathan on the floor, just close enough for their shoulders to touch. He remembers Jonathan's tenderness when he'd handled the old man's limbs, the softness of his touch.

Every death leaves a void, but these are different.

The phones are probably ringing upstairs, and Ezra doesn't want to think about his inbox, so he doesn't. He deepens his own breathing, slow inhales and slower exhales, and eventually Jonathan matches it.

There isn't anything he can say that will fix this, nothing to make it easier, but he can sit here, and breathe, and be proof that the world spins on.

9

Two weeks after the seder from hell and twelve days into his stint as Mom's replacement, Ezra meets Caroline.

She breezes in while he's fighting with the printer in the front office, failing to make sense of the chicken-scratch troubleshooting instructions scrawled on a Post-it note. He looks up at the sound of the door closing, poking his head out of the office in case it's a new client, and it takes him a moment to place her as the woman he'd seen coming out of Dad's office the night everything went to pieces.

"Good morning," he says a little cautiously, remembering the polite but displeased way Dad and Aaron had ushered her out the door. Still, Dad would kill him for being anything less than professionally courteous. "Can I help you?"

"Very possibly." She extends a red-tipped hand. "Caroline Lawrence. I'm here to see Mr. Friedman."

Ezra shakes it. "Ezra Friedman. Nice to meet you. You're going to have to be more specific."

Caroline laughs. "I suppose you're right. Which of them is available?"

"Do you have an appointment?"

"No, not exactly. But they know I like to stop by from time to time." She regards him for a moment, her dark eyes calculating. She's taller than he is—the three-inch heels probably help—and he stands a little straighter. "Are they in?"

"I'll have to check," Ezra says slowly. Something about her sets his teeth on edge, a feeling of unease creeping over him. "I'm sorry, ma'am, are you a vendor? I'm new, so I haven't met with everyone yet."

She smiles. Her lipstick is perfectly scarlet against her very white teeth. "Not exactly. I'm a potential investor."

Ezra startles. "What?"

"Mr. Friedman—either of them, I suppose—didn't tell you they were considering selling?"

It's innocent, the way she says it. Something flickers over Caroline's shoulder, just out of the corner of his eye, and Ezra doesn't need to look to know it's Zayde. "No," he manages. "They didn't."

Caroline hums. "Well, it's a very difficult environment for small funeral homes these days. My organization offers an opportunity for support, streamlining, increased profits—I'm sure it doesn't come as a surprise that Mr. Friedman would be looking into joining a broader community."

It *does* come as a surprise. Ezra has heard enough of his father's rants to know that *broader community* is just another way of saying *corporate conglomerates,* and that he would rather burn the place to the ground than sell it off.

"Right," he says, hoping his professional façade is still in place. "Let me just see if they're—"

"Ms. Lawrence." Aaron's voice is cool as he emerges from the stairwell, the carpet dampening his footsteps. "I'm surprised to see you."

She turns to smile at him, dismissing Ezra as if he's suddenly invisible. "Mr. Friedman," she says. "I just thought I'd come by to follow up on our last conversation. We ended it so abruptly."

Aaron stops beside Ezra, standing close enough to him to radiate brotherly protectiveness. It would be sweet, if it weren't totally unnecessary. "Like we told you, it was a holiday," he says. "And I think I also said we'd call you, not the other way around."

"Given the circumstances, I worried it may have slipped your mind," she says.

"Circumstances," Aaron repeats.

She cocks her head to one side. Her blond bob swoops with the movement. "I was very sorry to hear about the situation with your mother."

Aaron gives a tight-lipped smile. "Thanks," he says. "Well. Again, like I said, we'll call you if we're interested. Not that I don't appreciate your diligence."

"I believe in following up," she says a bit too sweetly, but she adjusts the strap of her bag over her shoulder. "I'll be going. Give my best to your father, of course."

"Of course," Aaron says. He doesn't move to show her out—Dad would murder him if he caught that, Ezra thinks, but he's amused enough not to do it himself—and she gives a last wave of her perfectly manicured fingers.

Ezra waits until the door has clicked shut behind her before he turns to stare at his brother. "What," he says, "the *actual* fuck, Aaron."

Aaron stops scowling at the door to look at Ezra instead, his mouth twisting at whatever he sees on Ezra's face. "Let me guess," he says. "She told you we're selling?"

"She tried to."

"Well, we're not." Aaron starts to run a hand through his hair, catches himself, and shoves his hands into his pockets instead. "Not that she'll listen to that. This is the fifth time she's been here in two months."

He brushes past Ezra to go into the office, probably to collect whatever he'd been coming up for in the first place. Ezra follows him. "Who does she work for?"

"Forever Memorials." Aaron opens a filing cabinet, riffling

through it until he comes up with a packet of intake forms. "You don't need to worry about it. Dad and I are handling her."

"Right," Ezra says, trying to keep the doubt out of his voice. "She looked very handled."

Aaron's ears go red at the tips. "It's under control."

"Aaron—"

"This isn't your problem," he says. "You made that loud and clear."

Forever Memorials, according to its aggressively bright, meticulously designed website, is a network of more than five hundred funeral providers across the United States and Canada, advertising *personalized, compassionate care at prices affordable for any budget.*

Scrolling through the site during his hypothetical lunch break, Ezra frowns as he skims the pages of suspiciously diverse stock photography, the listings of local funeral homes— or *funeral service partners*—and the seemingly endless casket and service options. He chews the inside of his cheek, then does another search for *Forever Memorials reputation with independent funeral homes.*

The first result is a thread from one of the forums he's heard Aaron mention. Everyone seems to have an opinion, from the people whose employers or families had joined Forever's network to the smaller businesses still clinging to independence. The people who sold to Forever were able to deliver lower prices to their clients, but the trade-off, Ezra quickly realizes, is the "body farms" that Aaron talks about with so much disgust: centralized morgues with embalmers and restorers working around the clock to prepare bodies before shipping them off to the funeral homes for the *personalized experience* that clients expect.

"And don't buy the whole 'Stay on as a manager' pitch," someone with the username LookAlive has written. "You'll get your joining bonus and an intro salary, and then as soon as the ink's dry they undermine everything your family built. It's all factory-farm bullshit. I sold my stock and quit to go to law school."

There are dozens of stories like that. Ezra forces himself to stop gnawing on his cheek before he draws blood. He sighs, rubbing a hand through his hair. There's a service he's supposed to help set up for in ten minutes, so it doesn't make sense to start working on something else. He gets to his feet, grimacing as his back protests the straightening of his spine, and grabs his suit jacket from the hook on the door as he makes his way to the chapel.

The family is already there when he slips into the room. Aaron is talking with the wife of the deceased, a tiny woman with a spray of white curls and tortoiseshell glasses that take up most of her deeply lined face, while a few middle-aged men, probably their sons, cluster a few feet away, shuffling through programs.

"There's just something that's not quite right," the woman is saying, her voice tinged with frustration. "I'm sorry, Mr. Friedman, I just can't put my finger on it."

"I hear you, Mrs. Green," Aaron says gently. "Do you want to go through the service again? We could choose another reading, if you'd like."

"No, it's not that." Mrs. Green wrings her hands. "I'm sorry. I'm just not sure."

Ezra meets Aaron's eyes across the room and offers him a sympathetic shrug, which Aaron returns with a *What can you do?* sort of grimace. Ezra tries to convey *Solidarity* with his eyebrows, then gives up and makes his way to the gathering room off the chapel to make sure that they're all set on tissues and water bottles and neatly packaged snacks.

He's not expecting to see anyone there and stops short when he sees a frail old man standing by the bookshelves of prayer books, regarding them with a furrowed brow. Ezra has his mouth half open to ask if he's lost before he catches the shiver of cold air, and understands.

"Sir," he says quietly, and the man turns toward him. His eyes are cloudy behind the thick glasses perched on his nose. "Is there something I can help you with?"

The dead man studies him for a moment, and then turns back to the shelves, making a vague gesture toward them.

"The books?" He studies the spines, cataloging the different movements' siddurim, and then something clicks. "Oh. Yours—the one you used—it wasn't here?" The man's face instantly brightens, and Ezra feels a rush of relief. "Okay. Got it. Give me— I've got it."

He abandons his stack of unopened tissue boxes on a side table and hurries back into the chapel, where Aaron and Mrs. Green have their heads together by the podium. Ezra hopes he's not too far out of line when he says, "Sorry to interrupt, Mrs. Green, but I couldn't help overhearing you earlier. I was just wondering—did Mr. Green have a favorite siddur?"

Mrs. Green lights up. "He did," she breathes. "Siddur Sim Shalom. He used it every morning." She turns to Aaron. "Do you have any copies? Could we have them available for the service?"

Aaron looks startled, but he quickly smooths his expression back into professional calm. "I'll make a few calls and see what we can do," he says. "Will you be all right here for a few minutes?"

She nods, all but shooing them off. "Yes, yes. Please, go ahead."

"Ezra, seriously?" Aaron hisses as soon as they're out of earshot, heading toward Aaron's office at a brisk walk. "I know you're trying to be helpful, but we've got, like, an hour before the service."

Ezra winces. "I know. I'm sorry."

Aaron rolls his eyes, opening his office door and motioning Ezra inside. "Maybe at least give me a heads-up the next time you decide to start altering the funeral arrangements," he says dryly, picking up the phone and dialing a number from memory. "Then at least I can block off the time to handle them. Hi, Sandra—it's Aaron Friedman at Friedman Memorial Chapel. Is Rabbi Marks available? I need a favor."

Ezra will give him this: Aaron knows how to use a connection. It takes him five minutes on the phone to convince the rabbi at one of the synagogues across town to put a box of siddurim together for them to have waiting in the office for Ezra to drive by and pick up. "Tell them you're from the Chapel and they'll hand them off to you," Aaron says when he hangs up. "Use the main entrance."

"Got it." Ezra traces the geography in his head. "I can be back in half an hour."

"See if you can make it less than that."

Ezra gets halfway to the parking lot before he remembers he left his car keys in his desk. He doubles back to his office to pick them up, only to nearly run into Becca, leaning against the wall by his door, scrolling through her phone. She grins at him. "There you are," she says, and then her smile fades. "Oh, you look busy."

"I have to run out to pick something up for the next service," he says. He slips past her to get his keys, saying over his shoulder, "Do you need me?"

"*Need* is a strong word," she says.

The circles under her eyes are a bit darker than usual, and there's a pale, drawn quality to her face. Ezra frowns. "You okay?"

She laughs, but there's no humor in it. "I mean, for a given value of *okay*. What with . . . you know." She gestures vaguely, as if to indicate *everything*. "I just wanted to stop by and see if you were free for lunch or something."

"I wish," he says. "Want to come with me? Not the most exciting quality time, but you can tell me about whatever's on your mind."

Gratitude floods into her face. Ezra loops an arm around her and steers her toward the door.

"So," he prompts as they pull out of the parking lot a few minutes later, "want to tell me what's going on?"

Becca draws one knee up to rest her foot on the passenger seat, drumming her fingers against her window. "Mom's called me, like, five times."

Oh. Ezra automatically tightens his grip on the steering wheel. "Have you talked to her?"

She shoots him a look. "What do you think?"

"Has she left you any messages?"

"Yeah. I only listened to the first one. Just a bunch of excuses and her asking me to call her back. I deleted the other ones." She pauses. "What about you?"

"So far? Radio silence." Not that he'd expected anything else. Mom has her patterns anytime there's a fight: She chases Becca down, waits for Aaron to come to her, and assumes Ezra will read her mind to reach out first.

"Doesn't that bother you?"

"Of course." Though this time around, maybe not as much as it should. It's partly that he's used to it, but mostly, he just doesn't have the brainpower to add one more thing to his to-do list. "But you know what she's like. Everything on her schedule, or not at all."

"That's the truth." Becca picks at the chipped yellow polish on her fingernails. When she was younger, she used to bite them until she drew blood. "I don't know how to stop being mad at her, but I also just . . . I don't know. I want to talk to her, but I don't want to hear her try to make excuses for what she did. To Dad, but to us, too, you know?"

Ezra swallows. "I know."

"And I just . . . I feel so stupid. I used to tell people that they were my marriage role models. And this whole time—"

"Not the *whole* time."

"Well, whatever. *Years,* Ezra." She slumps back in the seat. "*And* now you have to do her job for her, which I know you probably *hate,* even if you're not saying it."

"It's not that bad." Ezra checks the intersection, then turns them onto Morris Ave. "I mean, it's a lot of paperwork and spreadsheets, and I'm not used to spending so much time sitting down, but it could be worse. Mostly it's boring. So far the most exciting thing was Jonah accidentally sending the wrong obituary to the *Journal* and watching Melissa swoop in to do damage control."

"Oh, so *just* like helping people deliver babies." Ezra can't bite back a smile. Becca's always been the person in his family most supportive of his foray into birth work, despite insisting from the age of seven that she had zero interest in kids of her own. "Do you miss it?"

Ezra shrugs. "I'm still doing it. That's not the part of my job that got screwed over."

Becca hums. "That's something, I guess." She taps her fingers against her knee, then says, "Would it be really petty and immature of me to leave Mom a really angry voicemail and then block her number?"

It's such an un-Becca-like thing to say that he jerks them roughly to a stop at the next intersection so he can stare at her. "Seriously? Becca."

"Don't *Becca* me, you know I hate it." She crosses her arms. "It makes you sound like Mom." She pauses, considering. "Only worse, because I actually worry about disappointing *you*."

"You could never disappoint me," he says, and means it. "Have you talked to Dad about any of this?"

Becca scoffs. "Please. Talk to Dad? About emotions? You'd have more luck than me." She pauses. "*Are* you having any luck? Talking to him?"

Ezra hesitates, pulling them into the synagogue parking lot mostly on autopilot. It's not that he and Dad *aren't* talking— at least, not intentionally. But Ezra has barely spent more than a minute with him in the past two weeks. He's been trying not to take it personally. Maybe Dad's trying to figure out what he needs to say. What he needs to do.

When he does catch his father in the halls, Ezra does his best to smile, to project openness, offering a silent invitation. But when he asks if Dad needs anything, he gets a client folder and instructions to call the livery company, or send over an updated invoice. He might be more offended if Dad wasn't avoiding everyone else with the same determination, talking only when he truly needs to.

"I don't know," he says at last. He turns off the car. "You know me and Dad. It's kind of complicated."

Becca sighs. "Yeah," she says. "With the two of you, it always is."

10

Ezra's first memory is of the ocean.

The nature of the funeral business has always meant that real vacations, ones where no one left in the middle to manage a crisis, were few and far between. But the summer Ezra is three, Mom and Dad pack him and Aaron into the station wagon and drive to Narragansett for a week at the beach. Aaron takes to the water like a fish, but Ezra hangs back, overwhelmed by the vastness of the ocean, clutching Mom's hand and refusing to go in past his ankles, until Dad comes back and scoops him up, settling him on his hip and wading into the surf.

As he walks, Ezra clinging to him with arms and legs, he tells him about how waves work, about the tides, about starfish and dolphins and mermaids. Slowly, cautiously, Ezra relaxes his grip.

And Dad tosses him in.

The water closes over Ezra's head, and for a dizzying, terrifying moment, he's weightless. Floating.

And then Dad scoops him out of the water, and Ezra is sputtering, coughing, sobbing around the water in his throat.

"You're fine," he says, holding Ezra above the waves as he coughs and cries and clings. "See? It was just a second. And now it's over. That wasn't so scary."

When he catches enough of his breath to speak, Ezra says, "I wasn't *ready*."

"No," Dad agrees. "But that's why you had to do it."

He never quite let Ezra sink or drown, but he was always willing to let him flounder, to see if he'd figure out how to swim.

Ezra keeps following him into the water all the same.

Ezra's takeover of Mom's role is just one more exercise in treading water. He's not *good* at it—these systems are a web of sticky notes and scribbled passwords and software and spreadsheets—but Ezra holds it together to manage payroll and log their invoices and keep the files in order. Dad stops by once or twice, not to offer help but to verify that Ezra hasn't broken anything. Otherwise, Ezra barely sees him.

So it's a surprise when Ezra walks into the break room at eight in the morning and finds Dad sitting at the table with a mug of coffee at his elbow, reading the paper.

Ezra's first thought, lingering in the doorway and feeling like a creep about it, is that he looks better. Some of the puffiness has faded from around his eyes, and he looks as if he's slept more than a few hours. Ezra hopes he's moved past the initial shock of his wife leaving, and it's not just a side effect of the rush of business that has come in over the last few days.

The longer he hovers, the more Ezra feels like a stalker. "Morning," he chirps, pitching his voice into all the customer service zeal he can muster, striding into the room like he belongs there. Which, he supposes, he does now, and isn't that just a kick in the tits.

Dad startles like Ezra's started blaring reveille at him, looking around with wide eyes. "I forgot how quiet you can be," he says, and it's the most normal thing Ezra has heard him say in days.

"Sorry," Ezra says. The last thing the poor guy needs is a heart attack. "Too many years of playing hide-and-seek in the hallways."

"I hated when you did that. I was always worried one of you would end up closed in a casket somehow."

"That happened *one time*. And it was Aaron, which literally everyone should have seen coming."

This time, Dad chuckles. "I think you probably did see it coming," he says. "Since if I remember right, he was only in there about five minutes before you got him out again." There's something fond and a little wistful in his voice. "I don't know what he would have done without you."

Dad closes the paper, and Ezra takes the hint to join him at the table. The look on his face is one that Ezra has never seen on him before—thoughtfulness, uncertainty, concern. Maybe even regret. Ezra feels, suddenly, very conscious of how much he's changed since the last time he stood with his father in this room: the subtle differences in the shape of his face from the testosterone, the shadow of stubble on his jaw, the way the binder flattens his chest. All the tiny ways he's learned to change his posture, his expressions, his presentation, carefully taking all the softness of his femininity and folding it away like a winter quilt in summer.

He clears his throat and nods toward his father's coffee mug, pointedly nudging him out of his staring. "Top that off for you?"

"What?" The question does the job, at least; Dad blinks once, twice, and then leans back in his chair, embarrassment flashing in his eyes. "No, it's still hot, thank you." He pauses. "Do you have time to sit for a few minutes? I didn't—I feel like I haven't even thanked you, for coming to help."

"You're welcome." He *is* being paid for the work, not helping out of a pure sense of family obligation.

"Are you settling in okay?"

Ezra considers the potential responses to that and chooses a happy medium. "It's been okay," he says. "Different from what I'm used to, that's for sure."

Dad nods slowly, thick eyebrows drawn together behind his glasses like he's puzzling something out. "Aaron mentioned you were able to help with the taharah for Mr. Lowenstein the other day."

Ezra had never asked the man's name. "Jonathan needed an extra pair of hands."

"It happens sometimes." Dad watches him, eyes thoughtful. "Thank you for doing it. I know it's not something you enjoy."

The acknowledgment comes as a surprise. It's not that no one ever cared, growing up, whether Ezra and his siblings were comfortable picking up tasks around the Chapel. There was just an assumption that it would be done anyway. Ezra doesn't quite know what to do with being thanked. Especially not twice in one conversation. "I didn't want him to have to wait for someone else to come. I know how busy things are."

"Still. Don't think I didn't notice that you sprinted all the way to the other side of the life cycle to get away from doing funeral work."

Growing up in a world that revolved around death, when he was the only one who could *see* the specters of the dead around him, had sent Ezra running as far from it as he could. He'd thought about becoming a midwife, but one biology class his freshman year of college let him know that he wasn't cut out for medical or nursing school. Falling into teaching yoga had been more of a fluke than an intentional career move, an eye-catching flyer at his studio turning accidentally into a two-hundred-hour teacher-training course.

It was a friend from the program who told him about her

cousin who worked as a birth doula. He'd spent the afternoon after class in a research spiral, and something just—clicked. He was the only masc-presenting person in the full-spectrum training he enrolled in, which got him a few odd looks before he found a rhythm with his cohort. Mentioning that he had a uterus of his own helped, which he's never quite stopped feeling a little gross about, but it's not like he doesn't get it, a little. He has a harder time finding clients than the cis women he trained with, and he works harder for it. Even if he only keeps a few clients at a time, it soothes something in him to be there for the *beginning* of something, to be focusing on breath and joy and the opening of a book rather than the closing of a chapter.

It's not that there are never ghosts that show up at births. They're just usually there to help. They're the only ones that don't make him feel cold, the lingering shades of mothers and midwives and nurses, and when he meets their eyes, they nearly always smile.

"Ezra?"

Ezra shakes his head. "Sorry. Just—spacing." He can't stop thinking about the wandering ghost he keeps seeing, breaking all the rules like they're nothing.

The spark has gone out of his father's eyes, his client-facing mask settled into place, as if Ezra turned for half a moment and the tide rushed in to wash him away. "Well," Dad says. "Good to know some things never change."

He gets a respite from spreadsheets and ghosts when one of his clients goes into labor later that week. Ezra texts Aaron an entirely insincere apology, leaves Sappho with Ollie—"I knew you only wanted to live here for the free dog sitting!"—and spends the next ten hours doing the work he feels like he's actually good at.

Between Libby's curated labor playlist and her decision to sing through most of her contractions, the hospital room is far from quiet. A dreamy calm settles over Ezra all the same, an easing of the discomfort he's been unable to shake. He channels it into his hands and his voice and the steadiness of his own breath, helping Libby with positioning changes and talking her through her breathing.

It's eleven hours from the first phone call to the last push, but it's as smooth a birth as Ezra's ever attended. The relief of it hits him like a rush—he hadn't realized, until the cord is cut and Libby's daughter is contentedly nursing in her arms, how desperately he needed something to go *right*.

Ezra stays with them until they're settled in their recovery room, then makes an unobtrusive exit, waving an automatic goodbye to the nurses at the charge desk on his way out of the labor and delivery unit. He's a familiar enough face here that all of them wave back—including the one only he can see, a tall Black woman in scrubs that haven't been in style since the 1980s, her glasses propped on top of her head as she peers over the shoulder of one of her still-breathing counterparts. She meets Ezra's eyes and gives him a now-familiar nod of approval, and he manages not to get caught by any of the others as he subtly inclines his head in return.

It's five in the morning by the time he gets back to his car, and he wants a hot shower and eight hours of sleep, not necessarily in that order. Based on the sheer number of notifications on his phone, he's going to have to settle for an hour-long nap and as many shots of espresso as he can puppy-eye the barista at the coffee place near his apartment into putting in a single takeaway cup.

Instead he finds Jonathan sitting on the porch of the house when he gets back, Sappho sprawled on her back beside him, tail thumping enthusiastically against the floor as Jonathan rubs her belly.

She rolls up to her feet at Ezra's approaching footsteps, yanking her leash out of Jonathan's loose grip—"*Oof,*" he says—and tackling him down to the driveway, slobbering all over his face in greeting. He needs a shower anyway, so he lets her enjoy herself, powering through his leaden limbs to reach up and scratch her ears. "I missed you, too," he wheezes, trying to calm her enough that he can push her face to the side and look questioningly up at Jonathan, who's watching him from his spot on the stairs. "Hi? I'm confused."

Jonathan gives him a sheepish smile. "You just missed Ollie," he says. "I guess he was taking a walk and saw something he wanted to go back and photograph? He passed her leash off to me and said he'd be back in five minutes, but it's been fifteen. I was going to drop her back at your place, but I left my keys in my apartment again."

"You really need to find a spot out here to hide a spare," Ezra says, brushing gravel off his pants as he gets to his feet and picking up Sappho's dangling leash, looping it around his wrist. "Sorry about Ollie. He has a thing for getting the perfect shot. I'll yell at him once he's back."

"No need. We were making friends." Jonathan reaches out to scratch Sappho's ears and chin when she gets close enough for him to reach her, and she pants happily into his face at the attention. "She's a sweetheart. How long have you had her?"

"A little over a year." Ezra tries not to pay too much attention to how soft Jonathan's eyes are as he coos at her, or to how strong his forearms look where the sleeves of his sweater are pushed up to his elbows. "I meant to get a smaller breed, something that would be better for the apartment I had at the time, but I saw her at the shelter and . . ." He shrugs, a *What can you do?*, and Jonathan laughs.

"Yeah, I bet. A face like this? I'd have caved, too." He plants a kiss on Sappho's nose and gets up. For a mercy, he rolls his sleeves down as he goes. "Don't suppose you'd let me in?"

"Seems like a dick move not to," Ezra says, fishing his keys out of his pocket and unlocking the front door. Fortunately for Jonathan, it looks like he'd left the door to his actual apartment propped open. "I owe you one."

Jonathan shakes his head, giving Sappho one last pat on the head. "Consider it a thank-you for everything you've done to help me out at the Chapel."

Ezra blinks, taken aback. "You don't have to thank me for that."

"And yet," Jonathan says, smiling faintly as he lets Sappho go. "Here I am."

That smile sticks in the back of Ezra's head as he makes his way up the stairs to his own apartment, absentmindedly greeting Steve the gnome with a now-habitual nudge of his foot. Sappho's already pulling at her leash, so he unclips her, letting her pad away while he takes off his shoes. Everything smells like fresh-brewed coffee and—Ezra gives an experimental sniff—maybe cinnamon, and he can hear voices coming from around the corner, slightly muted beneath the soft strains of alt-folk music playing in the living room. He follows his nose to the kitchen, where he finds Lily and Noah sitting at the table, waiting for him.

"Hey." Lily breaks out in a smile. "You're not Ollie."

"No," Ezra says, a little caught out. "Apparently he ditched her with Jonathan so that he could go take some pictures. I ran into them on the porch."

Lily looks amused. "Yeah, that sounds about right. How did everything go with your client?"

"Baby girl, ten fingers, ten toes, all that good stuff. Nursing like a champ when I left." The coffeepot is blessedly full. Ezra fills the first mug he can find, patterned with multicolored mushrooms shaped like human butts, and slumps into the chair next to Noah. "What are you two even doing up? And why does it smell like a bakery in here?"

"We're making cinnamon buns," Noah says.

Ezra blinks. "Just because?"

Lily, peering into the oven, scoffs. "Of course not just because! We weren't going to, like, *not* acknowledge the fact that you just helped bring a baby into the world. What kind of people do you think we are?"

There's no good way to answer that. "Libby did all the hard work, I just made sure she and her wife didn't get steamrolled by the attending OB."

Lily makes a face. "Ick. Obstetric violence. You hate to see it."

Ezra hums into his coffee. It's fortifying. "I've seen worse," he says.

Lily wrinkles her nose. "At least now you'll have a cinnamon roll."

And that's really sweet of her, except . . . Ezra casts a wary glance at the oven. Noah grins.

"Don't worry," he says. "They came out of a box. She's basically defrosting them." Lily makes an outraged sound and smacks his arm. "Ow! What? You're the one who's always saying you can't cook!"

"*I* can say it. It doesn't mean you can!"

"You almost gave us all food poisoning last Thanksgiving!" Noah shoots Ezra a despairing look. "She tried to insist that turkey could be cooked medium rare."

"In my defense," Lily begins, and then huffs at the pointed slurp Noah takes from his mug. "Okay, okay. I still think we could have avoided the whole Friendsgiving dinner fiasco if you'd just let us order in."

Curious despite himself, Ezra asks, "Why didn't you?"

"Max wanted a home-cooked meal," Noah says. "The rest of us are just masochists."

"*Anyway,*" Lily interrupts, nudging Ezra under the table with her foot, and he realizes a little belatedly that he'd been starting to doze off into his coffee mug. "How are you doing anyway? I feel like we've barely seen you in a week."

"Fine," he says, immediate and automatic. He gets two identical looks of skepticism and has a flare of gratitude that Ollie isn't here, because if he were he'd see through the smile plastered onto Ezra's face. Has he gotten worse at acting like everything's fine? Or is it a side effect of being over twenty-five with a nonexistent skin care regimen that every micro-wrinkle of exhaustion is instantly visible? "Really," he adds. "I'm just tired. It's been a long few days."

The timer on the oven goes off.

"Ollie said things were still weird with your family," Noah says, checking on the cinnamon rolls.

Traitor, Ezra thinks. "They're not as bad as they could be," he says, out of long-ingrained loyalty. "But yeah, it's . . . weird."

Lily props her chin on her hand. "Has anyone talked to your mom yet?"

Ezra winces and shakes his head. "I'll have to," he says. "It's been over two weeks. She's going to think we're icing her out. But she doesn't like to admit when she's wrong, so it'll proba-bly . . ." He shrugs.

Lily's eyebrows have crept nearly up to her hairline. "Sorry," she says. "Is this the same mom who's been having an affair for, like, two years?"

"Yup."

"And she . . . doesn't like to admit she's wrong."

"Nope."

Noah sits back down, a plate of cinnamon rolls and a bowl of icing in his hands. "Big yikes," he says, then bats at Lily's hands when she reaches for the plate. "These *literally* just came out of the oven. What is *wrong* with you? I have met your mom, I know she raised you better."

"She did, but my dad is a total pushover," Lily says, flashing a sugar-sweet smile.

Noah rolls his eyes at her, but it's a practiced sort of fondness. They've been friends for years, and this is their second shared apartment. The two of them can point to everything in the apartment and recount its origin story, whatever adventure or inside joke or spontaneous flea market afternoon made them like it enough to bring it home.

Ezra wonders sometimes what it must be like, to be known like that. He has Nina, and Ollie, but he's never had someone who he could be fully, entirely honest with. Someone who knew all his secrets and wouldn't make him feel like he was out of his mind for sharing them.

Something nudges against his arm, and he blinks himself back into the room—*God,* he needs a nap—and stares at the shape in front of him until it resolves into a plate with a well-iced cinnamon bun, still steaming from the oven. He looks up and catches Lily's smile.

"You looked like you needed it," she says, so kindly it puts a lump in his throat, and he smiles back, hoping it doesn't look as watery as it feels.

"Thanks."

It stirs something at the bottom of his stomach, the way they extend this affection so easily, like it's nothing at all. It makes him feel unsteady, like a newborn foal struggling up onto its feet for the first time, unsure how to take a first step. Ezra takes a bite of the cinnamon bun to have an excuse to say nothing. It's delicious, so fresh that it nearly melts in his mouth, the icing sweet and creamy on his tongue, and he holds back a moan as his body remembers that it's been fifteen hours since he's last eaten. "Oh my God, these are amazing."

"I *told* you I can defrost things just fine," Lily says a little defensively, but she's grinning. "Oh, and—speaking of food. What are you doing next Wednesday?"

Ezra blinks. "Uh," he says. "I have no idea. I'd have to check. Why?"

"We do family dinner the third Wednesday of every month," Noah tells him. "Both apartments together."

Ezra pulls another piece off his cinnamon roll, eyes it, and then puts it on the plate. It's amazing, but if he shoves the whole thing in his face he's going to throw up all over the floor, which would just be depressing. "Isn't that what you do every night?"

"It's *optional* all the other nights," Lily says, like it's obvious. "And phones aren't allowed, and we actually try to cook something as a group instead of just ordering in."

Noah snorts at whatever look Ezra must have on his face. "Lily's allowed to chop vegetables and chop vegetables *only*."

"I graduated to stirring last month!"

"On a trial basis. With supervision." Noah blows her a kiss when she audibly kicks him under the table, then gives Ezra an open, inviting look. "Will you come?"

He hesitates. His default is to turn down activities like this or give, at best, a promise, a maybe, and back out later. They have too much potential for chaos and drama, and whenever there are more than three people in a room, he can never tell who he should be prioritizing to keep everyone happy.

But he can't quite shake off the yearning he feels around Noah and Lily's easy closeness, the warmth between them and Ollie and Max, the way the four of them are the sort of family that Ezra's always known existed. He *loves* his family, would throw himself in front of a train for them, but he doesn't think he's ever relaxed around them like his roommates relax around one another.

"Next Wednesday?" he asks, a little warily.

Lily nods. "At seven," she says. "We start dropping recipes into the group chat on Monday, usually."

Ezra should say no. He doesn't need anyone else to keep secrets from.

"Okay," he says. "I'll be there."

II

When Mom texts to ask if he'll come have breakfast with her, all Ezra can feel is relief.

If nothing else, he's glad that she was the one to reach out so that he didn't have to try to figure out a diplomatic way to open up the conversation that wasn't just *Hey, so . . . what the fuck?* He texts back a confirmation and tells his siblings nothing so that he doesn't have to field a thousand questions he doesn't have answers to.

Mom's new apartment turns out to be in a converted Queen Anne just off Waterman Street. It's a nice house in a nice neighborhood, pretty and well-groomed. None of that is surprising, given the amount of money in neighborhoods like this, but it *is* surprising that his mother can afford it.

"Maybe her sugar mama has a trust fund," he mutters, locking the car. It's kind of a gross thought and he nearly gags as he says it, but—well. He's allowed to be petty about the woman who broke up his parents' marriage. At least for a little while.

The door of the house opens as he heads up the porch steps. Ezra barely has time to recognize the casually dressed, beaming woman in the doorway as his mother before she's exclaiming "Ezra, honey!" and pulling him into a rib-bending hug.

"Oh," he says. He hugs back mostly on impulse, caught off guard. The angle of the embrace pushes his face into her hair, enveloping him, suddenly, in a smell so familiar he may as well be twelve or six or two again, held in the absolute safety of her peach-and-honeysuckle perfume. "Hi, Mom," he says, and to his horror, his voice cracks on the word.

Mom pulls back, though she doesn't let go of him. Her eyes glisten at the corners with the threat of tears. She puts her hands on his shoulders, looking up at him like she's searching for something.

"Oh, kiddo," she murmurs, her tone trembling between affection and regret. "How is it every time I think you're done growing, you shoot up another inch? Or is it all the yoga stretching out your spine?"

She's being playful, but her smile is tight, as if she can act, even if only for a few minutes, like everything is fine. "I keep telling you to try it," he says. "Otherwise you'll keep shrinking. That's why Grandma was so short."

"Oh, is that why?" Her eyes glint in the late morning sunshine—brighter than he's seen them in a long time. Months. Years, maybe. "I'll have to remember that. Maybe that'll be what finally gets me out to that studio of yours." She steps back, inclining her head toward the door. "Come inside, honey, I was about to start breakfast."

Ezra takes a breath, braces himself, and follows her.

The apartment she leads him into is bright and cheerful, windows open to let in the soft breeze and gleaming sunshine. He peers shamelessly into the rooms they pass on the way to the kitchen—living room and dining room and what he thinks might be an . . . art studio? Okay, interesting—and the impression he gets is one of softness and color and life. Every surface seems to have something on it, a plant or a book or a knitted blanket or a candle or an artisan incense holder. The walls are covered in prints and framed photographs and hanging bookshelves laden with battered paperbacks, spines crinkled with use.

Everything is texture and pattern, all of it mismatched intentionally, lovingly, miles from the disjointed jumble of the house Mom lived in with Dad for their thirty-two years of marriage. That was the disconnected disorganization of two people who could never quite figure out how to make their styles fit. This is maximalism for the sake of enjoyment, strange and misfit and mismatched objects collected and displayed for the simple delight of their existence.

It's also, he thinks, eyeing a framed Georgia O'Keeffe print on the wall above a photo of Provincetown, one of the gayest homes he's ever seen. It gives his own a run for its money.

Which is, he has to admit, horrifying.

"Ezra?" Mom pokes her head out of the kitchen. "Are you coming?" He musters a nod and follows her into the kitchen. Her lips twitch at whatever look he's wearing. "The décor?"

"It's very colorful." The kitchen is no different: mismatched ceramic mugs hang on copper hooks and an eclectic collection of cookbooks are arranged haphazardly on a shelf. The tiled backsplash is aggressively turquoise.

"Just a bit." There's fondness in her voice. "I was thinking I could make waffles—our sourdough starter needs feeding anyway, and you loved those when you were little. And I picked up some rhubarb jam at the farmers market the other day; it's early, so it's a bit tart still, but—" She breaks off with a frown. "Oh, hell. It's Becca who likes rhubarb. I forgot."

Food is his mother's love language. But here she is, suddenly unable to speak it. "I don't mind it."

Her troubled expression doesn't waver. "Are you sure? I could run out to the store, it's just a few minutes—"

"Mom," he interrupts. "It's fine."

He'd tell her not to cook if he had the slightest faith that she'd listen. Looking for any possible way to change the subject, he latches on to the pair of work gloves on the kitchen table next to a basket of gardening tools. "Do you have a garden here?"

Relief floods her face, and he tries not to feel sick about it. "In the back," she says. "It's still a bit of a work in progress, this early in the season, but it's such a nice day today." She hesitates, and then says, almost shyly, "I could show you?"

She leads him out to a small but functional little deck attached to the back of the house, furnished with a glass-top table and chairs, and down a few creaking steps—"Watch the banister, honey," she says when Ezra nearly stumbles. "We haven't gotten it fixed yet"—into the little fenced-in yard. There are raised garden beds arranged in a neat line and filled with the first blooms of spring flowers. Becca could probably name all of them—of his siblings, she's the only one to pick up Mom's green thumb. Behind the beds is a small patch of freshly turned earth, a mirror of the vegetable garden that Ezra grew up with, tucked against the back wall of the house. There's not much growth yet, but the rows have been marked out with string and popsicle sticks labeled in Mom's handwriting describing each one—tomatoes, carrots, lettuce, spinach. It's not the half-cursive scrawl that Ezra spends half his time at work trying to decipher off sticky notes and file labels, but the calligraphy she learned from Bubbe, copying her mother-in-law's smooth, confident strokes.

Something about seeing it here, so far from where he expects it, puts a lump in Ezra's throat.

Swallowing, he brushes his fingertips over the soft tip of one tiny green shoot. The whole space radiates love and care. It is quiet and lovely, and Ezra feels a pang of guilt, like he's betraying Dad just by allowing himself to relax in it.

Behind him, Mom clears her throat softly. "I still have some more planting to do," she says, setting her tool basket down between them. "I know you never really took to gardening, but if you wanted . . ."

He takes it for the offer it is. "Okay."

She hands him the gloves—they fit his hands—and slips into the gentle, instructing tones of his childhood, his mother demonstrating the distances to place between the seeds and the size of the stones they still need to pick out of the soil. On a strange autopilot, Ezra separates out the smoother, prettier stones; he will add them to the jars in the Chapel's foyer, for mourners to bring with them to burials and unveilings.

At last, Mom clears her throat. "How's your new apartment? Are you settling in okay?"

For all their differences, Mom and Dad tackle avoidance the same way. It's almost comforting. "It's fine. Good, I mean. It's an adjustment, I guess, living with people again, but it's good. Ollie and his roommate live upstairs and they're over all the time, so it's sort of like having four roommates instead of two, but Max is great. I like her."

"Mm," Mom says. She shapes a mound of dirt over a seed with practiced hands. With Ezra wearing her gloves, there's already dirt under her nails, visible through the clear polish she favors. "And how is Oliver?"

Also like Dad: She'll never forgive him and Ollie for breaking up. "He's good. Thinking about an MFA again. You know how he is."

"Is he seeing anyone?"

Ezra looks skyward in the hopes of divine intervention. "No."

She clicks her tongue, clearly disappointed, but for once she doesn't press.

Silence falls again, thicker now for having been broken.

"So," she says, resignation in her voice as she sits back on her heels. "Here we are."

Ezra keeps his eyes on the garden. He feels the weight of her gaze like a physical thing, like he's the one who's done something that needs to be figured out.

"You look good, honey," she says finally. "Settled. Is it weird to say that?"

He gives up and looks at her. "Not the weirdest thing," he says slowly, not totally clear where she's going with this. "I mean, people have definitely said weirder stuff to me."

"And you're . . . You feel okay? Happy, and everything?"

Ezra puts another small rock in his "to keep" pile. "This is feeling," he says, as evenly as he can manage, "like a loaded line of questioning."

He catches the lightning crash across her face before she smooths it away. "It wasn't meant to be," she says unconvincingly. She hesitates, and it's as if her hands keep working without her, using her thumbs to gently open another hole in the softened earth. "I want to say something, and I know it's not the right way to say it."

"My go-to is to set a timer and give two minutes of judgment-free questions that I reserve the right not to answer," he says. "Should I get my phone?"

She has the grace to look abashed at that. "No. But the fact that you had to ask means I probably shouldn't say what I was going to . . ." She sighs. "Are you *happy,* baby?"

Ezra blinks at her. "Am I what?"

"Well, it's just—" Mom lets out a hopeless, clearly embarrassed little laugh. "This past year, it's just—you're so *different.* I'm not just talking about your transition," she adds quickly. "Although of course—of course there's that. But you're—even the way you're sitting. You hold yourself differently. And I just wanted to know if you're *happy*, because it's such a change, and after the last few weeks that I've had, well—"

"Oh," Ezra says. He finds a weed that Mom must have missed when she was clearing the garden path and begins to work it free. "This isn't about me."

She flushes, but nods, and Ezra's not sure if he's offended or relieved to see her admit to it. The ease drains out of her posture, her shoulders hunching. "I knew you'd understand," she says quietly.

Offended it is. "Sorry, *what*?" The weed comes out with more force than he expected, dirt from its roots showering them both. "Please tell me how you got to that conclusion from *You look happy*, because you took a journey through some hoops and did not bring me along for the ride."

Mom gives him a lemon-pursed look, the one that means she knows he's trying to be funny to avoid conflict and she doesn't find it cute at all. "I just meant," she says, a hint of defensiveness in her tone, "that you're not exactly a stranger to— you know. Sexuality-related announcements that require some adjustment from your family members."

In the romantic comedy of his life, Ezra thinks, this would be a freeze-frame moment. *Ferris Bueller*–style. He'd widen his eyes, directly breaking the fourth wall, pleading, *Do you see the shit I have to deal with?* Every looks-directly-into-camera moment, sprung to life. He can't even say *Look at this heterosexual nonsense* anymore, because his mom is apparently not a heterosexual.

"Mom," he says. "When I came out to you in high school, I literally had a PowerPoint presentation about bisexuality, a reading list from the PFLAG website, and my girlfriend's mom on speed dial in case you needed to Talk to Another Trusted Adult." He emphasizes the capital letters, in case they aren't obvious enough. "I laid the groundwork for a *literal year* before I told you guys I was trans, and I *still* brought Ollie with me as backup in case I needed to bail out of the house—which, I'll remind you, I did. *You* blindsided the whole family in the middle of seder, on basically the one night a year when we all actually try to hold our shit together around company." He pulls off the gloves and sits back on his heels. The knees of his pants are stained already. "Are you kidding?"

She looks at him, wide-eyed, as if all of that was far more than she'd expected. "It's not like I planned it."

"That is so many levels of not the point, I can't even put it into words."

Mom looks at the ground between them. Her glasses make her eyelashes look long and full, but they aren't long enough to hide the misery. She closes her eyes for a long moment, taking deep, shaking breaths, and when she opens them again, she doesn't look at Ezra but past him, at the little garden.

"It's beautiful out here," she says. "Don't you think?"

She's not even close to subtle. Out of an unfounded hope that she's going somewhere with it, Ezra lets it slide.

The little fenced yard around them *is* pretty, a floral explosion, a wild splash of disorganized beauty so unlike the gardens his mother always favored at home, neat and tidy, the flowers arranged just so. The hands that made *this* garden, Ezra realizes, are clearly the same ones that designed the apartment inside.

They weren't, he knows just as surely, his mother's hands. His mom ran a home that was organized down to the smallest detail. Everything had a place. He's never bothered wondering what kind of home she might make for herself, if she had the chance.

"Yes," he says carefully. "It is."

Mom watches a pair of bumblebees circle a cluster of hydrangeas. "This was Judy's mom's place," she says at last. "She passed away last year and left it to her. Isaac wanted her to sell it, but she convinced him to let her keep it as a studio space."

Ezra watches her, saying nothing. She gives a little shake of her head, as if rousing herself from a dream. "She and Isaac had this horrible fight last month. God, I don't even remember what it was about—their younger daughter, I think. She wants to go to art school when she graduates next year, and—Oh, it doesn't matter now. Judy packed a bag and got in her car and she called me, and she said, Bobbi, I'm done, I'm leaving, and you can come with me or not, but if you're not coming, then that's it, I can't do this halfway anymore."

There are tears in her eyes, and Ezra digs his fingertips into his knees to keep from reaching for her. It's too easy to want to fix her sadness, the instinct born out of years of practice.

"I just," she says after a long moment, "could only think that I was going to lose her. So I finished the kugel I was making your father for dinner and I wrote him a note that said all I could think to say without hurting him any more than I knew I'd have to, and I left. I didn't even make it to the car before she was calling me back and saying that she didn't mean it, that she had overreacted, that she just needed a bit of time to be by herself and then she and Isaac would be able to sort things out again. So I went back inside and I threw away the note and I unpacked my bag, but that moment was enough for me to realize that *I* couldn't do it halfway anymore, either." She shakes her head. "I didn't mean for it to come out when it did, but it had just been boiling up for so long."

They don't have time to unpack *all* of that. "Okay," Ezra says slowly. "So, when I was in high school, you would have called that an explanation, but not an excuse."

Mom lets out a shocked laugh, less like he's amused her and more like he's punched her in the throat. "Ezra," she says, half a protest.

"What am I supposed to say?"

It comes out louder and angrier than he means it. He snaps his mouth shut, aware, in the way he has to be now, that to anyone strolling by on the sidewalk, he isn't a girl yelling at his mom, he's a man on the dirt with a middle-aged woman, raising his voice.

Mom is watching him, her face expressionless. "I've never seen you do that before."

"Yeah," Ezra says. "Well." There's nothing he can say to that.

After a moment, she sighs. "How's your father?"

"Jesus fucking Christ."

"*Language.*"

He bites back a response to that with the same ruthless efficiency that lets him suppress any possible noise of pain when one of his clients holds his hand when they push.

"Dad," he says, "is a disaster, just like anyone would be if their spouse of thirty-something years left without any warning to go move in with the wife of one of the most important people in his entire professional network. He's basically a zombie; work is pretty much the only thing keeping him from drinking himself into a coma. He's not sleeping, and according to Becca and Aaron, the six-minute conversation I had with him in the break room the other day was the longest he's talked to anyone other than a client since you left."

Mom flattens her mouth into one long, thin line. "I'm sorry. I shouldn't have asked you that."

"No kidding," he says. "And let's take Becks and Aaron off the table, before you go there next."

"You—" She hesitates. "You were at the Chapel?"

Ezra shrugs. "I'm doing your job."

"You hate it there."

"Someone has to do it."

Mom laughs, high and humorless and desperate like a sob, and puts her face in her hands, heedless of the dirt. "Oh, katchkaleh, what do you think of me now?"

He's never heard her Yiddish sound like this, heavy with despair and self-loathing, the language of his childhood affections abruptly steeped in misery.

"Mom . . ." Ezra rubs his eyes, giving himself a few seconds to *breathe,* counting the seconds in the spaces between inhale and exhale the way his yoga teachers had taught him: in for two, hold, out for two, hold. He wishes, for a moment, that he'd forgone his binder today, so he could let his ribs expand wide, wide, wide without the spandex tensing them back in.

"Okay," he says, once he's tamed his voice into something that resembles calm. "You can't just hide here forever. You know that, right? You have to talk to Dad. I mean, you have to talk to everyone, but you *really* need to talk to Dad."

"I didn't think he'd talk to me." It has all the weight of a confession. "Your siblings, either."

"I know they've been texting you," he says. "Aaron's called you at least once a day. *Becca's* called you. And Becca never calls anyone."

Which is true. Becca has horrible phone anxiety. Online food delivery was the greatest thing that had ever happened to her.

"I know," she says. "I suppose I just thought they were calling to yell, or—" She exhales a humorless bark of laughter. "All I've wanted to do is hide. This is just—" She shakes her head. "How do I apologize for something like this?"

"I don't think I can tell you that," Ezra says. "They don't cover cheating on your husband in yoga teacher training."

It's a blow below the belt.

"Sorry," he says, and then hates himself for it. Why is *he* apologizing? It kind of seems like he should get *one* jab in.

There's a part of him that wants to try to convince her to come *home*. Maybe Judy is the love of her life, and maybe she and Dad will have to split up, but they could figure it out, could do it together. Maybe this didn't *have* to be horrible and hurtful and miserable, and everyone could be okay again.

Wishful thinking, probably.

"Look," he says. "I'm spending enough time with Dad and Aaron to get a feel for how they're doing, and I see Becca four or five times a week these days. So I'll . . . see what I can do. I'll tell them that you're all in one piece and you haven't totally lost your mind. You need to talk to them, and I'm willing to be there as . . . I don't know, a mediator. But you can't just expect them to be ready to play nice. And you have to apologize."

Mom nods.

"Okay." He pauses. "And I really shouldn't have to say this, but they probably are not ready to talk to Judy anytime soon, so don't invite them over for happy-family Shabbat dinner or something."

"I wouldn't."

That's something, at least. He gets to his feet. "I should head out."

Mom frowns up at him. "You haven't eaten."

He will absolutely throw up if he eats right now. All he wants is a gallon of coffee and an opportunity to turn off his brain. "I need to get back to work."

Mom looks disappointed, but she nods. "I'll walk you out."

He follows her back inside. She hovers close to him as he washes his hands at the kitchen sink with floral soap so strongly scented it dizzies him. She keeps hovering as they walk toward the door, like she wants to reach out to touch him.

Is he grateful or disappointed that she doesn't try?

Ezra lets himself look more closely at the living room as they pass through it, trying to memorize as many details as he can. His eyes catch on a photo on one of the end tables, and he stops short. Mom walks directly into him, lets out a little "Oops!" of surprise, and then, voice curious, says, "Ezra?"

Ezra shakes his head at her, moving into the room and picking up the frame. It's a formal wedding photo, clearly taken within the past few years.

There are seven people in the photo, and Ezra recognizes five of them.

The two he doesn't recognize are both young women, one in her midteens, judging by the baby fat that clings to her cheeks, the other maybe in her very early twenties. They're both dark-haired, light-eyed, and beaming at the camera, wearing matching dresses in a floaty charcoal gray. Bridesmaids, probably. They stand on the outer edges of the group, one each on either side of Judy and Rabbi Isaac, just as nicely dressed, just as bright-eyed.

Next to Judy is Jonathan, smiling so wide his face looks ready to split in half.

On Jonathan's other side, his arm around Jonathan's waist, their heads tilted together in obvious affection, is a man Ezra's never seen alive. But he recognizes him all the same.

"Oh," Mom says, coming up beside him. "That's Ben."

He startles at the sound of her voice, barely managing not to drop the picture frame. He sets it down on the table with shaking hands. "Ben," he repeats, rapidly putting puzzle pieces together, faces and rooms and the shadows behind Jonathan's eyes. "Their son who died?"

Mom nods, reaching out to touch the frame. "Yes. A car accident, almost a year ago. Horrible. I don't think you ever would have met him, but he was at the Chapel quite a bit before he died."

"No, I never . . ." Ezra can't stop staring at the photo, trying to match this bright, beaming man to the solemn shade he's used to, who has broken all the rules Ezra thought he'd figured out. "Why was he there?"

"Isaac's synagogue has its own on-call chevra, and Ben volunteered with them for years. He's the one who got Jonathan involved. I still can't believe he went back to it."

Ezra nods, head spinning slightly. Mom touches his arm. "Are you okay?"

"Yeah." He shakes himself slightly. "Sorry, I— When did you say he died?"

"Last summer." There's a look in her eyes Ezra's never seen on any face but his own: haunted. "I don't think Judy's ever really forgiven herself for it."

Ezra frowns. "You said it was a car accident."

"It was," Mom says. Her hand lingers on the frame a moment longer. He realizes, for the first time, that she's not wearing her wedding ring. He's never seen her without it before. "He wasn't supposed to be out that night. Judy was supposed to drive something over to the temple for Isaac, and she asked Ben to go for her. The other driver hit him when he was on his way home."

He doesn't need her to tell him where Judy was instead.

12

When Ezra finishes talking, his siblings stare at him.

"Sorry," Aaron says at last. "I'm going to need you to go over this again."

Ezra had intended to spend today's breakfast telling them about Mom and Judy and everything that had come up in that shit show of a conversation. Instead, as soon as their waitress had left with their menus, he blurted out, "I've been seeing Judy's kid's ghost *everywhere,* and he's breaking the fucking *rules,*" and everything had promptly gone to hell.

Honestly, he's a little impressed that they're taking it as calmly as they are, but then again, neither of them are really the type to make a scene in the middle of an IHOP. Once they're back in the car, all bets are probably off.

"Okay," he says, wrapping his hands around his coffee mug to hide their shaking. "What do you want to know?"

"How about we start with why you never told us about the you-can-see-dead-people thing," Aaron says. "And go from there."

Ezra looks down. "I couldn't."

"*Why?*"

"I don't know." It's half the truth. There was never a conscious decision not to tell anyone—and by the time he realized it, he'd wrapped himself in too many layers of *No, sorry, just thought I saw something, corner of my eye,* and *I'm just talking to myself,* and *It's nothing, it's nothing, it's nothing.* The idea of undoing it all, of picking apart every moment he lied or pretended or pushed someone away, felt like throwing himself into the ocean and waiting to drown.

He'd tried, once. His first girlfriend in high school had loved ghost stories, loved mysteries, believed in the supernatural with all her heart and soul. If anyone was safe, he'd reasoned, it would be her. Instead, she burst into tears on the spot and accused him of making fun of her, of thinking everything she believed in was a joke. Ezra still remembers the way she looked at him, tear-streaked with betrayal. She'd never spoken to him again.

"I'm sorry. I just . . ."

Aaron makes a frustrated sound. "Did you think we wouldn't have believed you?"

"*Would* you?" Aaron might be the most religiously observant of the three of them, but he's always been a skeptic when it comes to believing in anything he can't see, rolling his eyes when Becca does tarot readings or refuses to make decisions when Mercury is in retrograde.

Aaron purses his lips. "Maybe not right away," he admits. "But you said this has been going on since we were kids?" Ezra nods, reluctant, and Aaron spreads his hands, the universal *Well?* "I would have believed you then. I believed everything you said when we were kids. You were the boss, remember?"

Aaron's steady and mature now, but growing up, he'd been a hurricane. Ezra was five when Mom first said, "Kids, be good. E—, you're in charge," when she left them to play together. Aaron was four years his senior.

"I didn't know how," Ezra says. That, at least, is the truth.

"That time in Mom's office," Becca says suddenly. She hasn't said a word since Ezra started talking when they sat down, her face pale and shocked. "When I was thirteen, and you—you *screamed*—"

Aaron gives her a bewildered look. "What are you talking about?"

Becca ignores him, looking at Ezra, so focused it feels like she's stripping back his skin. "You remember, don't you? You were telling me about how stressed you were with school, while I was freaking out about my bat mitzvah studying, and then you just went"—she lets out a sharp, bitter laugh—"you went white as a *ghost*—"

Ezra knows. He remembers his senior year of high school as a blur of college applications, homework, anxiety, and kissing people who turned out to be assholes in the way all seventeen-year-olds are assholes, but that day stands out in vivid Technicolor. He'd been strung out on energy drinks, annotating a copy of *Orlando* while half-heartedly babysitting Becca in Mom's office, when the ghost appeared. Becca's right, he *had* screamed—it was a girl, no older than Ezra, blood-drenched and blank-eyed, her neck bent at an angle that no neck should be.

She'd settled into normality half an instant later, soft brown eyes and a tumble of dark curls, but that split second of horror had been enough to scare the hell out of Becca.

"You told me you were just *letting out your energy*," Becca goes on. "And then you told me I should try it, too. That it would make me feel better. And it *did*, but then Dad yelled at us because there was a service going on and they could hear us down the hall. You told him that it was your idea, so I shouldn't get in trouble, and he grounded you for like a *month*. You had to miss homecoming!"

"I wouldn't have gone to homecoming anyway," he says, but he knows that's not the point. Not when she'd tiptoed into his room that night and given him a tearful hug, thanking him in a whisper for giving her a few precious minutes to let off steam. Now here he is, years later, stomping on the memory. Her momentary lifeline, that bright spark of connection, reduced to a diversion. "Becca, I'm sorry."

She glares at him—and then, unexpectedly, it drains away. "You must have been so *lonely*."

Yep, he'd have been more comfortable with their anger. The way they're looking at him now—Becca heartbroken, Aaron caught somewhere between bewilderment and hurt—is so much worse. "It was fine," he says. "I mean, it wasn't, like, tragic. Just weird."

Aaron narrows his eyes, his expression shifting to something calculating, almost thoughtful. "Is this why you started hating the funeral home?"

"I don't *hate* it."

Becca snorts. "Hard false."

Aaron ignores her. "You used to love hanging out there when we were kids. And then all of a sudden you just *stopped*. Mom and Dad had to start dragging you over when they needed help with stuff. Was it because of the ghosts?"

One ghost, really, Ezra wants to say, but doesn't. If he starts talking about Zayde now, he won't be able to stop. And he'll probably cry, which he refuses to do in public at seven-thirty in the morning. It's bad enough that the ghost of a middle-aged woman in a waitress's uniform has drifted from behind the counter to the booth next to theirs and is listening with interest; Ezra doesn't need their actual living waitress to follow suit. "I guess. It wasn't *just* the ghosts, but . . . I guess. Yes."

Becca looks like she wants to ask him something else, but Aaron clears his throat. "So why are you telling us *now*?"

"It just seemed too— With Mom, and Judy, and now I'm seeing him everywhere, I just—" He swallows. "There were too many connection points. And if he's sticking around because of something they did—because he died when Judy was supposed to . . . It's not like I'm used to them being *vengeful,* but what if . . ."

The more he talks, the more absurd it sounds.

"So he's just . . . what?" Aaron leans back in his seat. "Breaking all your 'rules'?"

He adds the air quotes but manages not to sound sarcastic as he does it. Ezra had stumbled through an explanation of what he's gotten used to from the ghosts he sees and how Ben has ignored just about everything Ezra thought he knew about how they worked. "Basically."

"Well, there has to be some kind of reason." Aaron looks like he's grappling with a nasty crossword puzzle, the last traces of hurt dropping off his face. Ezra relaxes slightly. Aaron moving into logic mode doesn't necessarily mean Ezra's not going to get a guilt-tripping meltdown later, but it's a good sign all the same. "Maybe it's, like, an emotional resonance kind of thing." Becca raises an eyebrow, and he says defensively, "What? I can come up with ghost ideas, too."

Ezra lets that go. "It makes a lot more sense now that I know who he is. The Chapel, our house—if he did chevra work, it makes sense he'd have an attachment."

Becca reaches for her abandoned plate. "What about at your apartment?"

Ezra shrugs. "Jonathan lives downstairs."

"Which is absurd, for the record," Becca says dryly. "There's *It's a small gay world after all,* and there's literally moving into the same house. Is New England queer geography challenging Jewish geography now? I just need to know if I should brush up on my six degrees of separation."

"Becca," Aaron chides, but there's a hint of a smile tugging at his mouth as he shakes his head. "She's right, honestly. It is weird. And what are you supposed to do, anyway? Help him stop haunting shit?"

"Trust me, if I knew, I'd be doing it." Ezra considers telling them what Mom said, about Judy being the person who should have been driving the night Ben died, but something stops him. If he knew more, maybe . . . He eyes the half-empty plates across the table, then dismisses them. His appetite has shriveled in his stomach. "I mostly feel like an idiot for not putting it together sooner."

"In your defense," Becca says, "there were one or two other things going on." She nudges the remainder of her waffle closer to him. "What are you going to do about Jonathan?"

Ezra pokes reluctantly at the waffle with his fork. "What do you mean?"

She gives him a pointed look. "The part where you could cut the sexual tension between you two with a knife?"

Ezra opens his mouth, then snaps his head around to scowl at Aaron, who has the decency to look sheepish.

"In my defense," he says, "I had to tell *someone*."

"Jail for you," Ezra tells him. "I don't know. I don't know! What am I supposed to tell him? *Hey, you're cute, and I'm possibly the first person you've flirted with since your husband died, but by the way, your husband's ghost is in the corner*? I don't see that going over so well."

"Valid," Becca muses. "Could be a mood killer." She props her chin on her hand, eyes thoughtful. "So, what, you're dead in the water? Horrible pun not intended. Does the husband-ghost thing just squash it for you?"

Ezra takes a too-large bite of waffle to avoid answering. If he were a better person, the answer would be that of *course* that squashed any likelihood he had of acting on his attraction to Jonathan, and even if it *hadn't* been an issue, he was a mess, and he wasn't about to ruin Jonathan's first venture back into the dating world by being . . . well, himself.

Unfortunately, he's probably *not* a better person, no matter how much he wishes he was.

13

Despite Ben being just one in a long line of ghosts Ezra's seen throughout the years, part of Ezra still expects something to have changed after putting the puzzle of his identity together. Some epiphany, a new understanding, a lightbulb moment.

But nothing changes. Life goes on.

Mom texts him constantly, asking for advice on the emails she's crafting to the rest of the family. He's also ended up on the permanent phone tree for Jonathan's chevra, and as much as his no-longer-a-mystery ghost makes him want to avoid Jonathan like the plague, he still says yes every time he gets a message asking for taharah volunteers. It's the way Jonathan performs the ritual, the look of absolute peace that settles over him, his focused tenderness.

He's just trying to *help,* he tells himself, tells Aaron, too, when he gives him those knowing looks every time Ezra and Jonathan pass his office.

He tries not to notice the way Ben appears almost constantly now, especially in the taharah rooms, always there at the edge of Ezra's vision as they wash and pour water and prepare the bodies for burial, watching them—no, watching *Jonathan*—with those soft, sad eyes. Sometimes Ezra catches his gaze, and when he does, Ben looks back and inclines his head.

His expression is always the same. A silent, unspoken *I see you.*

Ezra doesn't know what to do with that. He looks away first.

Becca

> I love you so much but I am BEGGING YOU to stop sending me clips from the Sixth Sense

Ok but consider: u do see dead people

also i use humor to cope and i feel like u shouldn't be able to judge me for how i respond to U LITERALLY SEEING DEAD PEOPLE

> . . . can you at least maybe limit to one a day

no promises 😇 😇 😇

He has all the best intentions to leave work early on Wednesday for Roommate Family Dinner. He has grand plans to stop at Bottles on his way home for wine—and may or may not have snooped through the communal wine rack in the living room, googling labels on his phone to discern everyone's tastes (with the exception of Ollie, who'd drink shoe polish if it came in a nice enough bottle)—and then get home with time to shower, change, and help cook.

Instead, he finds himself on the floor of the break room, Jonah's youngest daughter in his lap while the older two girls sprawl out with a set of coloring books Ezra unearthed from the depths of his mom's filing cabinet.

"I'll be ten minutes, tops," Jonah had promised, pushing the baby and the diaper bag into Ezra's arms while his phone rang. "If I don't get this livery guy on the phone before the end of the day, coordinating the routes tomorrow is going to be a shit show—"

"You said a bad word!" Shuli chirped gleefully. "I'm telling Mom!"

Jonah looked pained. "Go," Ezra said, taking pity. "We'll be fine."

Famous last words. He'd forgotten that girls under the age of ten are the most terrifying creatures on the planet. Case in point, the delicate flames Shuli is adding to the castle she's coloring, and the hopefully made-up song Alma is singing under her breath about a horse that eats children.

At least the baby's content to let Ezra feed her a bottle, but she's probably plotting world domination. Knowing her sisters, he wouldn't put it past her.

He looks up at the sound of voices in the hallway, half hoping to hear Jonah coming back, but it's Aaron, Jonathan at his heels. "I'm just saying you could consider it," Aaron is saying. "Not that we're not happy to have you, but you're going to get sick of spending all your time here eventually."

"I *like* spending my time here," Jonathan retorts, and then nearly runs into Aaron, who's stopped short to stare at the mess of small children, coloring books, and Ezra clustered on the floor. "Oh. Hey there."

"Hey," Ezra says. He hopes he's managed to catch all of Maisie's spit-up on the cloth haphazardly draped over his shoulder. "Jonah had to call Denny," he adds to Aaron.

Aaron winces. They've been using the same livery company since Zayde was alive. They're prompt, professional, and well organized, but the dispatch manager is hell to get hold of. "Say no more."

"We're drawing dead people!" Shuli announces. "Want to see?"

"Um, sure?" Jonathan crouches to look at her picture. "Wow. He's . . . on fire?"

"It's a ritual cremation," she says, with the kind of solemnity only the six-year-old child of a funeral director could muster. Alma uses her temporary distraction to steal her red crayon.

Jonathan tries to smother a laugh. "Of course it is." He glances up at Ezra. "So you do babysitting, too?"

"Only under duress." Maisie blows a spit bubble at him from the crook of his arm.

Aaron snorts. "Don't listen to a word he says. Ezra loves kids. That's why he works with babies when we're not making him work here." At Jonathan's curious look, he adds, with an unexpectedly proud note in his voice, "He's a doula."

"Oh." Jonathan blinks. "Cool."

"Which I still find terrifying, by the way. Like, you have to stay calm if something goes wrong but you aren't actually trained if something *does* go wrong, so you're just . . ." He waves his hands dramatically.

"Things don't usually go wrong," Ezra says. Not at any of the births he's attended so far, thank God. He's been hired specifically for miscarriage and stillbirth support, and those days are always awful, but it's an expected sort of awfulness, something he knows how to prepare for and recover from. "And there are actual medical professionals around if something happens."

Jonathan looks interested. "Have you ever had to catch a baby?"

"Only once." It had been his client's fourth, and none of the hospital staff had listened when she told them that her labors were fast and furious. The memory still makes him cringe. "Hopefully never again. My job is only supposed to be above the waist."

"Still cool," Jonathan says earnestly, and that familiar heat creeps up and over the back of Ezra's ears, staining them red. "It's an awesome job. I bet you're really good at it." Jonathan smiles at him. "You've got a good energy. You make people feel settled."

He holds Ezra's gaze as he says it. For a moment, Aaron and the girls and the baby in his arms seem to fade away, leaving just the two of them, alone in a quiet room.

And then Jonathan looks away, their connection broken. "I have to head out. Aaron, can you call me when you hear back from the suppliers?"

"Sure," Aaron says. He's looking at Ezra, not at Jonathan, and Ezra *does not want* to hear anything that's about to come out of his mouth. "I might have Ezra call you, if things get busy."

Traitor, Ezra mouths at him over Jonathan's shoulder.

"Great," Jonathan says. "Keep up the great art, girls."

"Thanks," Shuli and Alma chorus.

Jonathan shoots Ezra a last wave—Ezra refuses to be grateful that he's sitting on the floor and therefore totally unaffected by the way his legs feel suddenly like jelly—and leaves, the carpet muffling the sound of his footsteps as he walks away.

There's a beat of silence, broken only by Alma's newly resumed humming.

"Wow," Aaron says.

Ezra groans. "Please don't."

"That was *rough.*"

"I don't want to talk about it."

"I have never," Aaron says gleefully, "seen you turn red like that."

"Hey, girls," Ezra says. "Wanna help plan a murder?"

Jonah does come back eventually, though not before his daughters have spent ten minutes coloring a remarkably tolerant Aaron's fingernails with a set of highlighters. Ezra's running late for dinner, making the world's fastest trip to pick up a bottle of wine and pointedly ignoring the specter of an old man who keeps pointing insistently at a pinot grigio that's about four times Ezra's budget.

The look the ghost gives him when Ezra picks out a ten-dollar bottle of chardonnay could rival Mom's for withering disappointment.

He's sweaty and flustered by the time he gets home, almost tripping over his shoelaces as he comes through the door. There's music playing from the wireless speaker on the counter, bright and bouncy and maybe in Korean, drowning the solemn conversation Max and Noah are having over the rice cooker. Sappho, to Ezra's utter lack of surprise, is sitting squarely between Ollie's and Lily's feet as they dice vegetables at the table, watching them with eager eyes and clearly hoping for scraps. She doesn't so much as twitch her ears in Ezra's direction as he approaches, but Ollie looks over, his face lighting up.

"Hey," he says, putting his knife down. "We were beginning to think you forgot."

"I got held up at work," Ezra says. It's not like he *could* have forgotten, with the way the group chat has been *loud* the last few days while everyone else planned the dinner. But they all seemed to have such an easy connection that he felt clumsy and awkward even over text, so he'd just added the occasional thumbs-up and kept the chat on mute.

Ollie, who hasn't lost his ability to read Ezra like a book, softens slightly. "I think we've got dinner prep taken care of," he says, gentle in the way he always is when he can tell Ezra's contemplating running for the hills. "And I took Sappho for a quick walk earlier. Do you want to shower, and I'll make sure there's some wine for you when you get out?"

"I love you," Ezra says, meaning it, and Ollie snickers.

"Love you, too," he says. He gestures toward the hallway with his knife. "Go bathe."

Ezra goes, pausing to wave to everyone else and lean down to kiss the top of Sappho's head. She acknowledges him with a single wag of her tail but otherwise doesn't take her eyes off Lily's cutting board.

It's not as transformative as a nap, but he feels miles better after a shower and a change of clothes. He makes his way back to the kitchen once he's dressed, still scrunching product through his hair to try to tame his curls into less of a tangled mess. As promised, Ollie has a glass of wine waiting for him, and Ezra takes it gratefully as he slides into the seat across from him, peering at the ingredients scattered across the table and trying to remember the different recipes that had popped up in the group chat over the past week. "What did you guys decide to make, anyway?"

"Sundubu jjigae," Ollie says, and then, grinning at whatever Ezra's face is doing, clarifies, "Spicy tofu stew. With a few tweaks in the recipe because we didn't want to burn your taste buds off."

"I'm good with spice," Ezra protests, putting his wine down. Ollie gives him an *Are you, though?* sort of look, and Ezra concedes, "Okay, not, like, *spicy* spice, but I can handle heat!"

"You are so cute," Lily says, plopping back into her chair, having apparently just delivered her mushrooms to Noah and Max in the kitchen. She levels a perfectly manicured finger at

Ollie. "Korean," she says, then points to herself—"Indian"—and then, gesturing into the kitchen—"New Orleans and Jamaica. The spice heritage in this house is at a level you have *not* achieved."

Ezra can't argue with that. "Fair," he admits, because he's had enough meals with Ollie's sisters to know how willing they are to use chili oil as a hazing tool. "Can I do anything to help?"

Lily picks up a bundle of scallions. "Wanna do garnish?"

Having something to do with his hands is a relief, and Ezra gratefully accepts the knife and cutting board Ollie slides him. The work goes quickly, and before he knows it the five of them are gathered around the table together and he's burning his tongue off with all the grace he can muster. After too many days of tension and silence and grief, it's a sweet breath of air to be surrounded by laughter and warmth and the easy camaraderie of people who know one another well, who are happy to be in the same room.

By the time they're cleaning up, he has to admit to himself, finally, that he *likes* being here. He likes the energy that resonates through the room, working around one another with comfort, banter flying between the kitchen and the table, playful but never unkind. It goes against all his instincts to relax into this, but he makes himself do it anyway.

If he keeps his head down and doesn't do anything weird, maybe he can bask in this, just a little longer. It helps that Ollie keeps topping off his wineglass—*Ha, ten-dollar chard is a hit. Take that, judgy liquor store ghost*—because he's an asshole who knows that Ezra can hold just about any kind of liquor and stay fully even-keeled, but that wine turns him loose-limbed and relaxed like a cat in a sunbeam.

"Hey!" Ezra says, batting him away when he goes to do it again. "No! Shoo!"

"I'm helping!" Ollie protests.

"Do you think they broke up because Ollie has no respect for boundaries?" Max says in a terrible attempt at a stage whisper, her head lolling into Noah's lap.

"We broke up because we're *sexually incompatible*," Ollie says, enunciating in the way he only ever does when he's drunk-quoting his therapist. Ezra kicks him in half-hearted objection, because *hey*, but Ollie just absently pats his leg, easy and affectionate. "In that Ezra likes sex and I don't."

"Hey," Ezra says, out loud this time.

Ollie wrinkles his nose. "Sorry. In that Ezra likes sex but has issues about it, and I like sex *very rarely* but have issues about it, and for two people with our self-esteem problems and undiagnosed anxiety, that wasn't really a recipe for a successful relationship in the long run." He picks his head up off the armrest and looks at Ezra. "Right?"

Ezra shrugs, a little surprised at how much it doesn't sting to hear it. "Not wrong."

Lily props her chin on her hand, her wineglass dangling from her fingertips. "I *had* been wondering," she says, thoughtful. "You don't give off angry-ex vibes."

"If they gave off angry-ex vibes, we wouldn't have let Ezra move in," Noah points out. Max nods, waving a finger around in a clear *Cosigned,* and Noah pats her shoulder.

"Not angry," Ollie confirms. His words are sad and soft and kind. "Just, you know."

Ezra nudges him with his foot again, more gently this time. In some ways, it's the best breakup Ezra's ever had—no hard feelings or harsh words. But it's miserable in other ways, to be in each other's inescapable orbit, close enough to touch but never in alignment. They were only hurting each other by the end, though, only coming together at their most jagged edges.

They're better as friends, anyway. They were friends first, and are friends now. Ezra hangs on to that, when he's lonely, wallowing, and eight months deep into Ollie's Instagram feed.

"Ooh, he's sad again," Lily says. "Ollie, wine him."

Ollie perks up, reaching for the bottle of merlot on the coffee table. Ezra puts a protective hand over his glass. "*No,*" he says, and Ollie pouts, putting the bottle back down. "Safe word. Go away."

Noah squints at them. "Your safe word is 'safe word'?"

"No," Ollie says, grinning in a way that has never once been good news for Ezra's dignity. Ezra considers the space between the couch and the coffee table to see how much room there is, decides it's worth the risk of a head injury, and kicks Ollie off the sofa.

Ollie lands on the carpet with a *thump.* "Rude!"

To Ezra's immense relief, the conversation shifts away from their relationship—or lack thereof—and over to Noah's. Ezra hasn't met Noah's girlfriend yet, but he's heard enough secondhand stories and seen enough pictures to know that she exists at that terrifying intersection of gorgeous, talented, and genuinely nice, which he's always found unfair. Apparently, they've been talking about moving in together, which would probably mean Noah moving out. Everyone has an opinion. Max seems to have about six. Ezra lets himself drift to the sound of Lily lobbying for Noah to convince Grace to move in with all of them instead of the two of them finding their own place, only vaguely aware of Sappho climbing up to take Ollie's place on the couch and flopping against his side.

He's abruptly brought out of his comfortable, dog-covered reverie by Ollie announcing, "I think we should ask Jonathan if he wants to come over."

Ezra doesn't spill his drink everywhere when he startles back to alertness, but it's a close call. "What?" he demands, trying to rapidly catch up with whatever he's just missed. "Why?"

Lily sits up straighter, her eyes bright and delighted. "We should *absolutely* do that," she says. "Oh my God. Two birds! One stone!"

"What birds?" Ezra asks, alarm mounting. "There are no birds!"

"No, no, no, no, Oliver is *right,* we should totally invite him up," Max says, earnest in the way that only someone who has unexpectedly found themselves on the drunk side of tipsy can be. "He's all alone down there! Which—sad! No one likes a sad gay, Ezra, you should know that."

"I'm bisexual," Ezra points out.

"It's an *umbrella,*" she says, waving a hand and nearly knocking Noah's beer out of his hand. He jerks it out of her reach at the last second, making a face. "And you're single and depressed, and *he's* single and depressed, and you're constantly talking about him in the group chat—"

"I am *not*—"

Lily already has her phone out. "Would you like me to read you the receipts, or just start forwarding them back to you?"

Ezra changes tack. "He's not single and depressed," he says, trying to keep the desperation out of his voice. "He's *widowed,* and *mourning,* that is *not* the same thing. "

"Everyone's gotta get back on the horse sometime," Noah says mildly.

Ollie reaches up from the floor and pokes Ezra in the thigh. "You're the horse in this scenario," he says, sotto voce. "Or I guess he could be the—"

"I regret ever meeting you," Ezra tells him.

"Lies," Ollie says smugly, proving that Ezra has never had good taste in men ever in his life. Maybe he should take Nina up on her offer and they should just get married, IVF a bunch of kids, and move to a gay farming commune in Vermont.

No, it would never work out. Nina would be a terrible farmer. She'd break one nail and they'd be relocating to Brooklyn faster than it takes to milk a cow. Probably. Not like Ezra knows how long it would take to milk a cow. He takes out his phone to google it and pauses at the notification from Dad, already there on his lock screen.

He knows what it's going to say before he opens it.

Dad

Don't forget to count the Omer.
Yesterday was day 22.

It's a rule Ezra hadn't known before he actually started counting this year, that you weren't supposed to get an alert for the night you were actively counting, because that defeated the purpose of mindfully counting. Apparently it's kosher to get a reminder of what you counted the night *before*, though, hence Dad's go-to reminders.

Ezra texts back a guilty *Thank you*, then sets an alarm to remind himself to count later, because he's one thousand percent sure that if he slips away to do it now, he'll come back to find Jonathan standing in the middle of his living room.

Max's phone chimes with an incoming message, just as someone knocks at the door.

"What," Max says, all innocence. "Was I not supposed to text him?"

14

Ezra must have done something horrendous in a past life, because when Jonathan steps through the door, his smile uncertain but hopeful, he looks just as home-soft and comfortable as Ezra was worried he'd be outside of the Chapel. Ezra's gotten used to him in button-downs and sweaters. Seeing him in cuffed jeans and a too-large hoodie with a faded Brandeis University logo hits like a physical blow.

Ollie gives him a pointed nudge. "Shut your mouth before something flies into it."

Sappho breaks the awkwardness by greeting Jonathan with her usual enthusiasm, all but tackling him back against the door. Ezra gets to his feet to make sure she doesn't fully bowl him over, but Jonathan's grinning, the hesitancy disappearing from his face as he crouches to rub her ears. He looks up when Ezra reaches them, easy amusement deepening the laugh lines by his eyes, and Ezra wonders if it's too late to change his name and move to another state—anything to avoid the humiliating flutter that lights up his chest.

"Hey," Jonathan says, giving Sappho's chin one last scratch and rising to his feet. "Thanks for inviting me over. This was really nice of you."

"It was my idea," Ollie says, tossing an arm around Ezra's shoulders and grinning at Jonathan as he gives Ezra a playful shake. "You've met our Ezra, so you know how shy he is."

Ezra makes a mental note to steal one of every pair of Ollie's socks the next time he's up in unit 3, as he attempts to plaster on an expression that hopefully doesn't radiate *This is my ex, please ignore every word that comes out of his horrible face*, but Jonathan is already smiling.

"Oh, I don't know that I get *shy* from him," he says, and Ezra has to be imagining the hint of a spark in his eyes as they meet Ezra's. "I think he's just a little slow to warm up."

"I'm also right *here*," Ezra says, intimately aware of how hot his face is and how red it looks. The last thing he needs right now is Ollie and Jonathan teaming up, though, so he shrugs Ollie's arm off his shoulders and gestures back toward the living room. "You missed dinner, but we're apparently at the drinking-on-a-school-night part of the evening. Wine? Beer?"

"Wine's great," Jonathan says.

"Red or white?"

Jonathan tilts his head to one side, considering, and the weight of his eyes is far too heavy to just be thinking about wine. "Whatever you're having."

Whatever Ezra's having ends up being a glass of merlot and a lapful of Sappho, who sprawls out across both of them when Ollie—giving Ezra a pointed wag of his eyebrows, because he's the least subtle person on the *planet*—gestures for the two of them to take the couch, while he stretches out on the floor. There's enough room for them to share without touching, but Ezra finds himself tilting toward Jonathan anyway, their shoulders barely brushing.

If it bothers Jonathan to have him so close, he doesn't let on. He looks like he belongs there, leaning easily into the conversation that starts up around them again as if it never paused, responding to Max and Lily's energetic—though tactful, Ezra notes, avoiding any dead-husband questions—

interrogation about what he's been up to since the last time they talked.

It warms something in Ezra's belly to see Jonathan so comfortable here, in Ezra's living room, with Ezra's friends, and he realizes with a jolt that this is the first time he's *thought* of this place, these *people,* as his. It's like having Jonathan in this room was the puzzle piece he needed to make it feel *right,* to connect Ezra to it and make him feel *real,* and that's—that's—

No. Absolutely not. He gets up to pour himself a generous glass of water, steadfastly ignoring the look Ollie shoots him from the floor, and scoots himself to the far edge of the couch when he sits back down, chugging half of it in one go. Jonathan cocks a brow at him but doesn't comment, and Ezra's grateful for it.

He's even more grateful for the way Jonathan seems to sense that Ezra is none too subtly trying to keep from being pulled into the full group's conversation and smoothly pivots to asking Noah about his kombucha brewing instead. Ezra doesn't know how to feel about the way Jonathan seems to just—*get* him, to look at him and see him in a way that even Ollie never has. And he does it like it's nothing, like it's the easiest thing in the world, and Ezra doesn't know what to do with that, because no one has ever, in his whole life, made him feel easy to love.

Ezra looks at the wineglass he'd abandoned on the coffee table, still half full, and downs the rest of his water instead. If those are the kinds of thoughts floating through his head like they belong there, it's probably time to stop drinking.

Jonathan's eyes flicker toward him when Ezra settles back in his seat, empty-handed now, and he gives him another one of those *looks,* both thoughtful and knowing. He smiles, a quirk of his lips, a smile Ezra's seen from him more than once before, but this time—like it's the first time he's let himself *look,* even without meaning to—Ezra sees the invitation in it. Not something pointed or sultry, just . . . open, like an extended hand.

Like an offer.

Ezra bites the inside of his cheek. Tries to remember all the reasons he told himself this was a bad idea.

Instead, he remembers, like a shock of cold water, that the ghost he's spent the last several weeks trying to puzzle out is the guy Jonathan planned to spend the rest of his life with. The guy he lost too soon because the world is a horrible, brutal place where kind men lose their husbands for no good reason.

Ben must have been someone wonderful for Jonathan to still be wearing his wedding ring a year after his death, to still be close with his parents, to haunt the halls of the funeral home where Ben used to spend so much of his time. And Ezra's not—he's not a *bad person,* or at least he tries not to be, but he can't imagine anyone ever staying for him like that. You have to be willing to show your whole self to someone to get that kind of devotion, and Ezra's never been willing to risk it.

Ollie had known, he thinks sometimes, that Ezra was holding back. Maybe things would have been different, if he hadn't been so determined to keep his secrets so close to his chest, if he hadn't brushed off too many bad dreams and startles and poorly covered attempts to pretend he hadn't been staring too intently at something no one else could see. If in those too-rare, far-between moments when Ollie tried to push him to tell him what was really going on, Ezra had let him in instead of pushing him away.

Or maybe it wouldn't have mattered at all.

But Jonathan's an adult, right? That's what everyone keeps reminding him. He's a grown-up who can make his own choices, who can decide for himself what he wants, and if that's a reluctant psychic with anxiety, well—

Well.

"Hey," Jonathan says, barely loud enough to be heard over the waves of conversation happening around them, and when Ezra turns to meet his eyes, Jonathan's smile goes soft around the edges. But there's hesitance in it, too, and Ezra feels the recognition like a blow, the understanding that Jonathan is as off-kilter as Ezra is. "Do you want to go somewhere a little quieter?"

He should say no. The right thing to do is to say no.

He doesn't.

15

Jonathan's apartment is exactly like Ezra pictured it, during the few moments he let himself wonder about the rooms behind his door.

It's a quiet, calm space, all warm neutrals and soft fabrics and clean lines. But there's something empty about it, too, a consciously unfilled space, like the spots of darker paint left behind when you move a picture frame from one wall to another. He doesn't have to ask what's missing. It's obvious in the photos still clustered across the mantel, in the historical fiction novels crammed into the overflowing bookcases when Ezra knows that Jonathan prefers fantasy, in the winter coat hanging on the rack by the door even though it's spring.

"This is nice," Ezra offers, slipping out of his shoes.

"Thanks." Jonathan locks the door behind them. "I should probably be humble and say I can't take all the credit, but I absolutely should. If Ben had had his way, we'd never have bought a bed frame."

"Yikes," Ezra says, but it eases something in him that he hadn't realized was tense, to hear Jonathan reference Ben like that, simply and without pain. It's been over a year, he knows, but it's not like it's the kind of wound that just heals.

He does another quick, hopefully subtle scan of the room, in case the sudden mention of his name somehow summons

Ben's ghost from wherever the shades go when they're not making Ezra's life miserable. Ezra's not about to take it for granted that Ben's going to follow the rules.

Rules like *Don't hang out alone with the cute guy you're failing to talk yourself out of trying to kiss,* which Ezra's *also* breaking.

I'm going to hell, Ezra thinks, and looks up at Jonathan before he can let that train of thought go any further. "So, since we ditched the wine upstairs—"

"Way ahead of you," Jonathan says, just a touch too quickly, and slips past him to head into the kitchen, his fingers brushing over Ezra's waist as he passes. The touch sends a spark up Ezra's spine.

Going right *to hell,* Ezra thinks, and follows him into the kitchen.

The wine turns out to be a sauvignon blanc that looks several shelves nicer than the chardonnay Ezra bought earlier. They settle themselves at the little breakfast nook in the corner of the kitchen—a safer alternative, probably, than the cozy-looking sectional in the living room—and Jonathan opens the bottle.

"I wondered how much you'd had before I got there," he says, sliding a glass across the table to Ezra. "Max usually has to be pretty tipsy before she calls me in."

"I didn't realize you used to hang out with them," Ezra says. "They never said anything about it."

Jonathan shakes his head. "Not a lot," he says. "But from time to time. Max and I got off on the wrong foot when she moved in—I don't even remember why, honestly—but she always got about twenty times friendlier when she'd had a few glasses of wine, which I only ever found out because she used to show up at my door and demand that I play video games with her."

Ezra considers that as he takes a sip, playing it out against everything he's learned about Max over the past few weeks. "That sounds about right."

Jonathan looks like he's trying to bite back a smile as he nods at Ezra's glass. "Any good?"

"No clue," Ezra admits. "You've got the wrong sibling if you want real insights into wine. My standards are 'under fifteen dollars' and 'doesn't taste like vinegar.'"

Jonathan grins. "Okay, one for two," he says. "But before you think I'm shelling out major income on wine, I should probably say this was a gift."

Ezra *had* been wondering, mostly because any bottle of wine that looks like it might cost more than twelve dollars is a splurge in his book. "I'll give you credit for hanging on to it, unless your birthday was, like, five minutes ago," he says instead. "If I get a bottle of wine as a gift, it's gone in twenty-four hours. Less, if I share."

"Which you always do, I'm sure," Jonathan says. He runs a thumb through the condensation on the side of his glass, a probably absent-minded motion that draws Ezra's attention all the same. "No, I was just sort of . . . not saving it for a special occasion, I guess, but . . ." He shrugs. "Like I said, I'm getting used to living alone. Progressing to drinking alone seemed like something I should avoid."

Can't relate, Ezra thinks. "I know you probably get this all the time," he says. "And I'm like a year late. But I really am sorry about Ben."

Jonathan's smile fades, his right hand shifting to cover his left. "Thank you."

"And I'm also sorry that I shot you down when you first asked me out for coffee." He might as well get the awkwardness over with, right? "I just thought, you know—there was so much going on with my family, and I know you've probably figured this out but I'm kind of a mess even at, like, baseline? So I just kind of thought that if I was the first person you were flirting with since Ben died that you deserved someone who had their shit together, at least a little bit, and I didn't want to—"

"Whoa, whoa, whoa," Jonathan says, alarmed, and *yeah*, okay, so much for that filter. Ezra snaps his mouth shut, hoping he doesn't look as red as he feels, but Jonathan just shakes his head, the look on his face caught somewhere between amusement and chagrin. "Look, you're right, you *are* the first person I've—thought about, like that, since Ben, and I guess I haven't been as subtle as I hoped I was. But I didn't mean to make you think that I was just . . . trying to use you to rip off a Band-Aid, or something."

Ezra winces. "Ouch," he says. "I wasn't thinking that, but now I almost feel like I should."

"Oh." Jonathan ducks his head, rubbing the back of his neck. "Sorry. In my defense, I'm out of practice."

It's the first time Ezra's seen him look embarrassed, and it's such a novelty to not be the only red-faced person in a room. "You're not doing so bad."

They sit in silence for a few moments, the room quiet except for the hum of the refrigerator.

"Speaking of me asking you out, though," Jonathan says.

Ezra chokes on his drink.

Jonathan bursts out laughing. He gets to his feet and goes to the fridge while Ezra sputters and coughs, filling a glass of water and bringing it back. Ezra gives him a bleary-eyed glare—which probably loses a lot of impact from the fact that he's still wheezing around a lungful of white wine—and chugs it. "I'm so sorry."

"That was a murder attempt," Ezra rasps, setting the empty glass down. After a moment, he refills his wineglass instead.

"I said I was sorry!" Not that he looks at all apologetic. *Horrible man,* Ezra thinks, and is a little alarmed to realize that even the thought feels affectionate. "I just wanted to apologize if it made you uncomfortable. I haven't actually . . ." He starts systematically taking apart a napkin, tearing it into confetti with fidgeting hands. "Like I said. It's been a long time since I flirted with someone."

"I get it," Ezra says. "And look, you're not— It's not like you're not, um. Effective." Is he red again? He's red again. "I've been getting shit from Aaron all week for being a disaster around you."

Jonathan brightens. "Want me to get him off your back?"

"Are you kidding? It's basically the only thing he's calm about these days." Ezra thumbs a tiny chip in the base of his glass. "He's spending all day every day in triage mode, but if he can embarrass me about something, then all bets are off and we're back to normal."

Jonathan raises his glass. "I'll drink to that."

They do.

All the promises Ezra made to himself about not flirting with the married guy—and then not flirting with the not-married-but-probably-still-off-limits guy—seem suddenly less important, and the importance dwindles even more when Jonathan gathers up their glasses and they move to the couch. The soft lamplight paints Jonathan's brown eyes in dappled gold, and Ezra can't stop looking at his hands, at the way his long fingers toy with the fringe of the throw blanket tossed over the back of the couch and slide over the stem of his wineglass in a way that can't *possibly* be absent-minded anymore, and would be so much worse if it was.

It would be so much easier, Ezra thinks, if he was still properly drunk. He could lean over and kiss Jonathan's stupid, soft-looking lips, and if Jonathan told him he was out of his mind then Ezra could blame it on the wine and drag himself back upstairs and never speak to him again out of shame, but at least he wouldn't have to wonder anymore. And if Jonathan *didn't* tell him he was out of his mind, then Ezra would know that Jonathan was definitely out of *his*.

But he'd get to kiss him, to see what it *felt* like to kiss him, and that would be—

"Hey," Jonathan says. "You okay?"

"*Mm*-hmm," Ezra says, blinking himself away from Jonathan's collarbone—he'd ditched his hoodie at some point, revealing a deep V-neck shirt underneath, and it was a *very* nice collarbone—and back to the couch, and the warm golden light of the lamps, and the cold wine, and *fucking reality,* and maybe he's still a little drunk after all. Jonathan is watching him with a small smile that doesn't have any business looking as enticing as it does. "What?"

"Nothing," Jonathan says. He props his chin in one hand, leaning his elbow on the back of the couch. "You just— You're really cute."

"Oh my God," Ezra says. "Thank you for that. *Cute.* Kiss of death. Wow."

Jonathan laughs. He has such a good laugh. Ezra can't believe people used to make fun of it. "No, no, I meant it in a good way, really—" Ezra scowls at him, and that just makes Jonathan laugh harder. "No, really, I— You do this thing, do you know? You just look so focused but like you're trying not to look focused, and then when someone gets you out of your head you do this little *shake,* it's so—"

Fuck it, Ezra thinks. He's only human. He puts his wine down and reaches over to cup Jonathan's face in his hands. He waits just long enough to be sure Jonathan isn't going to push him off, and leans in to kiss him.

And it's—

It's a really good kiss.

Jonathan's mouth is as soft as it looks, and it's so *sweet,* so gentle. Ezra hears the *click* of crystal on wood as Jonathan sets his glass on the coffee table, and then his hands are on Ezra's hips, pulling him closer, and *that* shouldn't work either, not so smoothly. None of this is the sloppy, awkward fumbling Ezra had already half rehearsed in his head, and that, more than anything else, makes him pull back.

"Sorry," he says. He feels dizzy and knows he can't blame it all on the wine. "I— Sorry."

Jonathan blinks at him. "For what?"

Ezra bites his lip, and Jonathan's gaze flickers down to it. Ezra wants to groan, wants to fling himself off Jonathan's lap, wants to kiss him again and never stop. "You told me I'm the first person you've flirted with in a year."

"Yes," Jonathan says.

"And we've been drinking."

"A bit," Jonathan agrees.

"And—" Ezra gropes for another *and*. It seems like there should be at least one more.

"Ezra." Jonathan sits up straighter, and Ezra realizes, too late, that he's still straddling his lap. "You're not taking advantage of me. And I'd really like to kiss you again. If that's okay with you."

"Oh." Ezra feels—not dizzy, not drunk, but something very close. "Yes. I . . . yes."

Jonathan's hands move over his hips, warm and steady. *Sure.* The sureness of someone who knows what they want and is willing to reach for it, without second-guessing or spiraling, without worrying he'll say the wrong thing and mess it all up. What was that *like*? "If I'm being honest," Jonathan says, and Ezra flushes under the heat in his eyes, "I'd really like to do more than kiss you. If that's okay."

Ezra's tongue is heavy in his mouth, but not so heavy he can't manage the only word that matters. "Yes," he says. This *one* yes. "Please."

Jonathan smiles like the sun and pulls him back in.

Ezra wakes in darkness, in an unfamiliar bed in an unfamiliar room, and for the space of a breath, he isn't sure what woke him.

Jonathan is still asleep, curled around Ezra's back. His breathing is slow and even, warm against the nape of Ezra's neck. Ezra can feel his heartbeat, steady as a metronome.

He almost misses the figure in the dark.

Ezra pulls away slowly. Carefully. He manages to sit up against the headboard without waking Jonathan, and meets the eyes of a dead man.

Ben sits cross-legged on the dresser, his chin propped in his hands. He's in a sweater and slacks, his dark hair tousled. His gaze is locked on Jonathan, heavy with longing.

He looks impossibly real. Impossibly alive.

Ezra waits for him to disappear, the way he always has before. But this time, he doesn't.

He inclines his head.

And then he says, quiet and kind and clear as any living voice, "I think it's time we talked."

16

On the night of Zayde's tenth yahrzeit—ten years of hauntings, of constantly looking over his shoulder, of second-guessing everything he sees until he knows for sure it's real—Ezra writes down the rules.

The logic is this: The illusion of control is better than chaos. After ten years with no mystic revelation, no sudden understanding of the whys or the hows, all he can do is draw a box around the ghosts. So he writes the rules down and keeps them in his wallet. A reminder and a talisman.

First: *The ghosts can't move.*

Or rather: The ghosts are static, in one way or another—tied to a place, or a person, or an experience. In the early years, Ezra assumes that it's the body itself that holds the ghosts in place: He sees them in the funeral home, wandering the halls or sitting in the chapel or following their mourners through the showroom as if they could give their opinion on a casket, and with the exception of Zayde, who always seems to be there, Ezra never sees them once they're in the ground.

But then he gets older, and the ghosts multiply. At recess, he sees a woman with graying hair and horn-rimmed glasses keeping a watchful eye on the playground, and matches her face to the portrait of the founding principal that hangs proudly in the lobby. In high school, three weeks into his first year of choir, Ezra realizes that the pale boy two rows over, whose knit beanie never attracts a dress code violation, isn't singing too quietly to be heard—he's no longer capable of sound.

Wives who outlive their husbands last longer than the other way around, but he watches his grandmother fade in the years after Zayde's death. She calls him her *beshert*, her destined other half, and there are times when Ezra thinks she's nearly as haunted by his memory as he is. He talks to Zayde's ghost about her, when he's alone in the halls, not sure if he's convincing his grandfather or himself that it's only a matter of time until they'll be together again.

She dies in her sleep on a clear December night. Ezra sees her in the kitchen the next morning as if it's any other Tuesday, standing by the kettle, as though she can't understand why she can't make her morning tea. When she meets his eyes, her face fills with a strange, distant understanding. Ezra, relieved in a way he doesn't understand, tells her that Zayde is just a backyard away, that he's waiting for her, that all she has to do is follow him.

He makes it all the way to the front door before he realizes she's stayed behind.

It's only then that he realizes that Zayde never leaves the walls of the funeral home. That the yard that separates the house from the Chapel may as well be an impossible rift, that the space between his grandparents, even in death, is a cruel permanence.

Ezra refuses to attend a single service for a full six months after that, no matter how much guilt his mother layers on. His relationship to prayer has always been shaky at best, but for this, even rote recitation of words of prayer makes him feel like he's choking on dust.

Second: *The ghosts can't speak.*

He had talked to Zayde, in the first days after his death, following him through the Chapel's halls the same way he had when he was alive. He got used to Zayde listening in silent amusement while Ezra chattered absently to him about whatever came to mind. It took him almost two weeks to realize that Zayde never answered.

Before, he would have pulled on Zayde's sleeve to get his attention. After his death, he frowned at him, repeating "*Zayde, Zayde, Zayde,*" until Zayde finally looked down at him with exasperation, as if to say, *Well, what?*

He was a soft-spoken man, but never a silent one.

"Oh," Ezra said.

Zayde's eyes softened in apology, and Ezra sat down heavily on the Chapel floor.

Until that moment, with Zayde still right there in front of him, he hadn't grasped that he'd never hear his voice again. Ten minutes later, when Bubbe leaves the murmuring crowd in the upstairs chapel to come looking for him, Ezra was still crying.

And finally: *The ghosts can't hurt you.*

They don't touch him. They never touch him. They look at him, sometimes pleading, sometimes with eyes so utterly heartbroken he wants to claw his own out. But no matter how angry they look, how much their faces twist into silent screams, they don't even try.

They can't hurt you, he tells himself, year after year, nightmare after nightmare. *They can't hurt you.*

It's not until Ben that he remembers: There's more than one kind of hurt.

17

"You're not supposed to be able to talk," Ezra says, closing the front door firmly behind them.

It had taken Ezra several minutes to get past the shock, and even longer to ease himself all the way out from under Jonathan's arm—he's a cuddler, apparently, and protested Ezra's leaving without fully waking. Ezra had to try to pretend he couldn't see the absolute devastation on Ben's face at the sight of it. He pulled on his shoes, thanking every lucky star that he and Jonathan hadn't done much more than kiss after all, and it's Ben who inclines his head toward the door.

Now, sitting on the front porch, wrapped in a blanket he'd pulled off Jonathan's living room couch to ward off the chilly air, Ezra doesn't know what he's supposed to say.

The wind ruffles Ezra's hair and he shivers. Ben's hair doesn't so much as flutter.

"I think," Ben says at last, in that same soft, thoughtful voice, "that we're a little past what I'm *supposed* to be able to do."

There's nothing Ezra can say to that that won't sound absurd. "Why are you here?"

A faint smile touches Ben's lips. "Philosophical start."

"This isn't my usual rodeo."

"I'm an overachiever. At least, I was." He's not blue or translucent or spectral or glowing; he looks ordinary—

handsome and tired and rumpled around the edges. This close, Ezra can see the flecks of green in his hazel eyes, the occasional gray strands scattered through his dark hair, the stubble on his cheeks. Was he intentionally growing out a beard, or did he miss a few days of shaving?

Ezra can still feel the phantom touch of Jonathan's hands on his skin, the ghost of his fingertips skimming the line of Ezra's back under his shirt. "Oh my God," he says, horror mounting. "Could you see—"

"No," Ben says. "Though thanks for confirming there was something *to* see."

Ezra drops his head onto his knees.

Something brushes his back, a sensation like ice-cold water mixed with runny egg whites. He jerks back and whips his head up, shivers running down his spine. Ben's hand is still outstretched, like he'd tried to pat Ezra's shoulder in support, and he slowly pulls it back, looking down at it in a twist of discomfort and disgust.

"Sorry," he says, and the ease has dropped out of his voice so completely it's as if it was never there. What's left is something small and—Ezra's chest goes tight—*afraid*. He flexes his fingers, as if he can still feel them. "Did I hurt you?"

The question catches Ezra by surprise. "No," he says. "No. I'm okay, I was just surprised. It was cold, that's all."

Cold and unpleasant, but he doesn't need to *say* that. Ben nods, though, like it's a good enough answer, and wraps his arms around himself, looking down the dark street. It's a cloudy night, the moon hidden from view, and the light from the streetlamps is hazy against the fog. All the words turn dusty and dry on Ezra's tongue.

Ben breaks the silence, still looking somewhere beyond, where the streetlights fade into the darkness. "Jon and I used to sit out here all the time when we first moved in. I'm— I *was* a horrible sleeper, and then once I was in residency, I never had consistent shifts, so I never had a decent sleep schedule. I'd lie there and just not sleep, so eventually I just started getting up and sitting out here instead." He looks down at his hands, flexes his fingers again, then laces them together, resting them on his knees. "He always told me he hated waking up to an empty bed. Said he'd rather be awake with me than asleep alone. So we'd sit out here and drink tea in the middle of the night, and not even talk, and it would be . . . peaceful."

He looks down at his hands, rubbing them together as if to warm them. Can he feel the cold? "I hated that tea, but I drank it anyway, every time. He still does it, when he can't sleep. I sit with him, but he doesn't know I'm there."

Ezra swallows. "Are you? Always?"

"No. Only sometimes. I don't know where I am when I'm not here."

There's nothing Ezra can say to that. He chews the inside of his cheek until he tastes copper. "What can I do?"

Ben doesn't respond, just holds Ezra's gaze for several long, quiet seconds before he suddenly looks up and over Ezra's shoulder. His eyes widen, just for an instant, and when he snaps back to Ezra, there's something wild on his face.

"*Fix* it," he says, and then, abruptly, he's gone.

"*What*," Ezra says to the empty porch, and then nearly startles out of his skin when the door to the house opens behind him and Jonathan's voice, thick with sleep, says, "Ezra?"

He turns. Jonathan is standing in the doorway, backlit by the light in the hallway. His hair is rumpled and smushed to one side, his eyes bleary as he looks down at Ezra in confusion. "What are you doing out here?"

"I—" Ezra goes with what's easiest. "I couldn't sleep."

"Oh," Jonathan says.

He hated waking up to an empty bed.

He'd known this was a bad idea. He'd *known*.

It'll be so much worse, now, to leave.

Jonathan bites his bottom lip, like he can read the hesitation in Ezra's face. He says, uncertain, "Come back to bed?"

Ezra can still feel the trailing cold of Ben's almost-there touch.

But he can still feel the echo of Jonathan's hands, too.

"Okay," Ezra says, and gets to his feet.

18

Jonathan

Thursday, 10:04 A.M.

Everything ok? You left in kind of a hurry this AM

Granted it's been a little while since I've done this but I didn't think I was THAT rusty

Thursday, 3:17 P.M.

. . . that was a joke

Friday 11:23 A.M.

Are you free for a taharah at 1?

No sorry

Don't worry about it

Everything ok with you?

Just a really busy few days

Sorry

Don't apologize

It wasn't anything I did, right?

Seen Friday 11:30 A.M.

Aaron

Saturday 4:58 P.M.

Why is Jonathan texting me to ask if he screwed something up with you?

Ezra we have done such a good job in life NOT knowing these things about each other

(To be clear: he didn't do anything, right? I'm not really a fighter but I'll fight a dude if I have to.)

Haha, no

My honor is safe
Thanks though

OK but then why are you ghosting him

I'm not ghosting him

You kind of are, though

Whose side are you on?

The side of "do you
have any idea how hard
it is to find good
volunteers in this
economy"

Wow

Wait. This doesn't have
anything to do with like
actual ghost stuff,
right?? Like, everything
is okay with you?

I'll text him back.

THAT'S NOT AN
ANSWER

Seen Saturday 5:22 P.M.

Ezra doesn't mean to spend the next week avoiding Jonathan.

He does it anyway.

Work gives him an easy excuse. Suddenly the calls are
coming in nonstop, which means Ezra's processing paperwork and following up on invoices and helping with services
and there's always, always something to do. If he's too busy to
respond to Jonathan's texts, whether he's asking for help with
a taharah or just asking him to coffee, Ezra takes the win
where he can get it. It's a dick move, but every time he picks up
his phone and opens their text thread, or lets his thumb hover
over his phone number, or scrolls through Instagram and sees
another perfectly composed photo of Jonathan's office or
houseplants or latest Food Network–worthy meal, he remem-

bers sitting on the porch with the ghost of the man who *should* have been the one slipping back into Jonathan's bed, and he just . . . can't.

"For the record," Ben says out of nowhere as Ezra is taking a mug of reheated soup out of the break room microwave, "this was not what I meant."

"Jesusfuckingchrist," Ezra says, putting the mug down harder than he means to, then shaking scalding droplets off his hand. Ben is sitting on the edge of the table, chin on his hand. "What are you doing here? Is Jonathan here?"

"I don't think it works like that."

"Helpful." Ezra reaches for the freezer—he's pretty sure they keep some ice packs in there, or maybe some frozen peas—and lurches back when Ben appears between him and the freezer door. *"Seriously?"*

"You'll kill the nerves if you put ice on your hand," Ben says, and points firmly at the sink. "Cool water, not cold."

Ezra turns on the cold tap and sticks his hand under it. It helps, the cool water soothing like a balm. "Thanks," he says, trying to keep the grudging tone out of his voice as he flexes his hand, watching as the angry red blotches on his skin fade to pink. "Sorry. For snapping."

Ben shrugs. "I'm past being offended," he says. He leans against the counter, focusing on Ezra's hand. "You should be okay in a few minutes. Put a damp cloth on it when you turn off the water. Or paper towels, if you're not sure if the cloths are clean."

"Didn't realize you were such a first aid person."

Ben's mouth twitches. "Didn't realize I spent four years in med school to be called a *first aid person,* but sure."

God, of *course* he was a doctor. "Sorry." The pain's faded almost to nothing, but Ezra leaves the water running. "I didn't know."

"Guessing you and Jon had better things to talk about?"

No one else calls him Jon, Ezra thinks. "No. I mean—" He turns his eyes toward the ceiling, hopes he's not about to stick his foot in his mouth. "I try not to ask him about you."

"Why?"

"Seriously?"

"What? It's not like I'm competition."

Ezra's not sure about that. "Was there something you wanted, or are you just here to remind me about this awkward situation we're in?"

Ben looks amused. "You're acting like you're helping him cheat on me. I *want* him to be moving on. It's good for him."

"Maybe. But *I* know you're here. He doesn't."

"I'll give you that one."

They stand there for a few moments in silence, watching the water spill over Ezra's hand.

"I took this end-of-life planning seminar when I was in residency," Ben says suddenly. "The guy teaching it, he was insistent that we should all be talking to our families about what we'd want if something happened to us, even if we were young and healthy. Not just the 'Who gets your stuff?' conversations, but the hard ones—you know, power of attorney and DNR and whether or not to pull the plug if you're a vegetable. I came home and I was ready to just brush it off, but Jonathan freaked out, said we had to do it. I didn't realize he'd been soaking up every horrible ER case I told him about and putting himself in the next-of-kin shoes. I *hated* it. He made me do all the estate planning with him, and I complained through every minute. When we left the lawyer's office, after we got everything signed and notarized, we stopped at a red light, and I remember looking at him and just saying, 'Babe, I signed all that because I love you and it was important to you, but I swear to God if you die before me, I'll haunt your afterlife.'"

Ezra winces.

"Yeah. The irony isn't lost on me. I don't want to be haunting him," he says. "I just want him happy."

Ezra swallows. "I don't know that I'm the person to make that happen."

"Neither do I. But you've got a better chance than me." He pushes away from the counter. "Stop avoiding him, Ezra. You owe him that much."

Ezra turns off the water, and the stinging returns almost at once. "I know."

19

Rainbow Gnome Fan Club

Sunday 6:18 P.M.

Ollie

Hey who's around for
dinner tonight?

Lily

MEEEEEEEEEE

Are you cooking????

Ollie

I'm trying to make
myself cook

Which goes better when
it's not just me

Bc it means I'm less
likely to just be like
"oh hello sad pasta"

Max

OK hear me out tho

What if

Thai food

Ollie

. . . I could be convinced

Lily

👀 👀 👀

Noah

Work dinner :(#FOMO

Lily

Boo

@Ezra?? I feel like no
one has seen you in days

Pls send a sign of life

Still alive

Sorry

Work is just nuts

Ollie

. . . you have the dog
with you tho right?

Lily

Well, that's a relief

Promise to Ben or not, he doesn't go home.

He lets himself stay late, because he stands a better chance of not running into Jonathan if he avoids commuting hours. He brings Sappho to work so he doesn't have to go back to his apartment to walk her, sets up a little corner of Mom's office— now his—with a new dog bed and a small collection of her toys, and she seems content to sleep the time away.

Lily, Noah, and Max don't know him well enough yet to call him on the obvious avoidance. Ollie does, but for once—as if he's somehow sensed that Ezra can't handle one more thing—he seems to have chosen not to push.

Ezra will probably thank him for that, once he's back to sleeping more than three hours a night.

On the other hand, it's only because he's not going home to sleep that he's the one who takes Allison's call.

Like most funeral homes, the Chapel has 24-7 phone availability. Even on holidays and Shabbat, if someone calls needing help, someone will pick up the phone. Outside of business hours, there's a rotating schedule of staff on-call shifts, and the office phones are programmed to forward incoming calls to whoever's on shift that day. Zayde's philosophy was always that no one should ever go to voicemail, and he used to assign someone to stay in the office all night just in case something came in.

Cellphones and call-forwarding systems had been a welcome relief.

The job of setting the phones to redirect calls falls to the last person to leave the office each night. Ezra's done it for most of the past week before he drags himself out at nine or ten, at least an hour after even Dad has headed back across the yard. Late-night calls aren't actually that common—the one time he'd been on the on-call rotation, his phone hadn't rung once—so the sound of his desk phone ringing just after eleven makes him jump, his probably ill-advised coffee sloshing over his hand. Ezra swears, fumbling for a tissue to wipe his hand clean and hastily scooping the phone off the receiver before it can ring through to the answering machine.

"Friedman Memorial Chapel, this is Ezra," he says, schooling his voice to the professional calm that seems to come so easily to everyone else. "How can I help you?"

There's a pause, a sniffle, and then an oddly familiar voice says, uncertainly, "Ezra Friedman?"

Ezra blinks. "Speaking."

"It's Allison. Allison Collins. From yoga class? I don't know if you remember me, I— It's okay if you don't."

He remembers her. She's a sophomore at RISD, small and quiet, a regular attendee at his Yoga for Chronic Pain classes at the QCC, back when he could teach them. Her hair, which seems to change colors every time he sees her, is the loudest thing about her. "I remember you," he says, and then, because of where he is, and why he picked up the phone, softens his voice to ask, "What's going on, Allison?"

Allison takes an audible, hitching breath. "It's Nava," she says, and starts to cry.

The story comes in a jumble of sobs, anger and grief and frustration clashing together as she slowly forces out the words, stopping every few minutes to just cry. Nava is Allison's roommate, a bright-eyed, cheerful trans girl with a smile that Ezra can call to mind without any effort. Ezra never spoke to her much outside of the classes she attended, but he knows from Nina that she frequents several of the other QCC programs, especially the support groups and wellness classes. She was a sweet kid, quick to laugh and quicker to offer her time or her energy. She was always willing to stay after class with him to get all the props stored properly back in their closets.

And now, Allison tells him through her tears, she's dead. And no one knows what to do.

"She hasn't talked to her parents since she finished high school," Allison says, her voice quivering. It's taken them ten minutes to get this far, Ezra gripping the phone with white-knuckled fingers, his other hand pressed tightly to the side of Sappho's head, which she's come to lay in his lap. "They disowned her when she came out—they were super religious, they never understood her. She only made it here because she got a full ride, her art is so *beautiful,* and now— And I don't know what to do. I had to identify her, and they said they'd hold her—her body—but I can't send her back to those *people.* Only I know it would matter that she had a Jewish funeral, but I don't know anything about that and I don't know how we could afford—or if we're even allowed—"

A breath of cool air makes the hair on the back of Ezra's neck stand on end, and he jumps, turning, already half sure who he'll see. Zayde meets his eyes with solemn calm.

What? Ezra mouths to him. Zayde gestures to the intake sheet Ezra has been trying to fill out in a shaking scrawl with the few facts Allison has managed to get out. Then, to Ezra's surprise, he reaches past it to tap one of the few photos Ezra had brought with him to try to make Mom's space into something like his own. It's a picture of Ezra with Ollie and Nina at the Queer Liberation March in New York a few years ago, the three of them sharing a grip on a sign proclaiming YOUR REAL FAMILY IS THE FAMILY YOU CHOOSE. The ink on the poster is running from the rain, but they're grinning nonetheless, heedless of their wet hair and clothes. Zayde taps it again and then looks, more pointedly, back to Ezra once more.

Something clicks.

"Allison," Ezra says.

She hiccups around a sob. "Yeah?"

"I think we can help you," he says. "But I need to talk to someone. Can I call you back?"

It takes another few minutes to calm her down enough to take down her contact information, and the contact information for the medical examiner who currently has Nava in custody, and then to make sure she has someone who can sit with her and make sure she's not alone until Ezra can call her back. She's still sniffling when they end the call, but she sounds steadier, and there's a cautious spark of hope in her voice that wasn't there before.

Ezra hopes he's not about to kill that spark.

Ezra's not really expecting Dad to still be in his office this late, but sure enough, his door is open when Ezra reaches it, light from inside spilling out into the hallway. Ezra knocks on the frame and pokes his head inside to find his father frowning at his computer, carefully referencing a file on his desk as he types something up. "Dad? Do you have a minute?"

If his father is surprised to see Ezra there as late as he is, it doesn't show on his face. "Of course," he says, motioning Ezra into the room. "Did you take that call that just came in?"

"Yeah." Ezra takes one of the leather chairs. Sappho wriggles under the chair to curl up between his feet. He puts the half-filled intake form from Allison on the desk between them. "That's what I needed to talk to you about."

Dad frowns. "Okay," he says. "What's going on?"

Ezra takes a deep breath, steadies himself, and tells him.

Dad listens without interruption, his hands steepled in front of his face, brow furrowed but eyes calm. Ezra is almost certain that what he's asking for—for Dad to step into what's almost definitely about to be a landmine of next of kin and emergency contacts and family preferences and God knows what else in order to give Nava the funeral she'd want for herself, for the person she left her entire family behind to become—is far beyond the normal scope of what they do.

For all he knows, it's not even legal, or if it is, it has the potential to be so much messier than anyone could possibly want to deal with.

But when Ezra is finished, having run out of reasons why they should help, why it's the right thing to do even if it's going to be a huge pain in the ass, with horrendous amounts of red tape to cut through, Dad just says, very simply, "Okay," and takes the intake form.

Ezra blinks. "Okay?"

"Okay," Dad repeats. He skims over the form, then the half sheet of notes Ezra had scrawled on a piece of scrap paper next to it, and then nods. "I'll take it from here. Thank you."

"But—" Ezra falters. "Just like that?"

"Of course," Dad says, already reaching for the phone. "It's my job." He regards Ezra thoughtfully for a moment and then says, "When was the last time you slept, kiddo?"

The change in subject is jarring. "I— Last night?"

"For how long?"

Ezra opens his mouth. Closes it. "How did we start talking about me?"

Dad doesn't dignify that with a response. Ezra's almost grateful for it. "Why don't you head home," he says. "I'll have an update for you about this in the morning. We'll want your help on it, I think, if you don't mind—I want to make sure we do everything appropriately." Ezra can't do anything but nod, a little dumbly, and Dad gives a satisfied nod. "Good. Go get some sleep. I'll see you back here at seven-thirty."

His tone leaves no room for argument.

Ezra picks up Sappho's leash and goes home.

*   *   *

The door to Dad's office is propped open when Ezra returns in the morning, slightly high on the luxury of six and a half hours of sleep. The murmur of voices inside reaches him before he can knock, and Ezra hesitates for half a second when he recognizes them, before he makes himself take a breath and rap his knuckles against the side of the doorframe.

"That you, Ezra?" Aaron calls.

"It's me." Ezra steps inside and pulls the door mostly closed behind him, carefully avoiding Jonathan's eyes where he's seated next to Aaron across from Dad's desk. He's not surprised to see Ben there as well, leaning against the wall opposite the desk, languid and comfortable. He arches an eyebrow at Ezra as he enters, and Ezra pretends not to see it. "Am I late?"

"You're right on time," Dad says. "Grab a seat."

Ezra takes one of the small leather-backed chairs from beside the couch and pulls it closer to the desk, dropping into it. He feels out of place, the way he almost always has in this room, like the walls themselves are judging him for not wanting to be there. "What did I miss?"

"Jonah's going to go and pick Nava up from the ME's office in about an hour," Dad says. "He'll bring her back here. Allison is coming in at nine or so, along with Nava's aunt, who has apparently been her guardian since she managed to get emancipated from her parents. She's driving in from New York, so she might be a bit later, but she's given us permission to get her transferred and start preparations here."

Relief hits him like an ocean wave. "Seriously?"

"We got lucky," Aaron says. "The aunt was on all of Nava's emergency contact forms at RISD, and they were willing to give us her contact information. It could have been a shit show otherwise. I guess the aunt also kind of left the family fold, so she took Nava in when she left home."

"Our chevra sent a shomer over to the ME's office as well," Jonathan adds. "She shouldn't be alone."

"Thank you." Jonathan gives him a small smile, like Ezra hasn't been avoiding him for the past several days, and Ezra swallows around the gratitude welling up in his throat. "So . . . what happens now?"

"We'll wait to discuss arrangements for the service and burial until the family get here," Dad says, leaning back in his chair. "I think it would be good to have you there for that, Ezra—you knew her, but you know her community as well. It'll be important to let them know so they can be here for her."

"I didn't know her that well," Ezra says, and he's surprised how guilty he feels about it. "I mean, she came to my classes, and I spoke with her a few times, but it's not like we were . . . you know, close." An idea hits him. "Nina knew her, though. Nava came to a bunch of the programs she ran—I bet she could tell us more about what she might want and who she'd want us to call."

"Good." Dad turns to Jonathan. "If her aunt wants a taharah—"

"It should be with women," Jonathan says firmly. "She lived as a woman, she identified as a woman, women should be with her in the room." He glances at Ezra. "You agree?"

"Yes," Ezra says, a little surprised to be asked. "Of course."

Dad scribbles something down in his notes. "You'll get a group together?"

Jonathan waves his phone, a loose *Ready when you are.* "As soon as we have the timing, yeah."

"Thank you." Dad gathers up his papers. "I'm going to go make a few calls. Ezra, you'll reach out to your friend and be back to meet with Allison when she gets here?" Ezra nods, and Dad gets to his feet. "Good. Thanks for your time, everyone."

It's a clear dismissal, if a kind one. Ezra follows everyone else out of the room, faltering slightly when Dad and Aaron head off in one direction, Jonathan in the other. He hesitates, then turns to jog after Jonathan, catching his arm. "Hey."

Jonathan turns to him. "Hey," he says. If he's annoyed with Ezra for ghosting him after they hooked up, it doesn't show on his face. "I'm sorry about your friend."

"Thanks." *Friend* is a strong word, and he feels guilty about claiming it, but the world will be emptier without her. "I just wanted to apologize. And to thank you."

Jonathan cocks one brow. "For what and for what?"

"For not answering most of your texts this week," Ezra says, even though that's the least of it, and they both know it. "And for making sure that Nava gets the rituals she would have wanted. The way she would have wanted them."

"Oh. You don't have to thank me for that."

Ezra swallows. "I really do. It's not like the rabbis were thinking of people like me and Nava when they wrote this stuff down. And it'd be easier for some people to just say . . ." He trails off. "It matters. So thank you."

"You're welcome, then." He slips his hands into his pockets. "I need to make a couple calls, and I'm sure you have work to do. But we'll—we'll talk later. Okay?"

It's an out Ezra doesn't deserve. He takes it anyway, greedy and unapologetic.

In the end, it's beautiful.

Nina takes charge of setting up a phone tree with the kind of fervor only a program manager without programs to manage can muster, and within hours of the single conversation he has with her, Ezra's fielding calls from what feels like half the QCC. It's an outpouring of generosity that takes his breath away: someone from the comms team offering to help write her obituary, the development manager volunteering to set up a crowdfunding page to raise money to cover the funeral costs—"Not necessary," Dad says firmly, when Ezra tells him about it. "We have procedures for this. Tell them not to worry"—and even Ivy calling to ask if there's anything she can do to help.

"Just be there," Ezra tells her, surprising himself at how easy it is to say it. "Just come to show her she was loved."

They hold the funeral two days after Ezra picked up Allison's call, and the morning brings a break in the cold spring rain that's lasted most of the past week, blue sky and air tinged sweet with the promise of a sunny day. The Chapel is already buzzing with activity when Ezra gets there, his prescribed black suit and tie brightened with a pink, blue, and white striped pocket square. Aaron cocks an eyebrow at him when he sees it, but doesn't make a comment, just squeezes Ezra's shoulder and nods him toward the larger of their two chapel rooms.

"They're setting up now," he says. "Could probably use your help finishing up."

Ezra goes.

Nina meets him in the doorway with a hug, tucking her face down into the crook of his shoulder and then pulling back to adjust his tie, smiling sadly at him. "Look at you, a proper funeral director," she says, teasing as she boops his nose with one manicured finger. "Not a single pair of yoga pants in sight."

"They're under the suit," Ezra says, and she laughs.

Slowly but surely, the room fills. Ezra goes where Dad and Aaron direct him, helping people find seats and restocking tissues and keeping the flow of traffic into the room running smoothly, but it's not long before Dad takes him aside and tells him to take himself off duty.

"Go and sit down," he says, and the quiet kindness in the words reminds Ezra, startlingly, of Zayde. "We've got this one covered."

"But—"

Someone puts a hand on his shoulder, and the protest dies in his throat when he turns to see Becca, wearing a neat black dress and a familiar Friedman Memorial Chapel Volunteer Usher badge. "Like Dad said," she says. "We've got it."

He accepts her hug automatically, feeling vaguely bewildered. "What are you doing here?"

"Aaron asked me to come. Something about knowing you'd never sit down like a normal person going to a funeral of someone they knew without being totally sure we had coverage?" She reaches up to straighten his tie slightly. "Can't imagine why he'd say something like that."

Ezra blinks against the sudden stinging in his eyes. He looks past Becca, across to where Aaron is at the front of the room talking quietly to Allison and an older woman with covered hair who must be Nava's aunt Beatrice. Aaron meets his eyes and inclines his head, just slightly. "You didn't have to."

"I know I didn't." Becca gives him a gentle nudge. "Go be a friend."

There's an empty seat next to Nina at the end of a row, and Ezra drops into it with weary gratitude. She slips her arm wordlessly through his, threading their fingers together, and he squeezes her hand. Nava's casket is already at the front of the room, a simple sanded pine with an embossed Magen David, a candle burning at the head. Jonathan had texted yesterday to let Ezra know that he hadn't had a problem finding four women in his chevra to do Nava's taharah, that none of them had even raised a question at treating Nava as the young woman she was.

He catches sight of Jonathan now, in his own suit and tie, sitting in the back corner of the room and talking quietly to a middle-aged woman with thick-framed glasses and violet streaks in her hair—probably a RISD professor, if Ezra had to guess. To Ezra's surprise, looking around the room, he sees Ollie there as well, sitting between Lily and Max. He catches Ezra's eye and waves, and Ezra returns it. *Thanks for coming,* he mouths, and Ollie gives him a small smile.

The service itself is music and poetry and laughter and tears. Dad had gotten in touch with a local rabbi to offer a short reading and handle the brief liturgy, but most of the funeral is Nava's friends talking about her, singing about her, telling stories, and offering blessings. They're all so *young,* Ezra thinks, watching them, and it hurts, the quiet, dignified grief that they bring into the room. Allison's eulogy, delivered through tears, paints a picture of a girl of fierce conviction and an immense capacity for kindness. The story Allison tells about Nava's first trip to WaterFire, when they'd all gotten so tipsy that she and Allison had nearly fallen into the river together, has the whole room laughing. It makes Ezra wish he'd known Nava better, but even with the limited time he spent with her, he can picture the smile Allison tells stories about, the laugh he remembers lighting up a room.

A whisper of cool air makes him turn, and he looks up to meet Nava's soft blue eyes. Her dark hair falls in ringlets over her shoulders, the white dress she's wearing making her look younger than the short nineteen years she'd had to live. She smiles at him. The bright, easy smile that he could never help but return.

And then she's gone.

He holds Nina's hand, and lets himself breathe.

It's Chapel practice for staff to stay at the burial site until the last mourner leaves, there to answer any last questions, manage any last logistics, and make sure this last, sacred departure is handled with the same reverent care as every other piece of the funeral.

Standing beside Aaron, far enough away from the newly filled grave to be unobtrusive but close enough to be clearly available, Ezra watches Dad talking quietly with Allison and Beatrice as they head toward the car waiting to drive them away from the cemetery. From this distance, it strikes Ezra just how much Dad looks like Zayde, in the set of his shoulders and the arch of his brows, the way he holds himself as he opens the car door and offers his hand to help them climb in.

"Where are they doing shiva?" Aaron murmurs.

"Ivy's," Ezra says. She'd offered up her house to host, since Allison lives on RISD's campus and Beatrice came in from out of town. It had come as a surprise that Beatrice had given her blessing for Nava to be buried here in Providence at all, but she'd actually insisted on it.

"This is the home she chose for herself," she'd said in Dad's office yesterday, holding Allison's hand in one of hers, the other white-knuckled around a tissue. "This is where her family is now. It's where she would have wanted to stay."

Now Aaron says, "That was nice of Ivy."

"Yeah. Everyone's been—" Ezra's voice catches unexpectedly, and he clears his throat. "You've all been amazing. Honestly."

"It's what we do," Aaron says.

"Not like this. This was—this was special."

The expression on Aaron's face is one Ezra's never seen on him before. It makes him look older—but gentler than Ezra's ever seen him.

"Ezra," he says, like it's the simplest, most obvious thing in the world. "They're all special."

20

It's not until three days later, when taking advantage of another insomnia-inspired late night, that he catches the hole in the accounts.

With the stress and the lost sleep and the way the Forever Memorials rep seems to be haunting the Chapel's halls more frequently than any of their visiting ghosts, he's on high alert in case he messes something up purely by virtue of being too zoned out to catch an input error, going through everything with a fine-tooth comb before he hands it off for approval. He's on his third pass on the monthly profit and loss report, the cup of coffee at his elbow congealing into the sunken place that comes after room temperature and Sappho dozing under his desk, when his eyes snag on a set of numbers that don't look right.

Ezra frowns at the report, scrolling back through the input tabs, then hunts around on Mom's desktop until he finds the reports from the last few quarters, neatly organized by month. He'd known the place has never really been cash rich, and it's not like he's an accountant, but even his crash course in financial reporting was enough to send red flags—or at least orange ones—waving in the back of his head. He prints out this month's report, then the previous six months', highlights all the cells with the weird totals, then shoves them into a folder and bends to look under his desk.

"Hey, girlie," he says, and Sappho picks her head up to look at him. "We're gonna go for a walk, come on."

It's after eleven, and the house is dark and quiet when he lets himself in through the back door. He unclips Sappho's leash to let her trot up the stairs, no doubt heading straight for Ezra's empty bed. Ezra drapes the leash over the banister and follows, trying to keep his steps quiet so he doesn't wake Dad or Becca on his way to Aaron's room, muscle memory kicking in at the last second to keep him from stepping on the two creaky steps that made sneaking out as a teenager such an absolute pain in the ass.

Ezra makes his way down the hall to Aaron's closed door. He puts an ear against it for a moment, making sure he only hears snoring and not anything weird—he'd made that mistake once in high school, and never again—before pushing the door open, picking his way across the floor, and dropping all his weight on the side of the bed without preamble or warning.

Aaron flails awake with a strangled, half-slurred "*Whathe-fuck*," then promptly falls out of bed, hitting the floor with a jarring thud.

"What the *fuck*," he says again, clearly more awake now, then recoils when Ezra reaches over to turn on his reading lamp. "*Ow.* Ezra?"

Becca's voice, sleepy and annoyed, drifts down the hallway. "Aaron?"

"He's fine," Ezra calls back. "Go back to sleep."

Aaron blinks up at him, bleary-eyed and radiating disgruntled confusion. He looks as exhausted as Ezra feels. "What—" he starts again, and Ezra shakes his head, pulling the folder of printed reports out of his bag and handing it to him.

"We need to talk," he says. "Meet me in the kitchen."

Ezra has a pot of coffee brewing by the time Aaron slumps into a chair at the kitchen table, looking like he's aged ten years since Ezra walked out of his room. He puts the folder on the table, stares at it for a long moment, and then says, "Do you think Dad knows about this?"

"That you're about twice as financially screwed as you thought you were?" The coffee maker beeps shrilly. "You'd know better than me."

Aaron takes the cup Ezra passes him, running a hand through his hair. It flops back over his forehead, sleep rumpled and overdue for a trim. He opens the folder and flips through the pages before setting them down and rubbing his eyes. "How did this happen?"

Ezra shrugs. "My best guess? Dad's been charging clients wholesale prices across the board—if that—and still trying to keep up with expenses, and that stopped being sustainable . . . several staff cost-of-living and merit raises ago."

"*I* deserve a merit raise," Aaron mutters. "God. No wonder Forever's been circling us like vultures. You know Caroline Lawrence was here four times in the past two weeks?" Ezra raises his eyebrows. He had only caught her twice, one of those when Aaron was none too gently steering her out of his office, both of them looking like they'd just lost an argument. "How are we even paying the bills *now*?"

"I have no idea," Ezra says. "I mean, they're *being* paid—most of them are purchase orders or on autopay anyway—but if you look at the accounts receivable—"

"Yeah. There are transactions with names and dates that don't match up to invoices, bank transfers from accounts that don't line up with any of the accounts we have on file. And you couldn't find anything in Mom's files?"

Ezra shakes his head. "I looked, but Mom's system isn't exactly user-friendly."

Aaron looks up from the printouts, frowning. "What does that mean?"

"I don't know, that she's got thirty-something years of institutional knowledge and she labels her files in ways that don't make sense?"

"Seriously? You can't figure out how she organizes, and that's why we've got God knows how many months of undocumented income on our books?"

Ezra flinches. "Just because I'm picking up her slack doesn't mean I'm *Mom*," he snaps. "*I* didn't make this mess, I'm just trying to help clean it up. As usual."

"Spare me the martyr routine," Aaron shoots back. Ezra's halfway out of his chair—he can find another way to pay the rent, he's been doing this long enough and it's late and he's *tired*—before Aaron's shoulders slump, the fight leaving him as quickly as it came on. "Stop. I'm sorry. You're right."

Ezra sits back down, but he keeps a hand on the table, ready to push himself up again. Aaron puts his face in his hands, letting out a long, unsteady breath.

"Damn it," he says. "We're going to have to talk to Mom."

They end up at the park by the waterfront, as close to a neutral territory as they can find.

This close to sunset on a warm spring day, it takes them an extra ten minutes to find parking, the sky fading multicolored shades of orange and pink by the time they leave Aaron's car and make their way up the sidewalk. Ezra snaps a photo almost without thinking. The setting sun over the skyline is pretty enough to break through the exhaustion and crankiness that's hovered over him all day, and he has it posted on Instagram before he's even realized his fingers are moving.

Someone grabs him by the back of his shirt collar and

yanks sharply, and Ezra almost drops his phone, trying to flail out of the grip. "Relax," Aaron says, giving him an amused look as he lets him go. "Just trying to keep you from walking into the street."

"I would have stopped," Ezra says, wrinkling his nose at him like that will conceal the pounding of his heart. The light at the crosswalk switches to a walk signal, and they step off the curb together. "Probably."

"I'll remind you of that when you've got your legs crushed under some Whole Foods mom's Prius," Aaron deadpans.

The folder of spreadsheet printouts feels like a loaded bomb in Ezra's messenger bag. The mysterious transactions seem to go back months, none of them with the documentation they should have. He's pretty sure they don't have some kind of shadow benefactor—it's not that kind of business, community organized or not—but Ezra doesn't need an MBA to see that without those deposits, they'd be in the red every month. Far enough into the red that they'd be beyond screwed if they disappeared.

If Mom knows what that money is and where it's coming from, they can figure out what to do next. If she doesn't . . .

Ezra's not sure what they do if she doesn't.

They find a visible enough spot on the steps leading down to the water and sit down together, out of the way of the worst of the foot traffic. Ezra's phone buzzes as he sets his bag down, and he taps the notification absently, stilling when he sees the comment on the photo he'd posted outside the car.

> @with_bells_jon pvd skyline posts with
> no filter??? love to see it.

"Still playing hard to get?" Aaron says, far too close.

"Jesus, will you let me *breathe*?" He shoves at Aaron's arm until he stops peering over Ezra's shoulder to look at his phone. "And I'm not playing *hard to get,* things are just . . . weird right now."

"Right. I guess it can't be hard to get if you guys already—"

Ezra snaps his head up, abandoning his attempt at writing a reply. "We didn't— Who told you—"

"Like you didn't just confirm it for me?"

"It wasn't . . ." He has a brief, horrifying flashback to being sixteen, when Aaron caught him in the bathroom trying to use Mom's foundation to cover up a hickey on the side of his neck. "It's not like—a *thing*. And it didn't go that far."

"Ew," Aaron says, grimacing. "Please spare me the details. I have to work with the guy on a regular basis. I don't need any scarring mental images when I'm trying to have a conversation about chevra logistics." He cocks his head to one side. "Why isn't it a thing? I thought you guys were . . . I don't know, clicking or whatever?"

Ezra hesitates. "It's just . . . It's not a good time."

Aaron gives him a long, thoughtful look. It's a look that reminds Ezra uncomfortably of Dad. "He's a good guy, you know. You could do a lot worse."

Ezra shakes his head. "It's not me I'm worried about."

Aaron frowns but abandons whatever he was about to say when something behind Ezra catches his eye. "Incoming," he mutters, and straightens up just as Mom bustles her way into Ezra's line of sight, takeout cup in one hand and an overstuffed tote bag over her opposite arm.

"I'm so sorry I'm late," she says, setting everything down with brisk, obviously forced cheer. "I got caught up in a checkout line, and then my phone died." She kisses the top of Ezra's head before he can even think to tell her not to, then does the same to Aaron. "Have you been waiting long?"

"We're fine," Aaron says, just coolly enough that her smile

falters. It hits Ezra, maybe a moment too late, that this might be the first time they've seen each other since the seder. "You're not that late."

"Right," she says. She looks briefly at Ezra like she's hoping for solidarity. Ezra raises his eyebrows back at her, and she steels herself before turning to look at Aaron directly.

"Aaron, honey," she starts. "I know the last few weeks haven't been—"

"Absolutely not," he interrupts, and she breaks off immediately, the click of her teeth audible as she closes her mouth. "You're not going to do this now after a month of avoiding my phone calls and sending me half-assed apology emails instead. You either aren't ready to admit you fucked up or you still think you're somehow justified, because otherwise you would have been willing to talk face-to-face *way* sooner. We're only here having this conversation because we have to clean up the mess you left behind. And I'm not talking about Dad and Becca."

Mom deflates. "Okay," she says. "I'll—I'll help however I can, and maybe later we can . . ." Aaron's face darkens, and she presses her lips together. "Okay. I understand. Tell me what's going on."

Aaron nudges Ezra, and he pulls the folder of printouts out of his bag and hands it to her. "These are the profit and loss statements from the last four quarters," he says, watching her face carefully as she puts down her cup and opens the folder. "You've been logging multiple transactions a month, every month, for at least a year—and those are just the ones we found. No account information, no invoice attachments, no client names. It's like you've just been transferring money out of thin air."

"I pulled the bank records, so at least we know you weren't just making up transactions with no money behind them,"

Aaron says, leaning forward. He's not a big person, just tall, but he knows how to look intimidating enough if he wants to. "But that means you've had an income source that isn't in any of our files, that Dad and I didn't know about, that you've basically been funneling into the operating accounts to keep the business from going down. Which means that if those suddenly *stopped*—say, because the person running the transfers fucked off to—"

"Aaron," Ezra warns. He puts a hand on Aaron's shoulder, and Aaron breaks off with a sucked-in breath, his mouth tightening into a flat line. He sits back with a huff.

Mom is watching them both. She runs her fingers down the line of highlighted numbers on the page in front of her, and then sighs. "I meant to tell you when you were a little older," she says, closing the folder and resting her hands on it. "I wanted to wait until you were a little more established in the job, until I had more of an idea of—well, of who you were going to take after, I suppose."

Aaron narrows his eyes. "What's that supposed to mean?"

"Your father is . . ." Mom begins, and then stops. Sighs again, and pushes her glasses up and off her face so that she can rub her eyes. She's quiet for a moment, as if collecting her thoughts.

"Your father cares about what he does." Her tone is measured, not unkind. "And there are some parts of his work that he's very, very good at. He understands what people need when they're grieving, what they need to find closure and meaning and comfort. He understands the rituals and the history and the traditions. He has a brilliant way of making sure that every person who walks into his office leaves feeling like they've been cared for in a way that doesn't make them feel like they're the wrong kind of person, or the wrong kind of Jew. I might know how to network a group, but your dad's the one who knows people. I've always admired him for that."

She pauses, fingertips drumming on the cover of the folder. Ezra waits. He knows there's a *but* coming.

"But," she says, perfectly on cue, "he doesn't have a head for the business side. And that's not his fault, really. The funeral industry as a whole is—well. I don't need to tell you."

She doesn't. They've been listening to rants about the corporate funeral industrial complex from Dad—and before that, from Zayde—since they were still in booster seats. Frankly, Ezra's more than a little surprised that a representative from Forever Memorials had even gotten through the front door, let alone made herself a recognizable fixture. "He'd do everything for less than cost, if he could, because he's a wonderful person, but—"

"But that doesn't exactly cover payroll," Aaron says.

Mom shakes her head. "It would barely cover inventory," she says, and the wry almost smile in her voice sets off a wistful ache through Ezra's chest. "Your grandfather knew that. He always had a good sense for people. He set up a rainy day fund of sorts—a decent mix of investment accounts, liquid assets, that kind of thing." She looks down at her hands. "He gave me access to all of it before he died. He told me—" She laughs, a little damply. "He said I had a good head on my shoulders, and he knew I'd keep your father from running the place into the ground. It won't last forever, though. Especially if nothing changes in the way your dad runs things. I've been doing my best to replenish the accounts anytime there's anything spare, but . . ."

Ezra glances at Aaron, only to find his brother already looking back, his face a complicated mix of fondness and grief. He knocks their shoulders together and gets the faintest smile in return. "You didn't tell Dad, though."

She shakes her head. "No one knows except our accountant and the executor of your zayde's will. It would have broken your dad's heart if he thought Zayde didn't believe in him."

Aaron lets out a short, breathy exhale of a laugh. "Of course." Mom looks up at him. Aaron meets her eyes and smiles, a lopsided, unhappy twist of a thing. "Because the last thing *you'd* ever want to do is break Dad's heart."

Aaron drives him home.

Neither of them talk. The air in the car is thick with tension, both of them stewing in their own thoughts, and the tight-lipped look on Aaron's face is enough to keep Ezra from any attempt at conversation.

It's not even that he's angry. Fine—it's one more lie Mom told, one more secret she kept—but it's just been thrown on the pile. Ezra can't even blame her for it without drowning in hypocrisy, because it's not as if he hasn't been keeping secrets of his own.

So why does he feel like the ground's been pulled out from under his feet?

Maybe, he thinks, it's because he thought that even if he walked away, the Chapel would always be there if he ever decided to go back. Maybe it's the idea that it might not be, the realization that the threads tying it to their family are more frayed than the ties holding the family together.

He's still stewing in it, uncomfortable and unmoored, when Aaron pulls the car to a stop in front of Ezra's apartment. Ezra gathers himself back into the relative shape of a person, rolling his shoulders as he straightens up and unbuckles his seatbelt, and Aaron turns in his seat to watch him, expression wary.

"You gonna be okay?"

Ezra attempts a smile. "I'll be fine. Thanks for the ride."

Aaron eyes him for another moment, like he's considering turning the car around and driving right back to the Chapel instead. Then he sighs, runs a hand through his hair, and gives Ezra a *Yeah, I get it, but what can you do?* look that's so much a mirror of Ezra's own exhaustion that it almost makes him laugh. "Text me when Mom sends you the accounting stuff," he says. "Otherwise I'll just stress about it all night."

He says it casually, but his eyes are serious, and Ezra hears the undercurrent of concern that slips into the words.

Let me know that I don't need to worry about you.

"I'll hound her if I don't hear from her by ten," Ezra promises, opening the passenger door. "You'll have it as soon as I do."

Everything's under control.

It's impulse, more than anything, that makes him pause outside Jonathan's apartment. There's music playing, muffled but audible through the door, with just enough bass that the vibration of it buzzes against his skin when he reaches out to touch his fingertips to the wood. He wants, with a sweep of chest-clenching desire, to be on the other side of it, in the easy quiet of Jonathan's arms, soaking in his presence.

Jonathan's still a stranger to him in more ways than not. Half the time they've spent together has been in silence, the only sounds rushing water and the chant of millennia-old liturgy. How many conversations have they had with actual *substance*, not just logistics small talk made while Ezra spirals through all the ways he's been lying through his teeth just by omission? How—

God, why is he *here*?

He can hear Jonathan moving around his living room, the hardwood of the floor creaking under every step, and Ezra's fingers flex against the door, moving to knock. He presses his knuckles to his mouth like he can punish them.

The music is still playing, sweet and slow, building like a tide. Ezra closes his eyes and tries not to sway toward it.

The folder of printed spreadsheets in his bag feels like a pile of bricks. Tomorrow, he'll spend the day on the phone, getting the records of every transfer, finding out how much has been spent, how much is left. He'll sit with Aaron and they'll come up with a way to tell Dad that it's not just Mom who's been lying to him for years, but his father, too, who'd died without telling him the truth. They'll split the work the way they always have. Aaron will tell the story, will lay out the facts, will spin out the solutions. And Ezra will pick up the pieces that crumble before something else can be rebuilt, like waves washing away a sandcastle.

This is the part where he walks away. Where he goes back upstairs to where his roommates have been watching his dog for him, where he has the budding beginnings of a second family who seem, for some unimaginable reason, to want him to be part of what they've built. Where he sits on the floor by the couch and tells them everything about his grandfather's secret bank accounts and the latest addition to his mom's list of dirty laundry, while Ollie strokes his hair with a familiar hand. Where, after everyone says their good nights, he walks down the hall to curl up in his empty bed and call Nina until he can drift off to the sound of her honeyed voice as she weaves out a fantasy where they run away and no one expects him to fix anything.

He takes a breath.

He knocks on the door.

21

"You sound like a high schooler with a crush," Nina says. "And I mean that in the absolute nicest way."

Ezra had started this morning hoping to take advantage of one of his rare days off to spend several hours napping and then slip back downstairs and into Jonathan's bed.

Instead, he's in Stoughton, following Nina through IKEA. Ostensibly she's only looking for a new dresser, but he's seen her shop before. He made sure to wear good shoes. "I don't sound that bad."

Nina puts a vivid pink throw pillow back down on an equally vivid pink couch and cocks an eyebrow at him. "You just spent ten minutes waxing *No one's ever made me feel like this* poetic," she says, "and then clarified that you two are only doing—and I quote—'hand stuff.' "

Ezra crouches down to look at the price tag on an end table to hide the way he's sure his cheeks are going red. "I mean," he mumbles, "when you say it like *that,* sure."

"Listen, I'm not saying I blame you. I've seen his Instagram. Those forearms? Yes *please.*"

Ezra's face feels, if possible, even hotter. He's seen those forearms at work firsthand. "He's—" he begins, and then, knowing there's absolutely nothing he can say here that won't just bring that wicked glint of delight back onto her face, settles on finishing with "Yup."

"Oh, honey," Nina says, grinning. "You are *screwed*."

He *is*.

So much so that even after Nina's dropped him back at his own apartment and left him to flop face down onto his bed, face buried in a pillow that smells like his own conditioner and not at all like Jonathan's aftershave, he's still thinking about it. Over the past few days—and nights—he's learned that Jonathan can be gentle but brutal, teasing and slow and delicate, careful in a way that isn't about measuring what Ezra can handle or even what he needs, but like he knows exactly what to do to shatter Ezra to pieces, and intends to do exactly that with a quiet, devastating confidence.

Jonathan talks after sex, too, which is . . . new. Even with Ollie, who knows Ezra almost as well as Ezra knows himself, Ezra was usually too busy trying to pull himself back from whatever distant, tucked-away place his mind had gone to protect itself from the nagging curls of dysphoria and discomfort for pillow talk. But Jonathan doesn't seem to mind the way Ezra can't take himself all the way out of his head during sex, his tendency to need to squirm back into his binder or underwear halfway through, his inability to get completely naked with another person. He's comfortable in his own skin, but doesn't seem to care that Ezra isn't, and when his fingertips skim too lightly across Ezra's back or find a spot on his hips that makes Ezra jump, he never so much as frowns when Ezra twitches away. He just leans back and gives Ezra enough space to breathe himself back to something resembling calm, waiting, patiently, until Ezra reaches for him again.

"Sorry," Ezra whispers, the second or fourth or tenth time it happens—he's lost count, now, of how many times it's been. He pulls his shirt back over his head with shaking hands. "It's not you, I just—"

"Hey. It's okay." Jonathan shrugs into a zip-up hoodie as if in solidarity, though he leaves it open, his chest bare, and it's easier than Ezra expects to shift closer and rest his head there to listen to the steady beat of his heart. "No agenda. Okay?"

Ezra huffs. "Okay."

It's strange. Different. But bundled under Jonathan's soft sheets, the pressure of a warm body against his contrasting with the sweet, cool water Jonathan always coaxes into him as they wait for their heart rates to settle, listening to the quiet rumbling of Sappho's snores drifting across the room . . . it feels easy, somehow, to let himself talk.

They start with the safe things, hobbies and friends and funny-in-hindsight mishaps. But the conversations drift, as Ezra should have expected they would, into the quiet spaces of love and loss and family, the jagged places with the most potential to cut and bleed.

He tells Jonathan about growing up at the Chapel, about the constant uncertainty of being both invisible and on display. He talks about not realizing that other people didn't spend their days in close proximity to the dead and the mourning, that he owes most of his brutally dark sense of humor to the ever-present knowledge that death was as much a member of his family as his siblings or parents.

Jonathan seems more willing to talk about himself in the soft, dreamy darkness, and Ezra drinks in every piece of information like it's water in the desert. He learns that Jonathan left a full-time job when Ben died because he couldn't handle project management when his life was falling apart, that he started consulting so that he could make his own hours and spend more time coordinating the chevra. He learns that Jonathan is a trained and certified death doula—which Ezra hadn't even known was a *thing,* and the irony isn't lost on him—and that his hardest taharah cases are the clients he'd worked with before they died.

"My therapist hates it," he admits. "She says I'm turning my life into something that's obsessed with death. Like it'll make up for not being there when Ben died."

"Are you?" Ezra asks.

Jonathan's faint, joyless smile is answer enough. Ezra drags him in for a hug, and Jonathan tucks his head into the crook of Ezra's neck.

They don't talk any more that night.

He learns that Jonathan has a younger sister he loves dearly and doesn't speak to as often as he wishes he could since she moved to New Zealand for work two years ago, that his parents had the kind of brutal, vicious divorce that turned his middle school years into a miserable mess of custody battles and nearly made him swear off the idea of marriage for good. He learns that Ben's family—his cheerful sisters, his ever-affectionate parents, his doting grandmother—had become Jonathan's own before they were even married, that Judy had taken one look at him, seen something in him that activated some innate maternal urge, and all but adopted him, going so far as to tell him that if he and Ben ever split, he should still think of her as an extra mother.

And he learns that Jonathan has barely spoken to her since the night he learned about the affair.

It's the first time he sees Jonathan interact with someone with anything other than an easy grin and a kind word. Ezra catches him at the end of a phone call when he steps back into the bedroom after a badly needed shower, Jonathan's strong brows pulled together in the first scowl Ezra's seen from him.

"—and I'm not talking about this anymore," he's saying, his knuckles white where he's holding his phone. Ezra pauses at the door, uncertain, feeling too exposed in the towel he's wrapped around his chest, but Jonathan doesn't look at him.

"Judy, I swear to God—" He breaks off, jaw going tight, and then snaps, "*No*. I'm done. I told you, I'm done."

He hangs up the phone and flings it away from himself as he slumps on the bed, dropping his head into his hands and breathing like he's run a sprint. His phone bounces twice across the comforter and thumps to a dull stop against a rumpled pillow.

Ezra hesitates until he sees him start to shake. "Hey," he says, crouching in front of him. "Are you okay?"

Jonathan nods without lifting his head, his fingers digging into his temples. "I'm fine."

He's absolutely not. Ezra reaches up to gently take him by the wrists and draw his hands away from his face. He knows all about avoidance, has turned not talking about his feelings into an art, but he's never been able to watch it in someone else. "What did she say to you?"

Jonathan makes a sound somewhere between a scoff and a laugh. "It doesn't matter," he says. He pulls one hand out of Ezra's grasp and swipes at his eyes. "She's just— It doesn't matter." He swallows, then blinks down at Ezra. "Why are you naked?"

Ezra flushes. He hadn't noticed his towel making a break for it, but somehow the usual feeling of overexposed anxiety doesn't come. "Don't change the subject."

Jonathan shakes his head fondly, reaching down and wrapping the towel around Ezra's shoulders like a cape. "It's freezing in here. You should get dressed."

"Still changing the subject," Ezra says, but he lets go of Jonathan to better hold the towel in place as he gets to his feet.

"Imagine that," Jonathan says, and gives him a nudge. He smiles, but it doesn't meet his red-rimmed eyes. "Really, I'm fine."

Half a dozen offers of comfort flash through Ezra's head. *It's okay to miss her. I'm not talking to my mom, either, and it feels like shit. She doesn't deserve your tears. You can talk to me.*

You can talk to me.

Ezra's never been good at pushing. He bends down, kisses the top of Jonathan's head, and goes to find his clothes.

Despite all their conversations, tangled in bed or knocking their feet together at the breakfast nook in Jonathan's kitchen or across the mess of Ezra's desk at the Chapel, Ezra doesn't tell him about the ghosts. For all of Jonathan's seemingly ever-present patience and the apparently bottomless well of his heart, Ezra knows everyone has a breaking point. The snap in his voice and single burst of frustrated anger at Judy's call had shown Ezra the cracks behind Jonathan's easy smile. With a certainty that makes him half sick with guilt, he knows that learning Ezra's been talking to the ghost of his husband will make those cracks worse. Maybe even to the point where they can't be fixed.

He'll have to tell him. Especially now, with Ben *talking* to him, becoming more and more a person and less and less a shadow. Ezra knows that. But he hasn't been selfish for a long time, and maybe he can just have this. For a little while longer.

It's too easy to let that *little while* stretch out into the horizon of possibility, especially now, curled on his side with his head on Jonathan's pillow. He's pulled his underwear back on and stolen—*borrowed*—one of Jonathan's well-worn T-shirts, but he left his binder and the rest of his clothes scattered on the floor where they'd fallen, and the sheets are cool against his bare legs.

Lazily texting Nina and listening to the soft sounds of Jonathan moving around the kitchen, feeling sated and comfortable and safe, it's too easy to imagine a future of this. Easy nights in the same bed, the steady warmth of Jonathan's hands and smile.

He tries not to think about it. Tries harder not to want it.

He wishes he was better at it.

"Your roommates," Jonathan announces, coming back to the room with two mugs held in one hand and his phone in the other, "are bullying me."

Ezra bites back a smile, sitting up to take the mug Jonathan offers him. The steam is sweet and strong, scented with ginger and chamomile and lemon. Jonathan drinks coffee, but he defaults to tea in the evenings. Every time he makes it for them, Ezra wonders which blend is the one he used to bring Ben on those sleepless nights. "Yeah?"

"Yep." Jonathan settles into bed next to him, holding out an arm, and Ezra's body moves before he can think to question it, shifting to lean against his side. Jonathan hadn't bothered with a shirt when he left the bed, and his bare skin is warm and soft.

"What are they doing now?"

Jonathan hands over his phone, already open to a photo of Sappho's nose peeking out from under the edge of the coffee table in Jonathan's living room. The caption reads simply, *jaws theme intensifies*, and Ezra can't hold back a smile as he scrolls down to read the comments.

> @lilypaddington why is my daughter out
> past curfew

> @ollie_oop co-signed @lilypaddington this
> violates the dog custody agreement,
> @ezra_terrestrial what gives???

> @maximum_energy wait are we
> coparenting now? @with_bells_jon where's

the child support you can't just take the
family dog with no consequences!

@ollie_oop @maximum_energy THANK
YOU some people just have no respect

Ezra shakes his head, handing the phone back. "Sorry.
They got attached to her pretty quickly."

"I think the dog is a metaphor in this situation," Jonathan
says, but leans down and drops a kiss onto Ezra's hair. "Especially since your Ollie basically accosted me the other day
when I was taking out the trash to give me a shovel talk."

"He's not *my* Ollie," Ezra says, refusing to think about what
that shovel talk entailed. "I mean, anymore." He tries not to
look too closely at Jonathan's face when he asks, "Does it
bother you? That I basically live with my ex?"

"Not particularly." Ezra looks up, raising his eyebrows at
him, and Jonathan laughs softly. "No, really, I mean it." He
shifts his arm, still around Ezra's back, until he can cup the
nape of his neck, thumb stroking over the crook of where his
shoulder meets his neck. Jonathan takes a breath—that particular sort of inhale that comes with wanting to say something and cutting it off at the last moment. His exhale, when it
comes, is slow and quiet.

Ezra nudges him. "Hey," he says. "What?"

Jonathan drums his fingers against the side of his mug,
hums quietly, and says, "Why did you two break up?"

Ezra sits up, putting a little space between them.

Jonathan follows the movement. "I'm not jealous," he says
quickly. "But I guess I'm just— I can tell there's nothing romantic going on between you, but it still seems like you really
love each other, and I guess . . ." He gives a small, self-
deprecating laugh. "I've never had an ex that I stayed friends

with. Before Ben, I never had a relationship serious enough that there was an actual breakup. I think Ben and I . . . we could have stayed friends, maybe, if we'd broken up, but it would have taken . . ." He shakes his head. "Ollie told me you guys were just friends, right away. And I don't get how you can break up with someone who you loved for so long and not need some kind of . . . adjustment period. I mean, I know it's been a few months, I just . . ."

It's rare for him to stumble over his words like this, and that, more than anything, keeps Ezra quiet. He shifts a little closer and reaches to take Jonathan's hand, lacing their fingers together. It's Jonathan's left, and the metal of Jonathan's wedding ring is cool against Ezra's skin.

"I told you Ollie's mostly ace, right?" Jonathan nods. "Sex is . . . complicated for him. And—" He tries to muster a smile, but it feels brittle. "You already know it's complicated for me."

Jonathan brings their joined hands up and drops a kiss onto Ezra's knuckles. Easy, like it's nothing. "You're not complicated," he says. "You're great."

He says it so sincerely that Ezra has to keep talking before he starts kissing him instead. "I can be both," Ezra says, because casual dismissiveness is easier than accepting a genuine bit of kindness. "I contain multitudes." Jonathan laughs, and it makes Ezra smile despite himself.

"I am, though. Kind of complicated. Or at least inconsistent. And with Ollie . . . When things were good, we were great together. But when we didn't line up with what we wanted, or when we wanted, we just stressed each other out. He never really— If I was avoiding something, or I didn't want to talk about it, he just kind of let me get away with it, and we ended up just pretending things were fine a lot of the time, even when they weren't. There was this constant struggle to just be everything the other person needed even when it didn't feel right, and we just finally got to a place where we . . . didn't want to do that anymore."

Jonathan nods, his face thoughtful. "You still love him?"

"Yes," Ezra says, a little surprised at how little it hurts to say. "But I'm not in love with him. Not anymore."

Jonathan is distant as he nods, toying with Ezra's fingers. Ezra can see the wheels turning behind his eyes, but he waits, as patiently as he can manage.

"You should probably know that I'm still in love with Ben."

Ezra catches Ben's appearance out of the corner of his eye, as if the sound of his name summoned him from wherever he goes when Ezra can't see him. He feels a prickle over his skin, a shift in the air's pressure. "Okay," he says.

Jonathan hesitates, then looks at him. "Does that bother you?"

Ezra opens his mouth to reply with an immediate no, but something makes him pause. Without thinking, he lets his eyes drift to where Ben has perched himself on the dresser.

Ben only has eyes for Jonathan. What is it like, to be so close to the man you love, able to see him but unable to *be* seen, to be touched, to be heard? Ezra wants to hold Jonathan's hand, create a way for him to see what Ezra can see, to hear what Ezra can hear.

What kind of difference would it make if Jonathan could get that closure? If he could say goodbye?

Would it be enough to make him fall out of love?

Would Ezra want it to be?

Ezra breathes out, slow and steadying, like he can empty everything out of his lungs and leave only open space that maybe, if he's worthy of it, he can try to fill with the kind of goodness that Jonathan deserves. He kisses Jonathan's wedding ring and hears a sharp intake of breath. He doesn't know if it came from Jonathan or Ben. Jonathan's fingers tremble slightly in his, and then tighten, like he needs to hold on to something solid and real.

"I love how much you love him," Ezra says, and means it. "Loving him is part of what makes you who you are." He feels like he's standing on the edge of a cliff, horribly close to tipping over. He can see the abyss opening up below him, a deep, dark sea of uncertainty.

He chooses his next words with care. "You can tell me if I'm wrong. But I don't get the feeling that your heart only has enough room for Ben's memory and nothing else."

For a long moment, Jonathan's quiet. Then he puts his cup down next to Ezra's on the nightstand, turns toward him, and lays a hand on Ezra's cheek. His palm is smooth and cool, and Ezra tilts his face into it on instinct and holds himself still as Jonathan leans in.

The kiss is feather soft, with miles of secrets stretching out behind him, miles more reaching out ahead. He curls a hand around Jonathan's biceps and holds on, steadying himself against the rhythm of Jonathan's pulse through warm, solid muscle.

It doesn't go any further than that, chaste and light. All the same, it leaves Ezra shaking.

Jonathan pulls away. Ezra has to catch his breath before he trusts himself to open his eyes.

Ben is still on the dresser. Ezra braces himself, but there's no malice in his expression, no possessiveness. When Ezra meets his eyes, he inclines his head, as if giving permission.

"Will you stay here again tonight?" Jonathan murmurs. "Just to sleep?"

It takes Ezra a moment to reply. He feels tingly, as if he'd been kissed into trembling silence, rather than given a simple brush of lips. He swallows hard and says, "I'll stay."

Jonathan smiles. Over his shoulder, so does Ben.

22

Another night, Ezra brings it up first.

"You don't really talk about him."

They're sprawled together across Jonathan's bed, the covers a twisted mess somewhere around their ankles, neither of them particularly clothed, up far too late considering how early Sappho will wake them up in the morning. Ezra's binder is still on, and somehow Jonathan's underwear hadn't fully come off when they tumbled into bed after dinner, both of them flushed with wine and none too graceful. The orgasms had taken the edge off any tipsiness, but Ezra's still loose-limbed and sated enough to be half-drowsing against Jonathan's shoulder, torn between trying to keep his eyes open and trying not to creep on Jonathan's phone.

He blames too many consecutive nights without enough sleep for the words that slip out when Jonathan pauses to type a comment on one of Ben's sisters' posts, and Jonathan picks his head up, looking at Ezra curiously under the loose sweep of dark hair currently refusing to stay pushed back off his face. He doesn't bother pretending that he doesn't know what Ezra's talking about, and Ezra isn't sure if he's grateful or not. "Should I?"

"Yes? No. I don't know." Ezra shifts slightly, propping himself up on one elbow. "Maybe. I'm not sure."

"Very decisive," Jonathan says, but there's new tension

tightening the skin around his eyes that Ezra hasn't seen before.

"I'm sorry," he says, already trying to figure out a way to
walk it back. "Forget I said—"

"No, it's okay." Jonathan sits up, easing his arm out from
under Ezra's belly. He puts his phone on his nightstand and
puts his glasses back on, drawing his knees up and resting his
elbows on them.

Ezra still feels dizzy whenever he remembers that Jonathan spent a year alone and chose him, of all people, to be the
person who brought him back into the world.

"I don't know how to talk about him," Jonathan says at last.
"Not really. Not without feeling like I'm lying about him."

Of all the things Ezra expected Jonathan to say, that wasn't
one of them.

He feels, suddenly, very conscious of how much he *isn't*
wearing. Jonathan's voice is omen heavy, and he knows without asking that whatever is coming next will be something
that won't feel right to hear like this, sprawled across Jonathan's bed with damp thighs and kiss-bruised lips. He sits up,
pulling the duvet up to cover his lap and mirroring Jonathan's
posture.

It's not as good as wearing pants like an actual adult, but
it's something. "Okay," he says. Not prompting, but offering.
Inviting.

"I told you we got together in college, right?" Ezra nods.
"He was—I don't know. Hard to describe. Brilliant. Funny. An
asshole, but in the endearing way, which sounds horrible but
was unfortunately true." He twists his wedding ring around
his finger, that absent-minded tic that never fails to make Ezra
feel an unpleasant twist of rejection and shame. "He proposed
to me the same day he got into med school. Told me that he
was pretty sure my extended family would get past me being

gay if they knew I was marrying a doctor." He smiles, wry and a little wistful. "He was right."

Ezra tears his eyes away from the ring, the metal still gleaming despite the tiny scratches along its surface. If he doesn't look at it, maybe it won't hurt. "How long were you married?"

"Three years." Jonathan's smile fades again. "The first two years were great. The third one . . . wasn't. He was doing his residency, I was just finishing my MPH, we never really saw each other . . . It was a lot. We fought in college, but I always kind of put that down to us being literal babies who didn't know any better. When we were thirty, it wasn't as easy to make excuses."

Ezra chooses his words carefully. "What did you do?"

Jonathan shrugs. "We tried therapy. I was going on my own anyway. He was—" His mouth twists into what Ezra thinks might be an attempt at a smile. "They say doctors make the worst patients, and he was kind of proof of concept. He wasn't anti-therapy or anything, he just . . . I don't know. At first I thought we were just drifting, that maybe we just wanted different things, but the way he was acting, toward the end, I just— I knew something was wrong, something he wasn't telling me. He swore he wasn't cheating, that he was just working through something and didn't know how to tell me, and maybe he was, maybe he wasn't, but I don't . . . I don't know."

He breaks off, lapsing into silence. Ezra wants to touch him, but he knows, with every cell in his body, that it would be the wrong thing to do.

"We were talking about separating, when he died," Jonathan says at last. "That night . . ." He swallows. "Judy called him and asked him to bring something over to the Chapel for his dad, and I went out to get dinner with friends. When I left the apartment, I had a husband, even if I was constantly frustrated with him and wasn't sure I'd be married to him much longer. When I got home, I . . . I didn't."

"I'm so sorry." It feels as useless a thing to say as it was the first time, weeks ago, but there aren't any other words for it.

"It was a car accident. They told me he died at the scene. I asked if it was on impact, if he felt it, and they . . . they didn't answer. But I had to identify him, and"—Jonathan's voice catches, and he takes a trembling breath—"I just remember looking at his face, like I could find some kind of sign that he didn't suffer, that he wasn't in pain, but—"

Ezra reaches out before he can stop himself, stopping just short of touching him, but Jonathan catches his hand and tangles their fingers together, his grip so tight it's almost bruising. Ezra squeezes back hard, then moves across the bed to press their sides together. Jonathan leans against him, taking long, shuddering breaths, and Ezra intentionally deepens his own breathing, the way he would if he was teaching a class or talking someone through a contraction.

This is a labor, too.

It takes a long time for Jonathan's breathing to slow enough to match his.

"He didn't deserve to die in pain," he whispers, his voice thick around the edges with grief and unshed tears. "No one deserves to die in pain, not really, but he didn't— Whatever was going on between us, it fucking broke my heart, that I didn't *know*. And it was horrible, mourning him, because our relationship was so miserable by that point—I felt like a fraud for grieving, like I didn't really lose a husband. People kept trying to send me to these support groups for widows, and I had to try not to just say, like, no, it's not the same, those people lost the person they were going to spend the rest of their lives with, and I . . . didn't feel like I could even say that, because what if we weren't? What if he was going to come home and tell me he didn't want me at all, that whatever we had at that point just wasn't worth trying to keep, and . . . how was I supposed to sit in a room of people who lost their partners when they were so happy, and act like we were the same?"

"I don't . . . I don't think that's how it works," Ezra says. "It's not—it's not a competition."

"That's what my therapist said." He runs his thumb over the back of Ezra's hand.

They sit quietly, Jonathan's breath slowly, slowly gentling to match Ezra's once more, until they're inhaling and exhaling in tandem. Ezra can't stop thinking about the first time they sat like this, on the floor of the taharah room, each of them haunted in their own way. "How . . ." He hesitates. "How did you start at the Chapel? With all of that?"

Jonathan's mouth quirks up at one corner. "Ben started volunteering with the chevra a few times a month when he was in high school. When we got married, Isaac asked me if I'd consider doing the training, just because they can always use more people. And I knew it was important to Ben, so"—he shrugs one shoulder—"I helped out a few times, but I took about three months' leave after Ben died. When I went back, I was pretty sure that I could just go back into it, especially because— Well, I'd had this experience, right? I thought it would teach me empathy, and I'd be so much more compassionate and able to just lean into it, you know?"

"Vaguely," Ezra says. "Though from your setup, I'm guessing that's not what happened?"

Jonathan snorts. "I got through my first taharah, and then as soon as I left the room, I threw up on the floor, had a panic attack, and cried for three hours straight." Ezra opens his mouth on instinct, not even sure what he could say, but Jonathan squeezes his hand. "It was like this well just opened up and poured out of me, not just of grief but of—shame, I guess.

Because I was there with this stranger, bathing them and cleaning them and wrapping them for burial, and I didn't know who had done that for Ben. If he'd had that. I don't remember if I even agreed to a taharah for him for his funeral. His mom planned most of it, I was so out of it. But he deserved that." He looks at Ezra then, eyes too bright, even in the dim room. "I know he didn't get a gentle death, but did someone treat him like that afterwards? No one ever told me, and I couldn't ask. I was too scared the answer might be no."

"Oh, love," Ezra says, hoarse.

The endearment slips out, but Jonathan doesn't even seem to notice. He sniffs, pushes his glasses up to perch on top of his head, and scrapes the back of his hand over his eyes again, more intentionally now. "The guys I was with that day were great, actually. They stayed with me the whole time, talking about their worst times. Everyone *knew*, obviously, what was going on, but"—he shakes his head—"they told me that there was—that doing the work is . . . it's ritual, and continuity, and all of that, but that from what they saw, the people who really resonate with it, there's a— It heals something. Even if you don't really know what the wound is. And grief is . . . it never goes away, not really. There's always another part of you that needs to be treated gently."

He sighs, tilting his head to rest it against Ezra's. "Sorry," he says, and he sounds bone-tired, wearier than Ezra's ever heard him. "That was a lot. And probably not what you were looking for when you asked why I don't talk about Ben. I should have just told you I was worried it might be weird for you to hear about it."

"No, it's—" Ezra swallows. There's an epic's worth of *weird* in his feelings about Ben, but nothing Jonathan's just told him has made it any worse than it was. If anything, it almost . . .

No. Not the time. He shifts their joined hands so he can

put an arm over Jonathan's shoulders. "I'm glad you weren't alone," he says, and means it. "That there was someone there to talk you through that. That they gave that to you."

"So am I," Jonathan says. His thumb resumes its circles over Ezra's knuckles, a mirror of the motion he used on his own ring. "I don't know if we'd be sitting here like this now, if they hadn't."

Ezra thinks about trying to have handled the past few weeks without Jonathan's quiet, steady presence, feels a little sick. "I'm grateful, then."

Jonathan doesn't answer, just makes a small, almost sleepy sound, leaning more of his weight against Ezra's side. He's heavier than usual, and that seems wrong. Ezra wishes he felt lighter, some kind of proof that everything he just said was a burden lifted, not just resettled with all the same weight.

It takes him too long to realize that he's probably just falling asleep. Gently, Ezra disentangles them enough to maneuver them both under the sheets. He slides Jonathan's glasses off his unresisting face, folding them carefully and setting them on the nightstand, then puts his own next to them and turns off the light. He wriggles out of his binder, dropping it to the floor, and then curls himself around Jonathan's back. Immediately, Jonathan catches his hand again, tucking it against his own heart. Ezra matches his breathing to the rise and fall of Jonathan's back against his chest.

Ezra's just on the verge of slipping out of consciousness when Jonathan mumbles, "Thank you."

"Mm?" Ezra says.

"For listening."

Ezra closes his eyes. He thinks of all the reasons he shouldn't be here, all the things he should be doing to help Ben and fix things with Mom and keep the Chapel afloat and, more than anything, all the reasons he doesn't *deserve* this, the quiet trust Jonathan keeps putting in him, like Ezra can keep it safe.

Ezra swallows, exhales, and tucks his forehead between Jonathan's shoulder blades. "Always," he says, and maybe, if he's good enough, it won't have to be a lie.

23

The next time Ben appears, phasing into being on the window seat of Ezra's living room with all the warning of a hypnic jerk, Ezra speaks before he has a chance to open his mouth.

"You didn't tell me you were separating."

If Ben's surprised at this verbal pounce, he doesn't show it. He leans back against the window like a sweater-clad panther, all long limbs and easy grace. His boring clothing hides a figure Ezra knows from the photos in Jonathan's apartment is—was?—corded with lean muscle, honed from years of martial arts and morning runs.

Ben was tall and broad and toned and gorgeous. Ezra hits five-six on a good day, if he's purposeful about his posture, and his body still follows the map of his mother's and grandmother's, even after a year of testosterone redistributing his body fat.

After someone like Ben, what the *hell* is Jonathan doing with him?

Ben inclines his head, looking at him thoughtfully for a moment, and then he shrugs. "Does it matter?"

Ezra sits up on his yoga mat, abandoning the flow he'd barely started, narrowing his eyes. "Doesn't it?"

Ben skims the middle finger of his right hand over his wedding ring. Finally, he says, "I wasn't cheating on him."

"He thinks you were."

"I know." Ben sighs and looks away. He looks very *alive*, suddenly, solid and tired and real, shadows smudging the skin under his eyes and his shoulders slumping. The fading light of sunset paints him in shades of pink and gold, highlighting the strong line of his jaw, the flecks of green in his eyes. Ezra has seen the face of his death only once, that first moment of sight, when the afterimage of blood and viscera superimposed itself over Ben's handsome face, but he wonders if this is how he looked in the moments before the accident that killed him: world-weary and resigned.

He's silent for a long time. Ezra finds himself wondering if that was something he and Jonathan liked about each other: the ability to sit in silence, to gather their thoughts.

He's never been able to. Background silence is one thing—the hum of a city morning, rushing traffic and the distant barking of dogs, the natural silence that sinks into an empty room, the settling of an old roof and the echoing creak of floorboards or faint clanging of pipes; all of those are soothing and ambient, easy to relax into without care. This conversational quiet, the absence of sound as thoughts are gathered and Ezra's mind zeroes in on every possible place where he could be hurt, is something else.

At last, Ben sighs. Emotion and sound, without any actual breath. It's been years since Ezra has let himself wonder at the psychic physics of it, but now it seems impossible not to. How *real* is he? How much of him is an echo, and how much is something more?

"I knew about the affair," he says. "My mom and yours. That was the secret I was keeping. I knew, and I didn't know what to do about it."

"So you weren't cheating on him."

"No. God no." Ben rubs a hand over his face, long fingers scraping over the dark stubble on his cheeks. "I wouldn't have—

No. I know he didn't believe me. I just didn't know how to tell him—" He breaks off. When he looks back at Ezra, his eyes are conspiratorial. "He's such a romantic, you know? He wants so badly to believe that everyone loves like he does, and I've never met anyone else who loves like that. It's not just his heart, it's—it's a full-body experience with him. Heart and body and soul."

Ezra thinks of the way Jonathan looks at him like he's something precious, the way he can be simultaneously tender and devastating in the way he touches, the way he smiles.

He nods. It doesn't feel right to say *I know*.

"His parents are . . ." Ben's mouth twists. "They love Jon and his sister, but from what Jon told me, growing up with them was like living in a war zone. I think he kind of convinced himself that everyone grew up like that. I still remember the look he gave me the first time I mentioned that my parents did pub trivia together, like he was stunned at the idea that people would want to hang out with their spouse. And they *loved* him, like, from day one. My mom—" He huffs a laugh. "My mom took me aside before we'd even finished one meal and told me that if I didn't marry him, she'd never forgive me."

Ezra laughs, not quite sure if it's nostalgia or regret that makes him think of his own mother shooting significant glances at Ollie across the dinner table, not even bothering with subtlety. "Cute."

"Yeah. He loved it. Loved them. They were the marriage role models he didn't have growing up, y'know?" Ben's smile is a weary, unhappy thing. "When I found out about my mom—*our* moms, I guess—I just . . ."

"You couldn't tell him."

Ben looks at him. "It would've broken his heart."

Ezra thinks about Jonathan, white-knuckled and red-eyed, throwing his phone across the bed and folding in on himself after another argument with Judy, shaking like a leaf in the wind. What difference did timing make, if it was always going to break his heart in the end? Ezra draws one knee up, wrapping his arms around it. He plays it off as a stretch, not like he's shielding his own chest from impact. "But not yours?"

"Not the same way." Ben's chest rises and falls, another ghost of a sigh. "I was always more of a realist, I guess."

"So that's why you kept it from him?" It doesn't seem like enough, somehow, and he hears the skepticism in his own voice. "So he wouldn't be sad?"

"Residency was hard," Ben says, and the words have the edge of a confession. "I was miserable all the time, and I was taking it out on him, and I know he was frustrated with me, but we knew it was temporary, so we were— There was an end point, I guess. But when I found out about my mom . . ." He shakes his head. "I know I changed. But he looked up to my parents, and he knew that the years my dad was in grad school were the worst for their marriage, and he'd keep saying that we just had to look at them for an example, and we'd get through it like they did."

It's not hard to connect the dots. "You really think he'd have given up on you just because your parents' marriage wasn't as perfect as he thought it was?"

"I wasn't doing my best thinking at the time." Ben huffs out a short, humorless laugh. "I wasn't doing my best anything at the time. I shut down. Shut him out. It wasn't his fault. I just . . . I knew it'd just open the floodgates if I said anything. And he tried *so* fucking hard, and I knew he'd snap eventually, and then we were fighting all the time because he's not stupid, he knew I was keeping something from him, and—"

He clenches and unclenches his hands, a muscle twitching in his jaw.

The person in front of him is an unexplainable echo, but an echo nonetheless.

Ezra takes a breath, steeling himself. His lungs ache, as if he's been failing to inhale the entire time they've been talking, like his body has seen Ben's chest moving without air and wants to do the same.

"I don't understand what you want from me," he says. "You're everywhere, and I don't know why. I don't know what to do to help you."

It's the question that's been digging at him since the first time Ben appeared as a shade without a name.

He must want something.

Fix it, he'd said, the first time he spoke, but fix *what*? Between Jonathan and their mothers and, hell, even Ezra himself, that could be anything.

Ben doesn't answer at first.

"I don't want him to give up on love," he says so quietly Ezra barely hears it. "I don't want him to think that what we had, what my parents had, what my mom broke, what"—he laughs, low and bitter—"what *I* broke—I don't want him to think that's all there is."

Ezra swallows. There's a bird trapped in the space between his sternum and his lungs. "Every relationship I've ever been in has crashed and burned," he says. "And it's almost always been my fault, because I couldn't give them what they needed, or because I was trying too hard, or I was just too much for them to deal with because I was always running off to go deal with something at home or take care of my sister or—"

He digs his fingers into his palms until they sting. "If you want someone to be a good enough person that they can make him believe in love again, you should have chosen someone else. I'm not that person."

The smile Ben offers him is a small, crooked thing.

"Maybe," he says. "But you're the only person I have."

24

When Ezra was eleven, his parents had left him and Aaron in charge of Becca for the day while they went to a conference in Boston. Becca had been nursing a fever for three days, and Mom had needed to pry her off her legs in order to leave, giving Ezra half-distracted instructions for administering Tylenol as she stepped into her shoes, Dad yelling a reminder from the doorway that they were going to be late. After they left, Becca had hidden under her bed and cried herself to sleep, refusing to come out no matter how much macaroni and cheese or television Ezra tried to bribe her with.

Then, two hours later, she'd woken up screaming.

Ezra doesn't remember much of that afternoon. He remembers trying to call their parents, only to have his calls go straight to voicemail. He vaguely remembers trying to reach Uncle Joe, but Aunt Maddie had been in chemo that weekend.

He doesn't remember the decision to take Mom's car keys and try to drive Becca to the nearest hospital themselves, but he does remember talking Aaron—still six months away from his learner's permit—out of calling 911 instead because their parents had been worrying about money again, preoccupied to the point that they hadn't even noticed him listening at the kitchen door during one of their many arguments, and he was old enough to know that ambulances were *expensive*.

Melissa caught them trying to bundle a crying, vomiting

Becca into the car on her way to the parking lot outside the Chapel. She'd taken one look and snatched the keys out of Ezra's hand.

It was probably sheer dumb luck that she took speed limits as suggestions more than rules. They might not have made it to the hospital before Becca's appendix burst if she hadn't.

"What on earth were you two *thinking*?" Melissa had asked, sitting with Aaron and Ezra in the hospital after Becca had been rushed into emergency surgery, waiting for their parents to join them.

"I was just trying to help," Ezra said. He wiped his eyes. He was too old for crying. "Please don't tell Mom about the car."

"Sweetheart," she said, sympathetic. "Why didn't you call an adult?"

"We tried," Aaron said, more defensive than Ezra would have been. "They didn't pick up."

"Why didn't you come across to the Chapel and get one of us?"

Ezra looked at Aaron. Aaron looked back blankly. "You were at work," Ezra said, and hated how small his voice sounded. "And I was in charge."

Melissa glanced at Aaron, one eyebrow raised, and frowned at his answering shrug. There was something more careful in her voice when she asked, "And that means you couldn't ask for help?"

Ezra swallowed. He didn't like what he saw in her face. "Am I in trouble?"

Melissa regarded him for a long moment, and then sighed. "No," she said. "But next time, maybe consider phoning a friend before you jump right to grand theft auto."

She smiled as she said it, like that would lessen the sting. Melissa hadn't told his parents, but Ezra had still known. He'd been given a single job, and he'd messed it up.

And now, years later, he's about to do it all over again.

You're the only person I have.

The words sink into him, stones in still water. He's been *the only person* for most of his life, but it feels worse, somehow, to be a dead man's last hope.

Ezra spends three days dragging his feet and moving through his work like a zombie, too distracted by Ben's voice in his head to do anything other than act on autopilot. It's a relief when Becca ambushes him in the staff room, catching Ezra while he's trying to convince the ancient printer to stop choking on any document longer than a page and a half.

"Subtle," Ezra says, taking in her body language and deciding there's no point in trying to talk his way out of whatever she's about to hit him with.

Becca points at the table. "Sit," she says tartly. Ezra cocks an eyebrow at her, because he didn't spend ninety percent of his life parenting her just for her to start ordering *him* around, but he pulls out a chair and drops into it. Becca plops down across from him. "Were you and Aaron just not going to tell Dad about the bank account thing?"

Ezra opens his mouth, considers twenty or so possible answers to that question in order of pettiness, and then closes it. "It's on the to-do list."

It's not *high* on the to-do list. But it's on there.

Becca folds her arms across her chest again and scowls at him. "Aaron told me Mom gave you all the records and everything. I don't get why you haven't told Dad about it. When it was just mystery deposits, fine, whatever, but now you're just doing the same thing Mom did, and I don't get how that's *better.*"

He and Aaron had been going in circles about it since

Mom sent over the paperwork that put the accounts in Aaron's and Ezra's names, along with all of her records and notes. She'd been meticulous and consistent, calculating the cash flow shortfall twice each month and transferring over just enough to cover it, attaching the deposits to client invoices with no actual client records. To Ezra's surprise, she'd been transferring money *into* the accounts as well, a percentage of the money from the rare months when they pulled in a profit, supplemented with a portion of her own paycheck, because she was smart enough to notice that, generous as those accounts were, they weren't going to last forever.

He and Aaron had spent most of a day barricaded in Mom's office, going through the records with a fine-tooth comb to try to get a handle on just how bad the situation was and just how fucked they'd be if the accounts suddenly ran dry. It didn't seem like they were in any danger of doing so immediately. Most of Zayde's assets had, it turned out, gone right into them when he died. But like Mom said, they weren't a permanent solution. By Ezra's math, if nothing changed, they'd have two years left. Three, if they were careful.

But without that money, they were several thousand dollars in the red more often than they broke even. They'd need to bring in four or five more clients a month in order to even out over a year, and while they had the advantage of name recognition and fairly good standing in the community—or they *did*, before everything with Mom and Judy came out; Ezra's honestly got no clue what their reputation is like now, though it's not like things have been *quiet*—there are only so many people around to die in a given month.

And Ezra really doesn't need the kind of karma that comes with hoping a few more people drop dead just so they can make payroll.

"It's not exactly an easy conversation to have," he says at last.

Becca looks at him for a few seconds, like she's trying to read his thoughts through the lines of his face, and sympathy wins out over frustration.

"You know the longer you wait, the worse it's going to be."

Ezra realizes, in a heartbeat of horrible comprehension, that she's not just talking about Dad. For all the pieces of himself he tries to hide, to spare other people the worry of seeing him, his siblings have always known him better than almost anyone else. He looks away from her.

"Ezra," she says, softly now.

"I know." He doesn't need her to say anything else. "I just . . . I need to find the right time. The right way to say it."

Becca squeezes his hand. "Have you figured anything else out? About why he's still here?"

You're the only person I have, he'd said, like that was supposed to be a comfort. But Ezra can't stop thinking of that first night on the steps of the porch. The way Ben had looked at him, almost imploring.

Fix it.

Like Ezra knows what that means, when Ben couldn't be *more* mixed up in the mess of Ezra's life, between Jonathan and Judy and his own time, apparently, at the Chapel. There are more things to "fix" than Ezra can even wrap his head around. He swallows. "No."

"You'll figure it out," she tells him, with a surety Ezra wishes he could channel. "You always do."

He doesn't have her confidence, but he turns his hand to squeeze hers back anyway. "Thanks," he says. "So. What are we going to do about Dad?"

She lets him get away with the subject change, and he

loves her for it. Her lips twitch, and she lets him go, sitting back. "We could try to figure that one out together, I guess," she says. "At least we can all see everyone involved in *that* mess."

"Charitable of you."

"Is that Becca?" Aaron pokes his head into the room. "I thought I heard you. What are you doing here?"

"Interrogating me about why we haven't talked to Dad about Mom and Zayde's secret banking habits," Ezra says. "Thanks for spilling the beans on that, by the way."

Aaron salutes him with the coffee mug he's carrying. "You're welcome. And I had an idea about that, actually." He makes a face that hits somewhere between a smile and a grimace. "I don't think you're going to like it. But it's an idea."

"Solid start," Becca says. "Really getting a confident vibe here."

"Lag BaOmer is later this week," Aaron says. "I'm pretty sure Dad's still planning to do a fire, and since I'm pretty sure he's going to want to burn a bunch of shit down when we tell him about this anyway, we might as well, you know"—he shrugs—"two birds, one stone."

Ezra considers it. It's one of the few ritual holidays that he's always liked celebrating at home, mostly because their family observance has always been a backyard bonfire and staying up past bedtime, rather than putting on nice clothes and sitting politely at the table for fancy meals, which always made Mom stressed and Dad irritable. He'd been assuming it was off the table this year, given everything going on, but if it wasn't . . .

"It *is* one of his favorites," he says slowly.

Becca looks just as thoughtful, drumming her nails on the table. "I like it," she says. "What if we asked Mom to come?"

Ezra snaps his head around to look at her. *"What?"*

"No way," Aaron says at the same time, his voice mingling with Ezra's in a jumbled mess.

"No, hear me out," Becca protests. "It's Mom's mess, first of all, and she owes it to him to be the one to tell him and apologize, not have you guys doing it for her. And it's always been, like, one of the only holidays where they don't freak out at each other at least once. Maybe it can be, I don't know, an olive branch kind of thing."

"Shouldn't she be the one extending olive branches?" Aaron asks, flat and dry.

"It was just a suggestion," Becca says, but something about her seems almost deflated, and Ezra's never once been able to handle that look on her face.

"Let's ask Dad," he says. Both his siblings stare at him, and he shrugs. "It should be up to him if he wants her there. If he does, we'll invite her and tell her she needs to come clean. If he doesn't"—he grimaces, already scripting in his head; even if Mom did agree to come, at some point he'll end up taking over the conversation to keep it from going to hell, so it probably doesn't make a difference—"I'll do it, I guess."

Becca chews her lower lip. "Mom *should* do it, though," she says.

Story of my life, Ezra doesn't say, and gets up to wash the coffeepot so that they won't see the look on his face.

Dad, to no one's surprise, doesn't want Mom coming to the bonfire.

He stares at Ezra and Aaron like they've grown second heads when they ask him, thick eyebrows raised all the way up over the rims of his glasses. It reminds Ezra of being sixteen and asking to go to a coed sleepover, as if the sheer concept of the proposal was so absolutely absurd that his father couldn't believe he was being asked. It's almost reassuring to be on the receiving end of this again, a little spark of normality amid the mess of the last month and a half.

"So that's a no, then," Aaron says at last.

"That's a no," Dad says. "Is there a reason you two look ready to throw *yourselves* in the bonfire?"

"No," Ezra says. Probably too quickly. He clears his throat. "Do you need us to bring anything?"

The look Dad gives him suggests that he doesn't trust a word coming out of Ezra's mouth, but he seems willing to give him a pass for now. "No," he says, and then, considering, "You could invite Jonathan, if you'd like."

Ezra freezes. "I—" he says. He looks at Aaron for support—he gets absolutely nothing back—and manages an articulate, only slightly strangled "Why?"

Dad sits back in his chair, the imposing desk that used to be Zayde's stretching out in front of him. He steeples his fingers, eyes twinkling with amusement, which would be a relief to see if Ezra weren't currently drowning in empathy for every deer that ever stepped out onto a highway with no idea what was about to hit them.

"He mentioned once that he enjoys the holiday," he says. "No other reason. Unless there's one you think I should know about?"

"You're not as funny as you think you are," Ezra says, crossing his arms over his chest.

Dad chuckles. "Blame Melissa," he says. "She's the one who apparently caught you two—how did she put it?—'necking in the parking lot'?"

"Oh my God," Ezra says, dropping his face into his hands. "That wasn't— We weren't *necking*—"

"In broad daylight, too," Aaron says, clicking his tongue. "Where's the professionalism?"

Ezra's phone chooses that moment to ring, and he's never been so grateful to have a client go into labor in his life.

Broad-shouldered and bearded, Ryan hadn't made a secret of being perversely grateful to have spent most of the last several months getting side-eyed for his beer belly rather than dealing with invasive strangers commenting on his pregnancy. He has the personality of a field general, decisive and commanding, and Ezra thinks that's probably why he's gotten through this pregnancy with as much ease as he has. He'd gone the single-parent route deliberately, deciding at thirty-seven that if he wasn't partnered yet, he wasn't likely to be in a co-parenting position on any kind of timeline he felt good about. When he hired Ezra four months ago, he'd told him point-blank that he wasn't interested in the "gooey hippie" parts of doula services; he just wanted to make sure he had one guaranteed person in the room with him who wouldn't fuck up his pronouns.

"You'd be surprised how many people default to 'You got this, Mama,'" he'd told Ezra dryly during their last pre-labor meeting, breathing hard through his teeth while Ezra showed him an acupressure point, pressing firmly against his lower back. "I figure you have more empathy than most people would, considering. *Ow*, mother*fucker*, are you sure this is helping?"

"No pain, no gain," Ezra said, and met Ryan's scowl with a grin.

Practiced confidence or not, sixteen hours of active labor is enough to crack anyone's calm. Marcie, Ryan's midwife—who has, to her credit, not misgendered him once—assures them both that the baby's tolerating the contractions just fine, but Ryan's energy is flagging and he's been stuck at nine centimeters for an hour.

"This was the stupidest thing I've ever done," he pants, leaning hard on Ezra's shoulder to steady himself on the birthing ball. "What was I thinking?"

"You were thinking you're going to be an amazing parent," Ezra tells him, firmly keeping any kind of pain off his face even though he's sure he'll have finger-shaped bruises tomorrow. "Which you will."

"I'm going to be the kind of parent who reminds their kid how long labor took for their entire *life*," Ryan grits out. "Son of a— *Fuck*."

"Oh, that's promising," Marcie says brightly, pulling on a new pair of gloves. "Let's check your dilation again."

They hadn't planned on a water birth, but Ryan latches on to the offer of the tub as soon as Marcie makes it. He relaxes slightly when he sinks into the warm water, but Ezra catches the lines of pain and anxiety on his face. "Hey," he says, crouching down beside the tub. Ryan's on his knees, tall enough for his shoulders to be out of the water as he rests his arms on the ledge for support, his hands digging into opposite elbows. "You're doing great, okay? You're almost done. One more hard part, that's it."

Ryan laughs, tight and pained, and drops his head onto his folded arms.

Marcie meets Ezra's eyes over Ryan's shoulder and inclines her head pointedly. It's just the three of them in the room. Ryan's been pointedly reticent on his reasons for not wanting any family or friends with him, and it's not Ezra's job to pry, but it means he's not getting the partner or family support Ezra's used to supplementing, not providing completely. Marcie's look is clear: *Step it up.* She radiates a no-nonsense competency that makes her both excellent at her job and terrifying to work with. Ezra takes the hint.

"Ryan, hey," he says. Ryan opens his eyes, looking young

and scared and uncertain, his teeth digging so hard into his bottom lip that Ezra's a little worried he might bite through it. "Hey," he says again, and puts his hands on Ryan's shoulders. "You can do this."

Ryan shakes his head. "I can't," he says, and then drops his forehead back onto his arms with a shuddering groan.

"You can," Marcie says, her tone firmer than Ezra's but no less gentle. "It's time to push, hon. You can do it."

"I should have waited," Ryan says, not picking his head up. "I should've— I can't do this by myself. I—"

He breaks off at another contraction, and Ezra grips his shoulders through it. He catches Marcie's frown—she'd never do it if Ryan was facing her, Ezra's worked with her enough to know that, but he can see the concern on her lined, kind face. "Ryan," he says, squeezing his arms. "Hey. You're not by yourself, okay? We're right here with you." Ryan shakes his head again.

Ezra thinks, *Okay, well, fuck it,* and says, "Do you want me to get in with you?"

Ryan's trembling stills, and then he looks up.

His nod is tiny, but it's there.

Ezra takes the time to kick off his shoes, but Marcie's quick, jerking nod is enough confirmation that they don't have time for him to go change into scrubs. He climbs into the tub fully clothed, the water sloshing at the introduction of another body. As if on instinct, Ryan shifts around until his back is pressed to Ezra's chest, and Ezra holds on to both his hands, biting back a swear when he feels the bones in his fingers shift under Ryan's grip. "You've got this," he says. "Okay? You can do this."

"I can do this," Ryan echoes.

"That's what I like to hear," Marcie says. "Next contraction, you push."

When Ezra did his doula training, he had an instructor who insisted that at some point they'd attend a birth that felt different from anything they'd been at before. One that changed something fundamental in the way they worked, the way they felt.

"You might know it when you're there, you might not," she told the room. "But it'll settle in your bones, in your hands, and you'll remember it. The body always remembers more than you think."

He feels this one in his bones.

The water clouds with blood, but it never feels dirty, never feels wrong. The weight of Ryan's back against him means that he feels the ripple of feedback when Ryan passes the baby's head, then its shoulders. And then Marcie is scooping a wriggling infant out of the water, a wail escaping the tiny face as soon as he breaks the surface, and Ryan is crying and Ezra is crying, and it's the whirlwind of skin to skin and third-stage labor and a transition out of the water, the birth center staff and nurses filtering in and out of the room to help.

It's chaos, noise and movement, and the buzz of voices and bodies and *life*. Ezra feels more alive, more present, more *himself*, than he has in weeks, and through all of it, he doesn't once think of ghosts.

25

That night, Ezra dreams of water.

There's a mikvah in Providence, tucked behind the JCC, easy to miss if you don't know it's there. He'd gone only once, on a tour with his Hebrew school class to learn about the immersion ritual. At the time it seemed both old-fashioned and beautiful. The idea of ritual impurity had curdled unpleasantly, but the concept of something as simple as clean water washing away one part of life and gentling someone into the next filled him with a yearning he couldn't describe. He'd never gone back, but the memory would return to him at the oddest times—when he stepped barefoot into a puddle of new rainwater, doing the Penguin Plunge at Fogland Beach, the first time he swam while wearing a binder. It's always just a flash of memory, never anything more than the shimmer of clear water on mosaic tiles, but it surprises him every time.

In the dream, he's naked, looking down at the water as it laps against the walls of the pool. He steps carefully, feeling the cool water against his skin, *down, down, down,* until he's submerged to his shoulders.

"You have to go in completely," the attendant says in Zayde's voice, but when Ezra looks up, it's Ben there instead, sitting cross-legged on the floor, his chin in his hand. "If you don't go under, the ritual isn't complete."

Ezra looks into the deep water. He can feel smooth stone under his feet. "What's the ritual?"

Ben smiles, reaching out to rest his hand on top of Ezra's head, as if giving a blessing. "Rebirth," he says, and gently presses Ezra down.

The water closes over his head and the world rushes away. He keeps his eyes open. The water is clear, and through it, as he sinks *down, down, down,* far deeper than he should, he can see the delicate pattern of the tile floor, the pale skin of his body. His breasts float upward, his nipples hardened from the cold. He touches the soft tissue where it swells from his chest, and it doesn't feel foreign. He's aware of the place between his legs where the water feels colder against skin that runs hot, and when he lays a hand there, too, there's no sense of despair, no sense of yearning for something that isn't there.

Ezra opens his mouth and lets the water flow into him, his lungs and his veins, washing him clean from the inside out. He's a body in water, safe as the womb. He's a soul within the body, filling every space, every crevice, every cell.

He surfaces, water running from his mouth, from his ears, from his eyes. The spring is fresh, but his face tastes of salt.

Ezra gasps himself awake like he's surfaced from underwater. His bedroom is dark, only a faint sliver of moonlight trickling in through the blinds. The skin of his face feels tacky and tight, and when he reaches up to touch his cheek, his fingers come away damp.

His phone is in his hand before he knows he's reached for it. Jonathan's voice, when he answers, is a sleepy murmur, and Ezra winces. He hadn't checked the time.

"Ezra?"

"Hi," Ezra says. "Can I—" His fingers are shaking around the phone. All he wants, very suddenly, is to be *held*. He takes a breath. Swallows around the dry tightness in his throat. "Can I come over?"

"Wow," Jonathan murmurs, when Ezra finishes talking. "That sounds . . . intense."

They'd settled on the sectional in Jonathan's living room when Ezra stumbled in, shoeless and still in sweatpants, Sappho off leash at his heels for the walk down the stairs. Jonathan has his fingers in Ezra's hair, having detangled his sleep-mussed curls, stroking through the strands where Ezra's head rests in his lap.

It's grounding and soft, soothing the shivers that still ripple over Ezra's skin, lingering goose bumps from a dream that's just starting to fade into memory. He's grateful that his face is tucked against Jonathan's shirt, because he knows that if he sees the look that goes along with this touch, the tears he wiped off his face when he startled awake from that waterlogged dream are going to return in force.

"It's not usually like that," he says. He'd watched Jonathan's eyes get progressively wider as Ezra talked about Ryan's birth, but the quiet pride he's used to feeling after a job has turned fragile and indefinable. "I mean, it's always a lot, but I can usually leave it at the metaphorical office, I guess."

"Mm." Jonathan's hand settles on Ezra's waist, slipping under the edge of his shirt and running in slow circles over his hip bone, just above the band of his sweats. Ezra shivers into the touch without thinking, and Jonathan laughs softly. "It's not so bad, though, is it? Bringing it home with you?"

Ezra doesn't answer, closing his eyes and tilting his head into Jonathan's hip, letting himself soak in the scent of Jonathan's bodywash and laundry detergent. It's probably—

definitely—too soon in their . . . whatever this is to bring up the pile of baggage he has around parenting knocking around in his head after today. He shakes his head instead.

"I usually feel like I'm doing something wrong because I don't," he admits. "Bring it home, I mean. Same with teaching. I know people who do it where it's their whole identity. It comes into everything they do, whether they're at work or not. I'm always worried that someone's going to figure out that I'm faking it."

Jonathan, who had adjusted slightly when Ezra moved, slips his hand back into his hair, finger-combing it off his forehead. Ezra closes his eyes again. "What exactly do you think you're faking?"

Ezra scoffs. "Want the long list or the short one?"

Jonathan clicks his tongue, chiding, "Come on. You can't scare me off, I've already gotten attached to your dog."

Oh, I bet I could, Ezra thinks, but he sighs and sits up anyway, rolling his shoulders and drawing his knees up to loop his arms around them.

"Everyone I know seems to know who they are and what they're doing," he says. Sappho, curled under the coffee table, shifts in her sleep. "And I don't. I do what I do because it's about as far away from what I grew up with as I could get, and I was sick of constantly being surrounded by death. I tell people what I do for work and they act like it's something impressive or amazing, but it's . . . People have been doing this for thousands of years, and for most of that, none of what I do was even a *job*. I'm not special because I can keep someone calm or teach people how to move through a flow, I'm just—"

He starts to offer Jonathan a helpless, exasperated smile, but breaks off at the look on his face. Jonathan has one arm propped on the back of the couch and is watching him with a soft, amused sort of affection. "Why are you looking at me like that?"

Jonathan reaches out to curl a hand over the back of Ezra's neck. He telegraphs every movement, he always does, so Ezra's ready when Jonathan kisses him, slow and sweet and lingering. His thumb strokes over the pulse in Ezra's throat, and Ezra shivers a breath into the kiss, Jonathan's responding laugh caught between their mouths.

"You *are* impressive," Jonathan says when they part. He keeps his grip on the back of Ezra's neck and pulls, very gently, until Ezra takes the hint and slides into his lap. His body knows the motion now, and he settles his weight on Jonathan's thighs with familiar ease. "And you are special, and just because something's been done for years doesn't mean you're not still amazing for doing it. Do you know what I would have done if I was in that room today? Cried. Probably very loudly, and very unattractively."

Ezra doubts that. He has yet to see Jonathan do anything unattractively. And in any case, it's not the same. Ezra sits with people during what's often one of the best days of their lives. Jonathan volunteers to be there for the worst. It's not that Ezra doesn't see loss in his line of work—the nature of being a full-spectrum doula means that he sees nearly as many miscarriages and abortions as he does births—but it's not the same. "You handle bigger deals than that on a regular basis."

"I absolutely don't," Jonathan says firmly. He reaches up and brushes Ezra's hair back. It keeps falling over his forehead. "Why are you so set on acting like nothing you do is important?"

There are a thousand answers, and Ezra knows that there's not a single one he can give that'll take that brokenhearted look out of Jonathan's eyes. "I don't know," he whispers.

Jonathan cups his face, tilting his jaw up until Ezra has to look at him. There's still a question in his eyes.

There's too much Ezra wants to say and not enough words to say it.

Ezra kisses him instead.

It's a deeper kiss from the outset, and Ezra knows, from the moment that Jonathan's teeth scrape against his lower lip, that something's changed. The rain pounding against the porch overhang outside the window seems louder and stronger, and it takes a few seconds for Ezra to realize that it's the roar of blood in his ears that he's hearing as his pulse quickens, warmth spreading through him as Jonathan's hands slip under his shirt. He presses closer and Jonathan lets him.

"Bed?" Jonathan murmurs when they separate long enough for Ezra to haul his shirt off and drop it onto the floor, dragging Jonathan's off a moment later.

"Yes," Ezra says immediately, and yelps when Jonathan, laughing, stands up without dislodging him from his lap, hitching Ezra's legs around his waist. "Don't drop me."

"I'd never," Jonathan promises.

It makes Ezra's breath catch in the back of his throat, and he's still trying to settle his breathing when Jonathan sets him down in the nest of sheets he must have abandoned when Ezra called him earlier, the rumpled duvet already kicked to the bottom of the bed. Ezra reaches for him before he's properly made contact with the pillows, and Jonathan follows him down, catching him in a kiss when Ezra tilts his face up, and then another, and then another.

In here, the rain is louder, all the windows open to the storm. The air is thick with the scent of petrichor, pungent and sweet. Jonathan slides his hands up over Ezra's shoulders and biceps and wrists and then presses his hands to the pillow above his head, firm pressure that makes Ezra's heart stutter in his chest. When he flexes his grip, Ezra shifts so Jonathan can wrap just one hand around both his wrists, long fingers steady and sure.

"Okay?" he asks, the question brushed against Ezra's mouth.

Ezra nods. "Okay," he says.

Jonathan kisses him again, in appreciation or reward or both, and Ezra melts. He's gotten used to Jonathan kissing him senseless, but this isn't drifting out of his body and floating away to a place where the stimuli in his body and brain don't ever have to overlap. He feels present in a way that should be terrifying, but the panic never comes.

There's just the sound of the rain and the scent of their skin and the heat of another body against his.

"You good?" Jonathan murmurs, his breath ghosting the words over Ezra's neck. The hand not curled around Ezra's wrists trails down, over his sternum and lower, lower, lower. Heat blooms under Ezra's skin, following the path of Jonathan's fingertips, and his breath catches in his throat. "You seem different. More . . . here. With me."

"I—" Jonathan's fingers dip beneath Ezra's waistband. He shudders. "I feel more with you."

I feel more with you; as in, *I feel like I'm here, with you, more than I ever have.* And: *I feel more with you*; as in, *You make me feel, more than anyone else.* He tilts his head into Jonathan's next kiss, and arches into the touch that slips lower still, finding the place where he's wanting with unerring ease.

Jonathan breaks the kiss, punctuates it with one more, soft, deceptively chaste. "What do you want?"

"You," Ezra says.

He's barely been touched. But he feels like he's a live wire, every nerve singing. He wants—he *wants*.

Jonathan kisses the delicate skin under his eye. Waits.

Ezra says, in a voice he barely recognizes as his own, "*Please.*"

"Okay," Jonathan says, and then, "I've got you."

He helps Ezra slip his sweatpants and underwear over his hips and off, and then, with a devastating tenderness, takes him apart.

Ezra doesn't treat his body like a stranger. He spends too much time using it, needing to be aware of its angles and balance and rhythm, to be able to disconnect from it fully. Sex is—has always been—the same. He likes how it feels, he likes to be touched, he likes the way he can make other people feel good, but sometimes he just has to take himself somewhere else, somewhere where the parts of himself being touched or kissed or fucked belong to another kind of body.

He doesn't know what makes tonight feel so different. But it does.

Jonathan takes everything slowly, almost hesitantly, using his fingers and his mouth in careful counterbalance, never pushing too far, not going harder or faster even when Ezra starts to squirm. Ezra thinks he's teasing, playing like he has been all week, but then he catches the way Jonathan's other hand is trembling where he's holding on to Ezra's thigh and realizes that he's not the only one who's nervous.

Abandoning his grip on the pillowcase, he reaches down and laces their fingers together. Jonathan looks up at him, his pupils blown dark and wide, and Ezra thumbs over his cheek and then threads the fingers of his other hand through his hair. It's damp with sweat under his touch and catches when he tries to work his hand free, and when Ezra tugs, just to test his reaction, Jonathan sucks in a breath, eyes fluttering shut.

"Fuck," he says, pressing his forehead to the bare skin of Ezra's hip. "Fuck. Just—careful."

His voice has gone hoarse, the muscles in his back and shoulders so tense Ezra can see the tremors, and he bites back a laugh, surprised and delighted, the last of the tension he'd been clinging to leaving him in a rush. "Oh my God," he says, unable to keep the grin off his face. "Really?"

Jonathan picks his head up, scowling. "Because *you're* so calm," he says, and bites down on Ezra's inner thigh. Ezra lets out a yelp that turns into a choked moan when Jonathan licks over the spot he'd bitten, then sucks a bruise into the skin. Ezra knows immediately he'll be pressing on it for days, just to remember the feeling.

The sudden levity eases something between them, takes the heat that's been building down to a simmer. Jonathan holds his gaze until Ezra touches his cheek and gives a shaky nod, and then he dips his head back down between Ezra's legs and stays there. He works his fingers and mouth in perfect tandem until Ezra gasps and arches and begs, and when Ezra comes, Jonathan works him through it with determined care until he hits the edge of overstimulation and comes out the other side into another breathless peak. He looks up then, face wet and eyes wide, and Ezra doesn't stop, doesn't think, just reaches down and hauls him up for a frantic kiss.

"Ezra," Jonathan says against his mouth, tight and rasping. He's shaking. "Tell me—"

Ezra slips a hand between their bodies, and Jonathan drops his forehead to Ezra's shoulders with a whine. "Can we," Ezra says, floating on a haze of pleasure but still not sure how to *ask,* and Jonathan picks his head back up and presses their mouths together in messy, uncoordinated consent.

They never turned on the lights in the room, and they agree, by some kind of silent communication, not to change that now. Jonathan uses the flashlight on his phone to check the expiration date on the condoms in his nightstand drawer instead of turning on the lamp, and the cloudy moonlight coming in through the windows is all the light they have. It's enough, painting the room in silver blue, and Ezra finds himself unable to look away from Jonathan's face as he slips back between his legs, taking a shaky breath and running his fingertips over Ezra's hip bone.

He meets Ezra's eyes, his own wide in the dark room. Ezra reaches up and thumbs over his cheekbone, and Jonathan's face softens as he turns and kisses the heel of Ezra's palm.

The sound of the rain seems to pause when they come together, like the storm itself is holding its breath around them. It's a long, slow press, and Ezra closes his eyes at the warmth of it, aware of every tremor in his muscles, every one of Jonathan's ragged breaths, every place where their bodies are connected. Jonathan stills when their hips meet, and his forehead comes down to the crook of Ezra's neck, and he's shaking as badly as Ezra is.

"Ezra," he says, and there's something vulnerable and almost wondering in his voice.

I love how he says my name, Ezra thinks, wild and terrified, and he's already tilting his head when Jonathan bends to press a kiss to Ezra's throat, like he's trying to keep himself steady. Ezra wraps his arms around his shoulders and buries his face into the side of his neck.

He can feel Jonathan's pulse under his mouth, pounding almost as hard as the rain against the window. But there's a stillness inside him, like he's in the eye of a hurricane, tucked into a tiny space of calm while a maelstrom rages around him. "Please."

It's slow. Slow and deep and intense, and so much sensation Ezra thinks he could drown in it. He listens to the rain and the wind and the sounds of the room around him, skin on skin and heavy breathing and wordless pleas that he can't be sure are Jonathan's or his own. Sensation builds inside him, not like a tightening coil but like a wave, and when it crests at last he lets it carry him out to sea. He holds on, and when the roaring in his ears resolves itself into words, Jonathan's voice repeating his name in a litany that's nearly a prayer, he says, "Please, you can, please," and feels it in his bones as Jonathan shakes apart.

Afterward, curled together in the messy blankets, sweat still drying on their skin, Jonathan says, quiet and uncertain, "I've never done that before."

That makes sense, if Ben was Jonathan's first—only—everything. On the other hand, Ezra still can't totally feel his toes. "Beginner's luck, maybe."

Jonathan gives one of those soft, self-deprecating laughs that Ezra's slowly starting to get used to and tell the difference between. This is the one that comes when he's proud of himself but doesn't want to say it, because someone must have taught him not to sound anything other than humble, even when he should. "You're okay?"

Ezra hums an affirmation, a little afraid of what he'll say if he talks. Jonathan kisses the back of his shoulder, shifting to hold him closer. Ezra laces their fingers together.

He still feels stretched open and raw, and not just physically. But mostly, he just feels *good,* and it's such an unfamiliar feeling he wants to bask in it for a little while longer.

"God, it's really storming out there," Jonathan says, and Ezra has to blink a few times, rousing himself from the half doze he hadn't realized he'd slipped into, caught up in the warmth and comfort of Jonathan's bed and Jonathan's body. He picks his head up off Jonathan's arm in time to catch a flash of lightning outside the window. "Do you think—"

Thunder crashes above them, close enough to nearly rattle the walls. Ezra lets out a strangled yelp of surprise and is saved from absolute mortification by the fact that the startled sound Jonathan makes is even louder and probably half an octave higher.

There's an answering high yowl from the living room, and then the frantic patter of paws on hardwood as Sappho sprints into the room and leaps onto the bed, attempting to burrow between them. "Oh my God, no," Ezra groans, trying to push her off, but Jonathan laughs, shifting to scoop her up, all fifty-odd wriggling pounds of her, and depositing her on Ezra's other side on top of the sheets. She accepts this with only marginal squirming and promptly presses herself against his chest, and Ezra shakes his head in exasperated amusement, scratching her ears. At least she's outside the bedding. "So much for the afterglow."

Jonathan chuckles and lies back down, spooning up behind Ezra again. He reaches past Ezra's shoulder to stroke Sappho's head. She snuffles and leans into the touch. "I don't know," he says, and Ezra doesn't need to see him to hear his smile. "I think it's still okay."

His voice is soft, warm, tinged with sleepy affection. Ezra thinks, *You are the best worst decision I've ever made.*

Before he can talk himself out of it, he says, "Can I ask you something?"

Jonathan hums into his shoulder.

"My family does a fire for Lag BaOmer every year. And it's going to be— I don't know. But I was wondering—" God. Why is this so *hard*? "You don't have to, if you're busy, I know it's short notice, but—"

"Ezra," Jonathan interrupts, and Ezra stops talking with a grateful huff. "If you're asking me to come with you, my answer is yes."

"Oh," Ezra says. He feels relieved, and then embarrassed

about feeling relieved, and presses his face into Sappho's so he doesn't have to think about that more than he has to.

"Oh," Jonathan echoes, teasing but fond. He kisses the nape of Ezra's neck. "I demand multiple s'mores."

"Marshmallows might be kosher," Ezra warns into Sappho's fur. "I keep losing the fight on getting normal ones."

"Ugh. You're lucky you're cute," Jonathan says, and the warmth of his voice soaks into Ezra's soul, holding him buoyant and safe as he drops into the sweet emptiness of sleep, the rain a distant echo that follows him down, and down, and down.

26

Growing up, Ezra was taught that Lag BaOmer was meant to be a break in mourning, the one day in the seven weeks between Passover and Shavuot that people could get married and shave and probably a hundred other little things that Ezra never paid attention to.

What he did pay attention to was the part where every year, Dad and Uncle Joe built a fire in the connecting yard between the house and the Chapel, and even if it was a school night when they weren't usually allowed to have dessert, he got to have as many marshmallows as he wanted.

It's the little things, Ezra thinks, as he and Jonathan make their way up the driveway, that stick with you.

Dad and Aaron already have a robust fire going when Ezra and Jonathan show up. To Ezra's relief, they seem to have agreed to take it easy on them. Aaron teases Jonathan about cradle robbing and Dad makes a few playful remarks about keeping things PG-rated any time they're in the Chapel, because scandalizing someone into a heart attack probably won't be good for business unless they managed to scoop up the client. It's so close to a return to his old dark humor that Ezra lets it go without comment, even if Jonathan flushes red. The fire crackles cheerfully in the iron pit, and they sit around it in the lawn chairs Aaron pulled out of storage, while Dad pours them mugs from a large thermos of hot spiked lemonade, Zayde's own recipe of bourbon and lemon and honey.

It's warm and tart and tastes like old memories and rare bursts of sweet affection, and Ezra catches Jonathan smiling down at his cup, like he's tasting the same. He digs around in the milk crate by the thermos and makes Jonathan a s'more like he promised. The marshmallows are, in fact, kosher, and therefore taste like they've been freeze-dried, but Jonathan eats it anyway and lets Ezra kiss the sticky remnants off his lips.

Aaron throws a twig at them. "Hey," he says. "What did we just say about PDA?"

Ezra sticks his tongue out at him but goes back to his own chair, even if he does scoot it a little closer to Jonathan's. He'd gone back and forth about whether to bring Sappho with him and decided against it, just in case things go badly tonight— she hates raised voices, and the last thing he wants is to have her barking added to any potential yelling. He almost feels naked without her at his side, his hand constantly dropping down to scratch her ears before he remembers she's not there. "You guys did a good job," he says, nodding toward the fire. "It usually takes until later for it to get up this high."

"It only usually takes longer because we have to build in an hour of debating structure before we even get started," Dad says dryly. "For some reason, your brother didn't seem like he wanted to argue this year."

Aaron blinks back a look that would be all innocence if not for the marshmallows puffing out his cheeks.

Dad gives him an amused look that suggests he's not fooled.

He seems better, Ezra thinks, studying him. "Dad?" His father, reaching for the thermos on the ground to refill his mug, cocks a questioning brow. "Thank you. For doing this tonight. I know it's been hard, the last few weeks, and this—this is nice."

Dad replaces the cap on the thermos and sets it down, leaning back with his mug. He looks into the flames for a long moment, the firelight illuminating each line in his face, making him look older and more tired. "You know," he begins, "your zayde—" He pauses, glancing at Jonathan. "My father," he adds by way of explanation, and Jonathan nods. "He had a complicated relationship with his faith. But he liked this holiday. He liked the symbolism of it. He spent so much of his life either grieving or helping other people grieve, and this was the night that he could just look into the fire and . . . Well. I like to think that he used it to just take a mental rest for a little while, but who knows what he was thinking."

Aaron, watching him with thoughtful eyes, sends a tight-lipped look Ezra's way. Ezra shakes his head, a minute motion he hopes Dad doesn't catch.

Not yet. A little peace and quiet, a little while longer.

"Anyway," Dad says, giving himself a bit of a shake, as if rousing himself from a dream. "That's what I wanted tonight. A bit of normal in the middle of—well."

Well, indeed.

They're spared from having to break the silence when Becca emerges from the back door of the house, a tote bag over her shoulder. "Sorry I'm late," she says, crossing the yard. Like the rest of them, she's dressed for a cold spring evening, in jeans and boots and an oversize sweater. "Did I miss anything fun?"

"First round of drinks and Jonathan and Ezra being gross about marshmallows," Aaron says immediately. "What's in the bag?"

"Therapy," she says brightly and with no other explanation, plopping down in the empty chair between Ezra and

Aaron and making grabby hands toward the thermos. Ezra does some mental math and figures they're about half a cup away from breaking out the second thermos, and sure enough, Dad empties the first into the mug he pours for Becca, then tops it off from the second one when she looks at him with wide, hopeful eyes.

"Pace yourself," he says dryly as he passes it over.

"I am an *adult*," Becca says, sniffing, and earns one of Dad's rare chuckles. She pulls her legs up onto her chair and wiggles her fingers at Jonathan in a wave. "Hi. Is Ezra being nice to you?"

"Hey," Ezra protests, but Jonathan leans around Ezra's chair to grin at her.

"Just between us, I'm in it for the dog."

"I am *right here*," Ezra complains. Jonathan laughs, dropping a kiss to his cheek as he sits back. The easy affection makes Ezra flush, and he hopes the fire isn't quite bright enough to tell on him.

The sky tonight is dazzling, last night's storm washing away the fog and cloud cover that had hidden the stars from view for most of the past week. Ezra tilts his head back and lets himself look, catching familiar patterns but mostly just enjoying the sight as the quiet conversation around him fades to a background murmur, like the crackle of the burning wood. The heat coming off the fire keeps him from shivering, and Jonathan's fingers, laced through his, are cold at the tips but warm everywhere else. His eyes sting when the wind blows, but even that is a clean, piney sort of smell that reminds him of summer camping trips to Burlingame.

Jonathan squeezes his hand. "Not so bad," he teases, and Ezra wrinkles his nose at him.

"Famous last words," he mutters back, just as Becca finishes her mug.

"So," she says with forced cheer and exaggerated eyebrows. "Are we going to do this thing, or what?"

On the other side of the fire, Dad raises his eyebrows. "Are there plans I don't know about?"

Becca gives Ezra an expectant look. He sighs and drops Jonathan's hand. Jonathan cocks his head, puzzled, but lets him go without protest. "Kind of," he admits.

Dad's brow furrows slightly, and he glances at Aaron, who spreads his hands.

"It's a family thing."

"I see," Dad says. Wariness flickers in his eyes. "Should I be expecting your mother to pop out from behind the house after all?"

"Yeah," Becca drawls. "Because that's what we need."

Privately, Ezra had been holding out a hope that she *would* decide to show up and take a bit of responsibility, but apparently, it's not his night. "All right," he says, already feeling the ease of the night slip away. "So—here's the thing."

Dad, to his credit, listens without interrupting. Aaron holds up his end of the deal and does as much of the talking as Ezra does. They tell him about the off-book accounts, about everything they'd been able to figure out so far, about how long Mom had been padding their income and covering her tracks. Dad's expression is utterly blank, but Ezra feels horrible all the same, especially when he has to be the one to tell him what Mom said about Zayde. He tries to soften it as much as he can, to make it less about decades of financial distrust and more about the way Dad would prefer to help than to profit, but that doesn't change the fact that she hid it because she didn't trust him to keep them afloat any more than Zayde had.

"We just thought you deserved to know," Aaron says, when they run out of information and platitudes both and Dad still hasn't reacted beyond a few occasional twitches of his eyebrows. "And it's— Look, the financials are rough, I know we've only been scraping by, even with the extra money, but we've been looking at the numbers and I think we can find a few more places to trim so that we can get ahead of it a bit more. We probably can't fix it right away, but—"

"Aaron," Dad interrupts, and Aaron looks almost grateful to be able to stop talking, draining the rest of his drink and casting a longing look at the thermos by Dad's chair. "It's okay."

"Mom has been hiding money from you to the tune of *multiple hundreds of thousands of dollars,*" Becca says flatly. "In what universe is this okay?"

Dad presses his mouth into a thin line, and the puzzle pieces click together in Ezra's head.

"You already knew," he says. Dad doesn't answer, and a huff of disbelieving laughter bubbles out of Ezra's chest. "Didn't you?"

"Yes," Dad says.

One word, no elaboration. Aaron drops his head into his hands, rubbing his eyes, but Becca just gapes.

"Are you kidding me?"

"Becca," Aaron says, lowering his hands, but she's already on her feet.

"No, shut up," she says. "How long have you known? Did you know she was cheating on you, too?"

Dad blanches. "No. Of course not."

"Oh, *of course not,* he says, like we should all just be fine with the financial deception, but the secret affair is too far—"

"*Becca,*" Aaron says again, sharper now, and she whirls on him.

"What? Are you just okay with this?"

Aaron rubs his forehead. "No I'm not *okay* with this, but—"

"I only knew about the accounts because I got a copy of Zayde's will," Dad says. "He wasn't quiet about what he thought of the way I ran the business. But he knew he'd have to leave the Chapel to me if he wanted to keep it in the family. He always said marrying your mother was the best business decision I ever made."

"Oh my God," Becca says faintly. "It's no wonder none of us can fucking communicate, no one in this family can go more than a day without lying about shit!"

Ezra flinches. Jonathan's hand shifts from his back to his shoulder, like he's trying to ground him, but Ezra can't take his eyes off Becca. He doesn't like how close she's getting to the fire. "Becca," he warns. "Take a breath, okay?"

She snaps her head around to him so fast he sucks in a breath at how close the swirl of her hair gets to the flames. "Don't patronize me. You're as bad as he is!"

"I'm not saying I'm not," he says, dislodging Jonathan's hand as he gets to his feet. Behind her, Aaron eases himself up at the same time, though neither of them moves toward her. "I just really don't want you to set your hair on fire."

"Of course," she says sarcastically, but she does yank her hair over her shoulder, twisting it into a braid in sharp, jerky movements. "Because God forbid you deal with your own shit burning down before you start trying to handle someone else's, right?" Her eyes snap to Jonathan, and Ezra has half a heartbeat to think *Oh, please don't* before she's crossing her arms over her chest. "Have you even told him about Ben?"

Ezra closes his eyes.

Jonathan, very quietly, very uncertainly, says, "What?"

Heart in his throat, Ezra forces himself to turn toward him. "I—"

A twig snaps in the fire, gunshot-loud.

"Okay," Dad says. "I think we should all just—"

"Do fucking *not*," Becca snaps. She picks up the tote bag she'd brought out of the house with her—she never showed them what was in it, Ezra realizes—and starts toward the back door.

Dad gets up, as if moving to stop her.

Aaron catches his arm, shaking his head. "Let her go. She needs to cool off." His shoulders are a tight, set line, his grip hard on Dad's sleeve. "And you're right, we're not done here."

Ezra watches the play of emotions across Dad's face, all of them tense and none of them decipherable, but he gives a tight nod.

"Ezra," Jonathan says.

Fuck. Ezra digs his nails into his palms so hard he can feel the threat of broken skin. "Yeah," he says hoarsely.

Even when they were strangers, Jonathan never looked at Ezra like this. "What was she talking about? What about Ben?"

"I can't . . ." Everything from Ezra's rib cage to his throat is tight and hot, which doesn't make sense when the fingers closing around his heart feel so icy. "I was going to tell you, I just— I didn't know how to say it so you'd believe me."

"Believe you about *what*?" Jonathan's voice cracks on something almost like a plea, like he'd do anything for them to be having any conversation other than this one, and God but Ezra feels that in his bones so badly he could cry. "You're not telling me anything, you're just freaking me out."

"I know," Ezra says desperately. "I know, and I'm sorry, and I can explain, I swear I can—" He can't, but fuck, he can at least *try*. "I just need you to—"

Something red and orange catches his eye, and he breaks off, turning on instinct toward the house, half a heartbeat too slowly.

Ezra doesn't realize until Jonathan's grabbing his arm and yanking him against him that the crash ringing in his ears was the sound of breaking glass, the kitchen windows shattering, burst from the inside with a roar of too-bright flame.

27

The next hour happens like the hazy rush of a dream, vivid and impossible to touch.

Ezra feels all of it like he's watching through molasses. Jonathan's arms lock around him like a vise, and he realizes, distantly, that it's because he's trying with every fiber of his body to wrench free and run directly into the burning house. His head fills with the sound of screaming, and it takes him too long to realize that it's *his* screaming, Becca's name on repeat.

There are sirens, and people in turnout gear pushing him back. He can't see Dad or Aaron, doesn't know if he wants one of them to have run inside where he couldn't or if he needs them safe out here in the yard. Jonathan keeps trying to stand between him and the fire, using his height as an advantage, as if blocking what he can from Ezra's sight will somehow make everything okay.

Someone shouts, and Ezra gives one last wrenching jerk of his body and manages to break free of Jonathan's grasp just as the back door opens and someone sooty and staggering stumbles free. Ezra's moving before he can comprehend it, ignoring the first responders who yell at him to stop and catching Becca as she falls, her hands scrambling at his clothes and his arms and his face, coughing and crying and choking out his name. He crumples to the damp grass with her, holding her against his chest like he can press his own breath into her rasping throat. She's here and she's conscious, *alive, alive, alive,* and Ezra wants to scream and cry and pray all at once.

They live two streets from a firehouse—one of the neighbors must have called 911. It can't have been more than six minutes.

An eternity.

She refuses to let go of his hand, so he rides in the ambulance with her, stroking her hair back and murmuring soothing nonsense as the paramedics press an oxygen mask over her face and shine a penlight in her eyes. They're talking around and over each other, asking questions and noting down numbers, but all Ezra can see are Becca's glassy, frightened eyes.

"It's okay," he tells her, over and over again, until her grip on his hand slowly loosens from bone-crushing to frantic. "It's going to be okay."

The story comes out in pieces. She'd gone inside, had decided, on a whim, to take advantage of the empty kitchen to have a sacrificial bonfire of her own. Had piled the contents of her tote bag—family mementos and photos of her and Mom and a cluster of other knickknacks—into the sink, not noticing when her elbow knocked into the loose stovetop knob, the one that Dad's been meaning to have fixed, the one that turns the gas on if someone so much as looks at it the wrong way, the too-old gas lines decades behind modern safety standards. Becca had been too caught up to notice the smell of gas, her nose soaked with the scent of the vodka she'd grabbed from the freezer and poured over the contents of the sink.

All it took was the spark of the match.

"Am I in trouble?" she says, voice thick and half muffled by the mask.

"No," Ezra says immediately. He smooths the hair that's escaped from her braid back from her forehead. It's burnt at the ends—she's probably lost a good few inches. Better her hair, he thinks, than the rest of her.

He doesn't want to think about how lucky she is to be as unscathed as she is, the initial combustion knocking her off her feet and into a cabinet but not catching her in the sudden burst of flame. She looks so young, his baby sister, so scared and hurt, and he feels like a monster, for missing this much of her pain.

"Someone was looking out for you, kiddo," one of the paramedics says, checking her oxygen monitor and shaking her head.

The air in that house has always been thick with ghosts. Ezra drops his forehead to Becca's and swallows down a prayer of thanks.

Ezra's allowed to follow her back into the emergency department, but not to go with her when she's taken for a scan to make sure her disorientation and nausea aren't signs of a harder hit to her head than the one she remembers. He slumps back into the chair next to the empty bed, pushing his head into his hands and trying—failing—to get his breathing under control. A peek at his phone shows so many notifications that his heart rate ticks up again, and he shoves it back into his pocket, then pulls it out again when it starts to ring.

"We're in the waiting room," Aaron says without preamble when Ezra picks up. "Can you tell us anything?"

"I'll come out there," Ezra says, and hauls himself to his feet.

He lets the charge nurse know where he's going—she gives him a sympathetic smile and promises to send someone out for him when Becca's back in her room—and follows the signs out to the waiting room.

It's a weeknight, and not too badly crowded. Ezra scans the room, barely seeing the other people in it—an exhausted-looking young woman holding a miserably crying toddler in her lap, her hand pressed to his forehead; a group of what look like college students clustered around a girl with her ankle propped up on a chair; an older couple reading magazines with no indication as to why they're there; a middle-aged man and his irritated-looking wife holding a wad of sluggishly reddening paper towels to the man's head. Someone calls his name, and Ezra forces his body to turn until his eyes land on Aaron, standing at the edge of a clearly rearranged huddle of chairs and waving him over, and Ezra rolls his shoulders to steady himself before making his way down the stairs toward him.

He'd expected Aaron and Dad, but not Jonathan, whose face blooms into visible relief when Ezra approaches, his eyes searching Ezra's face as if to make sure he's all in one piece, like Ezra's the one who wasn't safe. Someone must have called Mom, too, because she's in the uncomfortable-looking chair next to Dad, pale-faced and clearly anxious. Judy sits in the chair between her and Jonathan, one hand holding Jonathan's and the other on the arm of Mom's chair, not touching her, just hovering close. Dad, his face a mirror of Mom's wide-eyed worry, seems to be mostly ignoring Judy. To Ezra's surprise, he and Mom are holding hands, their fingers laced together in a white-knuckle grip.

"She's okay," Ezra says when he's close enough to talk without raising his voice, praying that Mom reins in the impulse to get up and hug him. If someone touches him right now, he thinks he might scream. "They think she might have a concussion, but she's pretty sure she didn't lose consciousness. They just took her back to do some scans on her head to make sure there isn't anything they might have missed in the screening they did in the ambulance. She lost a few inches of hair from the fire and she's got a few burns, but—" His voice catches in his throat. He swallows what feels like a razor blade. "She's okay," he repeats.

Maybe if he says it enough, he'll believe it.

Dad drops his head into one hand, not letting go of Mom's. "Thank God," he says, and Mom curls herself over him in a hug, shoulders shaking. He puts his arm around her, and Ezra thinks, a little distantly, that this might be the first time he's seen them embrace like that in months. Maybe in years.

"Ezra," Jonathan says quietly. "Are *you* okay?"

Ezra blinks at him, trying to process the question. "I'm fine," he says. "I never got near the fire." A thought occurs to him, and he startles, his blood running cold. "Wait, fuck— how bad was—"

Jonathan's on his feet before the words make it all the way out of his mouth, taking him by the arm. "It's fine," Jonathan says, low and soothing, and something feral and frantic in Ezra's chest rears back at the sound. "It's okay, the fire's out, your dad called someone to stay and keep an eye on everything, just—"

"Did she say anything?" Mom asks.

Ezra tears his eyes away from Jonathan's, almost grateful for the excuse to look away from that earnest face, filled with concern Ezra doesn't deserve. "What?"

Untangling herself from Dad and wiping at her cheeks, Mom looks up at him from her chair. "Becca," she says. "Did she say what happened? How it started? Was she—" She casts an anxious look at Dad and then lifts her chin back to Ezra, eyes red-rimmed, almost gray within the sclera. Ezra wonders how long she's been crying, to look that drained. "Was she try-ing to hurt herself?"

"Of course she wasn't," Aaron says, horror in his voice. "What the fuck, Mom. What kind of question is that?"

"I don't *know*!" Mom swipes her hands over her eyes again,

then pulls her cardigan tight around her. "She's been so angry, and I haven't known how to talk to her about any of this. I don't know if she's— Has she been like that at home?"

"Wait," Ezra says. Alarm bells start to ring in the back of his head. "You've been talking to her?"

Mom shakes her head. "I've been trying," she says. "She won't answer my calls, but she's been texting me, and she's left a few voicemails. She never picks up when I try to call her back."

"Why wouldn't you tell me that?" It comes out angrier than Ezra wants it to. "I could have talked to her."

"That's not your job," Mom says, but something sparks in her eyes, uncertainty, maybe, or regret, and the words are so absurd that Ezra can't do anything but laugh, high and hysterical and loud enough that a few people look their way.

"Since *when*?"

Ezra has spent his entire life being the secret keeper, the confidant, the listener. He knows every wound, every unhealed scar, every place where salt water will sting. He's always thought that love is knowing all the best ways to hurt someone and never, ever exploiting them.

Maybe he's not a loving person after all.

"This has *always* been my job," he says, and it bursts out of him like the spill of viscera from a gut wound. God, how did he never realize how *furious* he was? He jabs a finger at his parents, who are no longer holding hands. "You two were so tied up in your own drama, in pretending everything was fine and making it look good to everyone else, as if people drowning in their own grief would ever *give* a shit about whether your kids looked cute or your marriage was healthy, and what, I'm supposed to believe that you just suddenly tried to start parenting like—like—"

It's so, so hard not to cry. He feels too hot, heat filling him up like a forest fire, like his body is a blaze of light in a vessel already lined with fractures, waiting for a single iota of pressure to send him scattering through the universe. Crying would make this emotional, would take away the truth of what he's saying, would take everything he's bottled up and tucked away and make excuses for it, just like they always have.

Jonathan's hands are firm on his shoulders. Keeping him in one piece.

He wants, more than anything, to be the one who gets to fall apart.

"That isn't fair," Mom says. She's on her feet, caught halfway between Dad and Judy, like she doesn't know who to lean on. "None of that is fair, Ezra, you—you're talking like we neglected you."

Ezra folds his arms over his chest, a mirror of her posture, each of them hugging their own torso like that's the embrace that would help. "I didn't say that. You're not listening."

"We're listening," Dad says. His tone is careful, like Ezra's, a spark waiting to go up in flames, and he doesn't want to fan them. "But I'm not sure what you want us to say."

Ezra wants to see the wreckage of his own feelings reflected back at him. To know he's not the only broken person here.

"Aaron," Mom says, turning to look at him, and Ezra forces himself to do the same. Aaron is as tense as the rest of them, but he looks torn, eyes flashing back and forth between Ezra and their parents. "Is that how you feel, too? Like you couldn't talk to us?"

Aaron opens his mouth. Hesitates. Ezra knows that look. That fear of being the disappointment, of letting them down.

"It's okay," Ezra says. He hopes he sounds like he means it. He thinks that he does. "No one's pissed at *you*."

Aaron's mouth twists. "You sure about that?"

"Ex*cuse* me."

An unfamiliar voice cuts through them like a shock of cold water after a hot bath. Ezra catches his breath and turns to look at the scowling nurse standing a few feet away, her face dark as a thundercloud.

"This is a *hospital,*" she says, low and furious, and Ezra becomes suddenly, nauseatingly aware of the people staring at them, the waiting room filled with that anxious, uncomfortable silence of people watching a spectacle of embarrassment with nowhere to go and nowhere else to look. The anger flooding his veins washes away, replaced with something sick and shameful, and he swallows hard.

"I'm sorry," he says, because no one else seems willing to talk. "It's—it's been a long night."

She looks at him with the absolute lack of pity of someone who has probably been on her feet for twelve hours straight and is having a much longer night than his. "Keep your voices down," she says. "Or I will call security and have you all escorted out."

He nods, looking down at the scuffed floor. He feels like a scolded child. The adrenaline flush has faded, leaving behind a shaky shiver of goose bumps over his skin.

The low murmur of voices begins to swell again around them, people returning to their own quiet conversations, their own little hurts and worries.

Aaron breaks first. "Fuck this," he announces. "I'm going for a walk."

He turns on his heel and stalks off in the direction of the hospital cafeteria, his shoulders stiff and his arms tight at his sides. Mom sits down heavily next to Judy, who hasn't said a word but looks shell-shocked as she draws Mom into a tight hug, carefully not meeting anyone else's eyes.

"Ezra," Jonathan says.

His hands slip off Ezra's shoulders, and with them, the weight holding Ezra inside himself, stuck in this moment of space and time, disappears. The world drops away like an exhaled breath.

"Ezra," Jonathan says again, but it sounds far away now.

"No," Ezra hears himself say, and starts to walk.

"Ezra—Ezra, God, will you *wait*?"

Fingers close around his upper arm and drag him back to reality, and Ezra stops walking abruptly, not quite sure if it's the shock of reorientation or some instinctive decision not to try to haul Jonathan bodily down the hospital halls with him. Ezra doesn't know how long he's been walking, whether it's been five minutes or twenty. The hallway around him is unfamiliar. He pulls against Jonathan's grip, half-hearted, just to see if he'll let go.

He doesn't, taking Ezra's other shoulder and turning him to look at him instead. "Hey," he says, and his eyes are wide, big and soft and concerned, and Ezra thinks he might have another breakdown if he's looked at like that for another second, so he jerks away. This time, Jonathan lets him go, but he stays close, his face unrelenting despite the hurt that flashes over his features. "Why are you running away from me?"

"I'm not," Ezra snaps. "This isn't about you."

"Okay." Jonathan absolutely doesn't believe him. He takes a single step back, as if to give Ezra room to breathe, and despite how much Ezra wants to cut and run, something in him wants nothing more than to bring him close again, to crawl into the circle of his arms where it's quiet and safe, no hurt sisters or loyalty-torn brothers or disappointed parents. "Are you . . . No. Okay. Dumb question. Of course you're not okay. Can I do something? What can I do?"

Ezra stares at him.

"Ezra," Jonathan pleads. "Let me help."

He says it like he's offering a blessing. Like Ezra's a body under his hands, to be cleaned and wrapped into the silent safety of a simple pine box.

"Why are you *here*?"

The words echo like a whipcrack through the hallway. It takes a beat for Ezra to realize that they came from him. "Is it because of what Becca said? About me and Ben?"

"No," Jonathan says, but he tenses. "I—I don't know what she was talking about, but you said you'd tell me when you're ready, and I'm not going to be the person who pushes you right now. This isn't the time to— Your sister could have *died*, Ezra, I'm not—"

"She could have," Ezra says. "Your husband *did*." Jonathan flinches, and Ezra thinks, with miserable surety, *See? I told you, I told you.* "Do you think I asked about him just because I wanted to know? He has been literally *haunting* me, ever since I moved into your house and had his ghost crawling all over my floors."

Jonathan stares at him, jaw open. Ezra doesn't think he's ever shocked him before, but the victory is hollow. "That's . . . that's not possible."

"Isn't it?"

Stop talking, something says in his mind. *Stop talking.*

He doesn't stop. "I know the secret he was keeping from you when he died," he says. Jonathan makes an aborted move, like he's going to reach out for him again, and Ezra strikes out, poison and fang. "I know he was spending half his time at the Chapel because you two barely talked anymore, and he was afraid to talk to you whenever he was actually around because he thought he was going to slip up." The color is slowly draining from Jonathan's face. Ezra keeps going. "I know he knew about my mom and his and he was lying to you because he thought you'd leave him if you knew they weren't perfect. I know he hated the tea you made him when he couldn't sleep. I know it was driving you crazy that you didn't know why he was spiraling and it still drives you crazy that you never found out. I know he's so worried about you ruining your life over him that he can't stop watching you to make sure you don't. So what is it? What's your endgame? I'm not him, Jonathan. Fixing me isn't going to make you feel better about what happened to him."

If he were a better person, Ezra knows, the guilt would flood through him now. He'd apologize. Say he didn't mean any of it. Say he's just lashing out because it's so much easier than letting Jonathan any closer than he's already gotten, letting him see all the cracks in Ezra's armor where the slightest extra pressure will shatter him for good.

Jonathan says, hoarse, "Ezra," and then stops. Like he doesn't know what to say next. Like he doesn't know if there's anything worth saying at all.

Ezra forces out, "I can't," and then, so robotic the voice doesn't even feel like his own, "I'm sorry."

He pushes past him. He doesn't know where he's going. Just anywhere other than here. Just *away*.

A desperate, hopeful piece of him waits to hear if Jonathan will come after him again.

There's nothing. Jonathan lets him go.

28

"Are you sure you're okay, honey?"

In an act of altruism Ezra absolutely doesn't deserve, the nurse he'd passed on his way out of the emergency department tracks him down and gives him directions to the wing where Becca's been transferred. She steers him back toward the inpatient rooms, clearly able to tell from a glance that he won't comprehend more than three turns' worth of navigation, and when she leaves him at the right wing she takes another moment to study him.

It's the second time someone's asked him that tonight, and he still doesn't understand why. He's not the one who almost got blown up in a fire or had his wife show up to the ER with her new girlfriend or had his maybe-boyfriend drop a psychic bomb in his lap about his dead husband.

"I'm fine," he says. "Thanks, though."

She eyes him for another moment, and then leaves him with an almost maternal pat on the back that makes his eyes sting. He's halfway down the hall before he realizes that he didn't even ask her name to thank her.

One more thing to apologize for. Add it to the pile.

Becca's scans come back clear of any swelling or bleeding, but between her ongoing dizziness and her blood alcohol level turning out to be just under the legal limit, the hospital admits her anyway. No one seems frantic or overly panicked here, and while the nurses and staff seem to be moving briskly, the calm eases some of his lingering anxiety. He asks after Becca at the desk, and the charge nurse checks his ID and pulls up a file on her computer, then points him down the hall. "Room 302," she says. "I'll send her room nurse in to give you an update."

"Thank you," he says, and she gives him a kind smile as she hands his license back. "Is there somewhere I can wash my hands before I go in?"

"Bathroom around the corner," she says, pointing. "And hand sanitizer outside each room."

He thanks her again and ducks into the single-use restroom, washing his face and hands and trying to push his hair into some semblance of order so that he'll look like an actual adult when he talks to whatever doctor or nurse comes into the room, then washes his hands again for good measure. When he studies his reflection in the mirror, he looks remarkably calm, tired and maybe a little red around the eyes, but not in crisis. "Okay," he tells his reflection. He takes a few deep breaths and runs through a few stretches, taking advantage of the privacy of the room—he's been wearing his binder for close to eighteen hours now and he probably *should* take it off, but the idea of walking around without it in a public place makes him feel sick to his stomach—and then, rolling his shoulders one more time, he unlocks the door and counts numbers until he reaches Becca's room.

She's asleep when he slips inside, the lights on their dimmer switch turned down to something soft and soothing. There's a clear IV running down to her hand where it rests on the blanket, a monitor clipped to the forefinger of the same hand, a nasal cannula still feeding her oxygen, probably a precaution against the smoke she inhaled. Someone has washed her face and braided her hair back, the ends a bit uneven where the burnt strands were cut away. She'll want to wash it as soon as she's discharged, maybe even before that, if she's allowed to shower. He wonders if he can ask a nurse for some shampoo that smells like something other than bland hospital soap.

No one else is in the room. Trying not to think about why, Ezra picks up one of the chairs tucked against the wall and carries it to the bed, setting it down as quietly as he can manage. Carefully, he reaches out to take her unwired hand. It feels small in his, her fingers long and slim. Pianist fingers, if she'd stuck with the lessons she'd started when she was six and abandoned the same year. Ezra doesn't really like his own hands—his fingers are short, and he always feels like they give him away to anyone looking to clock him. But they're good at what they do, his hands. He can adjust the angles of someone's hip or shoulder as they move through a vinyasa, can ease someone into an easier laboring position, can—now, after weeks of Jonathan's careful tutelage renewing Ezra's atrophied skills—wash someone clean of all they should leave behind.

He shifts his grip, just slightly, so that the tips of his fingers rest against the pulse at the base of her palm. It's strong and steady, each thump of her heart a balm against the lump in his throat.

"I'm awake, you know," Becca mumbles.

Ezra startles out of his chair. "Jesus, Becks," he says. "You scared me."

She blinks slowly at him, her eyes taking a moment to adjust in the dim room. "I'm sorry."

Her voice is small and uncertain enough that he's willing to bet she isn't just talking about being unexpectedly awake. "Hey, no, it's okay." He smooths a hand over her hair. "No one's mad at you."

She makes a little scoffing sound, skeptical. "Okay."

"For a given value of *okay*," Ezra clarifies. Becca laughs, tiny and wet. "Do you remember coming up here?"

Becca nods, then goes a shade paler at the motion. "They said I have a concussion so they want to keep me overnight." The nurse had told him that when she sent him up here, but he's glad to hear that someone told her, too, and that she was able to retain it. "And that I could sleep if I wanted to but someone would come wake me up every few hours."

"All right." Ezra waits. When it's clear she's not planning to go on, and the silence has drawn out long enough to thicken the air, he says, carefully, gently, "Becca."

She flushes, looking down at the blanket, fingers fidgeting against the weave. "I maybe drank a lot of the vodka before I poured it on Mom's stuff," she admits. "I wasn't trying to—"

"I believe you," he says, and is a little surprised, even as he says it, to find that it's true. She wouldn't lie about that. Not to him. She loves him too much for that. "You could tell me, though."

"I know."

"And I'd listen."

"I know that, too." She's quiet for a moment, her fingers tapping against his. "They told me everyone was downstairs in the waiting room, but . . . I don't want to see them."

Ezra stills. "Do you want me to go?"

She tightens her grasp on his hand, clinging. "No! No. I told them I wanted you, just not . . ." She looks away. "Not everybody."

He runs his thumb over her knuckles until she stops looking like a frightened prey animal and her shoulders settle again. "It's probably a good thing," he says. "Things got a little heated. It's probably better for them to cool off."

Her eyes brighten. "Really?" she says, propping herself up on one elbow. "What—"

"Absolutely not," he says firmly, and puts a hand on her sternum to push her back down. "Not unless you want to tell me why you've been yelling at Mom and not talking to anyone about it."

"Ouch," she says, but consents to lie back, falling silent again.

When she speaks again, her voice is quiet, almost distant. "Do you remember when I got my first period?"

Ezra blinks. "Kind of hard to forget. You were under my bed when I got home from school."

Mom had picked Becca up early after getting a phone call from the nurse that she was absolutely inconsolable about the blood on her underwear, refusing to calm down or shower or accept any of the pads or spare clothes the school kept on hand. She'd given Becca a What to Expect When Your Uterus Is Suddenly an Actual Thing and Not Just a Concept pep talk on the ride home, and Becca promptly had another freak-out. When Ezra got home a few hours later, he found her firmly tucked against the back wall of his bedroom, as far under his bed as she could get.

"Not my best moment," Becca says.

"I don't think any of us have our best moments at twelve."

"I know I had that whole meltdown, but I wasn't really— It wasn't like I didn't know what was going on. Mom gave me that copy of *Our Bodies, Ourselves* when I was, like, nine, and we had that ridiculous puberty class at school, so it wasn't totally out of left field, but there was just"—she gives a breathy little sigh—"the book, and the class, and God, *Mom,* they all made it sound like it was going to just be this whole huge life-changing thing. Like, hey, you're a *woman* now! Anything you do with your body can have *consequences*! Mom literally made me call Grandma when I got home from school, which was fucking *mortifying,* like I was some kind of menstrual debutante."

Ezra winces. He'd been bullied into making that phone call, too, and is pretty sure he'd have found it horrifying even if he *wanted* to be a woman.

"Anyway." Becca fidgets with the wire clipped to her heart monitor. Gently, Ezra pulls her hand away from it. "Do you remember what you told me, when I was done crying like a baby on your floor?"

"Only vaguely," Ezra admits. His strongest memories of being a kid and a teenager are grounded in sensation, not in words: He remembers wedging himself uncomfortably under the bed with her, the dusty smell of the underside of the mattress and the press of the bed frame against his shoulder, how wide Becca's eyes had been in the dark and the clutch of her smaller fingers around his hand. How she'd reached for him, absolutely sure that he'd reach back. "Nothing that traumatized you more, I hope."

She smiles. "You told me that something happening inside my body didn't change anything about who I was," she says. "That my period didn't make me a woman, not just because I was twelve and no one should be calling me a woman, but because I got to decide what I wanted it to mean, not Mom or Grandma or whoever wrote the books about puberty. Just me."

"Huh." It's familiar. Not a clear memory, exactly, but it's the kind of thing he would have said, even at sixteen and barely ready to touch the writhing mass of his gender identity with anything more than tentative fingertips. "What made you think of that?"

"I guess . . ." Becca chews her lip, her fingers tapping again. More a heartbeat than a waltz—*one-two, one-two*.

"When I left those messages for Mom, or listened to the ones when she called me back," she says at last, "I kept thinking, *Ezra would never say the things that Mom's saying.* Because Mom loved us—*loves* us—but she and Dad, they didn't know how to talk to us like we were *people*. Like we weren't just miniature versions of them. And I knew you would never make me feel like it's my fault that you were anxious or stressed or not sure what to do. And, like, I know we joke about it, but there are some things where it's like—I've always come to you, and not Mom. And I have friends who have older sisters—"

She breaks off, wincing, and he gives her hand what he hopes is a reassuring squeeze. He knows the difference between misgendering and whatever Becca needs to get off her chest. She squeezes back and continues, hesitant. "It's not like I'm the only person I know who says that their big sister—big sibling—is more like their mom than their mom is sometimes. But it's just that there are these moments where I just . . . I think I was treating you like you were, for real. Because Mom and Dad made it so hard to talk to them, but you were always there. You never made me feel like I couldn't come to you. And you always made it seem like it was fine. But it wasn't, was it? You had all that stuff you were carrying around, not just me and Aaron and Mom and Dad, but you were literally *haunted*, Ezra, and—and after everything that happened with Mom, when you actually let us see how stressed and over- whelmed you were, I just— I didn't want to—"

Her voice cracks and she falters, blinking rapidly. Ezra's heart breaks in two. "Oh, no, no, no," he says, and, less careful of the wires than he should be, he pulls her into a hug, feels her bury her face into his shoulder. "No. Okay? No. You haven't done anything wrong and I would never *ever* resent you or get frustrated with you or—"

"But you *do*," she says, half muffled into his shirt, and he pulls back enough so he can hear her properly. "I can tell. You've been so burned-out, and you're— God, Ezra, you're trying to fix things for people who aren't even *alive* anymore! How can I *not* feel like an asshole for—"

She stops, and pales. For a moment he thinks she's pushed herself too hard with the concussion and she's going to be sick, and he's leaned halfway over to pick up the bedpan when she says, horrified, "Oh my God. Oh my God, *Jonathan*. Ezra, I'm *so sorry*."

"What?" He startles, and then the pieces click together. "Oh. Don't—don't worry about that."

"Of course I'm going to worry about it," she says. "I can't believe I said— Did you two break up? God, you were finally doing something that made you *happy*, I'm such an idiot. Did I ruin it?"

"You didn't ruin anything," he says immediately. He takes her hands in his, squeezing hard. "Okay? Hey. You have never ruined *anything* for me."

She sniffles, nodding, and Ezra breathes out, sitting back in his chair and loosening his grip on her hands. "Honestly," he says, feeling suddenly too exhausted to stand, "you were right about what you said. I was lying to him, and I shouldn't have been. If anyone ruined anything, it was me."

Becca looks heartbroken, fresh tears spilling down her face. Ezra clicks his tongue and reaches over to pull a tissue from the box on the rolling table by the bed, dabbing her cheeks until she wrinkles her nose and takes it from him to do it herself. "You were going to tell him," she says. "I know you were."

"Maybe," he says. "But I didn't. And as secrets to keep go"—he toys with a loose thread on her blanket, then forces himself to let go before he starts pulling on it enough to make it unravel—"I don't know. I owe him about ten times that many apologies now. I said some things that I shouldn't have, and—I didn't deserve someone like him to begin with. I definitely don't deserve him now."

"Ezra," Becca says, with a particular note of exasperation he recognizes from a hundred lectures from Ollie and Nina about his self-esteem, but something in the way he looks must stop her from launching into one because she doesn't say anything more than his name, just sighs and presses the heels of her palms briefly to her eyes like she's steeling herself. "Okay," she says, and then picks her head up, fixing him with a look that's so like Mom's *I am the parent, actually, so do not bullshit me* expression that Ezra nearly laughs in spite of himself. "I'm going to ask you something and I don't want you to get mad at me."

"I don't think that statement has ever been followed by something good," Ezra says. She glares at him, and he puts his hands up. "Okay. Ask."

She looks at him for another moment, then takes a deep breath. "Are you *okay*?"

He opens his mouth to answer with the obvious: He's fine. Of course he's fine. It's his job to be fine.

Instead, to his horror, the tightness he'd finally managed to work out of his throat clenches, spreading up to his mouth until he can feel his lips start trembling, to his eyes until they're hot and stinging. He digs his teeth into the inside of his cheek and looks up at the ceiling, as if by counting the panels he can shove any trace of tears from his face.

"Ezra?"

"Just—" His voice breaks and he clamps his mouth shut before anything else can slip out. He pushes back the chair and stands up, his body moving like a possessed thing, and he takes a few steps away from the bed, as though a few feet of distance could take the question away.

"Oh, no, don't," Becca says. The bed makes an ominous sound and Ezra turns back around at the first rustle of her attempt to scramble at the wires, even before she lets out an-other frustrated "Fuck!" at the realization that she's connected to too many monitors to climb after him. "I'm sorry. Okay? Forget I asked. I didn't mean to make things worse."

"You didn't," he says, carefully untangling the few lines she's managed to fuss with and pushing her back onto the pil-low. And then, in case that's not clear enough, "You *don't*."

"You don't *look* like I didn't make things worse." She reaches out her hand for his, and he takes it. "Are you sure you don't want to talk about it?"

Ezra swallows carefully, looking down at their joined hands. "I think," he says honestly, maybe more honest than he's been in years, "that if I talk, I will have an absolute break-down."

"Oh." Becca hesitates. "You could, though. If you wanted."

A laugh bubbles out of him like he's taken a punch to the gut. "Thanks."

"I'm just saying. It's kind of your turn."

"I'll take a raincheck," he says, because he's only barely holding it together, and if she asks him one more time if he's okay he really will lose his absolute shit, and then they'll *both* end up admitted. "Besides," he says, "I think we're still doing yours, and I'd hate to steal the spotlight."

She tightens her grip on his hand until he feels the fragile bones in his fingers shift, and says, in a very small voice, "If we're still doing mine, can I have a hug?"

He gets up and shifts to sit on the edge of her bed, and when she leans into him, he folds her into his arms like he had when she was little, when she needed someone to tell her that everything was okay and their parents were too busy to do it themselves. Her fingers dig into the fabric of his shirt and she presses her face into his shoulder, squeezing until he feels the breath stutter in his lungs, and when he says, "Becks, Becca,

Becca-girl," in the fragile quiet of the room, she starts to cry—big, heaving sobs that rattle her in the circle of his arms like a bird throwing itself into the bars of a cage.

These aren't talking tears, he knows. He just holds her, because it's something he can do, something simple and uncomplicated and instinctive. A use for his body that doesn't hurt.

29

It's storming again by the time Becca's nurse finally convinces him to go home in the early hours of the morning. Rainwater spills over the edges of the concrete overhang and creates streaming rivulets that splatter against the pavement at the hospital entrance as Ezra steps outside, shivering in his thin jacket. He spends a few minutes just looking at it, wondering if maybe he should go and stand under one of the heaviest spots to let the water drench him clean.

Someone says his name, half muffled by the rain.

Jonathan is getting to his feet, leaving behind one of the cramped folding chairs by the valet station, and looking tired and a little worse for wear. He gives Ezra a look touched with uncertainty at the corners of his eyes and his mouth, and Ezra's chest clenches, guilty and miserable.

Of course he'd waited. He wasn't going to take the chance that Ezra would bolt home without taking responsibility for how shitty he'd been earlier. Ezra braces himself, his head already racing to find the right words for an apology he already knows will be useless.

"I'm sorry," he starts, but Jonathan shakes his head, coming over to meet him until they're close enough to talk without shouting over the rain.

"Later," he says.

"But—"

"Later," Jonathan repeats firmly. A promise, not a deflection. He studies Ezra's face for a moment, and then softens. "Are you okay? How's Becca?"

"Becca's fine," he says. "They're keeping her until the twenty-four-hour mark, probably. Kicked me out because she needs better sleep, apparently." He hesitates. "You haven't been here all night, have you?"

Jonathan cocks one brow. "I'm your ride home," he says. "I wasn't going to leave you here."

Because Ezra doesn't owe him enough apologies. "God," he says. "I am so sorry."

Jonathan shakes his head. "I went home for a bit," he says, which probably means he was there long enough to charge his phone, if that. "Aaron let me know she was being admitted overnight. But he's going to be tied up at your parents' house most of today, and I figured if I didn't come and get you, I wasn't sure how long it would take to track you down and have a conversation." His mouth pulls up on one side, humorless. "You can be hard to get hold of when you want to be."

They're less than an arm's length apart, but Ezra feels every inch like a chasm. He wants Jonathan to be the one to cross it, to fold him back up in the embrace Ezra had shoved out of earlier. Goose bumps shiver their way over his skin, from the chill of the air and the intensity of Jonathan's eyes, and his fingers shake with the urge to rub at his arms, as if he could scratch away the feeling.

How to fix this. If it even can be fixed.

After what feels like an eternity, Jonathan sighs, pushes his fingers through his hair—it stays where it's been shoved, a sure sign that he probably didn't sleep and definitely didn't shower—and says, "Okay. Let's go."

Ezra doesn't move. He must have heard that wrong. "What?"

"You look like you're going to keel over," Jonathan says, matter-of-fact tone softened by the look in his eyes. "You're running on fumes, and you're clearly—" He gives Ezra that little half smile again. "You're not doing great, whether you want to admit it or not. You need a shower, and something to eat, and something to drink that isn't coffee or alcohol, and then you need to sleep for about eight hours."

Ezra blinks. This isn't being yelled at. This isn't even being dragged into a car to be dropped home and dumped. "I—" he says, and stops, confused by the sudden lump swelling back into his throat. "I'm—" he tries again, but his voice catches.

Something unreadable crosses Jonathan's face, and then he steps forward, closing the space between them like it's nothing, like the impossible task of reaching out is no harder than breathing. He puts a hand on Ezra's arm, the barest ghost of a touch.

"Hey," he says, urgent and concerned. "Hey—Ezra, okay, you're scaring me now." He puts his other hand on Ezra's cheek, firmer contact, tilting Ezra's face up to his. "Talk to me," he says. "Are you okay?"

Ezra has been brushing away *Are you okay?* with smiles and winks and sarcasm and shrugs since he was too young to even know he was doing it.

He can't do it anymore.

The sound that comes out of him *hurts*, low like the dying moan of an animal worked to its limits. He crumples in on himself, doubling over as if applying pressure to his belly will keep his insides from spilling out onto the damp concrete. That horrible sound leaves him again, and again, and then he's crying, choked, desperate sobs racking through him until there's nowhere else to go, nowhere he can put the writhing, visceral force of what's inside him except here.

And then arms fold around him, pulling him up, and Ezra

can't do anything except reach out and cling, fisting his hands into soft fabric that stretches out under his fingers, burying his face in a shoulder that smells of sweat and smoke and rain. He presses his face tight against the warm fabric and takes in gasping breath after gasping breath, each exhale leaving him even more breathless, choking for new air and missing every time.

"Sweetheart," Jonathan is saying, too kindly, too gently. His voice is close to Ezra's ear, his hands a lifeboat. "I've got you. It's okay. It's okay."

Ezra keeps crying. He can't stop.

He cries through Jonathan walking them back to his car, bundling him into the passenger seat, and fastening his seatbelt for him when Ezra's hands shake too badly to do it himself. He cries the entire drive home, one of Jonathan's hands clutched in both of his until Jonathan says, "Easy, love, I have bones in there," and then, "Okay, okay, it's okay," when Ezra can't make himself loosen his grip. He cries when Jonathan parks the car and coaxes Ezra out and up the porch steps, not even suggesting that he walk Ezra up to his apartment, just unlocking his own front door with the hand not holding Ezra's tight.

He cries, and he keeps crying, and finally the world falls away.

It's the shock of cool water that finally brings him out of it, the pounding, high-pressure impact of the spray too steady to be rain. Ezra hitches a shaking breath, and then another, and slowly blinks himself back to awareness, connecting the picture-sound-sensation wires of his brain back to the receptors of his body.

He's sitting on the floor of Jonathan's shower, fully clothed except for his shoes. Lukewarm water is pooling in the tub underneath him and soaking into his pants and underwear, just cool enough to be uncomfortable. Jonathan's wedged into the tub behind him, wrapped around him like a life preserver and humming a wordless, half-familiar melody that's barely audible over the rush of the water, his thumbs rubbing even circles over Ezra's arms.

"That's a nice song," Ezra croaks, his throat raw.

Jonathan's hands still, and he starts to pull back, as if to turn Ezra to face him. Cold air rushes into the space where their bodies separate, and Ezra clutches at his hands, holding him in place with an embarrassing, desperate noise. Jonathan freezes for an instant, then murmurs, "Okay, here," and gives Ezra a nudge, guiding him to turn until he's as much in Jonathan's lap as he can be in the cramped, narrow space, his legs folded up over Jonathan's hips. He keeps one hand pressed between Ezra's shoulder blades to help him balance, the other cupping the back of his head, fingers moving in a slow, steady pattern against the short hairs at the nape of his neck. Ezra lets himself be pathetic for a few more minutes, pushing his face into the familiar crook of Jonathan's neck, even though he has to bend his own uncomfortably to manage it, grounding himself in the warmth of Jonathan's skin.

"Better?"

Ezra nods.

"Okay." Jonathan shifts under him, and the spray of water at Ezra's back gets a bit warmer. It makes him shiver anyway, but Jonathan just murmurs something wordless and soothing, squeezing the hand at the nape of Ezra's neck. "Can you give me some sign of life?"

Ezra feels wrung out and lighter, like someone has opened him up and scraped out everything infectious and festering inside him and left only healing flesh behind. He takes a deep breath, inhaling warm skin and steam and a little bit of water, and slumps a little more heavily. He has to swallow three times before he trusts his voice. "Yeah."

"Good," Jonathan says. He turns his head, just enough for his cheek to brush Ezra's. "You scared the hell out of me."

Ezra closes his eyes again. They feel swollen, too big for his eyelids. He wants to rub at them, but lifting his hands feels impossible. "Sorry."

"It's okay."

It isn't, and they both know it, but Jonathan seems willing to give him a few more minutes of grace. His thumb traces a slow pattern between Ezra's shoulder blades, and Ezra's tear-soaked brain slowly catches up to the sensation of sodden clothing clinging to his skin. The tightness around his chest registers next, what he'd been assuming was anxiety resolving into the recognition of his waterlogged binder. He forces himself to sit back, dragging his eyes open. "I need to—" he manages, and then breaks off with a cough.

Jonathan looks up at him, and then down at the hand Ezra has dropped to his own chest. For a moment Ezra thinks Jonathan might get the wrong idea. "Oh—fuck. Sorry, I didn't even think— How long have you been wearing that?"

Ezra makes a face, trying to express *You don't want to know,* and shakes his head. His shirt comes off easily enough, but it takes both of them working together to peel his binder away from his wet skin. The rush of air as he takes in a full, deep breath almost makes him dizzy, and he has to steady himself with one hand against the shower wall. Jonathan strips his own shirt off, letting it drop to the floor of the tub with a heavy *splat,* and Ezra lets himself be gathered close again, pressed skin to skin.

The beat of the water against his back is soothing, and the steam makes him feel sleepy and safe. He wonders if he could get away with closing his eyes again, just for a few more minutes.

"Hey." Jonathan taps his arm gently. Ezra blinks himself

back to awareness, lifting his head from where he's slumped back onto Jonathan's shoulder and looking down at him. He's still wearing his glasses, Ezra realizes with surprise, and his eyes are almost impossible to see behind the droplets coating his lenses. "When I said you should sleep, I didn't mean on the floor of my shower."

"I know," Ezra mumbles.

"And you're really, really going to regret it if you don't drink about a gallon of water before you crash."

Groaning, Ezra closes his eyes, and this time drops his head intentionally. Jonathan gives a soft, barely there laugh, and his hands fall to squeeze Ezra's waist. "Come on," Jonathan says. "I'll help you."

Ezra has never once, for an instant, deserved this man.

The feeling of drifting is gone as he lets Jonathan pull him up to his feet, helping Ezra balance against the wall as he reaches over to turn off the water. Ezra still feels thickheaded and weary down to his bones, but there's a new alertness now, like a fuzzy satellite signal that's just angled itself to send picture and sound into crisp resolution.

"Easy," Jonathan cautions, catching his arm when Ezra wobbles as he steps out of the shower.

"I'm okay," Ezra says, and is a little surprised to find that he actually means it.

Jonathan gives him a slightly skeptical look, but he lets Ezra go. Ezra doesn't argue, just strips out of the rest of his soaked clothes and accepts the towel he's given, then follows Jonathan down the hall to the bedroom and lets himself be bundled into a pair of sweatpants and a Henley a size too big in the shoulders and arms. He sits on the edge of the bed and drinks a glass of water, then manages to eat half an orange before his hands start shaking, nausea creeping back in around the edges of his stomach.

"I'm sorry," he says.

Not for leaving the orange unfinished. Jonathan takes it out of his unprotesting fingers, setting it back on the plate on the bedside table, and looks at him steadily. "I know," he says. "And we're definitely going to talk when you don't look like you're going to pass out."

Ezra opens his mouth to protest, to at least insist that he give Jonathan his bed back and go home, but Jonathan just looks at him, and the argument dies in his throat. "Okay." His head feels clearer, but he's exhausted down to his cells, and he feels loose-limbed and wobbly as Jonathan nudges him firmly under the blankets. "Wait, my phone—I should check on Becca. And—oh, shit, Sappho—"

"Is fine," Jonathan interrupts. "Ollie's got her. I checked in with him while we were at the hospital. Your phone is dry and on the bathroom counter." He pulls one of the blankets up from the foot of the bed and tucks it around Ezra's waist. "And probably dead at this point, but I'll plug it in for you. And I'll text Aaron and let him know that he can call you here if Becca sends any updates to your family chat. Okay? Now go to sleep."

He gives Ezra a firm but gentle shove, and Ezra's head hits the pillow against his will. It's soft and welcoming, and he immediately wants to sink even deeper. "I could take the couch," he tries to offer, but his eyes already feel heavier.

"I'm not dignifying that with a response. And you're not kicking me out of my bed or whatever you're about to try arguing next. I'm coming back as soon as I get your phone and hang up your binder so it doesn't die a sad, wet death on the floor of my shower. And then probably get us some more water because that was not enough for you to not wake up feeling hungover as hell."

Something swoops and flutters in Ezra's chest. He closes

his eyes so he doesn't have to think too much about it. "You're too good," he mumbles.

There's a pause, and then Jonathan's fingers slip into his hair, the softest ghost of a touch. "I am so fucking mad at you," he whispers. "But believe it or not, you deserve a little good."

Ezra doesn't know what to say to that. He turns his face into the pillowcase, breathing in Jonathan's shampoo and cologne where it's sunk into the fabric. He's dimly aware of cool lips pressing a kiss to his forehead, chaste and sweet, and then, at last, sleep pulls him under.

30

Ezra wakes up feeling worse than hungover, like he's cried all the moisture out of his body and all that's left is a headache and a dry-mouthed sensation of misery. The light coming in through the blinds is tinged with gold, hovering between afternoon and twilight. He must have slept through almost the entire day, but the panic he's expecting at the realization never comes.

Soft music drifts down the hallway, through the open door to the bedroom. Pushing the blankets off his legs, Ezra hauls himself out of bed, wincing when his body protests every move, every muscle aching and miserable.

"You," Jonathan says, when Ezra hobble-limps into the kitchen and half collapses into a chair at the table, "do not look like you feel great."

"I feel like I'm eighty," Ezra says, resting his forehead against the smooth wood. There's a quiet *clink* beside his head, and he opens his eyes to see a tall glass of water. "Thank you."

"Mm." Jonathan sits down across from him, his face unreadable as he watches Ezra drain most of the glass in one swallow, then the rest of it a bit more slowly. "You slept, at least."

"Yeah." Ezra rubs his eyes. "I owe you . . . a lot of apologies."

Jonathan raises his eyebrows. "True," he says. "You want to start now, or eat something first?"

Ezra puts the glass down. "Why do you keep doing that?"

"What?"

"This!" Ezra gestures between them. "I *yelled* at you. I was an asshole because I was freaked out and scared, and I was just trying to hurt you and I know that it *worked,* but you're just being . . . nice."

Jonathan props one elbow on the table, rests his chin in his hand. "It's very cool how you take something that would be a compliment from any other human being and turn it into an insult."

Ezra groans. "*Jonathan—*"

"Oh, stop." Jonathan gets to his feet. "Here's what we're going to do. I'm ordering dinner on your credit card, because I really *don't* want to talk to you about any of this until you're fed and hydrated. That's not altruism, by the way, I just don't want to feel like a shitty person if I yell at you and you pass out again. *You* are going to get the yoga mat stuffed in the back of my closet that I never use and go do some sun salutations or something."

Ezra opens his mouth. Closes it. Watches Jonathan pick up his wallet—when did Jonathan take his wallet?—and pull out a card, holding it up with a raised brow until Ezra startles back into himself enough to say, "Yeah, okay," and then, "Wait, what?"

"Also not altruism," Jonathan says, pulling his phone out of his pocket. "You're moving like you just got hit by a train, and it's a little pathetic."

"I feel like you're not usually this bossy," Ezra says, and immediately winces, because the last thing he remembers Jonathan saying before he fell asleep is *I am so mad at you* and he probably shouldn't be taking liberties like that.

Jonathan just snorts, putting his phone to his ear, because he's a dinosaur who still orders takeout over the phone instead of online. "You haven't seen anything yet," he says. "Go."

Ezra goes.

Twenty minutes of yoga does make him feel better, his body moving through the motions of an evening flow. It's habit and practice now to connect breath with movement and movement with breath, but it feels like the breath fills him differently than he's used to, as if there's more room inside him than there used to be. He angles his hips back into a downward dog and exhales, drawing his belly in toward his spine, and closes his eyes, listening to the steady *thu-thump, thu-thump, thu-thump* of his pulse beating in his ears. His muscles tighten and release, tighten and release, tension slowly draining away. He can feel everything: the weight of his unbound chest under his borrowed shirt, the ache in his shoulders, the texture of the mat under his fingertips. All the sensations that he usually pushes into the background like radio static have swept into a fullness of feeling. It leaves him dizzy, overwhelmed with how much his body can hold when he lets it fill up with light.

His body is buzzing by the time he spreads out for a final resting pose, letting all his weight relax down onto the mat. The stiffness he'd woken with has faded to a pleasant ache, and he closes his eyes again, tipping his head back and letting his throat and heart open toward the ceiling. Ezra breathes, each inhale sweet and cool, each exhale sweeter and cooler.

How long has it been, he thinks, as his pulse eases back to a resting heart rate, since he'd felt anything this fully? How long has he just been . . . drifting?

He thinks about the ever-present circles under Aaron's eyes, dark enough to have circles of their own. About how quick Becca is to complain, but never about anything that matters. About Dad, oscillating between pushing too hard and not bothering to push at all, expecting too much or losing trust at the slightest misstep. About the cracks in Mom's foundation, buckling under the weight of her secrets and her shame. About the weight of the grief behind Jonathan's soft smiles, the way he performs every ritual washing like he's seeking absolution.

Bodies separate from souls, as disconnected as the people they bury every day.

He thinks about the ghosts, the real ones and the ones they bring with them. Of old men and young women, English teachers and rabbis and kindergarteners and artists; of children lost to the miserable roll of genetic dice and parents lost to old age; of generations lost to the brutality of human hatred. The ghosts of the living, of fractured marriages and missing sisters and different bodies. The ghosts of dead husbands, gone in the blink of an eye and leaving a spill of confusion and guilt and shame and secrecy behind, of arguments never resolved and apologies never given. The ghost of a man who loved his father enough to lie and his mother enough to keep her secrets, who drank tea he hated on the porch with his husband just to make him happy, who never felt like anything he did was enough to make up for everything he couldn't be.

It clicks in his head then.

Fix it, Ben told him, that first night they spoke, and Ezra had been so certain it meant picking up the pieces of Ben's lost life, fitting them back together. But Ben's life existed at the edges of his own, and it had never been just Jonathan he looked at.

"Jonathan was right about you," he says to the empty room. "You do meddle."

There are things he feels like he has to fix, and things he knows, now, deep in the surest parts of him, that he simply wants to. How do you grieve a family? A marriage? Who prays over it, gives it the final dignity of clean linen and cool water? Does it get a funeral, or does it just lay itself down, mourned, but without mourners?

No one sits shiva for living ghosts.

Ezra lets his fingers relax. He lets a picture take shape in his head.

When he has it, solid and possible, he opens his eyes. He rolls his shoulders once, then puts away the yoga mat and steels himself to come clean.

When Ezra pads out into the living room, Jonathan is sitting on the couch, a bag of takeout on the coffee table and his phone in his hand. "I just checked in with your brother," he says as Ezra approaches him, glancing up. His smile is his real one, all the way to the corners of his eyes. "Becca's going to be discharged in a bit. He's going to pick her up and take her back to the hotel your dad— Oh," he says, breaking off when Ezra sits down next to him, taking the phone out of his hand and placing it on the table, then putting his hands on Jonathan's shoulders. "Okay. Hello. You look better."

"I feel better," Ezra says, and then, because his nerves are still singing, asks, "Can I kiss you?"

Jonathan raises his eyebrows. "Bold," he comments. "Considering."

"I know," Ezra says. "And I have a whole apology ready, and an explanation, and everything. But—just one?"

"For morale?" Jonathan says dryly, but he slips a hand into its familiar spot at the back of Ezra's neck and draws him in.

The kiss tastes like a forgiveness Ezra hasn't earned yet, and he sways against Jonathan, closing his eyes and letting it sink into him, filling every remaining space inside him until there's nothing left.

Ezra pulls away, but he doesn't go far. He tips their foreheads together, their breath mixing in the space between them. "I have a lot to tell you," he says. "And some of it is going to sound really weird. But I promise you, it's true."

Jonathan tilts his head, just far enough away that they can meet each other's eyes. He doesn't let Ezra go. "I'm listening."

31

Afterward, Jonathan asks for space.

He promises, with red-rimmed eyes, that he isn't angry—that it's just a lot to take in, and he needs some time to think, to process. He walks Ezra to the door and kisses him good-bye.

So Ezra goes home.

Sappho greets him with a full-body slam as soon as he comes through the door, slobbering all over his face. Ezra sits down hard on the floor to let her climb into his lap, and spends a solid few minutes just holding on to her, being showered with unconditional affection and drool.

He recognizes the pattern of Ollie's footsteps even before the floor creaks beside him. "So," Ollie says. "Long night?"

Ezra muffles an exhausted, soul-weary laugh into Sappho's fur. Ollie puts a hand on his back, half a rub and half a shake, rough and affectionate and entirely unromantic. "Thanks for watching my dog."

"Team effort," Ollie says. "I'm glad Becca's okay."

"I haven't talked to her today."

"She's back on Instagram." Ezra picks his head up, hopeful. Ollie already has his phone out, Becca's account open on the screen. Her latest photo is a selfie, still in her hospital bed, giving the camera a wrinkle-nosed, unapologetic smile.

@becksandcall F in kitchen safety. A+ in
unkillable bitch. CHECK YOUR STOVE
KNOBS, KIDDIES ☉ ☉ ☉

Ezra lets out a laugh, damp and relieved. That's his girl.

"So. At the risk of sending you running, you really look like you could use someone to talk to."

Ezra takes a deep breath. "No more running," he says. "And . . . talking would be good."

"Oh." Ollie looks surprised. "Gotta be real, I was kind of expecting more of a fight."

"I know." Ezra hesitates. "I'm sort of done fighting, too."

"Yeah?" Ollie raises an eyebrow. "'Done fighting,' like, going to actually let someone help you 'done fighting'?"

"Yeah," Ezra says. "Like that."

Ollie exhales and leans over to knock their foreheads together. "Good," he says. "About time."

Over the next few days, Ezra talks more than he has in years.

He tells his roommates everything. About the QCC furloughing half their staff, about going to work for the Chapel for the money rather than a streak of filial altruism. About Jonathan. About the ghosts—*all* of the ghosts, the dead and the living.

They take it . . . much more calmly than he expected. But then, Lily and Noah had asked him his sun, moon, and rising signs before they'd let him move in, and Ollie's been obsessed with paranormal investigation podcasts for years, and Max never makes any decision bigger than choosing a takeout option without pulling at least one tarot card.

Maybe he shouldn't have worried after all.

"You know," Max says thoughtfully when Ezra's voice finally runs dry, scratching Sappho behind the ears, "this explains so much about you. I know some jumpy people, but you are *so* twitchy."

"I actually don't know if that's ghost related," Ollie says, because he's an ass. "I think he's actually just like that."

"Rude," Ezra says, but he's smiling.

Lily props her chin in her hand, her eyes curious and considering. "Okay, ghost boy," she says. "So what's your game plan with all of this? I don't think running a haunted bake sale is going to save your family business."

Ezra shakes his head. "It's definitely not," he says. "And honestly, I don't want to spend any more time there than I have to. The QCC's supposed to be back up and running in a few more weeks, and I want to get back to my *actual* job."

"We all want that for you," Ollie says, patting his arm. "You weren't designed for a paperwork job. You hate math."

"I hate math *so* much," Ezra says.

Lying on the floor with his legs propped on the couch, Noah tilts his head back to look at him. "Do you even *want* to help? It kind of seems like you'd be a lot better off emotionally if you just burned the rest of the place down and took your chances with the insurance."

Lily leans over to grin at him. "Not a ghost person?"

"Hell, no." Noah shoots Ezra an apologetic look. "Not saying I don't believe you, just, you know. I've seen enough movies to know that hanging out in the haunted building literally never works out for anyone."

"All buildings are haunted," Ezra tells him. "Including this one."

Noah makes a face. "Please don't remind me." He sighs. "It's too bad, you know? I liked Ben. Shame we're gonna have to exorcise him."

"We're not exorcising anyone," Ezra says, alarmed. Sappho, as if sensing his tone, rolls out of Max's lap and pads over to shove her head into his chest. He scratches her behind the ears.

Noah gives him a thumbs-down. Lily rolls her eyes at Noah, nudging him with her toes. He bats her away, wrinkling his nose, and says, "So then what *are* we doing?"

Ezra hesitates, rubbing his hand over Sappho's ears. "I have an idea," he says.

The next part is what catches in his throat. He swallows around the knife of it. "I'm just going to need some help."

Three days later, he has breakfast with his siblings.

Becca still looks exhausted, circles under her eyes not quite covered by her makeup. But she's steady on her feet, and she hugs Ezra fiercely when he picks her up at Mom and Judy's condo, where she's been staying since she was discharged from the hospital.

"It's weird," she says, sliding into the passenger seat of his car with only a slightly pained tightening around her eyes as she settles her head back. She's gotten a haircut, the burnt ends trimmed away, healthy auburn curls loose around her shoulders. "But it's not bad, I guess. Mom's been trying really hard."

"You know you can say the word and come stay with me," Ezra reminds her, not for the first time, as he pulls away from the curb after an extra check of his mirrors. He can drive the route to IHOP on autopilot, at this point, but he always drives more carefully with Becca in the car. "My roommates wouldn't mind."

"I know," she says. He has his eyes on the road, but he still catches the look she shoots his way. "I made the executive decision to give you a break."

Ezra sniffs. "You have a concussion," he says. "Who can trust your decision-making, anyway?"

Aaron meets them at the restaurant, dressed down in jeans and a flannel despite it being a workday. He folds Becca into a squeezing hug as soon as she gets out of the car—"Ow," she protests. "You hit your head, not your ribs," he says, not loosening his grip. "Suck it up."—and then hugs Ezra as well, tight and firm, like he's trying to get a point across.

"Okay," Ezra says when Aaron lets him go, looking away with deliberate casualness as Aaron clears his throat and swipes a hand over his eyes. "Pancakes?"

"Oh my God," Becca says. "Yes *please*."

It's the first time the three of them have been together since the fire. With Dad's time taken up dealing with the insurance and the contractors coming in to repair the damage to the house, Aaron has taken over most of Dad's work. Even though there's only a hallway between them, they've barely had time to exchange more than a few words, and most of those about accounts or invoices or contracts or a request for Ezra to change into his suit to help with a service. Aaron tells them about the house as they give the menus their unnecessary skim, waiting for their waitress to come back with coffees and waters. They'd gotten remarkably lucky—other than the damage to the kitchen, the house is mostly unscathed, and the inspectors have already cleared them of any structural damage.

"You could almost say we were *supernaturally* lucky," Aaron says when he finishes, picking up his coffee and leering at Ezra over the rim.

"At this point, I wouldn't rule it out," Ezra says. Becca's hands are folded in her lap, and he nudges her under the table with his foot. "Hey," he says. "It's going to be okay."

She perks up somewhat when their food arrives, falling onto the pancakes and waffles with her usual enthusiasm. Ezra watches with affectionate horror as she pours enough syrup to induce a sugar coma onto her red velvet pancakes.

"Please slow down before you choke," Aaron says, Ezra's own affectionate exasperation echoed on his face.

"*You* slow down," Becca says, her mouth unapologetically full. Ezra raises his eyebrows at her, and she rolls her eyes but slows her pace from *college students descending on free food* to a slightly more civilized *lions discovering a freshly killed antelope.*

As they eat, Ezra lays out the fragile outline of his plan.

The Chapel, he explains, is in trouble. It was never intended to be a moneymaker, but there's a difference between not making bank and not paying the bills, and they hover too close to the latter. Without Zayde's extra accounts, they'd already be out of business.

A lot of that is Dad's insistence, whenever they can manage it, to keep prices as low as possible—if not lower. For him, it's about doing a service, not selling a product. Making sure everyone in their community who wants a Jewish burial can have one without their family going into thousands of dollars of debt.

So if it's going to be a service, then, Ezra reasons, it should be a service.

"A nonprofit funeral home," Becca says, frowning at the proposal Ezra slides across the table. He'd worked on it with Lily and Noah late into last night, Lily scouring state business statutes and Noah taking Ezra's ramblings and turning them into something visually brilliant and somewhat coherent. "Do you think Dad would go for that?"

She's devoured a plate of pancakes and all of her hash browns, and has made a dent in Aaron's. Ezra catches her eyeing his, and while he loves her to death, he pulls his plate a bit closer. "Which part?"

"I don't know, he's . . . You know how into the whole doing-Zayde-proud thing he is." Becca beams at Aaron when he flags down their waitress and orders another two sides of hash browns, looking only mildly pained about it, and then turns back to Ezra. "It wouldn't be a family-owned thing anymore, right?"

"Right," Ezra confirms. "But there are co-op funeral homes all around the country, and it's not like he'd have to totally stay out of it. The name could probably stay. He'd just be—I don't know, the executive director instead of the owner, or something like that."

Aaron looks thoughtful, flipping through the pages. "Someone would have to underwrite this, though, right?"

Ezra nods. He'd talked to Nina about it last night, and she promised to help him research. "There are definitely foundations we could look at."

Aaron winces. "None of us are grant writers."

"No," Becca says slowly. "But Judy is."

Ezra blinks at her, surprised. That's been one of the logistical areas he hasn't been sure how to work out. "Seriously?"

"I thought she was an art professor," Aaron says, frowning.

"She is, but she does grant writing on the side. I guess she started by doing some work for her department at RISD, and then it turned into a whole hustle?" Becca studies the shared plate of blueberry pancakes in the center of the table, preparing a plan of attack.

Aaron turns the plate so that the side with the most blueberries is closer to her. He tousles her hair gently, cautious of the bandage still taped to her brow, and sits back against the booth. "I guess she does owe us," he muses.

"True," Ezra says. He takes the papers when Aaron passes them back. "Do you think she'd go for it?"

Aaron nudges Becca. "What do you think?"

Becca puts her fork down, considering. "I think she would," she says at last. "Especially if Mom asked." She smiles, small and rueful. "Between the two of them, they have enough guilt to probably do just about anything we ask them to for the next . . . I don't know, twenty-five years?"

"I'll take one year of free fundraising," Ezra says. He tucks the printouts back into their folder, then, after a moment's hesitation, slides them back to Aaron. His hands shake, and he hopes no one notices. "Will you look these over again and help me figure out how to bring Dad in?"

Aaron looks surprised as he picks up the folder. Surprised—but pleased, too, and another knot of tension loosens in Ezra's chest. "Of course," he says. "We're going to have to move pretty quickly, though. I caught Dad with Caroline's business card on his desk the other day, and it looked a little too worn-out for him not to have been playing with it for a while."

That . . . is not a great sign. But also—

"Sorry," Ezra says before he can stop himself. "Since when is she *Caroline*?"

Aaron abruptly closes the folder with a cough. "We should plan to talk about this whole thing after work. Maybe grab a drink?"

"Aw," Becca says, propping her chin in her hand and smiling at them. "Bros night!"

It's not subtle, and they're definitely coming back to this later, but Ezra decides to let him get away with the subject change. "You have syrup *all* over your face," he tells Becca instead, and can't help but laugh when she sticks out her tongue.

Ezra and Aaron linger in the parking lot for a few minutes after Becca leaves, catching a ride to class from a friend. Ezra's

about to crack, to apologize for how he acted at the hospital—
he knows Aaron's never done anything but try his best, and it's
not his fault that their parents defaulted to the expectations
they had—but Aaron beats him to it.

"I talked to Jonathan yesterday."

Ezra doesn't drop his phone, or even fumble it, but he does
nearly lose his grip on his keys. "You did?"

Aaron nods, leaning against his car. "He told me you guys
talked."

He doesn't know whether to be grateful or not that Aaron
and Jonathan are . . . whatever they are. More than colleagues.
Probably closer to friends. "He asked for some time."

"He told me that, too." Aaron looks at him, arms crossed
and eyes thoughtful. "If it's any consolation, I don't think he's
angry anymore."

"What makes you say that?"

Aaron shrugs. "The way he talked about you."

Ezra blankly stares at him.

Aaron huffs a laugh. "Look. I spend enough time talking
to mourning people to know when they're trying to find excuses to stay angry and leave someone behind and when
they're not. He's hurting, yeah, and probably freaked, but"—he
shrugs again—"you two are going to be fine."

Ezra puts his hands in his pockets, phone and keys and all,
because he doesn't trust his fingers to stop trembling enough
to keep his grip. "I don't know," he says, and it comes out
rougher than he wants it to, tinged with a bitterness he doesn't
feel. "I don't know if we should be."

Aaron frowns, brow furrowed. "Why?"

"I just—" Ezra looks down at the cracked pavement of the
parking lot. There's a cluster of dandelions trying to force their
way through the concrete, a bright little burst of sunshine re-
silience. "I don't deserve another chance with him, you know?

Not after this. I owe it to him to tell him everything I can, to *do* everything I can, but—"

"Whoa," Aaron interrupts, firm enough that Ezra makes himself look up to meet his frown. "We're talking about the same guy here, right? The one who needs to be triple reassured that someone's gotten home safe if he's the last person to see them before they get in the car? The one who I've *personally* seen you talk down from, like, three different panic attacks after a taharah hit him too hard? The guy who's so wrapped up in feeling shitty about his husband that I, a *licensed death professional,* have had to tell him more than once he needs to *hang out with some living people*?"

Ezra opens his mouth, a defense already on the tip of his tongue, but Aaron just crosses his arms. "Plus I've seen him microwave the same cup of coffee four times in a row instead of making a new pot, which honestly should be a crime. The point is, he's a person, Ezra, not a saint, and he's not any less screwed up than you are—but at least he's *trying*. So why would you not deserve this?"

He's given Ezra this pep talk before, when he was sixteen and crying into a pillow because Kelsey Becket turned him down for homecoming because she was straight and he was, for all she knew at the time, not a boy. It had a lot more weight back then, when he hadn't actually done anything wrong. "I'm self-aware enough to know I'm a lot to deal with," he says. He doesn't mean it to be self-deprecating, but just . . . it is what it is. There's a reason people leave him.

He thinks, without really meaning to, of Ben, the way he watches Jonathan with so much regret in his eyes, the way he reaches out but can never touch. Ezra feels guilty every time Jonathan's fingertips brush his, each point of contact a reminder that he's here and Ben isn't. And he should be.

Jonathan deserves to have Ben with him, but he's got Ezra instead—nosy and neurotic, a shade too psychic for his own good but not enough to be useful. He still doesn't understand what makes Jonathan look at him with those eyes and smile at him in a way that he doesn't smile at anyone else, crooked and sweet. Jonathan could have anyone. Why the hell would he want someone like him?

Aaron has been studying him. When Ezra gives up on explaining, all but ready to try to make some kind of awkward apology and suggest they make their way back to work, Aaron pushes off his car and steps forward, putting a firm hand on Ezra's shoulder. He gives him a little shake, like he wants to be sure he has Ezra's attention, then exhales hard.

"All right," he says, and his eyes are steady and calm, the way he only is when he's instructing an intern or talking a grieving widow off a metaphorical ledge. "I'm only going to say this once and I need you to be cool about it and not brush it off like I'm joking. I know how you get with stuff like this, but I need you to listen. Okay?"

Ezra blinks, not sure if he should be confused or alarmed, but shrugs his free shoulder and nods.

"Thank you." Aaron looks at him, firm and unblinking and absolutely serious. "You are," he says, with incalculable slowness, "one of the best people I have ever known. You have taken so much shit it's not even funny, and you throw it back at people as something *good*. You take care of people. You've taken care of *me,* more than you ever should've had to. You taught me how to make people feel like they matter."

He squeezes Ezra's shoulder tight enough that Ezra almost wonders if it will bruise. "You're one of the best men I know. I am so proud of you. And I'm sorry I've never said that before now."

Ezra gapes at him. His ears feel stuffed with cotton.

His voice cracks, just barely. His eyes sting. "Um," he tries.

Aaron sighs, long-suffering but so fond it almost hurts to hear, and pulls Ezra into a hug. It's tight and fierce and Ezra feels pleasantly smothered, and wonders if maybe he'll go out like this, lovingly crushed to death in his older brother's arms.

It's not a bad way to go, honestly. If they didn't have shit to fix, he'd be tempted.

Still, he brings his arms up to hug Aaron back, smushing his face into his shoulder. He smells like diner coffee and the same cologne he's been wearing since his bar mitzvah. It's horrifically comforting.

"Thanks," Ezra says.

Aaron knocks their foreheads together. "Any time."

32

For all of Aaron's confidence, Ezra hadn't expected to hear from Jonathan anytime soon.

So it's a surprise when he raps his knuckles against the doorframe of Ezra's office the day after Aaron's parking lot pep talk. "Hey."

Ezra almost drops his laptop. "Hey," he says, and it's such a breathy exhale that he mentally kicks himself. "How—how are you doing?"

Jonathan shrugs one shoulder, mouth pulling up into a lopsided half smile. "Managing," he says. He nods to Ezra's backpack, half open on his desk. "Is this a bad time?"

"No." Ezra zips his bag. "I was going to head home, but I'm not—I'm not in a rush or anything."

Jonathan nods slowly. He hesitates, thumb tapping almost uncertainly against the doorframe, and then straightens up, slipping his hands into his pockets. "Come get a coffee with me?"

It's the easiest question Ezra's ever answered, even if he is about to go get his heart broken. "Sure."

They walk out to the parking lot together. The hallway is wide enough for there to be plenty of space between them, but Jonathan drifts close enough that their shoulders brush all the same. He curls his fingers into the straps of his backpack, and manages, by some miracle, not to reach for Jonathan's hand.

There's a rare chill to the late spring air as Ezra follows Jonathan to his car without protest, sliding into the passenger seat. Silence stretches out between them. He leans his head against the window and watches Jonathan drive as subtly as he can manage, taking in the line of his jaw, the tousled sweep of his hair, the way he defaults to propping one arm against his window, holding the wheel with the other with deceptive indifference.

They stop at a red light, and Jonathan glances at him, then clicks his tongue with an exasperated affection that catches Ezra off guard, reaching over and swatting at Ezra's knee where he's curled up in his seat. "Stop that," he says. "If we crash, you'll get your legs crushed."

"We're not going to crash," Ezra says.

Jonathan knocks his wedding ring once against the steering wheel, pointed. Ezra puts his feet on the floor.

The light turns green. Ezra counts his breaths in four-part rhythm, trying to lean into the place where he's settled into calm and quiet over the past week. The now-shared knowledge of Ben's ghost hovers between them, as surely as if he'd been there in the car for real, and Ezra has to resist the urge to twist around to look into the back seat to see if he's there after all.

"I've been going around in circles," Jonathan says, sudden and without preamble, like he's decided, mid-thought, to start speaking aloud.

Ezra waits to see if he's going to say anything more. When he doesn't, he prompts, hesitantly, "About?"

"Guess," Jonathan says, voice tinged with a tart sort of crossness that's almost a relief to hear. Jonathan's already proven himself a far nicer person than Ezra could ever hope to be, but it's oddly soothing to be reminded that he isn't all-forgiving. The SUV ahead of them takes a left turn with heartbeats to spare before the light turns red, and Jonathan stops the car at the intersection with a sigh. "I'm still trying to figure out why you just wouldn't tell me from the start."

I'm a massive coward seems like the wrong answer. "At first I just didn't think you'd believe me. I mean, I don't usually lead with 'Hey, just so you know, I'm a little psychic and it's a huge pain in the ass.'"

"That's . . . not unreasonable."

Ezra looks down at his hands. "And then I was just being selfish."

Jonathan snorts. "Right."

"What?"

"You've never been selfish for a second since I met you. To the point where I think whoever taught you the definition of the word should be beaten with a dictionary."

Jonathan executes the smoothest parallel parking job Ezra's ever seen, then turns off the car. He unbuckles his seatbelt and then, instead of getting out, twists in his seat to fix Ezra with a look that offers no outlet for Ezra to do anything but stare back.

"I don't know what you want me to call it, if I can't say I was being selfish," he says when Jonathan's expectant face becomes more than he can handle. "I liked you. *Like* you. Not past tense. And you make me feel . . . made me feel . . ." He trails off, has to intentionally relax his hands in his lap when his fingers curl of their own accord to press crescent pinpricks of pain into his palms.

We don't do that anymore, he tells them firmly, and rubs his palms over his thighs instead. "I didn't know who he was at first, and then when I did, we were already— I knew there could be something. And I knew if I told you, I'd lose you."

"You didn't know that," Jonathan says. "You assumed that."

"Right, sure," Ezra scoffs. "Definitely would have gone well. 'Hey, guy I've been tripping over myself about, I know we just met and we've got this weird chemistry going on that I'm pretending not to notice, but have I mentioned I can see ghosts? And one of them is your dead husband? Who also happens to be the son of my mom's girlfriend, because my life is an absolute soap opera?' Yeah. Sure. None of that would have ended with you dragging me into your car and driving me to the nearest ER with an open psych bed."

"Don't be ridiculous, I'd make Aaron drive you." He sighs, though, and drops an elbow to the edge of the steering wheel so he can rub his forehead. "And . . . fine, when you put it like that it sounds nuts, but I guess I figured you'd go for tact."

"Tact is for straight people," Ezra says without thinking, and then, at Jonathan's startled bark of laughter, smacks his head back against the seat, because *honestly*. "See? This is why I don't say things!" Jonathan shakes his head, but he's chuckling, a reluctant, exasperated sort of laughter that's nonetheless soft at the edges, and Ezra can't fully bite back his own smile, apologetic as it is.

"I *am* sorry, though," Ezra says, when Jonathan stops laughing at him. "I know that's probably not worth much, at this point. But I'm sorry."

"It's worth more than you think." Jonathan rubs his thumb over the worn metal of his ring, the gesture so familiar now that it doesn't hurt anymore to see it.

Then, to Ezra's surprise, he holds out a hand, palm up, across the center console.

It's an obvious, unmistakable gesture. Ezra can't help but stare.

"Not a trap," Jonathan says dryly, like he can read Ezra's mind, and wiggles his fingers.

Ezra flushes, caught, but reaches back.

Jonathan laces their fingers together—like it's easy, like it's nothing. Ezra can see, without even having to try, why Ben loved him so much even death wasn't going to make him leave him behind. His grip is steady. It shouldn't feel like coming home, but Ezra feels it all the same. For a moment Jonathan just runs the pad of his thumb over Ezra's knuckles, his face unreadable. "Can I ask about him?"

Ezra swallows. "Of course."

Jonathan takes what must be a steadying breath. Ezra waits, but no question comes. He looks less like he's trying to think of something to say, and more like he's trying not to cry. Ezra squeezes his hand.

"He loves you," he says. Because that's something he knows, beyond a shadow of a doubt.

Jonathan looks at him. "He told you that?"

He didn't have to. "Yes."

"You said the ghosts don't talk."

Ezra shrugs. "He's different. I don't know why."

A soft, sad smile curves Jonathan's lips. It's a Ben-specific smile, one for sharing memories and wishing for more time with someone who didn't have any other time to give. "Sounds like him," he says, voice damp around the edges. "Stubborn."

There's nothing Ezra can say to that.

Jonathan takes a shaking breath, and then another, and the glow of the streetlight is enough for Ezra to see his eyes shining. His thumb runs over Ezra's knuckles again and again, and Ezra isn't sure if it's absent or intentional, automatic or an attempt to self-soothe.

Finally, his voice little more than a whisper, Jonathan says, "I wish I could talk to him."

The words are brokenhearted, thick and choked with grief, and Ezra can't stop himself from leaning across the console to draw him into a hug. It's cramped and uncomfortable, an awkward-angled reversal of the roles Ezra hadn't realized they'd fallen into, Jonathan crumbling into Ezra's shoulder instead of the other way around. Ezra doesn't think about that, or the thought that this might finally be the last time he holds him like this at all. He just runs his fingers through Jonathan's hair and wraps his other arm tight around him, and when Jonathan buries his face in the crook of his neck, Ezra kisses the top of his head and holds him tighter.

He's been a fixer his whole life, but this isn't getting Becca to school on time or running notes back and forth between his parents when they didn't want to be in the same room. *I chose you,* he thinks, holding Jonathan tighter. *I'd choose you again. I'd choose you on purpose.*

"He loves you," he whispers into his hair, and Jonathan's hands fist in the back of his shirt, tense, his breath catching against Ezra's skin. "He loves you so much."

Jonathan shudders. "I know," he rasps.

"I'm sorry."

"You said that already."

"Not for not telling you. For . . ." Ezra swallows. "Because I'm here, and he's not."

For the space of a single heartbeat, Jonathan stills. And then he draws back enough to look at him with dark, unreadable eyes. He searches Ezra's face for so long that Ezra has another *I'm sorry* on the tip of his tongue, but before he can say anything, Jonathan cups his face and pulls him in, kissing the apology out of his mouth and then some, until Ezra's clinging to his forearms and dizzy enough to be grateful they're already sitting.

"Don't," Jonathan says, raw and hoarse. He doesn't let Ezra move any farther than a breath away from him. "Okay? Don't apologize to me. Not for that. Not for being here. Not when I—" He makes that broken half-laughing sound again, pressing their foreheads together. "Not when I just started feeling alive again."

Oh.

Oh.

"Okay," Ezra says. He feels whatever the opposite of sinking is. Of drowning. Is this what it feels like to fly? "Me, too."

This time, he's ready for Jonathan to kiss him. And the next time, and the next. And the next.

"You're buying coffee, though," he says, stopping Ezra from chasing his lips with a flat, pointed hand draped over his face like a starfish.

Yeah, that's fair. "Okay."

"And dinner."

"*Okay,*" Ezra says, not bothering to try to bite back a grin. "And breakfast tomorrow, I'm guessing?"

"Aren't you presumptuous," Jonathan says. He squishes Ezra's cheeks, then lets him go. "Come on."

"Do you even *want* coffee?" Ezra asks. "It's, like, nine o'clock at night."

"And yet," Jonathan says, and flashes a grin over his shoulder, so bright and gorgeous that Ezra's hand slips right off his door. "Here we are."

33

Over the next week, Ezra's apartment turns into a work zone.

Since the day he moved in almost two months ago, Ezra's never really felt alone there, even on those rare occasions when no one else was home. Unit 2 seems to hang on to bits and pieces of people, and Ezra could be the only person in the empty apartment and still be able to smell the strawberry tinge of Lily's shampoo or the spicy hints of Noah's cologne, to hear the echo of Max's bubbling laugh or sense the warmth of Ollie's grin. It's not the haunting feeling he's used to, of ghosts refusing to let go of a place they called home or a person they're determined not to lose, but something saturated in affection, as if the walls themselves have absorbed all that personality and love like rug fibers soaking up spilled perfume.

Tonight, it hangs in the air like humidity. The living room is full and busy and loud in the best possible way—Becca and Ollie bickering over a photo set on Ollie's laptop, trying to agree on favorites from the images Ollie took earlier in the week when Ezra snuck him into the Chapel in the golden light of early dawn, just in time to catch the sun coming in through the stained glass windows; Lily and Jonathan going through financial records and Rhode Island business statutes with a fine-tooth comb while they put together a draft proposal of articles of incorporation. Noah and Max and Nina have taken over every inch of the dining table not occupied by containers of takeout, tablets and laptops displaying different versions of their proposal. Noah's the only one still working, Nina and Max having devolved into flirting over half an hour ago, barely even trying to disguise it as bickering. Of their motley task force, only Aaron is missing, called out to do a removal with Dad across town, but even he's due to be back within the hour.

And Ben is there.

Not constantly. Not, Ezra thinks, even intentionally. But he flickers in and out of sight like he wants to be part of what they're doing—looking curiously over Noah's shoulder at the layout of the proposal, wrinkling his nose at one of the photos that Becca insists is perfect for a redesigned community website, watching Jonathan with a soft, affectionate expression that's so full of love it almost hurts to see.

But only almost. It never gets all the way to hurting, even when Ben looks away from Jonathan and meets Ezra's eyes instead, and smiles that rueful, *What can you do?* sort of smile before he vanishes once more. Sometimes Jonathan glances up before he disappears, like he can sense him after all, and he always looks right to Ezra, eyes questioning and uncertain. Ezra will nod, because he can't not, and sometimes Jonathan will smile—his Ben smile, soft and sad and wistful—but sometimes he'll bite his lip and duck his head, and Ezra will draw him gently away from the rest of the group to hug him in the hallway until his shoulders stop trembling.

"You can go home, if you want," Ezra tells him once, on their third escape of the night, stroking his hand over Jonathan's back while Jonathan makes a valiant attempt to pretend he isn't biting back tears. "Seriously. I'm glad you're here, but—"

Jonathan shakes his head and pulls away. "I'm okay," he says. "I just . . . I keep thinking maybe I'll see him, you know?"

Ezra runs the pad of his thumb over Jonathan's pulse. "If anyone could manifest ESP out of pure will, it would be you."

Jonathan huffs a watery laugh. "Sweet-talker."

"Hey," Becca says, poking her head around the corner. "Lovebirds. We're ordering dinner. Are you coming?"

"Absolutely," Jonathan says, pulling a smile out of somewhere so quickly and earnestly, Ezra's impressed. "Ezra's still in takeout debt."

"You can't milk that forever," Ezra says.

"Oh?" Jonathan gives him a syrup-sweet grin. "Can't I?"

"Ew," Becca says. "Please get a room."

It's a lot. The part of Ezra that squirms after too much time around too many people is constantly overstimulated and exhausted, and if he didn't feel so horrendously *loved*, he probably wouldn't be able to handle it at all.

But it feels good, in a way he doesn't know how to handle but is slowly starting to trust. It still doesn't make sense that this many people would be willing to put their time and their skills and their energy into helping *him*, when he hasn't done anything to earn it other than live here and exist, but as one day bleeds into another, and another after that, and no one crows "Ha, just kidding!" and leads everyone in an exodus out the front door to cackle at his expense, it finally starts to feel real.

"Oh my God." Nina closes the fridge, staring at him. "Is that what you thought we'd actually *do*?"

"Keep your *voice* down. God," Ezra hisses, flushing as he chances a look over his shoulder. Fortunately, no one seems to have heard her. "And *no*. I mean, not really. Not, like, literally. And not you, obviously. You don't have any better friends."

"Okay," she says, putting down the bottle of seltzer she'd grabbed and leaning back against the counter. She'd abandoned her heels when she showed up that night, but she still has several inches of height on him and doesn't seem to have developed any new qualms about using it to her advantage.

"I'm choosing not to be offended because I know you are just a tiny, crazy feral cat trapped in a human body—"

"Uh-huh."

"But even if we'd be willing to do something like that to you—which again, I cannot emphasize this enough, we *aren't*"—she takes his face in her hands—"you know this is, like, a *good* thing that you're doing, right? Like, even if you take your family out of it, this is an objectively good cause. So get over your inferiority complex, buttercup. You're cramping my style."

Determined to win this, he blurts out, "So if you and Max hook up, does that mean our engagement is off?"

"Oh, *sweet pea,*" she says, and pats his cheek with one manicured hand. Her smile is sweet with an edge of poison-tipped brutality. "One of us is going to be engaged by this time next year, but of the two of us, I would *not* bet on me."

She leaves him in the kitchen still sputtering for a response. When he finally makes it back into the living room, sure his face is still burning, he collapses into the couch and smushes his forehead into Sappho's belly, banking on everyone being too distracted by their own myriad tasks to notice him.

No such luck. The sofa dips next to him, and a familiar hand runs through his hair. "Hey," Jonathan says. "You okay?"

Ezra weighs the pros and cons and decides to pick his head up, turning just enough to squint at him. "Did Nina say something to you?"

"No, but she looks really pleased with herself, and you've told me enough about her that I'm not going to try my luck." Jonathan strokes his hair off his forehead. "Should I ask?"

"I will literally pay you not to."

"I'll put it on your tab. I think we're wrapping up for the night soon anyway. What time do you have work tomorrow?"

Ezra groans. "Bad. Bad o'clock."

"All those sunrise yoga classes and you're still not a morning person?"

"I have layers."

"I bet you do."

Ezra's trying to decide whether that's a compliment or not when the door to the apartment opens. Aaron steps in, still in his suit, and the look on his face is enough to make Ezra sit up, nudging Jonathan's arm until he shifts back to give him room.

"Aaron?" Becca gets to her feet, frowning at him. "What's going on?"

Aaron puts his bag down, shuts the door behind him, and leans back against it. "I just caught Dad on the phone with Forever Memorials," he says. "And we have a problem."

34

The problem, apparently, is that after everything in the last few months, Dad thinks they should just sell.

"You have got," Becca says, "to be kidding me."

Aaron grimaces, accepting a glass of bourbon from Jonathan—the good stuff, brought up from Jonathan's liquor cabinet downstairs, not the burn-your-lungs whiskey they have up here. "Wish I were."

Laptops and tablets and printed spreadsheets lie scattered and abandoned on every available surface, with everyone clustered on the couches and chairs dragged over from the dining room and, in Noah's case, sprawled out on the floor, which is his default even when there is room on the couches. Even Sappho seems to have figured out that it isn't playtime anymore, and after a few hopeful loops around the room with her fraying multicolored rope in her mouth and finding no takers for tug-of-war, she retreats glumly back to her bed in the corner of the room, chewing mournfully on one end of the toy.

Jonathan leaves the bottle on the coffee table, generous soul that he is, and comes back to the couch. Ezra slides down to the floor so Jonathan can have his seat, leaning back against his legs once he's settled. "I'm confused," Jonathan says. "Since when was that even an option?"

"Since always, honestly," Aaron says, taking a grim sip. He pauses to give the glass a considering look, then shoots Jonathan an approving nod before putting the glass down and rubbing his eyes. "We're a family-owned business with a multigenerational name and reputation; there have been corporate funeral homes trying to buy us out since—God, I don't even know. Years. Probably since we were in high school, maybe longer."

"But Dad *hates* the corporate system," Becca says, leaning forward with a frown. "Like, *hates* them. I've literally seen him rip up a business card *directly in front of the person who handed it to him.*"

"I know," Aaron says. "But with everything going on . . . maybe it's just too much for him. I mean, I've seen some of the offers, and they're not insubstantial. Not buy-an-island money, but definitely how-much-do-you-*really*-care-about-those-principles money. I think he always turned it down before because he thought he did enough good to balance out the places where he wasn't brilliant, with the numbers and the tough business calls, but . . ."

Dad's always been calm and steady around clients, has always put on a good face at home, but he's not, at heart, a deeply confident person. It would have been one thing for him to know about the accounts Mom was hiding from him, to keep that secret shame tucked away while acting like everything else was fine, but for Ezra and his siblings to know, on top of Mom leaving, and now the fire—

Ezra can't blame him for wanting to take a shortcut to retirement.

"Okay," Lily says slowly. "So . . . what? We're giving up on this? Your dad sells, someone else takes over, and that's it?"

"No," Ezra says immediately. It comes out with an odd little echo, and he belatedly realizes that both Aaron and Becca had spoken in unison with him.

"No," Aaron repeats. "I'll offer to take over for him and go

through with"—he gestures at the detritus around the room—
"with all of this myself, if that's the other option." He takes a
long drink of bourbon, clearly steeling himself and wincing
when he swallows, but his eyes are clear when he puts the
glass down again with a delicate clink of crystal on wood. "I
was hoping I wouldn't have to until I was, like, forty, but if it's
that or selling out to a body farm? Fuck no."

It's the surest Ezra's heard him sound about anything,
maybe ever. If it weren't for the circumstances, he'd be proud.

"Does he have an actual offer?" Max has her chin pillowed
in one hand, her socked feet tangled up with Nina's on the
love seat. "What kind of timeline are you looking at?"

Aaron shakes his head. "He wouldn't say."

That's not good. Ezra rubs his eyes. "Would he sign a con-
tract without talking to you?"

"Six months ago, I'd have said there was no way. Now?"
Aaron's mouth twists into a bleak, humorless smile. "I don't
know."

Which might as well be a yes. Fuck.

"Okay," Nina says, breaking the anxious silence. "Here's
what I think. It's one in the morning. No one's going to finish
anything useful tonight. We should break this up. In the
morning, one of you can go talk to your dad and try to talk
him off this cliff—"

"I'll do it," Ezra hears himself say.

Nina's eyelids don't so much as flutter. "Color me shocked.
Sure. Ezra will talk to your dad. And then we just need to . . .
I don't know, move our timetable up." She leans around Max
to look at Becca. "Is there a good time you could hit him with
this? Maybe zero in on the sentimentality?"

Becca wrinkles her nose, but she pulls out her phone, pre-
sumably swiping over to her calendar. "Huh," she says, raising
her eyebrows. "Maybe, actually." She waves her phone slightly,

as if any of them can see what's on the screen, and looks thoughtful. "WaterFire opens later this week. We've always gone to opening night as a family. I kind of figured we wouldn't, this year, but—"

"I don't know." Aaron sounds doubtful. "We tried that with Lag BaOmer, and look how that turned out."

Becca shakes her head. "This is different—public space, so he can't make a scene, and it leans into the whole *Look how important community is* thing, since half of Providence is going to be out there."

That's kind of what Ezra hates about it, ambience or not. "But," he says, a little weakly, "people."

He can't deny that it's a good idea, though.

Damn it.

"Okay," he says. "I'll get him there."

"Great," Becca says, all false cheer. "I'll try not to start any more unsanctioned fires."

Aaron snorts. "L'chaim," he says, and downs the rest of his drink.

The evening breaks off after that, the night's momentum decidedly stalled, everyone going their separate ways. Ezra doesn't fail to notice that Nina, for all she says she's going to take his bed since he's going downstairs with Jonathan, slips out the door with Max, but he's too tired to give her any shit for it.

From the gleeful look on Ollie's face, though, he's got it under control.

Jonathan's brushing his teeth when Ezra gets back from taking Sappho on a loop around the block. She hops onto the bed and immediately starts turning in circles to find the ideal spot, and has spread out across half the surface area of the comforter by the time he finishes washing up and turns out the hall light. "You're spoiling her," he says, taking in the way Jonathan's wedged himself into a corner of the bed so he doesn't have to move her over at all.

"Look at her face, though," Jonathan says, as Ezra scoops her up with a grunt and deposits her at the foot of the bed, pausing briefly to pepper kisses over her nose and ears before he crawls under the covers. "Cruel. Absolutely brutal."

"Tell you what," Ezra says, adjusting the pillow and dropping onto it with an exhausted sigh. "When she takes up all of *your* legroom at three in the morning, she can spread out."

"Deal." Jonathan leans over and kisses him, then reaches to turn off the lamp, plunging the room into quiet darkness. His arm slips around Ezra's waist, and Ezra shifts automatically to curl up against him. "Hey. Don't worry about this, all right? It's going to be fine."

"You're more of an optimist than I am."

"Maybe," Jonathan allows. "Or maybe I just think you deserve a break."

Ezra makes a face, even though he knows Jonathan won't be able to see it in the dark. "I don't get breaks," he says.

"Doesn't mean you don't deserve one." Warm lips press against the back of his neck. "Go to sleep, Ezra."

He doesn't.

Despite the heaviness in his limbs and Jonathan's soft, even breathing behind him, Ezra feels wide awake, anxiety making his skin tingle. He's spiraling and he knows it, and he isn't quite sure how to stop. Running through the logic of everything they've been working on doesn't work, and neither does reminding himself that his worth doesn't depend on how well he knows how to take care of other people or whether or not the Chapel goes under or goes corporate or doesn't go anywhere at all. He can't do anything but worry, pouring almost all his energy into lying still so he doesn't fidget Jonathan awake.

He considers, briefly, waking him up on purpose. An orgasm or two will probably knock him out, but on the off chance it doesn't help, they'll both be awake, and that won't do anyone any good.

When the clock on his phone reads three in the morning at his next miserable check, Ezra gives up. Carefully, he slips out of bed, shushing Sappho quietly when she wakes up with a snort at his movement, reaching out to scratch her ears until she snuffles and lays her head back down. When her breathing returns to its gentle snores, he bends down to kiss her nose, then gathers up his phone and his clothes and tiptoes out of the room. He gets dressed in the bathroom, then slips down the hall on cautious footsteps, pulling on his shoes and collecting his keys and wallet from the bowl next to the door. He remembers at the last second to scrawl a quick note on the whiteboard in the entryway—he's not going to give Jonathan a panic attack by leaving without a trace in the dead of night—and leaves the apartment as quietly as he can.

The Chapel is dark and silent when he pulls into the parking lot and lets himself in through the employee entrance, turning off the alarm. There's probably someone sitting shmira overnight upstairs—they rarely sit down here when the rest of the building is empty, for obvious *creepy-as-hell* reasons—and he pauses, just in case they call out, but he doesn't hear anything. Flicking on the hall light, he makes his way down to one of the taharah rooms, not really sure what's bringing him there until he's closing the door behind him.

It's too quiet. Ezra turns on the sink and lets his hand rest against the tap as the sound of running water fills the room, then sits down on the tiled floor, leans his head back against the wall, and closes his eyes.

The skin on the back of his neck prickles. A familiar voice says, "So, this is a little weird."

Reluctantly, Ezra opens his eyes. Ben, sitting on the floor next to him, raises one eyebrow.

"I mean," he continues. "Not that I have much ground to stand on, given everything, but still. There's wandering around in the middle of the night because you can't sleep, and then there's sneaking out of a perfectly nice bed to sit in a cold storage unit full of bodies. So. What gives? I thought you weren't doing this anymore."

"Doing what?"

Ben gestures at their surroundings. "You were doing such a good job," he says. "With the asking for help and the letting people in. What, you get one piece of bad news and it's back to the avoidance game? Jon's going to kill you, by the way. That wasn't a comprehensive note."

Ezra rubs his eyes. "Why are you here?"

"In general, or right now?"

"Either." Ezra looks down at the floor. The running water isn't making him sleepy or soothing the buzz in his head, not like he'd half hoped it would. "Both."

Ben doesn't answer. When he shifts slightly, stretching his legs out in front of him, Ezra can almost imagine that he hears the rustle of fabric, that he can feel the physicality of him, almost close enough to touch.

"I don't really know anymore, honestly," he says at last. "It's not like I got an instruction manual. I was here, so I stayed. I thought it was for Jon, you know? I wanted to know he was okay. And then I thought, maybe my parents, or"—he waves one hand to indicate the room—"even this place. I spent a lot of time here, over the years. I cared about it. Still do. Maybe I thought that if I could make sure everything would be okay without me, that I'd leave. But the longer I'm here, the more I feel like maybe there's a part of me that can't deal with the idea that they will be. No one wants to think their whole life will be fine without them around, you know?"

"Just because people can survive without you doesn't mean they're okay," Ezra says. "And even if they're not, you can't— you can't hang on to that. No one holds being gone against you. You did more than your best. You deserve to just . . . rest."

"And you think you don't?"

"It's not the same."

"Why? Because you're still here, and I'm not?"

No. Yes. Ezra looks at the floor again, and Ben sighs, a whisper of nonexistent breath.

"Ezra," he says. "What are you still afraid of?"

His whole world has been tied up in taking care of other people since he was too young to understand what he was doing until he'd built his entire identity around it. If he doesn't have that—if he can't fix things for the people who need him—he doesn't know who he is. He doesn't understand why anyone would want him, if not for that.

But he wants that. He wants it more than he's ever been able to admit.

If he can't say it to anyone else, maybe he can say it to Ben, here in this almost silent building, nothing but the sound of the water and the bodies of the dead, no one else around except the single person sitting a quiet vigil upstairs.

He lifts his head, steeling himself for the confession, but the room is empty.

Ben is gone.

35

Ezra knows, the moment it happens, that Ben isn't just gone, but *gone*, finally leaving for whatever place comes after this.

It's this realization—that his strange, unexpected ally won't ever flicker into being again—that pushes him into motion.

He can't spend another second in this room, in this terrible quiet. Ezra gets off the floor, turning the water off with shaking hands and switching off the lights, and he leaves on wobbly legs, like his body is trying to learn how to walk at sea.

Ezra has always looked at the ghosts he sees as something impermanent and transient. Even the dead can't stay forever, no matter how solid they look or how much they seem to cling to the living.

So why does this feel different?

He feels the cool air of Zayde's presence by the door and has to brace himself for longer than he wants to admit before he can bring himself to look up to face the inevitable disappointment in his grandfather's face. But there's only quiet concern in those old, sad eyes, an expression that reminds Ezra of being five years old and insisting to his mother that he could take care of Becca when she cried, that he could keep Aaron out of trouble.

He'd always thought that it was doubt that made Zayde give him that look. Now he's not so sure. Ezra swallows. "I did everything I could," he whispers, and has to swallow to keep his voice from cracking on the words. "I just. I need that to be enough."

Zayde's eyes soften, and it's so suddenly familiar, so absolutely the same way Zayde used to look at him just before he folded Ezra into a warm, tobacco-and-cologne-scented hug, that Ezra's knees nearly buckle.

Unlike Ben, Zayde has never spoken to him. Ezra's never known why. But even when he was alive, they didn't always need words. Zayde steps away from the door and leaves it free for Ezra to pass.

"Thank you," Ezra whispers, and goes.

A soft drizzle starts as he drives through the quiet streets, not sure what he's looking for, only sure that he can't go home. He craves a quiet that comes from predawn air and the slow murmur of the city coming to consciousness instead of the aching silence of the part of his mind that hears things others can't. By the time he ends up at the waterfront and turns off the ignition, the drizzle has turned to a steady rain, rattling against the roof of the car. Ezra gives himself a moment to just listen to the sound of it, head tipped back and eyes closed.

It's not a downpour, so he pulls up his hood and gets out.

He passes a few people on his way down the steps, mostly runners taking advantage of the empty sidewalks. When he gets to the bottom, he slips off his shoes and socks, rolls his cuffs a few more times, and dips his toes into the water. The Providence River is never balmy, even on the best days, and he shivers at the chill, his skin prickling into pins and needles before the numbness settles in. Ezra leans into the feeling, taking long, slow breaths as he swirls his feet back and forth, watching the ripple of the water under the glow of the streetlights. Sitting here, feet dangling into the river, he's seven and seventeen and twenty-seven all at once, memories of summer days and autumn afternoons and winter evenings with his parents and siblings washing over him like a wave.

So many of their family habits and traditions are tied up in ancient ritual, clung to out of a stubborn refusal to let one more thing die on the altar of assimilation. He sometimes forgets that they have places like this, too: stone and water and air, simultaneously solid and shifting, something they made for themselves and disconnected from the weight of loss and memory soaked into every inch of their home.

His phone vibrates in his pocket, rousing him out of the reverie. Ezra wipes his eyes and sits up, knowing it's Jonathan before he checks the screen.

He's going to have to tell him about Ben. He's used up all the secrets any one person could be allowed and probably more, but even if he hadn't, this feels so raw in his throat that he couldn't keep it to himself if he wanted to.

Ezra knows he left a note, but given the state he was in when he left, he can't even remember what he wrote.

"Please don't yell at me," he says when he picks up.

"I'm not a yeller," Jonathan says, in the tone of someone who's considering changing that. "Where the hell are you?"

"Down at the waterfront."

There's a beat of silence. "It's raining."

"I know."

Another beat, and then Jonathan sighs. "Don't go anywhere," he says. "I'll be there in fifteen minutes."

Ezra blinks. "What?"

"What do you mean 'what'?" Ezra can hear the rustle of fabric. "I'm coming down there."

"It's raining," Ezra protests.

"Yes, we covered that. Where in the park are you?"

He's in so much trouble. "Down past the bridge—where you can get your feet in the water." He hesitates. "You don't have to—"

"If you tell me not to come down there," Jonathan interrupts, sounding tenser than Ezra's ever heard him, "I will drown you in the river."

Ezra laughs, but it's hollow, and he's not even sure if Jonathan meant it to be funny. He's pretty sure he didn't. "Okay."

"You'll stay there?"

"Yeah."

"Good," Jonathan says.

The line goes dead. Ezra stares at the screen and wonders if it's too late to start swimming for safety.

Except that running away doesn't feel like sanctuary, not anymore. Sanctuary is a living room crowded with voices and color and cinnamon-scented tea; it's soft sheets and warm brown eyes and hands that hold him together as easily as they take him apart.

So he waits.

It's been barely ten minutes when the rain suddenly disappears. Ezra looks up and sees the umbrella first, and then Jonathan holding it, looking back at him with tight-jawed, frustrated uncertainty, like he can't tell if he wants to yank Ezra into a hug or push him into the water.

Ezra swallows. "Hi."

Jonathan doesn't answer, just folds the umbrella and sits down next to Ezra on the ledge. He draws his knees up, shifting to wrap his arms around them, and stares out into the water.

Finally, he says, "You can't keep doing this."

Ezra doesn't need to ask what he means. "I know."

"I thought we were on the same page here. I can't keep

chasing after you. I can't keep wondering if I'm going to wake up and find you gone. I need—"

He needs to not be left behind again. "I'm sorry. I wasn't—I wasn't thinking."

"That doesn't fix it."

"I know."

"You keep shutting me out."

"I don't know how to stop."

Jonathan closes his eyes. Ezra watches him, the way the rain clings to his hair and his eyelashes. He's handsome, but it's his soul that shines, and Ezra's never found him anything but beautiful.

"Ben—" Ezra closes his eyes. "Ben's gone."

Silence, except for the wind and the rain.

"I know."

Ezra opens his eyes, turns to look at him. Jonathan is focused on the horizon, where the first suggestions of sunlight have begun to break through the clouds. "How?"

"I don't know. I woke up and I just . . . knew." The droplets clinging to Jonathan's eyelashes aren't all rain. "It's funny. I didn't feel anything when he died. Had no idea until I got the call. I always felt like there was something wrong with me, like I didn't love him enough to feel the hole he left in the world. I went to this grief group, and everyone else would talk about how they just *knew*, as soon as the person was gone. And I didn't."

Ezra squeezes his hand. *I'm here. I'm here.* Saying it, in all the ways he can.

"When you told me he was still here," Jonathan says, slowly, like he's not sure what word will follow the one before, "I thought maybe that was why. Maybe I didn't feel him go because he hadn't. And I started to look for him, when I could see you seeing him—you get this look, did you know? Distant and focused, all at once. I couldn't believe I didn't see it before." He exhales, almost a laugh, and shakes his head. "I thought knowing he was here would help me figure out a way to say goodbye to him, but instead I just saw all the places where I couldn't let him go. And knowing you could see him, when I couldn't . . ."

He doesn't sound angry. Just tired, and sad. "Sometimes I think I was angrier that you told me at all than that you waited to. It was easier, when I didn't know."

Ezra opens his mouth, ready to apologize, but Jonathan cuts him off. "But this time, I felt it. Like you can feel the pressure change before a storm." He tilts his head back, turning toward the gathered clouds. They're both waterlogged now, but neither of them reaches for his abandoned umbrella. "Someone told me once that explaining grief is like trying to describe the scent of petrichor. How do you tell someone how you experience the smell of the rain?"

There are a hundred possible words to describe the scent of the rain and the clouds and the river stretching out in front of them. Ezra's been in the water for longer than he's ever been dry. If he has nothing else to offer, he knows how to help someone swim. "I know," he says. "I'm sorry I wasn't there. I should have been, but I wasn't."

"You were with him," Jonathan says. "Do you think he got what he needed?"

"I don't know." Ezra hesitates. "He asked me what I was afraid of."

"Did you answer him?"

Ezra shakes his head. The rain is lifting, light bursting through the clouds.

"This," he says. "I'm afraid of this."

Jonathan turns to him, a question in his eyes.

"You make me feel safe," Ezra says. Like a blessing of gratitude. "Like you don't need me to be anyone but who I am."

Jonathan doesn't waver. "Why does that scare you?"

He wants to draw into himself, protective and small, like he's a child again, listening to stories at Zayde's knee, the ghosts around him only the whispers of a family lost, of lives never lived, the ache of survival. "Because I don't know how to be worth that."

"You don't have to do penance for needing help." Jonathan touches his face with careful hands, running his thumbs over Ezra's cheekbones, sliding through rainwater and salt water. "You don't have to make up for needing to be loved."

Ezra stares at him, through the faltering rain and the gathering sun. His hands have moved as if under their own power, curling into the fabric of Jonathan's shirt.

"Ezra," Jonathan says. No one, Ezra thinks, has ever said his name like Jonathan does. "What do you *want*?"

What does he want?

He wants Dad and Aaron to do the work they care about, in the community Zayde loved. He wants Becca happy and safe and smiling. He wants Mom and Dad to be friends again, the way he remembers, before years of secrets drained their easy companionship away. He wants the QCC open in a building that's not falling apart, where he can teach gangly college boys stumbling through their second puberty how to move through the growing pains and through the hormonal rush and show middle-aged lesbians taking their first steps out of the closet how to follow the arc of their breath.

He wants to hold people steady while they bring new life into the world, to witness their awe when faced with the sheer power of muscle and blood and love. He wants to go home to a house full of people who make him laugh so hard his face hurts and smother him with the kind of affection that's only ever possible when a group of lonely people find the edges that fit together into an impossible whole. He wants to adopt four more dogs and start an herb garden and maybe grow a human heart under his own.

He wants to wake up in Jonathan's bed, to the scent of his skin and the way his eyes crinkle at the corners when he smiles and his horrible habit of microwaving coffee. He wants to learn how to make the tea Jonathan used to bring out to Ben on the porch when he couldn't sleep, not because he likes it, but because Jonathan does.

He wants to see a ghost out of the corner of his eye and let them be noticed, briefly real, and then be free of their weight. To let them exist without letting himself be haunted, to no longer fear turning into a ghost himself.

The last thing Ezra wants, in this life or whatever comes after it, is for Jonathan to let him go.

"I want," Ezra says, choosing his words with care, "to stay here with you and watch the sunrise."

Jonathan's lips part in a smile, something very like surprised delight flickering in his eyes, and Ezra can't do anything but lean forward and kiss him. He kisses him properly, one hand curled around his lapel, the other in his hair, and when Jonathan slides an arm around his waist and draws him closer, Ezra's shiver has nothing to do with the breeze whipping his soaked clothes against his skin.

"I love you." He presses the words to Jonathan's mouth, the safest place he can think to put them. "I love you."

Jonathan doesn't say it back.

Not in words.

By the time they leave the water, making their way back up to where they left their cars, the gathering sun has warmed them dry.

FROM: ivy@provqcc.org
TO: team@provqcc.org
SUBJECT: 🎉 And we're BACK! 🎉

My friends,

It is with great excitement, joy, and RELIEF that I send this
email: we are BACK IN BUSINESS!

After some of the most challenging months since the
Center's founding, I am overjoyed to let you all know that we
have completed all renovations and passed all inspections,
and have been cleared by the city to resume occupancy in
our beloved building.

I have so much gratitude for each of you for continuing your
commitment to our team and our mission during this time.
Given the unexpected extension of the furlough period, we
anticipated a significant number of staff resignations—yet
so many of you, the vast majority of you, are still here. From
the executive team, the Board of Directors, and the very
bottom of my own heart: thank you.

We anticipate that staff will be able to return to the building
as early as next week. Your supervisor will be in touch with

you individually and by program team to determine next steps, but we wish to extend an invitation for an informal welcome-back gathering this Thursday evening. We'll do a full tour of the renovated space, but our big focus will just be on reconnecting. We've missed you all!

Kelly will be emailing later this week with a full update on HR logistics, including plans to check in with each of you on your payroll information, benefits clarification, etc. If you have any urgent questions, you can reach out to her directly by email (kelly@provqcc.org).

Let's get back to work.

Warmly and with gratitude,

Ivy
Ivy Branwell

(she/her/hers) | link: <u>what are pronouns?</u>
President & Executive Director
Providence Queer Community Center

The Providence Queer Community Center officially reopens its doors on a sun-drenched Tuesday in August, three weeks after Aaron files amended articles of incorporation with the office of the secretary of state requesting nonprofit status for the newly restructured Abner Friedman Memorial Chapel.

Dad's reaction to the idea, when Ezra and his siblings brought it to him at the beginning of the summer, was a mix of surprise and relief that Ezra didn't expect. He listened quietly as Aaron ran through the financials and Ezra explained everything else, and when they finished he sat back in his chair, face thoughtful.

"So it wouldn't be ours anymore?" he asked at last. Not upset, not concerned. Ezra felt a little curl of hope. It was a good sign.

"You'd have to give up ownership," Ezra said. "And a certain amount of control, since there'd have to be a board of directors and—I mean, it's all in there."

"But if you stayed on as the ED," Aaron added, when Dad's brow furrowed, "you technically *can* be part of the board; you just can't vote. It's a whole conflict of interest thing, but we drafted a policy for it. And I know Uncle Joe took himself out of the loop, but if you wanted to keep family involved, we could probably get him on board—"

"No pun intended," Becca piped up, sitting next to Dad and holding his hand.

Aaron nodded. "So it would still be ours, in the ways that matter. In making sure that we can stay open, and do the work, and . . ." He trailed off, glancing at Ezra.

This was the part they worried about. Finding the balance between the head and the heart. "I think," Ezra said, choosing his words carefully, "that Zayde would have cared more about the doors staying open than anything else."

He could say it with certainty now. A steadiness he never expected to have. The years of anxiety, of flinching away from every movement in his peripheral vision, have been replaced with a surety of purpose—a psychic tingle at his shoulder, like a hovering hand, offering unspoken approval, warm despite the ever-present spectral chill. He sees Zayde less often, but each time he does, there's a new acceptance in the man's eyes. A growing contentment. Peace.

Ezra treasures those sightings in a way he never used to,

never sure which one will be the last. It will be soon, he thinks, and the sadness never fails to surprise him. But it's a good sadness.

Not all grieving has to hurt.

Dad looked down at the proposal they'd printed for him. Ezra held his breath, watching him flip through it, keenly aware of Aaron doing the same.

Then, at last, he sat back in his chair.

"We should call your mother," he said, and if it wasn't the most unexpected thing Ezra thought he'd say, it was close. "To look at the numbers. And maybe"—he hesitated, and then set his jaw—"to see if she'd take her job back."

It took Aaron three false starts before he said, "Are you sure?"

Dad gave him a wry smile. "Zayde always liked her," he said. "And I'm not above leveraging some guilt."

"That's the spirit," Becca said, and took out her phone.

Within a week, they had their amended corporate structure. Ezra's parents locked themselves in Dad's office for nearly a full day, but never got loud enough for Ezra and Becca, lurking outside the door and attempting to eavesdrop, to hear anything over the sound of the white noise machine Dad normally used for client privacy. But they emerged at the end of it with matching red-rimmed eyes and an agreement that not only would Mom come back to work, but Judy would serve as both a founding board member and a fiduciary sponsor, offering a starting donation that made Ezra's eyes water.

No *wonder* Judy's mom could afford that house.

They also seemed unsurprised to find Ezra and Becca in the hallway—and even less surprised that Aaron, who had claimed that eavesdropping at the door was beneath him, had been in his own office next to Dad's with a cup pressed to the wall, just as unsuccessful in hearing anything.

"We should probably also tell you," Dad said solemnly, as if the flat line of his mouth was enough to disguise the glint of amusement in his eyes, his shoulders more relaxed than Ezra could remember seeing them in years, "that we're getting divorced."

"I'm genuinely horrified that you felt like you had to announce that," Becca said.

"We're working on communication," Mom said, dry but not mocking, her eyes flicking to Ezra's. She didn't say anything, but he heard the quiet apology in her tone. It was a start.

The rest of the summer goes by in a blur of paperwork and government application forms, meetings with lawyers and accountants, staff announcements, and community tours. Ezra finds himself, for once, on the edges of the whirlwind of activity, not in the eye of it. His parents—whether by spoken or unspoken agreement, Ezra isn't sure—fall into determined sync, setting themselves to the project with organized focus. It reminds him of the way they planned his and his siblings' bar and bat mitzvahs, organizing guest lists and logistics and Torah chant practices with the precision of a military operation, but without the tension and stress and sharpness he'd seen from them then.

They seem, against all the odds, to have come out of this as friends.

"Weirder things have happened," Ollie commented, when Ezra came home in a bit of a daze after a spontaneous family dinner where Judy, of all people, had made an appearance that didn't end in any yelling or thrown cutlery. "I mean, we're still friends."

"Wow, big false equivalence," Lily said, moving over on the couch so Ezra could sit next to her. "Pretty sure you two didn't split after thirty years and an affair, unless Ezra's ESP comes with the best antiaging serum I've ever seen in my life."

"God, can you imagine?" Ezra mumbled into the arm of the couch. "I'd look so good."

"You look good anyway," she told him, ruffling his hair. "How many days do you have left there, now that your mom's back?"

He held up five fingers, feeling surprisingly conflicted about it. He's going to be glad to get out of there—for all that he's glad he's been able to figure out how to help in a way that will last, and desperately relieved that he's been able to pay his rent and his bills and keep Sappho in food and toys and vet care, he's more than ready to go back to work that's at least marginally less haunted. He's had three new doula clients sign with him in the last month, and that's put him over the top of what he'll need to break even, especially with the news that the QCC is finally set to reopen.

"Are you nervous?" Jonathan asks him the morning of the staff welcome-back party, as he and Ezra sit at his kitchen table sharing a tin of cold leftover quiche. These days, he sleeps in Jonathan's bed more often than his own. "To see it?"

"Kind of." Ivy had sent weekly emails throughout the construction and renovations, sharing photos and 3D-rendered plans and the occasional staff input poll, but it'll be different to be there in person. Ezra nudges the last mushroom toward Jonathan's fork and gets a pleased smile in return. "More about feeling it. The old building was drenched in all this history, you know? You walked on the floor and you could just feel everyone who'd been there since it opened."

Jonathan props his chin on his hand and gives him a wry look. "Wasn't that part of the problem? Given that the floor was literally rotting away?"

"I think it was the foundation *under* the floor, not the actual floor," Ezra says, but it isn't much of a defense.

"Also the wiring in the walls being a huge fire hazard."

"Also that," Ezra allows.

"So you're worried they stripped all the personality out of the place when they took out all the death traps?"

Ezra picks at a chip on the rim of his coffee mug. He'd knocked it into the counter a week ago when Jonathan had distracted him in the kitchen with a kiss, and the roughness of it under his thumb makes him grin, admittedly dopily, every time he sees it. "They were my emotional support death traps?" he tries.

Jonathan chuckles and gets to his feet. "Knowing you," he says, "you'll find new ones."

The death traps are, Ezra determines when he and Nina go in for their first day of staff reorientation, definitely gone. But he recognizes more of the original hardwood floors than he expects, pulled up and replaced over the new foundation. There are new fixtures, obviously—touches of chrome, drywall dividers replaced with clear or frosted glass, more clusters of cozy gathering furniture, and coworking desks with built-in outlets. But the collages of old photos still have places of pride on the newly painted walls, the mural in the lobby painted by one of the teen affinity groups is still miraculously intact, and even the staff break room still has nearly all its caught-out-of-time mismatched seating and handmade décor.

"I cannot believe they kept that horrible thing," Nina says in mild horror as Ezra flops gleefully into the battered old recliner, greeting its squashy, slightly smelly leather like an old friend. "That's a health hazard in and of itself."

"You just hate comfort," he tells her.

"You don't, though," she teases. "Or am I imagining the way your Instagram account is ninety percent pictures of your boyfriend's cozy bed?"

He doesn't deny it. There isn't really any point.

Boyfriend is still new. New and still a bit strange—not because Ezra doesn't want them to be something official, something recognized on family email chains and social media and a terrifying looming visit by Jonathan's mother to meet her in person, but because sometimes it feels like a word that's not big enough to hold the size of his feelings. Jonathan's nearly always the first thing he sees in the morning and the last thing he sees before he closes his eyes at night. He knows Jonathan's body now almost as well as he knows his own, knows his smiles and his nervous habits and the particular way he rolls his eyes when he figures out the trick in a crossword puzzle and finds it wanting.

"At least it's mostly pictures of my dog in my boyfriend's cozy bed," he says, the closest thing to a defense he can muster. "I mean, it could be a lot mushier."

The look Nina gives him speaks volumes of knowledge of just how many pictures do *not* make it onto the internet and instead live safe and sound on his camera roll, for him to flip through on the now rare nights he spends in his own bed.

He spends the morning before the QCC officially reopens with Nina, setting up the office they'll be sharing with two other program managers, and then bullying her into helping him put the finishing touches on the newly refurbished studio space. It's not just his—there are several other yoga instructors who come in to teach, plus the dance and theater and music programs that are run out of the same room. But it feels like his all the same as he unpacks boxes of blocks and blankets and mats into the closet and tests out his phone's connection to the sound system and hangs new art prints on the painted walls.

"It looks good," Nina says when they're done, slinging an arm around his shoulders and giving him a fond little shake.

His first instinct is to brush off the compliment. But he's trying to be better about letting people tell him when he's done something worth doing without squirming away from it. It's an uphill battle, but he's working on it.

And it *does* look good. The space is fresh and clean and bright, the floors still shining, sunlight streaming through the high windows. The scents of pine and rosemary still trace their way through the air, the last of the incense Ezra lit earlier slowly burning away.

New and gleaming, and not a single ghost to be found.

Ezra leans into Nina's arm. "It does, doesn't it?"

Nina ruffles his hair and lets him go. "You know I don't believe in fake praise."

"You flirted with our barista at Starbucks for five full minutes the other day for a free shot of espresso," he reminds her.

"And every one of those compliments was genuine—her eyeliner was *incredible*." She winks, her eye makeup still flawless despite a full day of moving furniture. "Are you going to be home for dinner on Friday? Max said she wants to do movie night."

"Oh, *did* she?"

Nina glares at him, clearly daring him to tease her. She and Max have been circling each other for weeks now. Ezra has no idea why they're playing chicken, but it's simultaneously infuriating and adorable. He wonders if this is how she and his roommates used to feel watching him and Jonathan.

Speaking of. "No," he says. "Jonathan and I are doing Shabbat dinner at my dad's."

"Ooh." She raises her eyebrows, all Max-related defensiveness apparently evaporating. "Drama?"

"I . . . think maybe not?" He nods toward the open door, and she flicks the lights off and follows him out. He locks the door behind them, and the key turns without needing to have the hinges propped up by a second person to realign the door-knob. "Everyone's going to be there, but I think it's going to be okay. Things have been good."

Nina eyes him skeptically as they head back to their office. "If you say so," she says. "Should I have some wine ready for you in case it all goes to hell, or is Jonathan gonna bundle you home and make sure you *decompress*?"

Ezra is absolutely not turning red, and if he is, it's only because he doesn't have her stamina for moving tables and organizing closet spaces. "You're not as funny as you think you are."

"I'm a delight and you adore me," she says tartly, then catches his arm when he rolls his eyes and tries to slip past her down the hall. "No, but really—are you going to be okay? I know how those dinners can get."

Ezra thinks about his family text thread, cheerful and teasing for the first time in months, about Becca calling him to tell him that she and Mom have been swapping recipes again, about catching Mom and Dad bickering in Dad's office without a hint of animosity, neither of them wearing their wedding rings but both using coffee mugs Ezra made for them in elementary school, handprint patterned and sloppily painted.

"I know," he says. "But I'm actually kind of looking forward to it."

"Your funeral, I guess," she says, and cackles when he groans.

The fire damage to the house had taken over a month to clean up and restore. They were, Ezra's been told time and again, incredibly lucky—not just with Becca's minor injuries, but in the overall lack of harm done to the interior of the house. Other than some smoke damage to the living room and stairwell, only the kitchen needed a gut renovation. They hadn't even had to move out, though Aaron had spent plenty of time complaining about eating all their meals at the Chapel. Dad had, to everyone's surprise, latched on to the project with a sort of fervent enthusiasm, recruiting Becca into touring sample kitchens at Lowe's and dragging Ezra into his office to look at paint swatches.

It took Ezra far too long to realize that this was probably the first time in his life that Dad had the chance to make a space that was *his*.

If he'd closed Mom's office door to give himself a five-minute cry about that, nobody needed to know.

The bottle of wine he picked up on the way over sweats in his grip, and he squashes the temptation to press it against his neck as he heads up the porch steps to his parents' house. Just Dad's house now, he reminds himself. August is in full swing, the New England humidity making his binder cling to his skin. Its days are numbered—there's a surgery date circled in bright pink highlighter on the calendar in his apartment, a matching one on the fridge at Jonathan's.

Six months and eighteen days to go, according to the countdown on his phone. A thrill of nervous anticipation goes through him every time he thinks about it, giddy and bright.

Jonathan opens the front door before Ezra can get his keys out, his grin easy and warm as Ezra abandons the search through his pocket. "You're late," he says, holding out a hand for the wine. "I was beginning to think you were making one last run for the hills."

"I promised to stop doing that," Ezra says, and leans up for the kiss he knows is coming. It's still strange, expecting that easy affection, to know before it happens that Jonathan's going to curl a hand over the back of his neck, to use his thumb against the hinge of Ezra's jaw to tilt his face up for a better angle. "When did you get here?"

"*I* got here on time," Jonathan teases, stepping back to let Ezra pass him. "Don't worry. Everyone's been very nice to me."

"Oh, I bet." His parents' fragile friendship isn't perfect, but if there's one thing they seem to be in agreement about, it's their shared adoration of Jonathan. "How's . . ." He gestures into the house, trying to encompass *all that,* and Jonathan's mouth tilts into a grin.

"Let's call it organized chaos," he says. "But friendly organized chaos?"

"Yeah?" Ezra strains his ears, but he can't actually hear anything threatening. "And that's not because no one's here yet?"

"No, you pessimist." Jonathan slings an arm around him, steering him through the living room. After the fire, Dad and Aaron repainted the walls a cool, calm blue and replaced the squashy couches of Ezra's childhood with a new sectional in supple brown leather. Other than the absence of Mom and Dad's wedding photos, most of the pictures on the walls and propped on the sideboard are the same. But the room has a quietly masculine feel to it now, more a sophisticated bachelor's den than a hand-me-down family home. It looks good, if still a little sterile. But he can see touches of his father's personality starting to find their way into the room—a framed Judaica print on one wall that's far more traditional in style than anything his mother would have allowed, a novelty Red Sox mug replacing the ceramic bowl that once held the television remotes. It makes Ezra smile to see it. To know it's never too late to figure out how to make a place feel like your own. "Your mom and sister are bickering over oven temperatures, but Aaron keeps telling me that's normal."

"It *is* normal," Aaron says, coming in from the kitchen, two tumblers of something amber and probably expensive in his hands. Despite the whirlwind of the last few months, he looks better rested and lighter than Ezra's seen him in years. Ezra hopes, probably in vain, that the new easy set to Aaron's shoulders has more to do with the funeral home's brightening future and less to do with the way he'd caught Caroline Lawrence sneaking out of Aaron's office two days ago, hastily sweeping her hair back into its bun. Aaron looked like a deer in the headlights when he'd caught Ezra's eye in the hallway, and had turned abruptly away to walk in the opposite direction.

Pointedly ignoring Ezra's smirk now, Aaron clears his throat and passes one of the glasses to Jonathan. "Judy's playing referee. She's weirdly good at it."

Jonathan's smile falters, just slightly, and Ezra instinctively presses his fingers to the inside of his wrist. He hasn't been in the room for any of the conversations Jonathan's had with Judy about the strange web of relationships they've ended up in—"If you two get married," Ollie asked once, curiously, "is she, like, a double mother-in-law?"—but he's seen the aftermath, red-rimmed eyes and shaky smiles, the beginnings of forgiveness.

"She raised three type-A kids with crazy competitive streaks" is all Jonathan says, though he laces his fingers with Ezra's and squeezes. "I'm just glad she and Becca are getting along."

"I think having her crash with them after the fire helped," Aaron says. "Apparently they watched a *lot* of reality TV."

"Never underestimate the power of *Bachelorette* reruns as a bonding tool," Ezra agrees, peering over Jonathan's arm at the contents of his glass. "Is that bourbon?"

"Brandy."

Ezra wrinkles his nose and leans away. "Since when do we stock that?"

"New bottle," Aaron says. "Dad's going full *Mad Men*." At whatever look Ezra gives him, he adds, "He's fine. He's exploring, not, y'know, drinking to cope."

Ezra believes it. Dad's been happier lately. Calmer, more relaxed. Probably drinking *less* than usual, not more. "Where is he?"

"I left him in the dining room, setting the table."

"I think he was considering place cards," Jonathan says. He tips his glass toward Ezra, offering, and Ezra shakes his head with a grimace.

"Nope. Gross. I'll grab something." He plucks the damp bottle of wine out of Jonathan's hand. "And put this in the kitchen."

He doesn't let himself feel a pang when he lets go of Jonathan's hand, because that would be ridiculous. He *definitely* doesn't let himself notice the knowing look Aaron sends him over the rim of his glass in response.

Mom scoops him into a bone-crushing hug when he steps into the kitchen, as if it's been months since they last saw each other, not hours. "Ow," he says, waving the wine bottle at Becca, who takes it from him with a coordinated flourish. "I literally saw you this morning."

"You were working," she says, pressing a kiss to his cheek and letting him go. She'd come—with his permission—to his sunrise yoga class, taking a spot at the back of the room and not once doing anything to act like his mom rather than a student. He'd drifted her way a few times, mostly to correct her posture, but otherwise hadn't singled her out at all. She'd given him a small wave on her way out, her smile proud on her slightly sweaty face. "So I didn't get to tell you how good a job you did." She cups his face in her hands. "You're a wonderful teacher, sweetheart."

Ezra ducks his head to avoid the look on her face. "*Mom*."

"What? You are." She makes a face. "Except for those side planks. Side planks at seven in the morning? I raised you better than that."

Becca grins. "I told you the beginner classes are on Sundays."

"She did," Judy agrees, standing at the counter and assembling a salad. "And you said, and I quote, 'I have birthed multiple children, I can handle a little abdominal pain.'"

"Traitor," Mom tells her.

Judy winks at her, then gives Ezra a warm smile. "Hi, Ezra. How's the reopening going?"

"Really well. Thanks." They're not quite at the hugging stage yet, but the way she's thrown herself into supporting the Chapel and helping Mom start to repair the damage the two of them did to Dad has made it easier to relax around her, to at least start to think of her as something like family. Her two daughters—Ben's sisters—followed Ezra and his siblings on social media last month. Ezra's pretty sure that the oldest is gearing up to give him a shovel talk about his intentions toward Jonathan. When he mentioned that to Jonathan, he'd looked like he couldn't decide whether to be embarrassed or touched.

"That's family, I guess," he'd said, cheeks tinged with pink.

Maybe it was.

The renovated kitchen barely resembles the old one. The Formica countertops have been replaced with granite, open shelving and smooth dark wood instead of the old cherry cabinets. It's clean and modern, but Becca's already making it her own. Glass storage jars of flour and sugar and coffee labeled with chalkboard paint in her sweeping calligraphy—passed down from Mom, who learned it from Bubbe—sit on a floating shelf along the back wall. There are fresh herbs thriving in a box by the window behind the sink, the plain dish towels Ezra watched Dad order to match the newly painted walls already swapped out for novelty ones patterned with teacups and leaves.

Out of the corner of his eye, he catches the slightest movement, and turns just in time to see Bubbe watching the bustle of the room with a small, satisfied smile, as if nothing could please her more than to see her old kitchen turning into something new. She catches his eye, winks, and blows him a kiss before flickering out of sight. Smiling, Ezra opens the wine and pours himself a glass, watching Becca peer into the oven while stirring a saucepan of something that smells absolutely incredible. He's never seen her at her internships, but he wonders if this is what she's like there, too: calm and confident and efficiently at ease, checking on dishes with an almost graceful sense of the space around her.

She closes the oven and turns to scribble something on a Post-it note stuck to the counter, then glances up at him. "What?"

"Nothing," he says, but he knows he's smiling. "Just excited for your cooking. I've been eating takeout all week."

"I heard," she says, giving him a look like she knows exactly how sentimental he's trying not to be. "Jonathan told me he's worried you're going to turn into a spring roll."

Ezra shrugs. "He should stop buying me spring rolls, then."

Becca finishes whatever updates she's making to her recipe with a flourish, then sticks her pencil into the headband attempting to contain the flyaways already escaping her messy bun. "Sure," she says, her look caught somewhere between a grin and a leer. "Because everything we know about Jonathan definitely says he's going to *stop* keeping you fed and cared for."

"Stop teasing your brother, Rebecca," Mom chides, winking at Ezra as she squeezes Judy's shoulder on her way to bring the bowl of salad out to the dining room.

Judy shakes her head, but the laugh lines around her eyes are deep as she smiles. "He's always been like that," she tells Ezra. "Ben used to complain that he couldn't keep up with the other med students competing for the worst food stories because Jonathan kept sneaking him lunches."

"A terrible person, truly," Ezra says.

The lingering grief in Judy's eyes is softened by the warmth on her face. "Your problem now," she teases, and he can't help returning her smile.

He still looks for Ben from time to time. He never appears, though Ezra knows he won't. Ezra thinks he still feels him, but in the simple, everyday ways he thinks that everyone still feels the touches of the dead—in the wistful curve of Jonathan's mouth when he pulls a well-loved Tufts sweatshirt out of his bottom drawer or when the clear, sweet opening notes of "Your Song" come up on the playlist he puts on when he's coaxing Ezra into a slow dance in the kitchen; in the still-fading tan line on Jonathan's left ring finger and the slim chain around his neck where his wedding band now hangs; the way the cool metal pools against Ezra's collarbone when they kiss; in the way Jonathan's eyes crinkle at the edges when Ezra makes him a too-sweet cup of that apple-cinnamon tea.

A thousand touches, but none of them haunting. Not anymore.

Becca pronounces the roast chicken ready just as Dad pokes his head in from the dining room to remind them that they have ten minutes until sunset.

"Doing okay?" he asks, clapping Ezra's shoulder while they wait for Becca to turn off the oven and Aaron and Jonathan to make their way in from the living room. "Been a busy few days."

"I'm good." After the constant exposure of the spring and the whirlwind work of most of the summer, the last few weeks of catching Dad only through quick text exchanges has been strange. The longest time they've spent together since Mom came back to work was a shared coffee break in Dad's office after Ezra finished a taharah. It had surprised him, how comfortable it was to sit with him and talk, the quiet that had come after the weeks of chaos and change. "Heard anything back on the paperwork?"

Dad shakes his head. "Not just yet. Soon, I hope." He lets Ezra go when Jonathan comes in, giving him a wink that's alarmingly close to the one he got from Mom a few minutes ago as Jonathan sets his drink down next to Ezra's wineglass and comes around the table to join them. Ezra leans into the arm Jonathan slips around his waist.

"Your brother's a menace," Jonathan murmurs against the side of Ezra's head, half disguised as a kiss to his temple.

Ezra tilts his head into the touch. "Yeah?"

"Something about taking me out for a Friendly Chat."

"Ooh, I heard those capital letters."

"He used air quotes and everything."

Ezra bites back a grin. "I think that's a compliment. He didn't try to get Ollie to 'go out for a friendly drink' till we'd been together almost a year." He catches Aaron's eye across the room and pointedly ignores the waggling eyebrows he gets in response. "He only puts on the scare tactics when he thinks someone's going to stick around."

Jonathan huffs a laugh into the top of Ezra's head, his hand slipping down from Ezra's waist to tuck into his back pocket. "Then I'm flattered."

"Okay," Becca announces, bustling into the room with a box of kitchen matches in hand. "I'm here, we're on time, let's light candles. The first person who makes a comment about fire insurance owes me twenty bucks in emotional damages." She shoots Aaron a warning look, and he grins, holding his hands up in defeat. "Good." She rolls her shoulders, then her neck, then looks around the room one more time. "Everyone ready? No last-minute announcements? World-shaking revelations? Dramatic declarations?"

Dad chuckles as Mom drops her face into her hands and Judy lets out a shocked, breathless "oh!" of a laugh that makes it clear she's still getting used to Becca's particular brand of humor. Becca blows Mom an exaggerated kiss, dodges Aaron's chiding swat at her arm, and then cocks one eyebrow at Ezra. A teasing question, but a question all the same.

He shifts so that he can nudge Jonathan's hand out of his pocket and shrug Jonathan's arm around his shoulders instead, reaching up to tangle their fingers together, his right hand to Jonathan's left. It's still a little strange to feel bare skin under his touch where he's used to smooth-worn platinum.

There's a part of him that shies away from how badly he wants to put a ring back on that finger, this soon and with this much intensity. There's another part that wants to dive in, fully clothed and headfirst, and let the rush of his wanting carry him away.

Becca's still looking at him, brow lifted and expectant, a glint in her eyes. She reads him better than anyone. Ezra loves her so much it hurts.

"Nothing new," Ezra says. *Nothing yet.*

Becca grins, her eyes darting to his hand in Jonathan's, but there's only warmth in her smile as she strikes a match. She lights the candles then blows out the match. Ezra closes his eyes.

Jonathan squeezes his hand.

Without opening his eyes, Ezra squeezes back. Steady and sure.

Becca's voice washes over him, words of blessing as familiar as his own pulse. Ezra turns his face toward the warmth of the candlelight, the dancing life of it bright even through his eyelids, and he lets himself, finally, breathe.

Acknowledgments

I am possibly a very strange person in that I delight in reading book acknowledgments. I'm even more delighted to finally be able to write my own.

To my wonderful, chaotic, impossibly funny dream agent, Ayla Zuraw-Friedland, who championed this book in ways I couldn't even imagine: I knew from that first phone call that you were the perfect person to make Ezra's story a published reality, and every day I feel luckier to have you in my corner. I'm sorry for making you cry on public transportation.

To the wonderful team at Frances Goldin Literary Agency, thank you for the endless support and for your unfailing dedication to your values. To Jade Wong-Baxter, who got my original query email and asked if she could forward it to the "brilliant new agent" who had just joined the team—thank you again! I'm pretty sure I still owe you a fruit basket.

Thank you to Laura Williams, my UK agent, who handled everything across the pond so smoothly I never even had time to get anxious.

To Jesse Shuman, my amazing editor, for approaching every draft of this book with a thoughtful tenderness I didn't think existed in the world of professional publishing, for putting up with my newbie texts, and for midwifing this manuscript into what it is today. To Serena Arthur, for joining our team so seamlessly at just the right time with your brilliant eye and your even more brilliant heart. Thank you both for loving Ezra just as much as I do, and possibly loving Jonathan even more.

Thank you to Jasper Levy, my authenticity reader, for the care and attention you brought to your notes, and for sharing so much of yourself with me and this book. I'm also sorry for making you cry on public transportation. Thank you to everyone at Ballantine Books who made this book possible: Kara Cesare, Jennifer Hershey, Kara Welsh, and Kim Hovey. A massive thank-you to my entire production and marketing team: Andy Lefkowitz, Sheryl Rapée-Adams, Linnea Knollmueller, Fritz Metsch, Elena Giavaldi, Amy Perez, Jordan Hill Forney, Kathleen Cook, Megha Jain, Robin Slutzky, and Abdi Omer.

Thank you to everyone who shared their wisdom, expertise, and industry insider secrets during the research phase of this book! Thank you to Emily Fishman and the Gender Task Force at the Community Hevra Kadisha of Greater Boston, not just for your time but also for the incredible work you do to ensure that every Jew can be buried with dignity and with gender-inclusive liturgy and ritual. Thank you to Stephanie Garry at the Plaza Jewish Community Chapel, the original nonprofit Jewish funeral home, for giving me a peek behind the curtain and for answering my many, many unnecessarily detailed questions. Thank you to Vicki Bloom, my beloved doula, for sharing your experiences as a full-spectrum doula and reminding me that there's so much more to this work than births. (Also for doula-ing my actual children into the world! It's the little things.)

To Emily Goodstein and the incredible team at Greater Good Strategy, thank you for your flexibility, incredible support, and unexpected (but delightful and delicious!) gift of Levain cookies to help fuel my twenty-four-hour revision retreat.

Thank you to Rebecca Mix and Andrea Hannah, for building the creative communities I didn't know I needed and without whom this book would never have left my hard drive. To the Story Grove: Thank you for believing in me and for pushing me to send out that last batch of queries. You were right—it made all the difference!

Thank you to Beth AuBuchon, Sheyla Knigge, Leslie Fannon, Naomi Ansano, Bri Hanschu, Chelsea Hollerud, and Rin Graham, my beloved coven, for your endless encouragements, manifestations, and willingness to read publishing emails before I did because I was too anxious to open them myself. I love you all to the stars and back.

To Andrea Towers, my buddy in writing-while-parenting: Thank you for listening to every complaint, every insecurity, and every moment of impostor syndrome. Thank you to Sarah Loch for reading this book in its very earliest form and seeing its potential to be so much more.

A massive, mushy-eyed thank-you to Deb Hecht for reading everything I've written since I was scribbling fanfiction on notebook paper while we were supposed to be playing sports, and to this day willingly diving into every Google Doc that comes your way. Your endless positivity continues to mean the world to me.

To my beloved queer found family: Thank you for allowing me to always be unapologetically, absurdly, entirely myself. Thank you to Paloma Griffin for your brilliance, your compassion, and your gigantic heart. Thank you to Jay Geris, for inspiring me to love the things that bring me joy with wholehearted enthusiasm and delight. Thank you to Zoë Shannon for coming into my life at the exact moment I needed you—and changing it for the better in more ways than I can count.

To my parents, who let me apply only to colleges with programs in creative writing, and never so much as suggested a backup plan: Thank you for always believing this writing thing would work out, even when I didn't. You were right!

Thank you to Heather, my first baby and my first rabbi, for being my teacher and never letting me forget that we're here to do something good.

To Rafi and Yael: Thank you for reminding me that the stories we tell aren't nearly as important as the way that we tell them. Everything I do is for you.

And to Ziv, the Jonathan to my Ezra: Thank you for always seeing me, and for teaching me to be seen. I love you.

RULES *for* GHOSTING

SHELLY JAY SHORE

Random House Book Club

Dear Reader,

Okay. Let's get into it.

How do you feel about ghosts?

I've always been taken in by the idea of a non-spooky ghost story. To me, ghosts were never nearly as scary as living people. The idea of opening up to the dead? Easy. The possibility of a vulnerable conversation with a living person? Hard pass.

I wrote *Rules for Ghosting* as a way of exploring a character who became so used to being haunted by the dead that he forgot how to really live—but to write that story in a way that shows how things like joy, community, laughter, family, and even romance can sneak their way into your life, no matter how determined you are to close yourself off to them. No matter how little you believe you deserve them.

At its heart, *Rules for Ghosting* is about connection. It's about loving your family even when you don't like them, and deciding that maybe you like them after all. It's about falling in love when you least expect it, and realizing that your friends do, actually, have your back. It's about Jewish guilt and Jewish joy, about queer community and messy situationships. It's about how the ones we love never really leave us—even when we kind of wish they would.

We tell ghost stories as a way of talking about the things that we're missing, but more often than not, they tell us more about what we still have than what we've lost. As you read *Rules for Ghosting* and meet Ezra, his friends and family, and their many ghosts, I hope you get to spend some time with your own ghosts—whether they're familiar old friends or you've just given yourself a chance to notice them. Whatever form they take, tell them I say hi.

Thank you so much for reading *Rules for Ghosting*. I hope you enjoy!

xoxo
Shelly

Questions and Topics
for Discussion

1. Ezra observes a set of strict spectral rules when it comes to the ghosts he reluctantly sees. Do you believe in ghosts or have you ever had a paranormal experience? If so, what is your "theory" of ghosts, what they're like, and how they reach us?

2. In the book, Ezra is haunted—literally and figuratively—and burdened by the expectations that are foisted upon him. Is there a time or place in your life where you felt similar weights? What about a time in your life when you felt the pressure of high expectations? Did you feel motivated to rise to the occasion or paralyzed by the fear of failure?

3. Ezra often finds himself needing to step in as the Friedman family mediator, and he's grown accustomed to taking the temperature of every room he enters and acting accordingly. Do you think people get assigned roles in their family? Did that happen to you? How do the stories families tell, and the stories we tell ourselves, shape our identities and expectations? Have you ever had to challenge those personal narratives or family myths?

4. Ezra's father jokes to Ezra that he ran to "the other side of the life cycle" to get away from the funeral home. What

conceptions of birth work and death work did you have before reading the book? Did anything surprise you?

5. Usually, secrets can shake a person's trust in someone else. But Ezra reveals his clairvoyance to his siblings in an attempt to open up to them, even though he doesn't tell Jonathan until much later. Do you think some secrets can build trust once revealed?

6. Our culture is obsessed with death. From *Ghost* to *Pushing Daisies* to *The Sixth Sense*, we have a cultural refusal to let death be final—and, as a result, ghosts are a constant fixture in books, movies, television, and even podcasts. Why do you think that is? How does *Rules for Ghosting* subvert your perception of a "ghost story"? Of the rom-com?

7. Shelly Jay Shore puts the "fun" in "funeral." How do humor and tragedy, the macabre and the whimsical, go hand in hand? Why do you think we joke about death so often?

8. *Rules for Ghosting* is as much about a found family as it is about a family of origin. Discuss the importance of friendship in this story. Why do you think it's valuable, and what does it provide that other relationships might not?

9. Discuss the novel's contrasting main themes: love and grief, life and death. How are they at odds and how do they work together?

10. What moments do you think sparked the biggest changes in Ezra's character throughout the book? What moments

come to mind in your own life? By the end of the story, how has Ezra's growth affected his relationships with others?

11. *Rules for Ghosting* spends a lot of time with Jewish funeral practices. What rituals or practices around death, dying, and funerals show up in your culture? What other kinds have you learned about? Do they resonate with you? Why or why not?

12. Discuss the novel's title. Did your understanding of it shift while reading?

13. Bobbi, Ezra's mother, spends a lot of time fretting about what her family thinks of her choices. Could she have handled her revelation better? Do you think her children responded the right way? At what point do we draw the line between an obligation to others—and to family—and the pursuit of our own personal happiness?

14. Besides the obvious, why do you think Ezra kept Ben's appearances from Jonathan for so long? Would you have done the same in his position?

15. If Ezra and Jonathan had a sequel, what do you think it would be about? How do you think Ezra handles his power of seeing ghosts in the future? What do you think is next for Ezra and Jonathan? What do you want for them?

A Q&A with Shelly Jay Shore

Let's go back to the beginning. How did *Rules for Ghosting* start for you?

Like any good Jewish kid, I have to give credit to my mother! The earliest spark that eventually became *Rules for Ghosting* started from a conversation we had following my grandmother's funeral, when she remarked that the people who drive the "family cars" at funeral homes (courtesy cars to bring the family to and from the cemetery) must hear absolutely outrageous conversations. From there, I knew I wanted to write a funeral home novel!

You've written a book that seems to have everything: humor, heart, romance, drama. It wrestles with some big questions about family and the expectations that they foist upon us. Why was this important for you to explore?

Rules for Ghosting was always going to be a family story that juggled families of origin, families of choice, and how we make ourselves into different people based on who we're with and what we think they want from us. So many of us spend our whole lives trying to differentiate who we are from who our parents wanted us to be, but I wanted to show that you don't have to know who you are in order for someone to love you for it.

Ezra grew up in a funeral home, but works as a yoga teacher and a doula. How did you choose that career path?

From the very first draft, I knew that Ezra was going to have a physical career, and one that somehow involved working with the body. Physical bodies and the characters' relationships to them—their own and others'—play a huge role in the book, and Ezra's chosen career had to fit into that narrative. The yoga teaching actually came before the doula work, but once I knew he was going to be a doula, there was never a question about him doing the full spectrum of doula practice, which includes working with people experiencing pregnancy loss and abortion, as well as birth. There's a bit of irony there, too—that Ezra did his best to run from anything involving funeral work, but reproductive work has elements of life and death, endings and beginnings. There were a few deleted scenes that went more deeply into the different aspects of that, as well as Jonathan's death doula work—maybe in a special edition? (Wink, wink.)

What's one challenge you had writing this book?

Not making a dramatic twist about Ben being secretly alive and ending the book with him in a beautiful throuple situation with Ezra and Jonathan. I will neither confirm nor deny deleted scenes or an alternate ending!

Did you learn anything about yourself while writing this book? Is there a message you want readers to take away from it?

I wrote and revised *Rules for Ghosting* during some of the most acute parts of the Covid pandemic, at the same time that I was parenting an infant, was mourning my grandmother's death, and had just lost my full-time job. Even though I was writing a funeral home book, I never set out to write a grief book. Writing this book really made me realize how reluctant we are not just to talk about grief, and the way we're irrevocably changed by it, but that so many of us are reluctant to let ourselves feel it at all. But I quickly learned that grief has a way of creeping up on you, especially if you're trying to push it away. If there's anything I'd like my readers to take away, it's that, whatever you're running away from feeling—whether it's grief, joy, or anything else—that's probably the thing you need to let yourself feel the most.

And for the final question, something just for fun! If *Rules for Ghosting* were to become a movie, who would you want to see cast?

A sad confession: I am not nearly sufficiently aware of who's who in Hollywood to be able to answer that question, other than my dream casting for Jonathan would have been a mid-thirties Dan Levy. The most important thing to me would be to see an unapologetically Jewish, trans, and queer cast, and for the body diversity of the characters to be reflected— neither Ezra or his mother are thin, Becca isn't tall, etc. The next most important thing: Sappho should definitely be played by a rescue mutt. I'll take her home with me when they're done filming!

JUDE VALENTIN

SHELLY JAY SHORE (SHE/THEY) is a writer, digital strategist, and nonprofit fundraiser. Her writing on queer Jewish identity has been published by *Autostraddle*, Hey Alma, and the Bisexual Resource Center. She lives with her partner in New York, where she attempts to wrangle two large dogs and two small children while single-handedly sustaining her local Dunkin' Donuts with year-round iced coffee orders. *Rules for Ghosting* is her debut novel.

shelly-jay-shore.com
Twitter: @shellyjayshore
Instagram: @shellyjayshore

ABOUT THE TYPE

This book was set in Minion, a 1990 Adobe Originals typeface by Robert Slimbach. Minion is inspired by classical, old-style typefaces of the late Renaissance, a period of elegant and beautiful type designs. Created primarily for text setting, Minion combines the aesthetic and functional qualities that make text type highly readable with the versatility of digital technology.